Hemingway
Was
Murdered

Hemingway Was Murdered

Elizabeth Ritter

ABSOLUTELY AMAZING eBOOKS

Published by Whiz Bang LLC, 926 Truman Avenue, Key West, Florida 33040, USA.

ISBN 978-1-951150-66-2

For information contact:
Publisher@AbsolutelyAmazingEbooks.com

To the American Bar Association Derivatives and Futures Law Committee for the erstwhile great good sense to hold annual conferences in Key West, else I might never have found my island home and family.

To Michael Morawski, CEO of the Ernest Hemingway Home and Museum, for providing the opportunity to live on the Hemingway property, and to Ernest and Pauline for sharing their home with us for so many years.

To Tippy, who will be remembered for having deeply enriched the lives of the Hemingway cats.

To Dave, Katie, Erik, and Drake, for the crazy, swirling, immeasurable love of this family.

Author's Note

Pablo Picasso famously said, "Learn the rules like a pro, so you can break them like an artist." To that end, I have meticulously researched the lives of Pauline Pfeiffer and Ernest Hemingway, so that I could write a believable book of fiction about their marriage.

In appropriating the most famous suicide of the 20th century and portraying it as a murder, I recognize that there are those whom, possibly, I will offend. Scholars and readers who venerate Hemingway may perhaps take umbrage at his portrayal as an oafish lout, deserving of eradication at every turn, and those who admire Pauline might conceivably be offended by her depiction as a neurotic manipulator. No offense is intended. I have simply caricatured their personalities so as to provide a credible foundation for a work of the imagination.

Indeed, I have a deep respect for Ernest Hemingway, Hadley Richardson, Pauline Pfeiffer, Martha Gellhorn, and Mary Welsh. I also have an abiding admiration for those who devote time, energy, and scholasticism to the study and analysis of the Hemingway *gestalt*. I have relied heavily on their numerous primary and secondary sources to craft this tale.

And perhaps I feel an especial artistic license, particularly when it comes to Pauline. During the years that my husband and I lived on the Hemingway Home property in Key West, Florida (my husband was the Executive Director of the Museum), I felt a distinct, palpable relationship to Pauline. After all, since the 1850s, Pauline and I have been the only two wives ever to be able to call this singular bit of real estate "home."

Of course, she was the mistress of the mansion, I only of the little apartment above the cat cemetery. Still, I was able to walk the same gardens in the evenings, watch the same sunrise over Pauline's coconut palm, swim in the same magnificent, mystical pool, and commune with the progeny of Ernest's many cats. And it was something about Pauline's personality, her determination, her mettle, that put the idea for this novel into my head in the first place.

As to specifics, I have utilized the general timelines of Ernest Hemingway's life and events—as well as those of Hadley, Pauline, Martha, and Mary – to construct this tale. That said, I have taken numerous liberties with occurrences and dates to suit my story.

I hope and believe that Pauline and Ernest, wherever they may be, are drinking a cocktail and enjoying a laugh at my audacious charade. I hope that readers can share that amusement.

– Elizabeth Ritter

Key West, Florida 2020

Hemingway
Was
Murdered

Prologue

Key West, Florida, July 1951

Pauline needs to move, to get out of the pool, to walk inside the melancholy, cavernous mansion. It is late evening. The towering limestone walls of the house, limned against the dimming tropical sky, seem to arch menacingly over the silver-green water of the pool. Jinny will have supper waiting for her. She needs to go inside.

Pauline makes a few feeble, laborious steps through the water, then stops. *If only Elizabeth were here tonight, with me in this pool.* She wonders briefly if perhaps her friend would be able to offer some solace, or even pardon. She remembers her own former invincibility, and then begins to consider clemency.

But she is sidetracked by a movement in the grass, a tiny flicker caught in the corner of her eye. She moves toward the rough concrete ledge that encircles the magnificent salt-water pool, and peers intently into the darkening yard. The St. Augustine grass is thick, a dull gray-green, and cut long. The gardener keeps it trimmed that way – says it is healthier, better able to survive the long days of brutal Florida sun. But the tall grass harbors so many tiny animals, little fugitives from the cats and raccoons, like the pin-head mites that bite and prick and sting. Pauline squints, wondering what is hiding in the grass, what may be looking back at her. For a moment, she is afraid.

She shakes her head. *It's nothing,* she chides herself. At least it is not a snake, or a rat, or a scorpion. It is no more than the movement of a grasshopper, or a fallen tree frog, or one of the ubiquitous green geckos that populate the island and waken tourists in the night with their mating screeches.

Native islanders are inured to their eerie sounds; it is only tourists passing through who are bothered. Pauline continues staring, but there is no more movement. With the stillness, her momentary diversion is forgotten, her thoughts glide backward, and she is lost again.

"Pauline, it's time to come in, the sun's gone down." Jinny's voice calls faintly from the main house, not for the first time this evening. It is past the dinner hour. Jinny will have made a simple, light meal – fish caught that afternoon from the waters of the Florida Straits, and fragrant Cuban yellow rice, just for the two of them.

The sisters are the only occupants of the mansion now, and Jinny's footsteps echo dully on the dark heart pine floors as she pads out to the pool to call Pauline to dinner, yet again. Jinny rounds the corner of the pool house and watches her sister, floating on her back in the salty water; Pauline is oblivious to the falling light, to the cooling day, to Jinny's persistent calls.

"Pauline," Jinny says again, exasperated. "Dinner's ready, come on in." Pauline is unresponsive, eyes closed, floating in the salty water. Jinny kneels by the poolside. She reaches down to the shiny surface and splashes water on her sister's upturned face. Pauline's eyes pop open. She lets her legs sink, leaden, until her toes touch the bottom of the pool. She stands, and stares at Jinny as if at a stranger, mute. Jinny sighs resignedly, knowing it will take effort to rouse Pauline from her solitary, watery reverie.

"I'm going back in," Jinny says. "I'm putting the food on the table, and if you're not there in five minutes, I'm starting without you." She pauses, waits for a reply. When none is forthcoming, she shakes her head and walks wearily back to the house. Her sister's heartache and pain weigh her down; for the thousandth time Jinny attempts to slough off the decades-old anger that could easily consume her.

Pauline watches her sister walk away. Her mind feels foggy, almost blank. Jinny wants her to come to dinner. She should get out of the pool and go inside. But her body feels like dead weight beneath her; every movement comes only with great effort. She closes her eyes.

Pauline leans back into the water to watch the rising, pale moon peeking through the coconut palms. She looks down at her legs, eerily misshapen in the water's refraction. *Elizabeth was correct: I do look like I have frogs' legs.* But Elizabeth is gone now, only faithful Jinny is left, and Pauline is alone. Alone in her saltwater pool, floating with her valueless regrets.

She turns onto her back again to face the now blue-black sky studded with stars, and the solitary moon. Closing her eyes, she lets the cool water buoy her, embrace her.

It has been a long time since anyone held her. Her thin hands paddle the water, and she thinks about parents, lovers, husband, sons, friends – all the hands that have touched her. They are all gone. Her only companion now is Jinny.

Pauline opens her eyes. The moon has risen farther in the northeast sky – the palm trees are silver in the moonlight. She sighs. *I gave everyone good reason to leave.* She pushes the thought away, and hastily suppresses the threat of losing Jinny as well.

"I'm coming," Pauline calls weakly, only vaguely aware that her voice will not carry into the house.

Minutes pass. Pauline is no nearer making it inside to dinner. The cooked fish will be cooling by now, beginning to gel around the edges. She senses a niggling anxiety, a vague acknowledgement that she is risking Jinny's irritation. But her thoughts, like seaweed heavy around her ankles, detain her in the water.

Pauline shivers. She considers the consequences of bearing these maddening echoes, alone – with no exoneration, no compassion. The water now feels so cold, and she is chilled to the bone. Her frailty, her illness, her mortality weigh her down. It is a physical struggle to keep her head above water. She tips her head back and prays, *God, please don't let me die out here tonight, alone. Please.* She knows that she is coming late to the altar, perhaps in vain, to plea for some relief.

Pauline begins to cry, silently, motionlessly. Tears slip down the sides of her face, into the salt water of her pool. *Who am I to weep, or to grieve?* After thoughtlessly creating so much heartache for others, is there not a prohibition from weltering in personal sorrow? Pauline feels regret for those she hurt so deeply, and pity for herself. Her thoughts drift away. She has again forgotten about Jinny and the now-cold dinner.

Jinny's plaintive voice brings her back abruptly to the present. She is calling again. Pauline jerks her head and blinks, coming out of her trance. She swims to the opposite ledge of the pool and rests her cheek against the cool siding. She lifts her head, then slowly climbs out of the water. She picks up her terrycloth robe, lying where she had dropped it, and slowly wraps it around herself. She moves clumsily across the flagstones of the poolside and sits down on her favorite mahogany bench.

If Jinny has to call again, she will surely be irritated. Pauline picks at a splinter on the bench seat and peels it off, revealing a paler wood underneath. She muses that her sister's forbearance seems unending, if undeserved.

The soft white robe engulfs her, and she leans back against the weathered wood. Pauline looks up into the high, swaying fronds of the coconut palm beside her. She planted this palm when they first moved into the house. It is now the tallest tree on the island. She dips her head toward her chest and sits motionless, swaddled in remorse.

Pauline pulls the comfort of the thick robe more tightly around her, shivering now in the cool tropical night. She stands and begins to walk toward the house. Her small steps across the smooth flagstones are shuffled, tentative. She must go inside to dinner. She cannot risk further exasperating Jinny.

She walks across the yard, slowly padding through the broad-blade St. Augustine, so thick it cuts at her bare feet. As she nears the back door, she pauses again and to look at the lilting African tulip tree, heavy with gaudy orange blossoms. She stares up into the branches, and wonders if her penitence can have any effect, any saving grace at so late a juncture.

Getting no answer from the tree, she slips through the back door into the kitchen, and slowly propels herself down the long corridor to the dining room. As she walks, her slim fingers trail the cool plaster of the wall. She reaches the doorway of the dining room and pauses, leaning for a moment against the heavy wooden molding. Jinny glances up, her fork poised in mid-air, obviously having decided to eat her meal alone. The two sisters stare at each other with mutual disappointment and sorrow.

Jinny shifts her tiny frame in the large oak chair. She is dwarfed by the massive antique Spanish monastery table that fills the dining room. Smaller than her sister, her pale blonde hair and pretty, child-like features give her an elfin quality.

Jinny does not say anything when Pauline enters; she turns her attention back to her dinner.

Pauline shuffles forward and sits down. She contemplates her plate, as if she is not sure what to do with it. Her long illness has made food anathema; eating is an unpleasant chore. She sighs. With an effort, she lifts her fork, and pauses.

Jinny looks up. Her sister is lost in a daydream again, and Jinny is torn between irritation and empathy. They leave for California in the morning, to see yet another round of doctors, but neither is sanguine about the trip. The insidious genesis of Pauline's illness has not responded to medication.

Pauline is hazily aware that she needs to comply and do this simple thing: eat her dinner. But her overabundance of guilt and sadness intrude. She does not know whether, after tomorrow, she will see Florida or her beloved mansion again. She attempts to collect herself, and inclines her head to conceal any emotion from Jinny.

She says a silent prayer, wishing Elizabeth would come; Elizabeth could perhaps provide some reassurance. She wonders silently, *are there some sins that can have no resolution other than complete abandonment?*

In silence, Pauline begins to put small bites of food into her mouth. Jinny looks up once or twice, but her sister's sadness is palpable and overwhelming. Yet Pauline is still her anchor, the essential heart around which Jinny's world revolves. *She needs me*, Jinny thinks for the thousandth time. *God in heaven, she needs me.* After all this pain, all this hurt, Jinny is the only one left to help her sister.

Pauline, absorbed in reverie, sips her water and briefly focuses her attention on the condensation shimmering down the sides of the tumbler, the ice long melted. She puts the glass down and continues to eat, but tastes nothing. She looks at Jinny and forces her lips into a wan smile. She lets her head drop back down. The sisters continue to eat, in silence.

PART ONE

~Springtime~

CHAPTER ONE

France, April 1926

The *RMS Mauretania* was berthed at the gritty, cheerless dock of Cherbourg's industrial harbor on a cold, rainy pre-dawn April morning. The pier was dotted with slow-moving, late-night workers ending their shifts and with stevedores starting the new swing, walking briskly down the pier toward recent arrivals. The ship had left her home port of Southampton the previous evening and had continued across the Channel on the last leg of her journey, carrying remaining cross-Atlantic passengers to the continent.

The grand liner had been the largest moving structure ever built when she was launched in 1906, and in the twenty years since her inaugural sail she had more than fulfilled the expectations of Her Majesty's admiralty. The British government had leant the venerable Cunard Line over a million pounds to construct the luxury liner, and another million to build her sister ship, the *RMS Lusitania*.

Both were designed to sail upwards of twenty-four knots, enough to surpass their German counterparts, and the *Mauretania's* massive steam turbine technology had proven up to the task. She had seen valiant service in the World War, and afterwards had been meticulously refitted to recapture her Edwardian opulence.

The ship's public rooms boasted twenty-eight different kinds of exotic woods, exhibiting the cabinetry, turning, and joinery of more than three hundred master craftsmen. Corinthian marble columns, straw wood paneling, and Italian tapestries adorned the multi-level first class dining rooms, and a magnificent central staircase, constructed of dark walnut and luxuriously frosted with deep ruby-red carpeting,

1

connected the first and second stories. For those passengers who chose an alternative mode of conveyance between floors, the novelty of shipboard elevators, each encased in startlingly bright, ornately carved aluminum grills, provided swift transport.

Although it was quite early in the day, Pauline had left her stateroom to visit the Verandah Café on the boat deck. She knew it would take several hours to complete the disembarkation process, and she wanted to spend some time alone before enduring the harried jostling of departure. Pauline climbed the circular metal staircase up to the enclosed sight-seeing area, and pulled herself up into the room.

The back walls of the café were festooned with meticulously carved replicas of sailing ships, ships' wheels, and lighthouses. Photographs of dazzling Cunard Line christenings decorated the walls, the foregrounds featuring Edwardian ladies in plumed hats, long dark coats, and fur collars, standing Lilliputian before the massive keels and brandishing bottles of champagne tied to deck ropes. Walnut shelves dotted the walls and sported painstakingly carved and painted wooden sculptures of seagulls, pelicans, and terns, all screwed securely to their artificial maritime tableau.

The two outer walls were comprised of floor-to-ceiling paned windows providing a panoramic view. Oblivious to the interior decoration, Pauline walked toward the glass wall and reached for the handrail that ran along its perimeter; she leaned against the smooth wooden rail and looked out over the city in the early morning light.

Cherbourg was covered in fog, and small, indistinct points of light poked dimly through the haze, as if the electricity had run down during the night. The wind buffeted the windows of the enclosed deck, pelting droplets of rain against the misty glass. Pauline let her mind wander.

Soon she and Jinny would leave the ship, take the train into Paris, move into their hotel, and start the process of finding an apartment. Pauline expected Jinny would take charge of the details; she was extremely capable at that sort of thing. And it really did not matter much to Pauline, so long as she was close to the throbbing, stimulating nightlife of Parisian urbanity.

Back in New York, Pauline had read thrilling accounts of the bohemian culture that was burgeoning in Europe, and in Paris in particular. The colorful newspaper and magazine stories had tantalized her, and she had been drawn as if by a magnet.

Pauline finished her contemplation of the bleak morning sky, and crept carefully back down the narrow, curving staircase. She walked the padded plush carpeting of the ship's elegant hallways and returned to her stateroom to finish packing the heavy travel trunks. The stewards had brought them in the night before, and the trunks now filled the small room.

Just as Pauline finished packing and snapped shut the locks on the last case, Jinny appeared at the door.

"Come on, I'm hungry," Jinny said. Pauline smiled at her and surveyed the trunks, glad to have the task completed. The sisters left the small stateroom and ambled slowly up the grand staircase to the main dining salon. Soon they were seated for their last on-board breakfast.

The Cunard Line's elegant porcelain china plates and coffee cups were placed before them, efficiently and generously filled, and they began to eat. Their conversation was halting and measured by long pauses; both were absorbed in thoughts of Paris and the adventures before them.

Pauline was slated to begin work as a fashion editor at *Vogue*, in a relatively new office of the famous magazine. The

Paris office had been open only six years. It was the perfect position for an ambitious woman, particularly one who was young and wealthy, to establish herself among the litterateurs and artists of Paris.

Jinny had no such focus or ambition; she had accompanied her sister seemingly on a whim. She didn't have a strong interest in European travel, but she had long evinced a desire to get away from the rural, albeit elegant, family home in Arkansas, and Pauline's new posting provided as good a reason as any to leave.

As she ate, Pauline reminded herself that, once in Paris, she needed to keep the provincial roots of the family's business fortunes to herself. Her father was now a successful banker, but it was cotton farming that had provided the family's initial wealth. She would also need to be vigilant to ensure that Jinny, who often acted without regard for social convention, remained similarly discrete. Pauline did not want their pastoral heritage to prejudice her longed-for acceptance into eccentric, avant-garde Parisian society.

The sisters were extremely close – they were almost like twins in their affection for and devotion to each other. But they had strikingly different personalities: Pauline, steady, calculating, self-absorbed; and Jinny, unpredictable, introverted, altruistic. Even so, they had learned to tolerate each other's demeanors and, for the most part, accept each other's foibles.

Another immediately obvious difference between the two: they did not dress at all alike. Jinny often chose pants over dresses, and was given to bold cuts and colors, much to the chagrin of their mother. And even though she had often been referred to as a tomboy – an unfortunate label back home in Arkansas – Jinny was by far the prettier of the two Pfeiffer daughters.

Jinny was blond and blue-eyed, in contrast to Pauline's darker aspect, and Jinny's features were classic: shining almond eyes, a delicate nose, small rose-shaped pink lips. In comparison, Pauline's was an atypical beauty; she had broad planes to her face, angular cheekbones, a longer, almost Roman nose, large brown eyes, and a generous, wide mouth. Despite their differences in physique and personality, however, the two sisters shared an unwavering devotion to each other, and they apprehended one another's moods and proclivities instinctively.

This morning, Pauline sat carefully on the edge of her dining chair. Her sheath dress was of pale blue silk *crêpe-de-chine*; she loved the way the undulating fabric swayed closely around her hips when she walked. As Pauline sipped her coffee, one hand moved to caress the puff of dove-gray chiffon at her décolleté. *Perfect*, she thought, precisely the right outfit for her arrival in Paris.

Pauline replaced her coffee cup in its saucer, then absentmindedly ran her fingers over the long, glossy strand of perfectly matched pearls that fell down the front of her dress and were casually knotted just below her waist. A black woolen travelling coat, gray gloves, and a slim satin clutch lay on the empty chair beside her. She adjusted her dark gray felt cloche and absently crossed and re-crossed her ankles, sliding the black leather heeled pumps back and forth under her chair.

Pauline's outfit had been purchased in New York, but it had been carefully chosen for Paris. She was exceptionally conscious that she needed to begin as she meant to go on in her new city; Pauline wanted assiduously to avoid any action or appearance that might brand her as a vulgar American.

In contrast, Jinny was dressed as she was any day, for comfort. Dark blue sailor slacks swung easily around her slim legs, and were topped with a square-collared, winter-white wool skimmer jacket. Low-heeled black flats completed her outfit. Her head, as always, was uncovered: Jinny refused ever to wear a hat.

"Well, are you excited?" Jinny asked absently, and then shook her head and laughed. "A stupid question, of course you are." She smiled at Pauline.

Jinny hoped that this trip was a pivot point, a jumping off into a better future, although she was not sure exactly what that might entail. Jinny still was not sure whether she was leaving something behind or headed toward a goal. Then again, she thought, it really did not matter. The change itself was more important to Jinny than understanding the purpose of the journey.

Pauline, on the other hand, was very certain about her future. As she had told her sister, Pauline's intent was to enthusiastically explore the Parisian artistic community, to fully experience, as she had phrased it, "the uncommonly spectacular."

"Yes, excited," Pauline said, replying to her sister's query. "I'm excited, and happy, and any other good adjective you can think of." Pauline had been more than ready to leave New York, her dull job as a proofreader, and the endless line of pleasant but impecunious beaux. Her keen anticipation of an electrifying existence in the American expatriate cultural heart of Europe was all-consuming. She itched to get off the ship.

"Well, I will be your enthusiastic cheerleader," said Jinny, smiling over the top of a porcelain coffee cup; she traced her finger along the tiny arc of the cup's silver "C" monogram. "*'Whither thou goest,'* sis," Jinny murmured. She picked up a piece of toast, covered it in orange marmalade, and took a bite.

Pauline looked at her sister contemplatively, her coffee cup arrested in mid-air.

"You know, Jinny," Pauline said quietly, replacing her cup in its saucer and looking thoughtfully at her sister, "that phrase, that bit from the Bible, it's often mis-used in wedding ceremonies." Jinny cocked one eyebrow, and waited. Pauline took another sip of her coffee, and continued. "It's from the Old Testament, and it wasn't said by a woman to a man; it way said by Ruth, to her mother-in-law, Naomi." Pauline paused, tilted her head to one side, then continued.

"Their husbands had died in a war or something, they were on their own, alone. Women without husbands were treated horribly back then, and so Ruth was throwing her mother-in-law a lifeline, telling her she would stay with her. '*Whither thou goest,*' and all the rest. Woman to woman, not woman to man. Your use of the phrase is much more apt than some naive bride's." Pauline took the last sip of her cooling coffee.

Jinny was mildly surprised at her sister's remembrance of their Catholic catechisms, and pleased that she had elicited Pauline's measured approval. They finished their meal in silence and went out on deck to wait for the whistles to blow.

CHAPTER TWO

"**L**et's go find Ichabod Crane and ask him for recommendations for drinks and dinner." Jinny's voice was soft but resolute. Pauline was pleasantly surprised at Jinny's invitation to consult the hotel's cadaverous concierge; she had anticipated that it might be difficult to coax Jinny to go out on the town.

It was almost dusk, and the light shone pale and evanescent through the tall windows of their Paris hotel room. They had briefly rested after settling into their suite late that afternoon, and Jinny, though tired, was clearly trying to accommodate Pauline's desire to explore. Pauline was grateful for it, and she languidly and with evident pleasure ran her hands over the clothes hanging in her open wardrobe trunk. She picked out a short evening dress, slip, shoes, and hat. Jinny, as usual, did not bother with her attire, and casually pulled on a coat over the pants and shirt she had been wearing.

"Come on," Jinny chided, "let's get moving. Chop, chop, little onion." Pauline laughed, and began leisurely to dress. Jinny waited, leaning up against the door frame, silently watching her sister put on clothes and make-up. Finally, Pauline was ready. She walked across the room and hooked her arm in Jinny's.

"Let's go," she smiled and tugged on Jinny's arm. The sisters walked down the hallway to the metal grill door of the elevator, and pushed the button. When the elevator arrived they slid the grill open, stepped inside the polished, wood-paneled enclosure, and pulled closed the creaking metal grate behind them. As the elevator descended to the lobby, the two women stood close together, heads almost touching, softly chatting.

In the lobby, the concierge – tall, gaunt, and painfully thin – stood behind a massive registration desk that dwarfed the small entryway. The desk was of dark oak, its frontispiece heavily carved with pendulous hanging grapes, weeping apple saplings, and drooping lemonfruit limbs. The lobby was poorly lit, but the dim atmosphere suited; it was calming, and quiet. A small green accountant's lamp cast a pleasant low light over the guest registry, which was the sole occupant of the huge desktop. The highly polished surface gleamed in the soft glow.

The skeletal attendant stood silently, patiently waiting, his long-fingered hands resting lightly on either side of the registry. Like the specter of Washington Irving's imagination, he stood guard behind the desk, erect, severe, his pencil-thin moustache twitching, watery eyes peering over the top of wireless-rimmed glasses. He smiled fawningly when the sisters entered the lobby.

"Why yes, my dears," the concierge sighed breathily in response to their queries. "I have plenty of suggestions for you." He smiled and simpered at them, and fluttered his bony fingers. Then he quickly reached under the desktop and pulled out a telephone book, which he immediately dropped on the floor. The concierge quickly bent to pick up the book, and smacked his head loudly against the top of the desk.

Pauline and Jinny could barely keep from laughing. Effortfully maintaining serious demeanors, they finally received the concierge's considered suggestions, carefully written in a florid hand on thick paper, and then quickly left, before they started giggling openly at him.

The sisters hurried out the revolving lobby doors, bumping into each other as they rushed outside. They fell out onto the sidewalk, burst into laughter, then walked quickly away down the sidewalk, arm in arm, giggling. They were relieved to have spared both themselves and their benefactor any embarrassment.

They decided to have a couple of drinks. Back in New York, Prohibition had made it hard to find reliably good liquor, and they were looking forward to choosing from a full cocktail menu. The first *boîte* they found was an inviting, café-style restaurant, with casual seating on the sidewalk and what looked like a welcoming wood-paneled bar at the back. It seemed a good place to start the evening.

Once seated comfortably on banquettes at the back bar, Pauline rested her head against the padded leather and smiled at her sister. She raised one finger and beckoned the waiter to their table.

"*Garçon, une bouteille de Veuve Clicquot, s'il vous plait.*" She smiled at Jinny and winked. "Might as well start with a bang." Jinny laughed, and shook her head. Pauline looked around the softly lit bar and relaxed into her seat.

Both sisters were silent, but not uncomfortably so, surveying the new scene and pleasantly anticipating what might happen next. The waiter returned with the bottle of champagne, an ice bucket, and two bowl glasses. He made a fine show of opening the bottle and pouring. They watched, appreciatively. Pauline raised her glass to Jinny's and clinked them softly together.

"Here's to us, my dear sis – whatever this might bring, let's hope it's wonderful fun." Pauline smiled. Jinny didn't respond, but simply nodded, and took a sip. Jinny's head was bent too far over the top of the glass as she drank, and the bubbles went up her nose. She sneezed, and Pauline laughed.

"You're going to have to get over that, Jinny, or you'll look like an American rube." Pauline said as she sipped, making sure that the bubbles did not have a similar effect on her.

"Well, perhaps my role is to make sure I show you what *not* to do, dear sis," Jinny replied, continuing to drink the sparkling amber liquid.

For some reason, Jinny's comment deflated Pauline a bit. She made an effort to suppress the uncomfortable feeling. Pauline didn't want to be unhappy tonight, she just wanted to enjoy herself. She beckoned to the garçon, who deferentially refilled their glasses. They continued to drink in comfortable silence; each occupied with her own thoughts.

There were other occupants of the bar: two middle-aged women gossiping over half pints of beer; an old man staring sullenly at a half-full glass of red wine, a handsome collie lying quietly under his chair; a young couple, giggling and caressing over cocktails. Pauline looked at the other patrons bemusedly, and then her thoughts turned to the vaguely understood specifics of her new position.

The trans-Atlantic job application-and-offer process had been effected in truncated fashion. The whole procedure – an initial importunate inquiry from Pauline followed by several letters of recommendation from her father's obliging business associates – had been concluded in a series of overseas cables, without much detail as to precise responsibilities. Whatever the duties were to be, however, Pauline was confident and cavalier that she would be more than capable of performing them.

The waiter poured more champagne. Pauline nodded and smiled in thanks and relaxed back into her thoughts. She was certain that this new stage of her life would bring, not just the intrinsic pleasure of having captured the job at *Vogue*, but also exciting indulgences and adventures. Right now, all she wanted was pleasure.

The new job would, she hoped, bring attendant amusements – fine food and wines, lovely and decadent wardrobes, perhaps even romantic diversions. Pauline had decided she would place no unnecessary limitations on her conduct or expectations; she would do nothing that would impede her ability to enjoy herself.

"Penny for your thoughts," Jinny inclined her head toward Pauline, waiting for an answer. Pauline smiled.

"It's going to be the real start of my life, Jinny," Pauline said, and tapped her fingertips on the tablecloth. "This, what we're doing right now, this is the very start." She paused briefly, smiling. "And I plan to drink an awful lot of champagne." Pauline tilted the bowl toward her lips. "Like this."

Pauline quickly threw her head back, and suddenly choked on the bubbly liquid. Recovering, she inclined her head forward and sputtered into the glass, her eyes watering.

Jinny chuckled, watching Pauline repeat the earlier gaffe. She waited patiently, knowing Pauline had more to say.

"I plan on being a famous editor," Pauline continued intrepidly, showing no embarrassment at her *faux pas* with the champagne, "and having a staff of slavering assistants, and driving a stupidly expensive sports car." She hiccupped, and continued, "With no lid."

"What do you mean, 'no lid'?" Jinny asked, laughing.

"No lid, silly, you know, nothing above me." Pauline waved her arms above her head, champagne bowl still in hand, sloshing a little bit out one side. The champagne puddled on the seat beside her, but she ignored it and continued to drink, enjoying her slight inebriation.

"You mean a roadster, silly." Jinny offered. She sipped and smiled at her sister, waiting for further expansion.

"Yes, that, a roadster. Oh, and a man." Jinny watched her sister's face split into a grin. "Yes, a man. A big, rich, important man. Oh, and a scandalous man – that's what I am going to do: be famous and have a disgracefully shocking love affair, and over here no one will be able to say 'boo' to me about it."

Pauline tipped her head over the champagne and touched her lips to the glass. This time, taking care, she managed to swallow it without misstep. Jinny tilted her head sideways and gazed softly at her sister.

"You know, honey, I think that's precisely what you will do. And I'm just going to sit on the byway, and watch the circus roll by." Pauline looked up sharply.

"No, don't sit by, Jinny," Pauline said, suddenly quiet. "Don't sit on the byway – please don't just watch me go by." Pauline's playfulness was gone; the alcohol had exaggerated her emotions and she looked pleadingly at her sister. Jinny immediately moved her arm across the table and covered Pauline's hand.

"Don't worry hon, you won't ever be alone." Pauline let Jinny's hand rest on hers, then, shrugging off her momentary gloominess, pulled her hand away. She changed the subject.

"I'm ready for something new Miss J. Let's get going." Pauline quickly picked up her purse and gloves, and slid to the end of the banquette. Her brief discomfort apparently forgotten, Pauline stood and steadied herself against the edge of the table. She picked up her glass and finished the last of the champagne. Then she turned and walked back through the bar and out into the street. Jinny followed. Together, the sisters stepped carefully along on the cobbled sidewalks, out into the long Paris night.

CHAPTER THREE

They had been in Paris for a week, and Pauline had just a few more days before she was expected to report at the *Vogue* offices. She wanted to make the most of it. Jinny and Pauline had fallen into a routine of sleeping late, shopping in the afternoons, and in the evenings dropping around to a party or two. Before the parties, they usually visited a bar, meeting writers and painters, each *artiste* more flamboyant and outrageous than the last. It was as if there were an unspoken contest within these bohemian circles to see who could most shock the *bourgeoisie* conscience. The atmosphere of the city was electric and spontaneous, and radical behavior the norm. It was immensely fun, sometimes enervating, but always exciting.

One evening, the sisters were headed to a private party that promised to be full of the usual concatenation of painters, musicians, writers. Neither Pauline nor Jinny knew the hosts, but it did not matter; the expat community in Paris was fluid, and forgiving of gate crashers.

The party was being held in small brick house on a quiet street. Loud music thrummed from the windows, and throngs of people could be seen inside – dancing, talking, drinking, laughing. Jinny and Pauline walked up to the front door, knocked and, when no one answered, went inside. They surveyed the revelers and Pauline pointed, raising her arm discretely to elbow level, at a man across the room.

"Look, over there, he's a writer," Pauline whispered to Jinny. Jinny was familiar with her sister's shorthand: Pauline believed she could tell a person's artistic passion by their clothing. "Musicians wear black, writers wear tweed, and painters wear dangling *Gauloises*," was Pauline's maxim;

Jinny was amused at how often this turned out to be correct. They moved across the room toward the man in tweed.

He was accompanied by a petite, curly-haired, bobbed blond, who appeared to be his inverse in all respects. The man's aspect was calm, staid, solid; the woman, on the other hand, was a howler. Pauline and Jinny watched as the little blond climbed up on a tabletop and began to dance enthusiastically; the man seemed entranced and gazed up at her with bemused approval.

Pauline glanced at Jinny and noticed that her sister was staring raptly at the blond, similarly captivated by the wildly gyrating dancer. Pauline recognized that it was just this sort of person – tempestuous, unpredictable – who seemed to appeal most to Jinny.

"That's your kind of dancing, isn't it?" Pauline asked Jinny. Jinny did not respond, her eyes focused on the girl on the table. Pauline was not sure Jinny had heard her. Jinny swayed to the music and continued to watch the blond with fascination and admiration. Pauline, realizing she would not be able to divert her sister's attention, walked away to go find the bar.

She located a table full of mismatched glasses and bottles, and poured two tumblers of wine, taking one back to the still-enthralled Jinny. Pauline handed her the drink and, when ignored, set the proffered wine down on a cocktail table, already littered with empty glasses and toothpicks. Pauline decided it was futile to try and engage Jinny. She began to mill alone around the room through the mass of revelers, smiling at half-heard bits of conversation, watching the continual refilling of empty glasses held in outstretched hands.

As the evening progressed and the wild-eyed, boisterous blond became more and more inebriated, Pauline noticed that Jinny's glow intensified. When the little woman finally fell off the table on which she was spinning, Jinny watched her laughingly fall into the outstretched arms of the man, who appeared to be her husband. Pauline glanced at her sister; Jinny's expression was aggrieved, as if she wished she had been the one to have caught the little blond.

The husband walked toward the front door through the revelers, carrying his unconscious burden in his arms, and apologizing for alternately hitting shoulders and backs with the head and feet of his insensible wife. Pauline found Jinny, and gently pulled her arm. She spoke softly into her sister's ear.

"Hey there, let's get out of here. Time to fall into bed ourselves." Jinny continued to watch the man carry the woman outside, presumably to their car or to a waiting taxi. Jinny did not acknowledge her sister.

When the man finally made his way down the front steps with his bundle and disappeared into a cab, Jinny turned to Pauline and nodded; they began their exit through the sweat and now-stale perfume of the partiers. Jinny's disappointment at the departure of the fantastic table-dancer was obvious.

Pauline felt sorry for her and wished she could do something to ameliorate her sister's discontent. She hoped that Jinny's letdown this evening would not cause her to mope and avoid future outings. She also wished that Jinny would not, as she had so many times before, take a single unfortunate incident and turn inward toward a dark, depressing place.

As they walked home on still sidewalks, the streetlights intermittently casting their shadows in front and behind, Pauline decided that she would not let that happen; she would force Jinny to go out, to enjoy herself, to be happy. She did not want Jinny's capricious emotions to interfere with her own pleasure and gratification.

CHAPTER FOUR

The following evening, Pauline was pleasantly surprised when Jinny excitedly tugged her out the door to yet another *fête*. Jinny had apparently recovered from her frustrations of the previous evening, or at least was successful in hiding any lingering malaise. She told Pauline that she had heard about this evening's party from their phlegmatic concierge, but that she only had an address; Jinny murmured absently that she had not quite caught the name of the host.

Pauline was surprised at Jinny's happiness; if Jinny wanted to go out, that was good. It was a sign that she was not giving in to her usual debilitating melancholy, which would surely spoil Pauline's good mood.

The evening was cool and pleasant, a slight breeze ruffled Pauline's silk skirt and tugged at the chiffon scarf carelessly wrapped around her neck. They walked down narrow streets in the seventh *arrondissement*, near the Palais-Bourbon. The neighborhood was an odd admixture of government buildings, small, dingy *pensions*, and a few understatedly elegant private houses. The sisters had walked in this area before; it was home to a diverse group of expat artists and writers.

Jinny still did not know how to confidently navigate the Paris streets, but Pauline had developed an uncanny knack for negotiating *les rues et les instructions*. As they walked toward the address Jinny had provided, music doppled from successive apartments in competing wafts. They walked silently, enjoying the rival descants.

The sisters finally reached their destination and looked up an agreeable row house, clean red brick, neatly appointed and fronted by low, clipped shrubbery in a well-tended stone planter. It was by flanked by two disreputable-looking apartment buildings. The brick house, and its occupants, were obviously more affluent than their neighbors. The sisters walked up the low rising steps and rang the bell.

A maid, in full uniform, answered the door. Pauline and Jinny, surprised at this unusual luxe, were ushered in and made their way down a long, narrow hallway leading to the back of the house.

They could hear the Victrola playing a Cole Porter song, loud and jaunty. They walked down the hall, which was covered in deep red-flocked wallpaper and crammed with paintings and photographs. Pauline paused to stare at a single photo.

The photograph was of a blond curly-haired woman standing beside a man on the deck of a boat. The woman was smiling and holding up a large fish, clearly her trophy catch. The man beamed adoringly at the woman in the photograph. With abrupt recognition, Pauline poked Jinny in the rib and pointed to the picture.

"Look!" Pauline exclaimed, "this is *their* house! It's the dancer from last night and her husband – this is *their* party!" Jinny stared blankly at her, then turned and quickly walked away down the hall.

Watching her sister's receding back, Pauline suddenly realized that Jinny had already known whose house this was. *No wonder she was so keen on coming out this evening*, she thought. Pauline hurried after Jinny, occasionally glancing at the wall of pictures. She would have liked to stop and look more closely at the photographs; she wondered who else might be in them.

The sounds of the party grew nearer, and suddenly Pauline was in the main salon, full of sound and smoke and music. The blond and her husband were bearing down on

Jinny. The woman beamed at her, and spread her thin, pale arms wide in a welcoming embrace.

"Good evening, Miss Pfeiffer," said the man, addressing Jinny, "we're so glad to see you both," turning his gaze briefly to Pauline. Pauline stared blankly, realizing that not only did Jinny know who these people were, but in addition, they somehow already knew Jinny.

The man continued, with just the faintest glimmer of a smile playing around his lips. "Last evening was a bit of a blur. Perhaps we should start the introductions over again." Pauline glared at Jinny, who gave a quick, dismissive shrug of one shoulder. Jinny turned and addressed herself to the blond.

"I'm so glad to see you are doing well," Jinny purred. "I was concerned that you might have been ill after last evening." The blond smiled engagingly at Jinny.

"Well, aren't you the angel!" The distinct Alabama drawl sugared out of her mouth. "That was so kind of you to send flowers! I'm doing fine." Glancing up at her husband, she continued, "and I plan on doing even better this evening!" Her husband put his arm softly around his wife's waist and pulled her to him.

Pauline cocked her head sideways and stared fixedly at Jinny, marveling at her sister's covert identifications, as well as her clandestine floral overture.

"Well darling, perhaps we could enjoy an evening that doesn't conclude with my carrying you to the car." The man's words were spoken without admonition, but rather with a teasing pleasure. Jinny, the husband, and his wife all laughed conspiratorially.

Jinny leaned in a bit closer to both of them so that Pauline was slightly behind her, deftly positioning Pauline outside the threesome. Pauline leaned over Jinny's shoulder and hissed *sotto voce* into her ear.

"*Flowers*? You didn't tell me you knew these people, and you sent her *flowers*?" Jinny responded by turning more of her back toward her sister, attempting to cut Pauline out of the conversation completely. The little blond, however, with deft and practiced politesse, maneuvered slightly around Jinny and held out her tiny hand, palm downward, toward Pauline. Circles of diamonds sparkled at her wrists.

"We haven't met, dear," she smiled sweetly at Pauline. "Well, apparently we *have* met but I don't really remember." The little woman laughed, and her blond curls bounced as she spoke. "I'm Zelda, in case I didn't make that quite clear last night, and this is my husband Scott." Zelda pointed over her shoulder and continued, "My darling husband, who has apparently forgotten that his parched wife needs another drink." Zelda winked at Pauline, and with a vague wave of her hand indicated that she was well on her way to a repetition of the previous evening's drunkenness. Jinny glowed at Zelda and responded enthusiastically.

"I'm right behind you," Jinny said, speaking only to Zelda. "Let's go find a couple of cocktails." Zelda beamed at her, hooked her arm in Jinny's, and abandoned her husband and Pauline. Zelda and Jinny quickly headed toward the cocktail bar at the back of the room.

"Well, they seem to have made fast friends – fast," Scott murmured as he stared at the two women. He seemed not at all embarrassed by his wife. Indeed, his insouciance led Pauline to imagine that if she announced that Jinny and Zelda were off for an evening cruise on the Seine, the man would simply nod and smile. His was clearly a passion that would willingly put up with rather a lot.

"Jinny's always been this way," Pauline offered, "she's an easy person to love," and immediately felt that she had perhaps unwittingly overstepped. "I mean, people love her, all kinds of people." She thought to herself, *I need to shut up and just stop babbling, or this will only get deeper.* Scott smiled indulgently and nodded.

"I can see that. So is Zelda." They sipped their drinks silently, coming to an unspoken agreement that clearly, the best thing to do was to change the subject. Scott obliged.

"Are the two of you here on business or pleasure, as they say?" He smiled at her and lit a cigarette, and Pauline watched his elegant, long fingers as they snapped close the lid of his handsome silver lighter, which he casually slipped it back into his vest pocket. Scott looked supremely charming and at ease. Pauline wondered what his background was – his family, his money, his social standing; her analysis of people usually fell along those three lines.

"I just got a job here – fashion editor, at *Vogue*," Pauline answered. Pointing toward the bar she continued, "Jinny, my sister, came with me to help me get settled." Scott nodded and murmured a blandishment; he did not seem as impressed with her new position as she had hoped or expected. This piqued Pauline's interest in him even more.

"And what do you do, Scott?" Pauline wondered if the tweed jacket had been an accurate predictor. He smiled vaguely and peered around the room, as if looking for an answer.

"Oh, I'm a writer, after a fashion." He took a long drag on his cigarette.

"Oh, really?" Pauline responded. "And what is your *nom de plume*?" He looked at her absently.

"My *nom de plume*? Well, I suppose I haven't got one. Just use my name." He paused. "It's Fitzgerald. Scott Fitzgerald.

The man spoke in a self-deprecating manner, not inviting further inquiry. He took a long pull on his cigarette and, seeming not inclined to elaborate on his response, changed the subject once again. "May I get you something to drink?" he asked politely, bending his patrician face toward her. Pauline gladly accepted, and watched Scott make his way through the tightly packed crowd.

She was intrigued; the name was familiar. Pauline had heard of Fitzgerald's writing, which was receiving some mild acclaim. She'd been told his prose was elegant; she thought, *his writing must match his looks*. She watched him as he crossed the room and dealt with the bartender. Scott seemed to have a sophisticated gracefulness about him, but it was coupled with a guarded aspect. Pauline wondered at the dissonance. *Perhaps having money hasn't fixed whatever problems he has.* As she watched him, Pauline wondered briefly how much of a problem the wife would become.

Scott returned with her drink, and Pauline thanked him and took a sip. The music thrummed around them, and Scott surveyed his guests, looking for an empty glass or an unlit cigarette. Pauline observed his urbane composure, and wondered again at what made her feel that his demeanor belied an almost palpable sadness. She took another sip of her drink.

Then, without a word of apology, Scott disappeared. She stared at the back of his jacket as he moved quickly toward the far end of the room. She then looked around and noticed that Jinny and Zelda were nowhere to be seen. *Oh well*, she thought, *I guess I'm not doing well at mingling tonight.* She gazed lazily around the room.

Pauline knew no one at the party, but at the same time, there was a great freedom in being anonymous. She was about to duck back out to the long red hallway to look at the pictures, when a solid-looking young woman sidled up to her and gave Pauline a shy smile.

"You're American, aren't you?" The woman's accent was pure Midwest; she seemed to be looking for someone to rescue her from the sea of foreign artists and writers.

"Yes, my name is Pauline Pfeiffer, I'm from New York." Pauline avoided giving her Arkansas pedigree. She had already decided that she would present herself as a New Yorker living in Paris.

"My name is Hadley Hemingway," the woman responded. "I'm from St. Louis. My husband and I live here now, but I don't think of myself as anything but a Missourian." She was a sweet-looking woman, almost childlike. But there were lines in her face that bespoke adult worries and concerns; she was no child.

Pauline guessed her age at about thirty, a bit older than herself. Hadley's clothes were bland and frumpy and somewhat worn. She looked out of place among these chic, young artists and aesthetes. This gathering was clearly of the erudite cognoscente in Paris, and Pauline wondered what this drab woman's connection was to it.

To Pauline, Hadley looked like she had come directly out of a St. Louis suburb and still belonged back there, in a little house with a yard and a garden and about ten children. She certainly did not look like she belonged in Paris, at this party.

"I worked in St. Louis for a brief while, right after I graduated from college," Pauline offered. "I was a reporter for the *Times-Dispatch*." Hadley brightened.

"Oh, then perhaps you know my husband – he is – well, was, no I guess is – a reporter too," Hadley stammered, and smiled awkwardly. "Worked on the *Kansas City Star*, and now does some contract work here. But mainly, he's working on fiction. Short stories right now."

So that was the answer, thought Pauline, the husband was another American expat writer, come to Paris to find his muse. And she was the dutiful wife, tagging along and putting up with it. By the looks of Hadley's clothes, so far the writer-husband must not be much of a success. Pauline decided to be benevolent with this meek woman.

"Well, perhaps our paths may have crossed. What's his name?" Pauline hardly expected that she would have ever run into a bumpkin, Midwestern reporter from Kansas City, but she was trying to be polite. This poor woman clearly was at sea and needed someone to talk to. And, as Scott, Jinny, and Zelda had all disappeared for an indeterminate amount of time, Pauline was free to oblige this misfit young woman for a while. She peered over Hadley's shoulder distractedly, looking at the pictures on the red-flocked walls as she waited for a response.

"It's Ernest, Ernest Hemingway," said Hadley. "He's standing right over there." Hadley pointed toward the back of the room, toward the cloth-covered bar.

The large man was standing in front of the bar, instructing the bartender on the mixing of his drink. He was unusual in appearance. Pauline's first impression was that he, like his wife, was out of place. Not in the same way as she – not inadequate or unsure or tentative – not at all. Just the opposite. It seemed to Pauline as if the man were somewhat outsized, as if there were a kind of mutation about him, that he was just a little bit oddly larger than anyone else in the room.

Back in New York, there had been a pharmacy near Pauline's apartment that hung advertisements in all its windows, large posters depicting extravagantly cheerful customer happily engaged in utilizing health or dental products. When Pauline occasionally did a favor for a neighbor and walked her dog, upon passing the pharmacy the little terrier would bark uncontrollably at the gargantuan human faces, spreading its miniature forelegs legs in an aggressive stance and yapping wildly until Pauline pulled him away down the sidewalk. When Pauline first saw Ernest Hemingway, standing at the bar in Zelda and Scott Fitzgerald's living room – larger-than-life, loud, and annoying as he belligerently ordered his cocktail – the first thought she had was, *this guy would drive Tippy out of his mind.*

Hadley watched Pauline staring at her husband. Pauline was watching the bar fixedly, and had turned her back to her new acquaintance. Hadley tapped her softly on the shoulder.

"Would you like to meet him?" Hadley asked. Obviously, she felt that he was the more important, the more interesting half of their couple. Most women would have continued chatting with a new acquaintance, particularly when meeting someone from their own country in a foreign land, getting to know more about them and telling more about themselves. But Hadley almost immediately abdicated her role as a conversant and offered to introduce Pauline to her husband. At this small tipping point in time, Pauline assented.

Hadley took Pauline's hand, and they walked to the bar, toward Ernest. As they made their way through the guests, Hadley's eyes never left him. Pauline watched her; she could see this was a woman who adored her husband. Perhaps too much so. Pauline had seen that look before, that look of a woman who poured herself into a man, and then got lost. She took care of him, had his babies, cleaned his home, and cooked his meals. But the woman herself, she was gone. Pauline suddenly felt sorry for Hadley.

They approached the bar, and Hadley gently touched Ernest on the arm. He did not turn, did not act as if her touch had registered. His cocktail, a Negroni, had been put in front of him, a deep liquid blood red.

"Let's see where we are now, son," Ernest growled at the nervous bartender. From the detritus of toothpicks and cocktail fruit and spilled, sticky sweet vermouth on the bar, it looked as if this had been at least the third or fourth attempt at mixing the requested drink. The young barman looked up, his face haggard, clearly begging the man to accept this latest proffering and carry it off to another room, so that he could do his job in relative peace. The barman's hopes were not to be realized.

Ernest took a long swig of the cocktail, and his face contorted into a theatrical grimace. He slammed the glass down on the bar.

"Gad almighty boy!" Ernest bellowed. "How many times do we have to do this?" Although his question was framed as a complaint, Pauline noticed that his first "taste" had drained most of the glass. Ernest glared at the barman and demanded, "*Again.*" He slapped a heavy palm down on the bar. "And this time, when I say a jigger of gin, I mean a *man's* jigger, not a bloody fairy's dribble." The bartender cringed, and began to try to concoct the drink yet again.

Ernest's words were offensive, but somehow no one watching the spectacle seemed to mind, least of all Hadley. The conversation went on, swirling around him just as before. The anxious bartender complied, once again, with yet another attempt to please this ogre of a man and fulfill his petulant, demanding requests. Hadley smiled benignly at her husband, and the partygoers around him continued to laugh and occasionally glance at him with insouciant acceptance.

It seemed to Pauline as if almost everyone around Ernest colluded to satisfy the indulgence of his whims and desires. His presence seemed to pervade the larger space around him; he sucked the air out of the room, leaving onlookers to turn to him for exhaled oxygen.

In later years, it was a phenomenon Pauline would witness many times, in cities and towns and villages all over the world, in grand hotels and bars and living rooms, with celebrities and acquaintances and drunks and vagabonds. Even when they abhorred him, they all circled around Hemingway.

Pauline stared at him, mesmerized. Ernest continued to bluster and bully, and Pauline found herself unable to stop watching the sideshow he spontaneously created around him. At that moment, she felt the force of revolving poles of two strong magnets: Ernest was both intriguing and repellant. And, for some reason, she found his antics – however, foul or irksome – weirdly humorous.

Pauline wondered briefly, what a chore it must be to be his wife. At the same time, she considered that, however difficult, life would never be dull around such a circus of a man.

CHAPTER FIVE

Pauline found Ernest and Hadley to be an enigmatic couple. He was large, handsome, his physical energy exudant in every movement, while she was mousy, quiet, seemingly too timid to be able to attract and keep the attention of this bear of a man. But perhaps, Pauline thought, that was the attraction. Perhaps Hadley liked being the submissive, overwhelmed wife, and perhaps he enjoyed his supremacy over her. Pauline did not think it a positive or salubrious type of partnership, but she found Hadley to be a pleasant enough person, if a bit boring.

As the Fitzgerald's party went on into the evening and Ernest's bouts of ranting and declaiming persisted, Hadley and Pauline continued to chat. Having been abandoned by Jinny and feeling the onus to indulge this needy companion, Pauline, surprisingly, found that she really did not really want to make the effort to mingle. So she sat with Hadley, and listened to her talk about Ernest, their baby, and what had brought them to Paris. As she chatted, Hadley kept a constant, watchful eye on her husband, waiting for the next pause in Ernest's diatribes to perhaps try and draw him into their conversation.

At one of these intermissions, Ernest huffily left the companions he had been sarcastically berating at the bar and made his way over to the two women. Pauline and Hadley were side-by-side, on a brocade settee in the corner.

"Hey, Tatie," Ernest bellowed at his wife, "move over and give me a seat." Ernest squatted between them, practically sitting down on top of Hadley. Pauline wondered if their marriage was always like this – a mountain sitting on top of a little molehill. Hadley moved quickly and slid obediently as far

31

to the other end of the settee as she could without actually falling off; she looked expectantly at Ernest and waited for him to direct the scene.

Pauline found their marital *pas de deux* irritating, and at the same time mildly interesting: it was like watching two children struggling over the same toy. Ernest leaned back and a swig from a short glass; it appeared he had abandoned Negronis for whiskey. He turned to Pauline.

"So, what is it that you do, young lady?" he demanded of Pauline. "You a writer, a painter, or the concubine of a writer or a painter?" He laughed at his own mildly objectionable joke and waited for her response.

"I'm a writer," Pauline responded tartly. "A fashion writer. Actually, an editor." Pauline immediately regretted responding so defensively to the question; she wished she had been able to toss back a witty riposte. Unfortunately, none had occurred to her.

"*Fashion* writer?" Ernest laughed sarcastically. "And what do you find to write about? Hem length? Zipper function? The effect of the plunging neckline on the morality of the next generation? Or is that too deep a subject?" He took a long drink of his whiskey. "Too deep a subject – *ha*, 'plunging.' *Ha*." He belched, and laughed drunkenly at his own weak pun.

Although Pauline was irritated by his condescension, she felt a momentary discomfort that perhaps there was a kernel of truth in his crude commentary. Though his comments were crass and vulgar, Ernest had touched a nerve.

She had already silently acknowledged that she was not in the same league with all these intensely creative people surrounding her in Paris. They were real artists; they lived and breathed their craft. She was not a writer; she only edited others' writing. Pauline had at one time been a good reporter and was becoming a decent editor, but Ernest's words exacerbated the feeling that what she was doing was facile, and probably not as important as whatever it was that he might be working on.

Pauline had read sections of various manuscripts from aspiring writers during the past weeks – so many of them carried around their writing like a mother cat carries kittens. Even at parties, they were happy to pull a manuscript out of a coat pocket and request a reading, *"with comments, please,"* asked diffidently and importunately. Some of the manuscripts were terrible, but a select few of them were, Pauline knew, exceptionally good. This minority, indeed, was destined to become famous; Pauline recognized that she was privileged to be present, watching great artistic fires fan into blazing flames. But at the same time, she acknowledged that she was not *doing that,* creating art – she was merely an editor, and therefore a spectator.

And so, when Ernest ridiculed her job as a fashion editor, Pauline felt herself becoming defensive. She knew that he was at least in part right, and she was irritated by his ability to put his finger on her weakness.

Pauline suddenly felt compelled to show this boor of a man that she was not what he thought – she was not just some little rich girl whose father's influence had guaranteed a journalism degree from a good university and a fancy job at a magazine in Paris. Pauline had read and studied the classics; she knew good writing. It occurred to her that if Ernest Hemingway were on a worthwhile journey, she would be able to tell by reading his work. And so, she told him that.

"I'd like to see what you've written, Mr. Hemingway," Pauline said, curtly. "I'd like to see for myself what kind of a writer you really are." He seemed taken aback by her words.

"Are you offering to be a critic?" He challenged her. Pauline met his eyes, directly.

"Well, I'm an editor, that's my job and I'm good at it. I'd be happy to read your work, that is, if you won't be offended by my telling you the truth." Ernest stared at her as if he, for once, was at a loss for words. Pauline smiled, which seemed to disconcert him even more.

Ernest's discomfiture gave Pauline a delightful frisson of pleasure. She felt like a mouse playing a game of tag with a lion. Her words seemed to make him cautious, to set him on edge. He didn't quite know what to make of her, and Pauline was surprised to find she liked that.

The party swirled on into the night. Later, when Pauline was finally at home and in bed, she lay quietly in the dark and pondered the evening. Her thoughts sleepily turned to Hadley and her enigmatic husband, Ernest.

Pauline had enjoyed setting the over-large man off his pins; it had given her pleasure to challenge him. At the same time, she was not sure it was a position she would ever be able to maintain. He was such an imposing, overbearing figure. It had been intoxicating to be able to best him, even momentarily, but it was a little frightening as well.

Her sleepy thoughts turned briefly to Hadley; Pauline did not like how this boorish man treated his wife, however unexciting and prosaic she might be. And then, hazily, Pauline found herself imagining what it would be like to be alone with him, with this inscrutable, perplexing man. She imagined herself in a face-off with him, with no one else around. It would be exciting to try and get the better of this intriguing personality.

Drifting off to sleep, Pauline thought, *I should get to know him better*. Then an intruding picture of Hadley jerked her suddenly awake. Ernest was, if nothing else, a married man with a dear little wife. Married men were off limits. Pauline closed her eyes again, and breathed deeply, pulling the comforter up under her chin and settling into her pillow.

Hadley. Pauline mused sleepily. *Hadley needed a friend.* And there was certainly no reason not to become friendly with her. And if that friendship brought Pauline into occasional acquaintance with Ernest, well, there was nothing wrong with that.

Pauline was not unused to or uncomfortable with mental contortions and justifications; she had long experience in the rationalization of any ruse, as long as it benefitted or pleased her. And seeing Ernest every so often would be an amusing distraction.

And it would be easy – Hadley was so eager for friendship, particularly from another American. Pauline, if she had been able truly to acknowledge her intentions, would not have been proud of herself. Later on, much later, she would find comfort in the slim defense that she had eventually come genuinely to like Hadley. Pauline fell into a comfortable, easy slumber.

CHAPTER SIX

Jinny and Pauline slept late the next morning. They had been among the last guests to leave the Fitzgerald's, and they certainly had been over-served. Pauline woke up with a thick headache and a heaving stomach. She sat on the edge of her bed, elbows on knees and forehead on palms, trying to stop the room from spinning. She hazily mused, incongruously, that she had never gotten back to the red-flocked hallway to look at the rest of the pictures. Pauline sighed.

She had ended up spending the entire evening talking with Hadley. She had listened to Hadley talk endlessly about her son and her apartment and her husband. Pauline leaned forward and cradled her belly in her hands. What a night. What a boring, depressing night.

She sat up and attempted to alleviate her nausea with deep breaths. Finally, she stood and went into the kitchen to make coffee and begin another day. As the coffee brewed and the familiar, bracing scent acclimated Pauline to a new morning, she replayed the last evening's events. Pauline resolved that, in future, she would attempt to avoid, in any way she could, Hadley Hemingway and her train wreck of a husband.

As the weeks passed, however, Jinny and Pauline began to see Hadley and Ernest with some frequency. The Hemingways seemed to be, inexplicably to Pauline, embraced by the talented cadre of artists and writers in Paris, and were welcomed at their parties. And although this meant seeing the Hemingways more than she would have liked, Pauline put up with it; she was happy that Jinny remained amenable to going out every evening and socializing. Jinny, for her part, was not particularly fond of the Hemingways either, but liked the group of bohemians they associated with, and so tolerated their occasional presence.

The sisters fell into a routine. Pauline's work schedule was undemanding, and the duties were interesting. Monday through Thursdays she worked full days, editing whatever copy her bosses put in front of her. Friday mornings they had staff meetings, compiling the previous week's work, sorting through copy, and getting it ready for the managing editors to put in final form for future publication. At noon on Fridays, Pauline was free to begin her weekend, and Jinny was usually waiting for her.

Pauline was pleased that Jinny had embraced life in Paris and was obviously enjoying herself. Pauline no longer worried whether Jinny would fall into a depression; Jinny was too busy having fun.

Jinny had found a little apartment for them in the fifth *arrondissement*. Pauline coveted one of the more glamorous townhouses inhabited by the wealthier crowd of literary and artistic expats in more fashionable areas, but she learned to like the atmosphere of the Left Bank and *le cinquième* – the atmosphere was irreverent and enchanting.

Their little *pension* was one of the nicer ones, light and airy and charming, with beautifully high ceilings. It would do, and Pauline was, for the time being, satisfied with it. Jinny and Pauline spent their Friday afternoons and Saturday mornings trolling the local flea markets for interesting sketches or paintings to hang on their walls. They bought lace curtains for their windows, and enjoyed leisurely hours decorating their apartment.

One Saturday, Pauline carefully picked out a costume for yet another round of evening parties, daydreaming about the admiring glances she would receive. As she was getting ready for the party, Pauline wondered aloud if they would see the Hemingways that night. Jinny responded with a noncommittal grunt.

Ernest always ended up being, in some way, the center of attention at every party, and Jinny had begun to be more and more irritated by him. She had come to intensely dislike how Ernest always called attention to himself, sometimes drunkenly and weirdly challenging anyone within hearing to a boxing match. At other times he simply sat in the corner of a room, ruminating, and people were somehow ineluctably drawn to him, as if to discover and ameliorate the source of his brooding. Hadley, always, was a hovering satellite around her sun.

At these times, Pauline would often pull Hadley away from Ernest, and they find someplace to sit together and talk. Over time, their conversations became more intimate. Hadley told Pauline about their little boy, John, who Ernest had nicknamed "Bumby," about Ernest's writing, about her piano playing, about their money problems – whatever came to her mind. Pauline sat and listened, outwardly empathetic and inwardly evaluative; she wondered how any married couple could be so inherently and obviously mismatched.

Before they left their apartment for the evening, Pauline carelessly threw a black feather boa around her shoulders, topping a dark purple sheath dress studded with sequins and hemmed with a tossing fringe. Jinny wore a pair of tailored black satin tuxedo pants, a white dress jacket, and a red paisley ascot tucked casually at the open neckline of her silk shirt. Pauline's new shoes were black calf-skin heels with pearl buttons up the side; Jinny's were patent leather ballet flats.

They took a cab to the address they had been given and were deposited on a quaint, quiet street with weathered cobblestones, crooked sidewalks, and flickering gas streetlights. It was clear which brownstone was this night's destination: every window blazed with light, and the raucous din of a banjo and a ukulele swam through the open windows. They paid the cab driver and made their way inside.

The first person Pauline saw as she entered was Hadley Hemingway. Hadley spotted Pauline immediately and her face broke into an open, grateful grin. She gestured for Pauline to come sit beside her. Ernest was nowhere in sight.

"I'm so glad to see you!" Hadley said. "A friendly face, and one that speaks good American English!" Pauline was surprised, once again, that this antique little woman was married to such an obviously worldly, if loutish man.

"And I'm glad to see you, too, Hadley." Pauline sat down beside her, and – oddly – patted her leg. Patting was not usually Pauline's style, but Hadley's neediness somehow inspired an uncommon empathy in Pauline.

"Ernest is off somewhere – I think he's at the bar." Pauline was not at all surprised. Whatever the event, one usually found Mr. Hemingway at the bar. "I think he's trying to get one of his special drinks made here – a "peroni" or something. Sometimes I wish I drank more, just so that I could keep up with him." Hadley sounded wistful, and her words carried a sadness. "Of course, it's fun to watch him."

That summed it up pretty well, Pauline thought. She could see the years of marriage ahead of Hadley: Ernest having fun and Hadley sitting on the sidelines, waiting to go home to bed with a man who she probably wasn't sure was completely hers. It was ineffably depressing. Hadley continued.

"Did you know Ernest has started a book about bullfighting? It's terribly exciting." Although surprising to hear it approvingly from Hadley, it seemed entirely in character for Ernest: bullfighting, Pauline thought, would fit perfectly his outsized, truculent personality.

"You don't mean you are interested in such an awful thing, are you Hadley?" Pauline asked.

"Oh, well," stammered Hadley, not wanting to appear unladylike but at the same time clearly animated, "it's as Ernest says, you can't imagine how beautiful it is until you've seen it." Pauline was astounded. Here was this little mouse of a woman, coming alive, red in her cheeks as she talked about, of all things, bullfighting.

"Excuse me, Hadley, it's just somewhat hard for me to believe – you like bullfighting?"

"Well, yes," Hadley whispered excitedly, as if revealing a secret. She continued, even more animatedly, speaking quickly. "We've been to Pamplona twice, to see the running of the bulls, and Ernest has taken me to the *corrida* several times. At first, he didn't think I would be able to handle it, but I surprised him. In fact, some of the men had to leave, but I loved it." Hadley's face was alight, shining. "One time, the toreador gave me the bull's ear at the end – just after he slipped in the last sword." This last revelation made Pauline feel slightly sick to her stomach.

A severed bull's ear. And Hadley's comment about the sword – it was astounding to Pauline that Hadley should speak so casually, and approvingly, of this. This kind of thing would of course appeal to Ernest, but Hadley? Pauline had trouble absorbing it.

"Hadley, I don't understand. How can you actually like that kind of thing?" Hadley leaned toward Pauline in response and continued.

"Well, let me tell you about the *verónicas* – do you know what a *verónica* is?" Hadley said, smiling, her eyes blazing. Pauline shook her head. "Well, you know that the toreadors use a red cape – a *capote de brega* – to enrage the bull, and also to entice it. They use the cape to make the bull charge –

41

just a little bit of red cloth, think about that! – and then, when the bull is almost upon them, the toreador swirls it, swirls the cape – that swirl is the *verónica* – and the bull runs under the *capote* and past the man. It's a beautiful thing to watch." Hadley's eyes glowed as she described this, and Pauline could see that she was entranced by the memory. "You know, I was pregnant with Bumby last year at Pamplona," Hadley added softly.

Next to her husband, her son was Hadley's favorite topic. This was her signal accomplishment, her pride, the baby she had produced. Hadley continued.

"I told Ernest, you know, I liked showing this to our little boy even before he's born. Ernest knew we were having a boy – never even considered that it might be a girl and, of course, he was right." This kind of extraordinary comment rolled off Hadley's tongue matter-of-factly, as if she were talking about the weather or politics. Pauline was stunned, and somewhat repulsed.

"You're amazing, Hadley," said Pauline. "Not one woman in a thousand would have gone to a bullfight during her pregnancy, not even one who enjoyed them." Hadley smiled at her.

"Well, no one else is married to Ernest." Hadley often liked to reiterate this attainment. She had proudly adopted Ernest's likes, his desires, his wants, even his beliefs. If he liked bullfighting, then she liked bullfighting. "I wanted to see the toreador kill a bull," she said. Another remarkable statement, coming out of this diffident woman's mouth. Pauline wondered, not for the first time, if this was what Hadley actually believed, or only what Ernest had induced her to believe.

"I'm surprised, Hadley," Pauline mustered. "It seems to me that would just be too gruesome to absorb. What makes you want to witness that?" Hadley hesitated only a moment and then replied.

"Well, I see how interested Ernest is in this, so I know there must be something to it. And really, there can't be anything more gruesome about it than, say, giving birth. Now *that* is a ghastly experience." Hadley leaned in toward Pauline as she confided this, as if sharing a confidence with a co-conspirator. As she finished her sentence, however, she seemed to realize an error, speaking of childbirth to an unmarried woman.

"Oh, I mean, of course, you wouldn't know about that," Hadley said quickly. "And maybe I just had a bad experience, I'm sure not all women go through that, it's just ...." She trailed off, unable to get out of the hole she had dug for herself. It made Pauline feel even sorrier sorry for her.

"I understand, Hadley," Pauline said obligingly. "I haven't had the experience but I suppose, from the beginning of time, that it has never been what one would call a pleasant event for a woman to endure. I have often wondered if it were just a grand joke that God was playing on half of humanity. Seems like The Almighty could have come up with a better strategy." Hadley laughed, grateful for Pauline's kindness in lifting her off the hot seat. Hadley changed the subject, continuing with her defense of bullfighting, and of Ernest.

"Really, you know, Ernest says it is an art form. Really, an art form. Wait until you see it one day, Pauline – it will change your mind." Pauline doubted that anything could change her mind about witnessing the hot and bloody death of an angry, captive animal, but she held her tongue.

She wondered again, briefly, at the sway that Ernest had over Hadley. If he wanted to see a toreador kill a bull, then she wanted to see the plunge of the sword. If he believed that his child would be a boy, then she believed that as well. And

Pauline had come to suspect that it was not imagined or forced or fabricated – Hadley truly believed and felt and wanted all those things, whatever it was Ernest espoused. It was extraordinary to Pauline, the power that this man had over his wife. Pauline wondered fleetingly about what it would be like to be with such a man, to be overpowered, overwhelmed. She wondered how she would respond. Hadley looked at her, and her eyes lit up.

"Pauline, I have a wonderful idea. When we go to Pamplona in a July, why don't you and Jinny come with us? I tell you, you will *love* it." It had never occurred to Pauline to go on vacation with the Hemingways, much less to travel to Spain to watch a bullfight.

"That's kind of you, Hadley, but really, I'm not sure that's my cup of tea." Hadley looked immediately disappointed.

"Oh, think about it, please. Why not? What else do you have planned for your summer?"

Hadley had a point on that front. Jinny and Pauline had talked briefly, and to no real end, about what they might do during the slack days of summer. The *Vogue* offices, like most of Paris, worked on a skeleton staff during July and August. People who could afford it went to the seaside or to the mountains. The sisters had talked about both options but had not come up with anything firm yet. Hadley pressed on.

"Please, at least ask Jinny. She might think it's a fun idea! And I know you'd enjoy it." The more Hadley urged, the more Pauline began to consider the idea. She had never been to Spain and, as conflicted as she was about the couple, the prospect of being around Ernest was not entirely disagreeable: he was like watching a car crash, you couldn't look away.

As she pondered it, the thought of traveling to Pamplona became more intriguing. Ernest was, in his way, a powerful man, that was apparent, and Pauline had always found powerful men interesting. Besides, she thought, once we get there, no one can force me to go to a bullfight. There would be lots of other things to do and see, she supposed.

"Well, let me think about it," Pauline responded, "and talk with Jinny. We have no other plans, and it's awfully kind of you to invite us to come with you." Hadley brightened at her friend's acquiescence. Just at that moment, Ernest appeared, towering beside them, swaying somewhat as he approached his wife, and reaching for the back of her chair for support.

"What are you two chickens clucking about?" he said softly, diminishing the crudeness of his words with a gentler timbre in his voice, and, with a surprisingly tender touch, placing a hand on Hadley's shoulder. Pauline considered, that was the thing about Ernest: you could never predict whether he would be a lion or a lamb. And, with Ernest, sometimes the lion would roll over, and sometimes the lamb would kick. He was an enigma to Pauline.

"I invited Pauline and Jinny to come to Pamplona with us in July." Hadley smiled brightly up at Ernest, but he did not seem pleased to hear she had made this invitation.

"*Hunnh*. Well. Not sure that's your style, Pauline," Ernest grunted. "You'd get those pretty clothes of yours very, very dirty." He stared at Pauline, waiting for a response.

His words, his demeanor, the look in his eyes – all were a challenge to Pauline, and she had always appreciated a challenge. The good Catholic girl in Pauline knew it was wrong to be attracted in any way to a married man, and yet the forbidden fruit was tantalizing. The harder part, even for someone as self-concerned as Pauline, was acknowledging that she was intrigued, not just by a married man, but by a married man whose wife had become somewhat of a friend.

45

To further complicate the stew of emotions, the circumstance was more difficult still because the attraction itself was conflicting. In short, Ernest was not easy to like. The more she knew of him, the more Pauline found that equal parts of him repelled and attracted her. And part of her just wanted what she was not supposed to have. But she was playing a game, and not expecting it to go as far as it did. Not expecting it to have the consequences that it would ultimately have.

When Ernest looked at Pauline and she saw disdain in his eyes, as if he thought she wouldn't be able to stomach a bullfight – something his meek little wife had not only endured but actually enjoyed – Pauline couldn't help but rise to the bait.

"Actually, Ernest, I can't think of anything I'd enjoy more," Pauline said evenly. Hadley looked at Pauline, mouth agape, obviously wondering at what had precipitated this astonishingly rapid change of heart. Ernest continued to glare at both of them.

Hadley, to her credit, recovered quickly enough to grasp Pauline's hands and tell her how happy she was. She began to prattle about how much fun all of them would have. If Hadley noticed Ernest and Pauline exchanging defiant stares, she remained intentionally oblivious.

CHAPTER SEVEN

No one would have expected Jinny and Pauline to travel to Pamplona to watch something as crude as bullfighting with a couple as bourgeois as the Hemingways, least of all their urbane, natty Uncle Gus. Gus was their father's younger brother, and, in Pfeiffer tradition, he was an extraordinarily successful businessman. But unlike the senior Pfeiffer, Uncle Gus seemed to want to invest as much time in family as he did in his capital ventures. Gus had always been a doting and delightful uncle, and had made as much time as he could to be present in his young nieces' lives. Gus had never married, a "confirmed bachelor," as their mother quietly but insistently referred to him.

Pauline had sensed from the time she was a little child that there was an unidentified sorrow about Uncle Gus. The source of his pain was not clear to her, however, until she was much older. Being a homosexual in early twentieth-century America – or at any place in the world, at that time – carried with it not only its own difficulties and depressions, but also alienation and isolation. One way that Uncle Gus occasionally relieved his solitary sadness was by expending lavish attention on and devotion to his nieces, and his love for Pauline and Jinny was liberally reciprocated.

As a child, Pauline knew Uncle Gus was different, and in ways she liked. He always dressed carefully and fastidiously, and – unlike most grown-up men – he unfailingly smelled good, of soap and shaving cream and bay rum. He wore two-tone, wing-tip shoes, and gaily colored socks, all year round. He combed his hair sideways, across the top of his head. This last was in a vain effort to cover a growing baldness, but Pauline thought it dashing and fashionable. In later years,

Pauline found the wistful poignancy of those wisps of hair inexpressibly endearing.

When the sisters received the cable that Uncle Gus would be visiting them for a week in Paris, they were delighted. There was a long month in front of them before they were to leave for Pamplona, and Uncle Gus' visit could not have been more perfectly timed. Jinny was in the middle of a fruitless effort to learn how to paint, and so his impending arrival was a good excuse to rid their apartment of half-finished canvasses, dried up paint brushes, and messy smocks. Pauline was certain that as soon as Uncle Gus' visit was over, Jinny would move on to some other similarly absorbing project at which she would be equally inept. But for the time being, his imminent visit was a useful expedient to clean up their apartment.

On this trip, Uncle Gus was using the Paris sojourn as a waystation: he had business in Germany. His primary commercial endeavor in the United States was in pharmaceuticals, and several medical firms in Berlin and Munich were anxious to have an American business conduit. Pauline was looking forward to talking to her uncle about his plans and finding out what new profitable ventures might be forthcoming.

The sisters met his ship at Cherbourg early on a surprisingly chilly June morning, on the same dock at which they had disembarked just a couple of months earlier. Pauline spotted him first, and excitedly nudged Jinny.

"There he is!" she exclaimed and started to move forward in the crush of the welcoming crowd. Uncle Gus was on the gangplank, making his careful way down the footbridge in small, delicate steps. When he saw the two sisters, his face split into a wide grin, and he threw his arms open wide, absentmindedly hitting the two passengers on either side of him.

Gus did not seem to notice his fellow travelers' irritated, indignant reactions, he just kept smiling and moving forward. His gleeful expression indicated that he could not wait to envelope his nieces in a hug. Finally, he reached them, and threw his arms around both of them at the same time. Pauline felt like a little girl again, being held firmly in her uncle's warm embrace. The threesome stood, clasped in each other's arms, oblivious of the log jam they were causing.

They parted, a bit awkwardly, and then began to move toward the piles of stacked trunks that were being off-laded. They soon found Gus' luggage, including one mid-size box especially dedicated to his several chess sets; Pauline recognized the box, and correctly perceived that it meant Gus did not intend a brief stay in Europe. He was an enigmatic man, and briefly she wondered again what his plans were.

They located a baggage handler with a cart. Uncle Gus meticulously directed the loading of the bags and boxes, and the three began to navigate the thick, pressing crowds to find a taxi at the end of the pier. After more explicit directions as to the transference of luggage from cart to taxi, Uncle Gus tipped the handler and the three climbed into the cab, the sisters settling on the back seat. Uncle Gus insisted on occupying the small perch of the jump seat behind the driver.

Pauline glanced out the window and saw the baggage handler staring incredulously at the wad of paper money in his hand; obviously, he had been tipped handsomely. The handler looked up smilingly and waved in thanks at the back of the cab as it moved away from the pier.

Pauline began to remark on the lavish tip, but Gus silenced her with a soft wave of his hand; he did not want her to comment on his extravagant tipping. Gus was always uncomfortable with any type of recognition of his generosity.

"I'm hungry," Gus sputtered, as if to introduce a new topic quickly.

"You mean you didn't get enough to eat on the ship?" said Jinny, teasing. "That's odd – to my memory that's all there is to do on a crossing!" She smiled indulgently at her uncle. Gus fidgeted on his little seat and barked through the tiny window into the driver's compartment, "Find us a café, *maintenant, s'il vous plaît!*" The sisters laughed and smiled at their uncle's obvious attempt at diversion.

The cabbie drove quickly through the dockside section of Cherbourg, and eventually deposited his passengers at a small café directly next to the train station. Gus gave detailed orders to the driver as to the further conveyance of his luggage to the train baggage handlers; he then went further to repeat the instructions in small, sharp scrivening on a piece of elegant card stock produced from his breast coat pocket.

The driver, with blank expression, accepted the written repetition of reserved train time and ticket numbers, and nodded obsequiously, tipping his head and touching his fingers to the rim of his cap. Underneath the cap rim, the driver's face showed effortfully veiled annoyance, but he did not want to offend what promised to be a good tipper. He was not disappointed. Uncle Gus reached into his wallet, pulled out several bills, and palmed them to the driver. The driver looked down furtively into his hand. Then he looked up quickly, smiling, and took off briskly to deliver the luggage as instructed.

The three Pfeiffers walked across the wooden boardwalk of the depot, into the café. They ordered coffees and croissants, which were promptly served by a waiter dressed in the uniform of the *Mantes-la-Jolie* rail line. Jinny thanked him; she supposed that the servers rotated between café cars on the train and the station restaurant. Pauline and Uncle Gus ignored the server and began to sip the steaming coffee.

After a little while, a small dog trotted up to their table, seemingly unattached to anyone. The sisters and their uncle looked around them, searching for an owner for the pup. Seeing no one who obviously belonged to the dog, Uncle Gus patted his lap and the small brown mutt jumped up.

Uncle Gus held his plate of crumbs under the dog's chin, so that the dog could lick it clean, and then in turn did the same with Pauline's finished plate, and finally with Jinny's.

The sisters were bemused by their uncle's sudden and indeterminate attachment to a stray dog, but kept silent. Uncle Gus neither acknowledged nor responded to their shared querying glances, but simply kept talking, about travel, finances, business, all the while scratching the little dog's head. It was yet another example of their uncle's iron unwillingness to talk about anything he chose not to address.

When the dog was done being petted, it jumped down and wandered slowly away, sometimes stopping to relieve an itch with a hind paw. Uncle Gus took one last look at the dog, just a glance as it walked away, and then brought himself back to the full attention of the rest of his cup of coffee and to their genial, if prosaic, conversation.

Pauline wondered at the meeting – between dog and man – and speculated as to how many casual encounters Uncle Gus had engaged in during his life. She wondered how often he had keenly sought attention, received it from a stranger, and then placidly turned back to the present, and on with the daily business of living. Finding no ready answer to her question, she pushed the thought away, and turned her attention to uncle and sister.

The three finished their coffee and croissants, paid the bill, and walked arm in arm down the boardwalk to the waiting train.

CHAPTER EIGHT

After once again checking on the receipt and storage of his luggage, Uncle Gus and the sisters climbed into the train car and settled into their seats to continue their journey on to Paris. As the train rumbled through the lush green of the French countryside, they made plans to drop Uncle Gus off at his hotel, and pick him up later that evening to take him to a party.

It was to be one of their expat artists gatherings, at the home of yet another "lost generation" young writer. Pauline had heard that phrase – "lost generation" – applied to this group of attractive, talented young people they had fallen in with, and she was mystified by the appellation. To her, they did not seem lost at all. They seemed, Pauline thought, to know precisely who they were and what they wanted. They were quirky, unusual, and talented – sometimes fabulously talented. And a bonus: to a person, both the men and the women knew how to drink.

Pauline was anxious to introduce Uncle Gus to this crowd. She suspected he would enjoy the excitement, the titillation, the pure animal agita these intensely interesting people created. Their energy permeated every conversation; it crackled in the air around them. Also, Pauline wanted to show off. She wanted Uncle Gus to see that they had arrived, they had made it, they had entered a totally foreign world and were successfully sailing the waves. It was a puerile emotion, she knew, but Pauline wanted him to see how much she had grown up.

They arrived at his hotel about seven o'clock, and the evening sun cast a warm haze through the windows of the hotel lobby. Uncle Gus was sitting in the lounge, waiting for them. He was dressed like a dandy, down to the spats; his hair was brilliantined, his face full of happy expectation. They climbed into a cab and gave the driver the address.

That evening, the party was at the home of John Dos Passos and his lover, Katie, two of the less eccentric but still interesting and exceptionally talented members of the tribe. Even so, Pauline assumed the evening would hold more of the same unpredictable revelry; the parties were never dull, no matter who threw them.

The cabbie dropped them off at the Dos Passos' home. After they made their way inside and were divested of their coats, Pauline led Uncle Gus into the main salon. She had planned to introduce him to some of the more voluble men, thinking that's what he would most enjoy. But of course, the first person they saw, literally ran into when they walked into the room, was Ernest Hemingway.

Hadley was sitting on the side arm of a long sofa, holding two drinks, having been made the keeper of Ernest's glass as well as her own. Pauline noticed this small servile function and was again irritated and intrigued at the same time. What power of human coercion could turn a wife into a maid, a lover into a servant? Pauline shook her head at the disquieting thought; she would never let herself be put into that same kind of situation with a man.

Ernest had backed up into them as they had entered the room and had bumped hard into Pauline's shoulder. He had taken no notice of the collision, simply had flexed his arms and solidified his stance. Although it had been Ernest who had collided into her, it was Pauline who moved away, accommodating the big man's space.

Ernest was facing the interior of the room, standing at the edge of a Persian rug. Pauline stared at Ernest and at another man who was standing in the middle of the carpet's medallion, facing Ernest. Both men had their arms flexed in front of them, fists clenched. Both were shirtless. Pauline recognized with a start that the edges of the rug were meant to be the boundaries of a boxing ring. Oh no, she thought, realizing that Ernest had managed to coax some benighted soul into agreeing to box with him; he was priming for the fight.

Ernest's reluctant opponent was a small, lean man, his thin arms bent awkwardly in front of him. He stood forlornly rooted to the middle of the carpet, his pleading eyes darting wildly, looking for any possible escape.

Ernest jumped from one foot the other, occasionally moving toward his unwilling competitor and jabbing at the air in front of him, knees flexed, moving backwards and forwards in the "ring." His petite opponent grimaced each time the large fist came close to his face. As Ernest's jabs persisted, the smaller man continued to dart glances around the room, searching for rescue or reprieve.

Once again, Pauline was repelled and fascinated at the same time. She did not understand how this churlish man could capture her attention. But the lure was inescapable; she gazed at the two men, one large, sweating, undeniably handsome, and the other meek and milquetoast—an impossibly lopsided face-off. She could not pull herself away. Indeed, she did not make much effort to do so.

Ernest's poor victim in the self-aggrandizing charade was a young artist named Emmanuel Radnitzky. Pauline recognized him from previous parties and had been told that he had shortened – and in her opinion immensely improved – his given name by truncating it to "Man Ray."

Pauline had been told of Man's artistry. He was an accomplished painter, but an even better photographer. Man referred to his photographic work as "Rayographs," and the few that Pauline had seen were magnetic, provocative, electric. He was one of their crowd who was destined for great and deserved fame. Pauline shook her head, staring in disbelief at the absurdity of the bizarrely asymmetric boxing match.

Despite the machismo of his name, Man was not an athletic man, nor a particularly masculine one. In fact, he was slightly effeminate, though well-built in a slim way. He had dark, manicured hair, but it now hung mussed and falling over his forehead; he panted, more in fear than in the effort of the match.

Man was short and slim-hipped. And although his lithe body appeared not physically weak or incapable, he looked extremely forlorn, standing in the middle of the rug, cringing at Ernest's barked instructions as to how he should hold his arms, where he should punch, and where he should expect to get punched. In fact, Man looked as though he might be sick at any moment.

Pauline was surprised when Uncle Gus, surveying the situation, moved swiftly across the room and slid sideways around Ernest, placing himself directly between the two men. Gus glanced back and forth at the antagonists for a few moments, and Pauline watched a decisive expression move across her uncle's face. He paused just a moment, then took a deep breath, straightened his shoulders, and stood stock still, immovable in the middle of the Persian carpet.

Ernest's body tensed, then his arms fell limply to his sides. He appeared shocked, and scowled at the intruder. Man, on the other hand, looked at Uncle Gus as a Christian might have regarded an avenging angel, swooping in at the last minute to kill a lion.

"What the hell do you think you are doing?" Ernest yelled at Gus. Pauline could see spittle arch from his mouth. He clearly was not used to anyone interfering with his games.

Hadley sat still and wide-eyed at the end of the couch, not moving, not doing or saying anything. It hurt Pauline to look at her face; she did not like the fact that Hadley seemed scared. Uncle Gus continued, unperturbed.

"Excuse me, this young man appears to be somewhat ill," Uncle Gus said softly, nodding at Man. Gus leaned over and picked up Man's shirt from the corner of the rug where it had been deposited. He handed the shirt to Man, then gently took him by the arm. "Come with me," Gus said firmly. Man slipped on his shirt, and allowed Gus to pull him to the side of the room, walking steadily and unhurriedly. The two men went through a set of large French doors and out into the garden, where a bar had been set up in a corner of the yard.

Pauline watched them walk outside, her uncle's arm lightly resting on the younger man's shoulders. Through the open doorway, she saw Gus order drinks for both of them, and then watched as the two men moved quietly to a bench among the greenery. They sat together, softly talking. As Pauline watched them, she heard Ernest roaring behind her.

"Who the hell was that old fart?" stormed Ernest. He addressed his query to no one in particular. He spun around to face Hadley, and she started at the force of his glare. She sat still, mute. Jinny hated scenes like this; she had already developed an unremitting antipathy for Ernest over past events like this one. Jinny strode across the room toward him.

"Oh Ernest, just shut up," Jinny shouted at him. "Did you ever stop to think that none of us cares whether you need to prove that you have the biggest poker in the room? Did it ever occur to you that we're all getting kind of sick of watching you pretend to hit people, just to gratify your ego?"

Pauline was shocked to hear Jinny talk like this. Although she knew Jinny was no ingenue, it was surprising to hear her well-bred sister erupt like a fishwife. Pauline assumed that

Jinny had recently expanded on her vocabulary from their new Parisian friends, and although surprised, Pauline was not unhappy that Jinny had turned her verbal guns on Ernest.

At the same time, Pauline felt acute embarrassment that, after her expounding to Uncle Gus about their fine and interesting new acquaintances, the first person he had met was this American boor. In addition, Pauline was also disturbed at the obvious embarrassment that Ernest's tirades and antics inflicted on Hadley.

Ernest stood still in the center of the rug and glared at Jinny; Pauline flirted with the absurd notion that he might actually start boxing with her. Then slowly he turned and walked away.

Ernest found Hadley, still sitting on the arm of the couch, and leaned toward her, as if for support. Hadley looked stricken; mutely, she handed him his shirt. It was clear she was not used to Ernest being bested, and certainly not by a woman, or an old man. Pauline, Jinny, and the other party guests moved away from the Hemingways, and attempted gamely to begin new conversations, refresh drinks, and erase the disagreeable aura of unpleasantness that had just occurred.

Pauline searched for Uncle Gus and Man, but they were no longer in the garden and she could not locate them elsewhere among the guests. Jinny and Pauline continued to mill around the party, but assiduously avoided Ernest and Hadley. A little later on, they witnessed the Hemingways' early, somewhat sheepish departure.

Around midnight, Uncle Gus showed up with Man in tow. They both looked happy, certainly happier than Jinny or Pauline; it had been a stressful evening. Pauline wondered vaguely where the two men had been. The sisters and their uncle made their goodbyes and headed back out into the evening.

Pauline was surprised when Man appeared alongside Uncle Gus, clearly intending to join them in their cab. Whatever was going on with them, it apparently wasn't over for the evening. They all tumbled into the cab and rested into their seats.

"What an odious young man," Uncle Gus said as the cab pulled away from the curb, referring, obviously, to Ernest. Man smiled at Gus and patted his knee.

"You are a life-saver. Literally." Man laid his head back against the leather seat. "I'm sure he would have beaten me to a pulp."

"Men like that are just trying to get over their own inadequacies," said Uncle Gus softly. He returned the pat, and his hand remained floating gently on Man's thigh. The air in the cab was still, and no one spoke. Suddenly, Man broke the silence.

"I rarely say something this definitive, but I can unreservedly say this," Man spoke quietly, yet firmly. He leaned his dark head against Gus' shoulder and relaxed his slim frame into the curve of the older man's body. "I truly hate that man," he sighed, "and I think I always will. If I could find a way to rid the earth of men like him, I would."

Uncle Gus turned his head and stared out the side window of the cab. He smiled quietly to himself.

CHAPTER NINE

After Uncle Gus's visit and his departure to Germany, their relationship with the Hemingways was altered. Jinny's antipathy toward Ernest was now open and notorious, and Pauline's queasiness about his treatment of Hadley had deepened. Pauline genuinely liked Hadley and found Ernest's treatment of her increasingly distasteful. At the same time, she found herself wondering if Ernest were perhaps goaded into acting the bull, simply because of Hadley's meekness.

Pauline could not disavow his sometimes-loutish behavior, but then again, she wondered how much of Hadley's irritating domesticity and docility precipitated his conduct. She also found herself thinking less of Hadley for letting herself be treated like a piece of furniture. Were Pauline in her position, she thought, she certainly would not acquiesce to him as Hadley did.

Whatever conflicting feelings Pauline had about the Hemingways, she was unfortunately and annoyingly committed to the trip to Pamplona. It now seemed like a great folly, but Pauline was hesitant to back out. Even though the Hemingways were part of the excursion, Pauline found that she was interested in discovering what drew so many fanatics to the famous San Fermin festival.

And so, when Hadley called a few days after the boxing fiasco, asking about getting together to plan the trip, Pauline assented. She did not say anything to Jinny, assuming she would be furious after what had happened at the Dos Passos' party and refuse to go on the trip. Pauline did not know how she was going to resolve any of this; she just moved forward, unwilling to find sufficient reason to stop it.

Pauline went to Hadley and Ernest's flat the morning after Hadley's call. Hadley ushered her into the apartment, and proffered a seat on a dilapidated, fraying couch. Pauline sat, gingerly, and Hadley plumped down at the other end of the couch.

Hadley had left Bumby across the hall with an elderly neighbor woman for a few hours, and so was free from her mothering duties. Indeed, she was free from mothering both her child and her husband. Ernest was busy writing, as he was most mornings. That was his pattern, Hadley had explained. It seemed somewhat affected to Pauline: the Hemingways were poor as church mice, yet Ernest spent part of their meager funds – most of which Pauline understood to be Hadley's scant inheritance – to rent for himself a small atelier where he removed every morning "to work."

He had not yet shown Pauline any of his manuscripts, as he had promised to do. She assumed it was because his writing was no good, or that he thought poorly of what he had written, or feared that she would critique him harshly. As to the last, she thought, he was very probably going to be correct. Pauline was a good enough writer in her own right, but at the magazine she had blossomed as an editor and critic and was becoming more and more confident in her assessments. She imagined, not without some pleasure, that this would cause Ernest a bit of heartburn.

"We're planning on taking the train next Tuesday to Bordeaux," Hadley said, animatedly, to Pauline. "And from there we're renting a car and driving south across the border to Pamplona. It's about a three-hundred-kilometer drive, so we'll have plenty of time to talk in the car. Have you and Jinny gotten all your things ready to go?" Hadley's face shone. She was so obviously looking forward to this trip, and to their company.

Pauline was still mystified as to how this drab, sweet mid-western American housewife had become enamored of bullfights. She admitted to herself once again that she was intrigued, and that she had begun to wonder what exotic experiences they might encounter in Pamplona.

"We're nowhere near ready, Hadley." Pauline responded. "You know me, I always pack a million outfits, when two or three will do. Jinny doesn't care a whit about clothing, so she packs nothing, and then is surprised to find herself without underwear when she gets to her destination. We are a maddening pair to travel with." Hadley laughed and pulled herself up off the couch to go make a pot of tea.

Pauline noticed that Hadley got up more like an old lady than a young woman of thirty, scooting her bottom forward on the cushions, knees apart, and then heaving her shoulders forward for leverage and lift to rise. It was a very unladylike movement, unattractive and depressing. Pauline had seen her old aunts, as they progressed in years, get up from chairs and couches this way – she did not expect someone close to her own age to do it.

And Pauline was sure that Hadley would never have stood up that way had Ernest been in the room. Hadley seemed, more and more obviously, to act one way in front of Ernest, and another when he was absent. What was it about him that could have that effect on another human being? Pauline wondered briefly what tectonic plate shifts it would take to make her act the same way if she were in Hadley's shoes. She shook her head; Pauline was certain she would never let herself devolve to that state.

In addition, it seemed to Pauline that Hadley knew that she might be on the verge of losing something, losing Ernest's interest, losing any remaining ability to entice, lure, attract him, to keep him loving her as he once must have had done. It was sad to watch. Although they were close in age, Pauline felt as if Hadley were of an older generation, a matron.

"Can I help you, Hadley?" Pauline called out to the tiny kitchen. She wanted to stop Hadley from making tea. She wanted to break out the martini glasses and get drunk with her. She wanted to make Hadley put on a pretty dress and go out to a *boîte* and dance with strangers and throw her head back and laugh. Pauline wondered if perhaps she could ever convince Hadley to do that.

Altruism was not a customary feeling for Pauline to indulge in; she wondered if it was genuine, or just a transitory state. She had never been what anyone would call kind or generous or empathetic. Pauline's musings were interrupted when Hadley poked her head around the corner of the kitchen doorway.

"No, of course not. This will only take a minute, dear." Pauline sank further down into the couch. It was depressing to see Hadley looking and acting like a drab hausfrau. Pauline thought once again, I would never have let this happen to me, were I in her position.

Pauline looked out the window at the dreary Paris afternoon, at the chimney pots poking up from the tarry, smoky skyline. The scene did not help her mood. She thought that perhaps a change of pace in Pamplona, with the sunny Spanish landscape, might improve not only her own outlook, but that it might also do something for Hadley as well.

Pauline had committed them to the Pamplona adventure. She thought that she could still cajole Jinny into coming, and that Jinny's presence would be a help. Perhaps the two sisters together could bring about some improvement in this hapless woman's pitiable life.

"Here we are," Hadley said setting down her tray. The scene was so prosaic, so American, they might as well have been back in St. Louis. The cheap aluminum tray held a floral-patterned china tea service. Hadley poured the tea, tipped in some milk, and passed the cup and saucer to her guest. Pauline noticed a slight chip in the rim of her cup, and found it dispiriting; she sighed inwardly. Pauline looked at Hadley's face, turning slightly jowly at the jawline. *Good grief*, she thought, *I will never let myself turn into that, never.* If Pauline were ever to be married to someone like Ernest, she was sure she would not let herself become dominated, overpowered as had poor Hadley.

Pauline's mind began to wander, as she listened to Hadley drone on about babies and recipes and cleaning products. What would she do, Pauline mused absentmindly, sipping her tea and ignoring Hadley's chatter, what would she do if she were Ernest's wife? Would she ever have sufficient reason to become the second, the helpmeet, the one holding his drink as he boxed in the center of the room? Pauline was certain not.

Suddenly she felt a keen desire to read his work, if for no other reason than to compare the distaste engendered by his presence with any that might be found in his written words. If he held true to form, it would be a pleasure to give him all the nasty edits she could muster. Hadley got up to add more hot water to the teapot. Pauline listened to her bustling about and called out to her.

"You know, Hadley," Pauline called out to the kitchen, "Ernest asked me to edit some of his pieces. I'd like to get started on that. Do you happen to know if he left anything for me to begin working on?" Pauline's words were met with a sudden silence.

After a moment, Hadley appeared in the small doorway to the kitchen, a dish towel twisted tightly in her hands. She was mute; she stared at Pauline. The silence was long and heavy. "He promised a manuscript to me," Pauline continued, "but I think he's scared to let me read it." As soon as the words left her mouth, she wished she could retract them. Pauline watched Hadley knot the dishtowel even more tightly, squeezing it between her fists.

"I didn't know he had offered you anything. I'm surprised. That's unusual for him." Hadley's voice was calm, a monotone, almost sedated. She stared at Pauline. "He usually takes his drafts to Gertrude." The air between them was still, and neither of them spoke for a long moment, then Hadley continued. "Sometimes he lets me read his things – but I didn't even know you were interested." With that last comment, she turned and went back into the tiny kitchen. The sounds of cutlery against porcelain, glass against metal, and water splashing on the drainboard began to flow again.

Pauline sat in the dreary sitting room and waited for Hadley to finish refreshing the teapot. When she returned, Pauline carefully, but purposefully, responded to her.

"I love editing manuscripts," Pauline's tone was conciliatory. "You know, it's what I do for a living – well, sort of. I have been wondering what kind of stuff your husband writes. He seems like such an unusual character, so I have been thinking that what he writes must be similarly unusual." Hadley looked defensive. Her dishtowel was gone, but her hands were still knotted together, rigid in her lap.

"Ernest is a writer's writer." Hadley said, defensively. "He's not playing at this. It's his life. It's why he gets up early. He leaves me, he leaves the baby and it's hard. I know it's more important to him than anything else." Hadley looked at the floor. "I know that I come second. I accept that." Pauline stared at her. She looked at the translucent, splotchy skin on Hadley's reddened cheeks, at the transparent hurt on her face. Ernest had molded this woman exactly as he wanted her. And again, Pauline thought, what is it about this man that he can do this, that he can have this kind of power over a woman? He must have a latent sovereignty of some kind, and he had clearly used this authority over his wife to his benefit. Pauline again turned to Hadley, and decided to press her point further.

"Since he won't give me anything," she importuned, "would you let me see something he has lying around?"

"Good heavens, no!" Hadley immediately erupted. Although Pauline had anticipated a negative answer – Hadley was too much of the mouse to do anything else – she was surprised by the aggressive vehemence, and it was unattractive to witness.

They were clearly in dangerous waters, and Pauline had gone into an area that was patently off-limits. His writing, their marriage, their family, they were all intertwined, and Hadley would be fiercely protective of all of it.

Pauline abandoned her queries and withdrew to the safer territory of their upcoming trip. She reiterated that she and Jinny were woefully behind in their preparations, she asked Hadley to tell her more about the travel arrangements. Pauline feigned excitement and anticipation.

"Tell me, what kind of weather should we plan for?" Pauline dutifully sipped at her tea, carefully avoiding the chip on the rim. "What should I pack?" Hadley relaxed at the introduction of a different topic, and responded affably.

"White cotton, Pauline, that's what you need, a lot of white cotton." Hadley said, clearly relieved that the discussion was off Ernest and onto something more comfortable. "It gets unbearably hot there. I wear a little white scarf around my neck, soaked in water, and the evaporation cools me. It's also nice to be able to untie it and just wipe the dust from your face." Hadley sipped her tea. "And I cover my arms – long white sleeves – and wear a long skirt. You'll be most comfortable that way."

When Pauline considered that prospect – hot, dusty days, shrouded in white cotton and needing to wipe down with a wet cloth – she could not help but feel again the niggling uncertainty about the trip. They drank their second pot of weak tea and ate the limp cookies Hadley had proffered. Pauline began to feel that she needed to escape the drab apartment as quickly as she could. After the minimally acceptable interlude, Pauline made her careful goodbyes, promised to talk with Hadley soon, and fled.

She spent the rest of the afternoon walking around the quiet Parisian streets, thinking. Later, when the sun was just beginning to set over the city skyline, she sank deeper and deeper into an uncharacteristically gloomy mood. How had she gotten herself into this mess?

Pauline and Jinny could have had a pleasant time simply staying in Paris and relaxing during their summer vacation, or going off to Nice or Geneva. But now she had committed them to heading off to a provincial country town in the wilderness of Northern Spain. And although Pauline somewhat liked Hadley, her presence had certainly become depressing, and her husband continued with his propensity to exhibit at times the most inexplicably ill-mannered behavior. *Why then,* Pauline wondered, *why do I still want to go?*

CHAPTER TEN

"**J**inny, would you please sit down. You're making me nervous." Jinny was pacing back and forth in their living room; it was several hours before they needed to leave for the train depot. The Hemingways and the Pfeiffers were booked on the same slow, late-night train to Bordeaux, and the afternoon preparations for the trip had been unpleasant. Pauline and Jinny had bickered over packing, wrangled over their dinner, and generally were in sour moods. Pauline was questioning, once again, how she had ever come to agree to this ridiculous trip.

She thought that perhaps this had all come about as some sort of compulsive delusion. Although Pauline still professed antipathy toward Ernest, she found that she kept thinking about him, and had even developed an odd fascination with him. He was undeniably handsome, even if he was an oaf and a loudmouth. Pauline sometimes daydreamed about Ernest, and would catch herself, looking guiltily around her to see if Jinny could detect what she was thinking.

Just as uncomfortable was the fact that, although she admittedly was growing more and more to like Hadley, Pauline looked down on her. In recompense, or perhaps penance, Pauline convinced herself that, even as she seemed to be developing an odd obsession with him, she looked down on Ernest as well. The Hemingways were not of Pauline's social class, she decided, and in addition, they were not of her intellectual caliber either. Still, there was something about Ernest that kept her interest, even if for no other reason than to find an opportunity to belittle him in some way.

Pauline knew that Jinny was also feeling apprehension about the impending week in Spain. It did not, however, make

Pauline any more sympathetic to her; she was too preoccupied with her own gloominess to empathize with Jinny.

The early evening sunset streamed in their windows, and cast a lazy orange glow across the room. Jinny suddenly stopped pacing, turned to Pauline, and snorted.

"What the blazes is wrong with you, Pauline?" Jinny glared at her sister. "You've been miserable since we agreed to this godforsaken trip. I thought at least we might be able to have some fun along the way to this bloody carnival you're dragging me to, but I can see that's not going to happen." Pauline was familiar with Jinny's unpleasant moods; once she was fully in the throes of one, only time would release her. Pauline sighed. It was going to be a long, miserable evening.

"I don't know, Jinny, but I'm no happier than you are to be here right now. At the very least you could be civil." Jinny stood up abruptly and scowled at her sister. Pauline could tell that Jinny wished she had a glass to throw, to shatter against a wall, to make a dramatic and satisfying smash.

"You know," Jinny said menacingly, "you are selfish Pauline. I'm going along with this because of you, and only because of you, and you can't seem to find it in yourself even to be pleasant to me." Jinny huffed. "You're mooning after that oafish windbag of a man, trailing off after him like a school girl – which is incredibly embarrassing to watch, by the way – and I'm supposed to be your 'convenient chaperone'; you're treating me like one of the pighands back home on the farm. Gad, I can't stand you right now." Jinny folded her arms across her chest and slumped down onto a chair. Her words shocked Pauline into a surprised silence. When she gathered her senses to respond, Pauline's anger and indignation fueled her words.

"How dare you?" Pauline retorted. "What do you mean, implying that I'm interested in Ernest Hemingway? Good grief, he's as much of a pig as you are right now." It occurred to Pauline fleetingly that they both had just managed to throw porcine barbs at each other; it was one of the lowest cuts they had.

"Oh, stop the hogwash, Pauline," Jinny continued. "You are disgusting. And you pretend to like that mousy little Hadley, and yet you're practically throwing yourself at her husband. You make me sick." Jinny stared resolutely out the window, refusing to look at her sister.

Pauline tried to come up with a rejoinder, disabusing Jinny of everything she had just accused her of, but she could not form the argument. Pauline sat, stunned and silent, staring mutely in front of her, unable to meet Jinny's eyes. The reddening sunlight pouring through the apartment windows was turning darker by the minute.

CHAPTER ELEVEN

Jinny stormed out of the apartment, and Pauline sat unmoving, alone. Her sister's words jangled in the air around her. As painful as it was, Pauline silently admitted that she had begun to consider Hadley less and less, certainly thought nothing about their son, and was becoming more and more interested in Ernest. Hadley had been unfailingly kind to Pauline, but at the same time she was almost a non-entity.

It was Ernest who had begun, almost imperceptibly, to consume more and more of Pauline's thoughts. But there she was, Hadley, with that baby, being the dutiful wife, dutiful mother. If Pauline had been able to step away, to jump off the merry-go-round she had climbed onto, perhaps she would have been able to stop the desecration she was about to set in motion. But she was not.

Pauline found that she couldn't stop herself – nor did she really want to – from her daydreaming obsession with Ernest. Nothing bad had come of it – yet – and Pauline suddenly recognized that she did not want the titillation to stop. She wanted to keep playing with the beguiling, dangerous, lovely little fire that she had started.

After their scene of throwing insults at each other, and partially acknowledging to herself her uncomfortable secret, Pauline felt she needed to make amends with Jinny. She left their apartment and went to the local café. Jinny was not there, and Pauline suddenly felt tired and defeated.

She sat down at an empty table near the sidewalk, and looked out at the bustling evening street traffic. She ordered a cocktail from the white-coated waiter. When it came, she accepted the glass gratefully and began to sip, savoring the soft punch of the alcohol.

Not a great start to this trip, she thought. Pauline continued to sit, alone, as the sun finally set over the skyline. She watched the chimney tops turn to dark gray smudges in the darkening sky.

Ah well, she mused, *I've ticked off my sister, slighted my friend, and am having uncreditable thoughts about her husband.* She threw back the rest of her drink, and realized with sudden clarity that she had no intent of changing her behavior. Slowly, she stood, placed a couple of *francs* on the table, and turned slowly to make her way back home.

CHAPTER TWELVE

After a short, fitful night's sleep in one of the train's sleeper compartments, Pauline awakened early to the sound of running water in the miniscule water closet. Usually one or the other would have called out a sleepy good morning through the door, but this morning Pauline knew that neither she nor Jinny felt much like camaraderie. She pulled on a travelling dress, pulled up her stockings and slipped her feet into comfortable shoes. She brushed on some face powder, applied lipstick, and peered at her face in the small round mirror of the compartment wardrobe. *That will have to do*, she thought, and walked out of the room, headed toward the dining car.

Pauline chose a table and, as she had the night before at the café, sat alone. She looked absently out the window at the early morning sun shining brightly on the high summer landscape. A waiter appeared, looking trim in his bright white jacket, and offered her the breakfast menu. Pauline waved it away.

"A whiskey, please, neat." She glanced at the waiter, then turned to stare out the dining car window. Pauline did not want to deal with censure, even mildly from a waiter. Trained to conceal emotion and ignore insult, the waiter nodded, bowed briefly, and moved away to the bar to fetch the drink.

When he returned and placed the glass of amber liquid in front of her, she turned her face directly to his and thanked him coldly. She stared at the waiter defiantly until he turned and walked away down the narrow aisle. Pauline began to sip her breakfast. The next thing she knew, there he was.

"Well young lady, you've started drinking rather early in the day." Ernest sat down heavily on the red leather banquette across from her.

"Yes, I'm taking a page out of your book." She turned a slight smile on him. It struck her that this was the first time they had been alone together in the daylight; usually they saw each other only at parties, well after the sun had set. Now she looked at Ernest in full daylight, the sunshine falling full on his face.

Pauline was struck by what an incredibly handsome man he was. She noticed the scar on his forehead, and the thick brown lock of hair falling over his brow. He had a close-cropped mustache, and Pauline felt a sudden, almost irresistible urge to reach out and touch it.

"You must admit," Pauline continued, "you do seem – as a matter of course – to start drinking rather early in the day, Mr. Hemingway. When did that become a habit?" Pauline sipped her drink and stared steadily at him.

"You make assumptions, Ms. Pfeiffer." They continued with their formal banter, teasing, testing each other. Ernest ordered a whiskey. Their light repartee continued in seemingly harmless fun, and for some reason there was no dredging up of the rancor that they had felt over those last months in Paris. Pauline indulged a warm, private pleasure in looking at his handsome morning face, freshly washed and shaved, and in listening to his deep, surging laugh. She watched his immense hands as they cradled glass after fragile glass of whiskey.

He was so handsome – Pauline could not pull her eyes away from him. Everything about Ernest in that moment seemed charming, entrancing, powerful. As Pauline watched the sunshine playing off the planes of his face, she resisted the urge to touch him, to place a finger on the ruddy skin of his cheek. *It must have something to do with the sunshine,* she thought. The light did Ernest very well, particularly as it goldened. He looked so attractive and, for some reason, sitting alone with him in the almost empty dining car, swaying back and forth with the rhythm of the train, Pauline seemed to lose some of her constant focus on herself.

"You are a remarkably interesting and engaging man, Mr. Hemingway," she offered. "I wonder that you haven't run for political office." Ernest threw back his head and laughed, and his laughter was deep, engaging, musical. Pauline saw the other few remaining diners turn to stare at them. She didn't care.

"You are unusually solicitous with compliments today, Miss Pfeiffer. But I want to talk more about you. Tell me about your piggy little town – where you grew up – Piggott, I think? Is that it?" Pauline did not care that he was being condescending about her birthplace; she felt the same way about it and was glad to have fled. She told him so.

"Yes, a decidedly piggy little southern town, Mr. Hemingway. Close-minded, provincial – everything that is best about America, yes?" He smiled at this and swirled the whiskey in his glass. He formulated his response.

"Well, that's certainly the case for a great deal of what we call the heartland of our fair country," he said, "but I want to hear particulars. I want to hear about your house, and your mother, and your father, and your dog, and what you liked to eat for breakfast. I want to hear about *you.*" Pauline stared at him, discomposed.

Until this point, they had never really talked about anything other than the facile, the surface, the obvious – and now he was asking her to tell him something personal, something deeper. She looked down at the white tablecloth and glanced only as far north as his bulky hands, then began to speak.

"Surprisingly, I think you actually might like Piggott," she began didactically, as if by rote. "It truly is quintessential America. We have lots of land, lots of livestock, we farm ten thousand acres of cotton – it's a rather large operation." Pauline looked up to see what effect her words were having. Ernest seemed interested, and so she continued. "My father is a banker, and my uncle owns a pharmaceutical company, but the bulk of the wealth was originally built on the land – and the people." If Ernest tumbled to the reference to Uncle Gus, he did not show it. Pauline continued.

"We employ, I don't know, perhaps two hundred workers, both in the fields and in the house. My father has a man to oversee the agricultural end of it; my mother holds sway over the 'big house' – that is to say, as opposed to the overseer's home." Ernest had ordered another drink for her, and when it was delivered to the table, Pauline picked it up and took a sip.

"It is a classic Southern plantation lay-out," she said. "The white owners always have lived in the large colonial, the overseer in an unprepossessing farmhouse down the lane, and the workers and, used to be, slaves, in various shacks all over the place. We didn't think much about that when we were growing up – it was just the way it was." Pauline paused, and again searched his face for a reaction. Ernest looked down into his glass, his brow furrowed.

"Don't you sometimes get snow in Arkansas? Isn't there a real winter climate there sometimes?" He seemed genuinely interested in the tedious details Pauline was outlining.

"Well, yes, I suppose so," she replied. Ernest continued to frown.

"Then what would happen to the people living in the shacks when it got cold? What would happen to the slaves and the workers?" Pauline was surprised at his intensity; she thought a minute about his question.

"Well, they had fire pits in most of the separate smaller dwellings, and the kitchen, which is also freestanding, has two huge fireplaces. There is also a forge in the blacksmith's shop, and that produces a lot of heat. I suppose, when it gets really cold, folks congregate wherever there is the biggest fire." Ernest looked at Pauline steadily, but with an unsatisfied demeanor.

"I suppose that is the way it is all over," he said, swirling his drink. "And not just where you come from. Workers, poor people, the uneducated – they always get the short end of the stick, don't they?" Pauline was not sure whether she had offended him or engrossed him: he was impossible for her to read.

Just as she was about to try and give some justification for their privileged-caste lives in Piggott, she noticed a small man with nicotine-colored fingers staring at them from his table in the corner of the dining car. Ernest followed her gaze and the man spoke to Ernest in staccato Spanish. Ernest smiled and nodded in response.

"What did he say?" Pauline asked. Ernest grinned slyly at her as he replied.

"He complimented me on having chosen a beautiful wife." Ernest picked up his glass and tossed it back, draining it. He set down the empty glass on the white tablecloth, and stared at Pauline, waiting for her response.

"Well, he's certainly correct. You did choose a beautiful wife."

"No, there you are wrong, Miss Pfeiffer," Ernest countered, and gazed at Pauline fixedly. "Hadley is many things – faithful, obedient, grateful, perhaps pretty – but she is most decidedly not beautiful." Pauline was stunned and a bit sickened by Ernest's analysis of his wife. He might as well have been referring to a dog. Although she would not have disagreed with his conclusions, Pauline would never have expressed them.

"I'm not sure it's appropriate for me to make comment on that," Pauline said, somewhat primly, even to her own ears. She was feeling the effect of the alcohol on an empty stomach, and her head had begun to swim.

"Bull." Ernest spat the word at her, and for the first time that morning she saw the familiar belligerence on his face. "You flirt with me, you 'make comment' on my wife by your very presence here." Pauline stared at him, attempting to compose a response.

But in that hazy, slightly drunken moment, all self-righteous, dignified, civilized rebukes left her, and she inexplicably felt only one desire – to reach across the table and turn over his rough, brown hand, and place her palm against his. She found she had nothing to say.

CHAPTER THIRTEEN

The movements of Pauline's hands, so small compared to his, were slow, deliberate, feline. She was intentional with every inch she moved her hand closer toward him, and though she knew there was no ordination, no permission or concession for what she was doing, she felt strangely calm. More than that, she knew that once she passed through this door, she would not retreat. And she knew Ernest would not either.

"You have big hands, Ernest." It was a silly, inane comment, and Pauline addressed it to the hands, not the man. He responded with uncharacteristic softness.

"And you, my dear, have inquisitive hands." Now speaking to her in a low, measured tone, his irritation somehow completely dissipated, he looked down at her fingers playing on his skin, her hand finally coming to rest softly, like a leaf, on his calloused palm.

They sat like that for a while, staring at their own hands. Pauline imagined they both had an inkling of the enormity of their intentions, although she was not sure either of them cared. In that moment, another small tipping point in time, she jumped. She abandoned all thoughts save those of her fixation on him.

Ernest brought his other hand on top of Pauline's, and gently turned it over. He began to draw circles on her palm. He continued his small movements up and down her wrist. The alcohol had made them both slow, languid, soft. He did not speak, nor did Pauline. She did not look at his face, just stared at the movements of his finger. No other diners remained in the car, and the waiters, if they were looking, watched from behind the closed curtains of the bar.

Pauline knew as she watched the languorous movement of his hands that something had changed. She gazed at Ernest, in their intoxicated encounter, and knew with certainty that she wanted to have the experience of this man. And all the enormous sacrifices that desire would engender were, at that moment, opaque to Pauline. *I don't need to say anything*, she thought, *I just want to watch this happen.*

CHAPTER FOURTEEN

Pamplona, Spain, July 1926

Ernest and Hadley had rented a room in an ochre-stuccoed *pensión* directly off the main square in Pamplona, and had located a similar room across the hallway for Jinny and Pauline. After the long, awkward car ride, they had arrived late in the afternoon, and Pauline was tired, hungry, and irritable. All she wanted was a shower, a good meal and a glass of wine. She did not want to talk, to sightsee, or to interact with anyone. She wanted to be left alone.

When they reached their lodgings, Pauline dealt disagreeably with the desk clerk, who reeked of garlic and wine and sweat. After signing the coffee-stained register, she snatched the key from his hand, and trudged spitefully up the narrow staircase to a room on the third floor. She abandoned her suitcase in the foyer for Jinny to carry upstairs. Jinny, too tired to argue, stared disconsolately at her sister's back as she climbed the staircase behind her.

Hadley had suggested that they dine together that evening, all four of them. But before they had even peeled their dusty travelling clothes off, Pauline found herself extraordinarily – and unwarrantedly, irritated with her sister. Jinny made a small mention that she wanted to go out and explore Pamplona, and Pauline began to hurl insults at her.

"You've been a pain in the neck all the way here, and now you want to continue to be a pain in the neck and act like a silly tourist?" Pauline fumed. "Well, go ahead and do that by yourself." Surprised and hurt, Jinny left the room. Pauline slumped on the bed.

From what she had seen so far, it was clear that Pamplona was not Paris - not by a long shot. That had been obvious from the views through the grimy windows of the old car they had driven from Bordeaux: it had been unending, arid wilderness, unrelieved by any hint of civilization. Pauline had inquired at registration, and had found that there was no room service, and no valet. She began to wonder if the electricity and water would be turned off at a certain hour.

Pauline was sorely regretting her decision to come to this godforsaken place. Prompted by the need for food and something to drink, Pauline soon made her way alone back downstairs and out into the glaring evening sun. She did not want to be with Jinny, and certainly not with the Hemingways. Pauline walked slowly along dusty sidewalks, until she came to a bar with the beguiling name of *Las Tres Damas.*

The doorway leading into the bar was narrow and low, and the walls of the building were thick, and covered in the same light brown stucco of their *pensión*. Pauline stepped into the dim atmosphere; the smell of yesterday's spilled beer was heavy and sour. She waited for her eyes to adjust to the weak light, and scanned the interior of the bar.

The early-evening crowd included several tables of men wearing white shirts, red sashes, and red berets, worse for wear after a day in the streets. More men, similarly dressed, leaned heavily on the long wooden bar, protecting their glasses of beer.

Several of the men looked up at Pauline suspiciously as she walked in, and she realized that it was probably unusual for a woman to be alone in a place like that. But now on her own, she decided she was going to lighten her mood, and that a few disconcerting glares from strangers were not going to deter her from getting a drink.

Pauline signaled to the bartender, pointed to a table along a side wall, and sat down. She waited for service, irritated by the muffled chuckling from the other patrons. Finally, the bartender came around from behind the bar and shuffled to her table. He asked, in rapid Spanish, what she wanted.

Pauline responded in English that she wanted a bottle of wine, "*Good* wine," she instructed. The bartender gazed limpidly at her, unfazed. Pauline sat mute, glaring, and then repeated her request in a strident, if somewhat shaky timbre, hoping to make it clear that she was not going to be intimidated. She reached into her pocket, pulled out a handful of pesetas, and said, again in English, "Here, take that, get me my wine, and stop staring." Immediately, there was a burst of laughter from the doorway.

Ernest filled the small space, his face alight. He stared at Pauline as if delighted by her performance. He walked over to the bartender, put a hand on his shoulder, and spoke to him in low, rapid Spanish. The bartender smiled, gave Pauline a slow, conspiratorial grin, and returned to the table with a bottle and two glasses.

"What did you say to him?" she asked. Ernest raised one corner of his mouth.

"I told him you were my mistress, that my wife had just caught us in bed, and that you had nowhere else to go." Pauline's initial reaction was lividity. She had decided that their inebriated meeting in the dining car that morning was a one-off, a consequence solely of intemperance. There was no way she would ever allow herself to be interested in this bearish, bellicose man. Ernest continued to stand over her, to bear down upon her.

Pauline felt the heat rush to her face, her hands clenched tightly in her lap. She tried to conjure up biting words to spit

85

at him, to make him go away. But nothing came to mind. He stood watching her, a calm, placid smile on his face.

To her surprise, his imperturbability began to have a strange effect. Although Pauline's first reaction had been to rebuke him, Ernest's equable, beatific smile in response to her irritation elicited a concomitant reaction. She began to breathe more slowly as she contemplated his expression. As she stared at him, she began to feel calmer.

Pauline looked down at her hands and then up again at his face, oversize and handsome in the smoky bar. She relaxed her hands, and then suddenly felt the same urge she had experienced in the dining car: she simply wanted to touch his face.

Ernest immediately noticed the change in her demeanor, and slowly sat down in the empty chair across from her. It was the first time, but certainly not the last, that Ernest Hemingway would win a contest of wills with Pauline Pfeiffer. He gazed at her, serene, unhurried, self-assured.

"Well, I suppose we should drink something now," Ernest said quietly. He continued to smile warmly at her. Pauline thought about his ability quickly to switch moods: she knew he was able to turn off his charming manner like a light switch and become suddenly pugnacious. And although in the past she had seen Ernest at his uncouth worst, he was now being invitingly soft. Pauline wondered how long that would last.

Ernest poured two glasses of pale red wine. They sat, mostly quietly, sipping the thin, sweet wine, until Ernest broke the silence.

"Move your chair closer, Pauline." This was the first time he had spoken her given name. She liked the way he said it; slowly, she moved her chair around the small table, closer to him. She reached for her glass, drained it and then tapped its side; Ernest obligingly refilled it from the bottle on the table.

"Say it again," she said, picking up her glass. Ernest took another drink, then set down his glass softly on the dark wood.

"Say what?" He did not look at her as he spoke.

"Say my name. Say it again." Pauline's voice was soft, almost imperceptible in the gentle murmur of the bar. Suddenly, Ernest reared back on two legs of his chair, flung his head back and broke the calm with a barrel-chested laugh. Just as quickly he leaned forward, took Pauline's face in both hands, and kissed her full on the lips.

"*There*," he thundered. "That's your name." He smelled of sweat and liquor and hot afternoon dust. What surprised Pauline was that she did not respond with anger. She merely gaped at him. Her mute reaction elicited another round of laughter from him. "Well," he said, "either you're really ticked off or really stoned." He took another drink of his wine. "And I don't think you're stoned." Pauline still said nothing. Finally, she broke her silence.

"No, I'm neither," she replied. Pauline looked down uneasily at her hands. She knew that she had enjoyed the kiss, and that she should not have. She knew that she wanted another, and that she shouldn't. Pauline fidgeted in her chair. Feeling an urgent desire to exit this tricky mental impasse, Pauline decided to change the subject.

"You asked me to edit some of your pieces," Pauline attempted, "and I still haven't seen any of them." Ernest stared at her, aware that the bull was backing away from the toreador, moving the discussion away from dangerous ground. He decided, for the moment, to fold his *capote*.

"Yes, I'll let you do that." Ernest said, and heavily dropped his hand to the table. He took another drink. "I've never read any of your magazine, and heaven help me if I ever do, but I like listening to you talk, you're smarter than any of a hundred people that I've met, and that counts for something."

His compliments were double-edged, more insulting than not. Still, Pauline felt pleased that he was going to let her read his writing. The small amount that she had found in print was moving; his vivid prose style intrigued her. With her usual self-focus, it had made her wonder how he might write about her. Pauline took another long drink of the wine, enough to make her bold.

"If you were to put me in a book, Mr. Hemingway, how would you write about me?" Ernest paused, and despite his inebriation, appeared to take this seriously. Then he surprised her.

"I have thought about that before," he replied. Pauline cocked her head and re-crossed her legs. She waited. Ernest took a deep swig of his wine, draining the glass, and poured another. His expression became intense, and he looked penetratingly at Pauline. "Have I ever told you about my iceberg theory, Ms. Pfeiffer?"

"No," she said. "Tell me." Ernest began, obligingly, beguiling, boldly, to expound upon his theory of writing. Pauline listened, not moving, still as stone.

"Write what you know, Pauline," Ernest began. "Write only what you know." He took a long pull from his glass. "You know what an iceberg is, don't you?" She nodded. "Well, an iceberg is eighty percent unseen – the vast, menacing bulk of it is underwater. But a geologist or a hydrologist or whatever-the-blazes kind of scientist it is who studies these things, they *know* icebergs, they know what's underwater, what others can't see. But they know it, and they have the *cohones* to tell you about it. Nobody else can. Everything else is bull." He took another long, pulsing drink, head tilted back, his Adam's apple moving in tandem with his slow swallowing. Pauline stared at his neck, captivated.

As he explained this to her, she thought about what she had heard others' say of his writing, and she realized it was true. What would become his famous economy of language seemed simple, but it was deceptive – and this was the key: you had to know what you were writing about, an inch wide and a mile deep. Otherwise, don't write about it. It was a valuable lesson. He stopped and studied her.

"You realize what that means as it pertains to you, don't you, Pauline?" His use of her Christian name again startled her. But she was stunned speechless at his next words. "It means," Ernest continued, "that I won't write about you until I've had you in my bed."

And with that comment, Pauline's obsession took a sharp turn. Although she had already grudgingly admitted to herself that Jinny was right – she *had* been daydreaming about this man – she now passed beyond those thoughts. She was no longer the ingenue, fancying herself as a seasonal inamorata. In one drunken, decisive moment, fueled by red wine and Spanish heat, Pauline Pfeiffer decided to become Ernest Hemingway's wife.

CHAPTER FIFTEEN

Pauline awoke the next morning, disoriented, confused. The bright morning sunlight had already uncomfortably heated the cotton counterpane, and was glaring off the white bedroom walls. As the fog of sleep lifted, she remembered where she was, and why. Pamplona. *Oh hell*, she thought, *what on earth am I doing here?*

She then remembered Ernest's words to her the evening before. She closed her eyes and replayed his overture and her response to it. Was that real? Had that really happened? She lay in the small bed a long time, scrutinizing her thoughts. Finally, Pauline opened her eyes and blinked at the bright sunshine. Yes, she realized with sudden clarity, that was what she was here for: there was a quarry to attain.

Pauline sat up and threw her legs over the side of the bed. Her overwhelming, immediate need was for coffee. She dressed quietly, trying not to waken her sister.

"I'm awake, I can hear you." Jinny knew the sound of her sister's morning preparations. Slowly, she sat up and stared at Pauline. "Good grief," Jinny complained, "I wondered when you were going to get up. I'm starving."

Jinny clearly was in a fractious mood, and Pauline did not feel up to tackling a fighting match with her; she didn't respond. Jinny got up off the bed and snatched some clothes off the bedside chair. "Let me get some clothes on," she snapped, "and we'll go find coffee and food." Pauline watched her sister quickly pull on pants and a loose shirt, and together they walked, unspeaking, downstairs.

They soon found an outdoor café with an empty table. The sisters sat down under a large, tattered umbrella, and gratefully ordered two *cafés con leche y azúcar* from the smiling, chubby waiter. Without their having ordered it, the waiter soon brought out a plate of *tostada de queso*; he smiled, ingratiatingly, and gestured beneficently toward the browned, cheesy bread. Pauline eyed the plate suspiciously, but Jinny tucked into the small meal with gusto. Pauline sipped at her coffee, sweet and milky and restorative. She thought about the events of the day to come.

"You know, Jinny," Pauline offered, "what most people know about Pamplona's San Fermin festival is the crazy jostling and hightailing down the streets with the bulls, but it's a lot more than that." The night before, after Ernest's bold statement, they had continued talking on well after midnight, and Pauline had learned a great deal from him about the festival. She had listened raptly as he had told her about the highly stylized bullfights in public arenas built for the purpose. She was surprised to remember most of it, and even more about the extemporaneous street events.

"The bullfights," Ernest had explained, "the public ones in the arenas, those aren't the main events for the locals. What most people don't know is that bullfighting here is not just a spectator sport; it's a true community event, this festival is a time for family gatherings and parties – sort of like Thanksgiving – but spread out all over the streets, and not for just one day, for a whole week."

Pauline thought about Ernest's vivid explanations and began to recount them to Jinny. As she spoke, Jinny stared at her sister, chewing on the now-gooey mass of bread and cheese, mute. Pauline continued.

"Ernest told me all about it," Pauline said animatedly. "We're going to see just the tip of the iceberg when we go to the formal fights. What we need to look for is what's happening in the streets." Pauline repeated Ernest's words, that, by far, the more popular contests were not those staged in the arena, with toreadors in elaborate costumes and capes, but rather they were the street fights, the *touradas ã cordas*.

What people can experience, he had explained, if they are lucky enough to be there at the right time, are the bullfights that take place in small cordoned-off public squares and dead-end streets. Smaller bulls were brought from wooden pens behind homes and public houses, and people gathered in whatever small space they could find to watch, not a red velvet clad toreador with gilt epaulettes, but a man from the streets waving a ragged towel or shirt at an angry bull, controlled only by a small rope. The citizens of Pamplona would hang out their apartment windows, looking down into the makeshift "arenas," walls of humans forming pulsing barriers.

Ernest had described these street bullfighters: while not as elegant as the famed toreadors, they were just as brave and the fights just as exciting as those in the big arena. The makeshift, alleyway fights could occur anytime, and seemed to happen spontaneously, no advertisements, no prelude, just a humming outside in the street, and then it happened.

"And afterwards," Pauline continued to repeat Ernest's account to Jinny, "everyone gathers together in bars or homes and they celebrate with wine and fruit and cheese and good bread." As Pauline recounted all this, she could see Jinny was unimpressed. Jinny ate the last of the toasted bread and looked at Pauline, clearly nonplussed.

"Look," Jinny said, when Pauline finally paused, "I'm glad you think you've found something interesting here, but frankly it all sounds just as unpleasant as it can be." Jinny finished her coffee, and sighed. "I'm going to try and find somewhere to get away from the crowds, perhaps go on a nice long hike, and I'm going to rest and try and relax, somewhere away from human beings, until we can head for the train back to Paris. That's my plan," Jinny concluded. "Go have a ball."

Pauline looked at her sister, and exasperation and embarrassment overtook her. She had repeated to Jinny all of Ernest's flamboyant explanations and commendations about bullfighting, and Jinny had rejected it, ridiculed it. Pauline realized glumly that she had perhaps sounded like Hadley in her repetition of Ernest's words, and her shoulders drooped with dejection. She sat in silence, not responding to Jinny's dismissal.

Then Pauline's sullenness began to turn to anger; she did not like being made to feel the fool. She looked at Jinny, shook her head, and without speaking to her sister, got up and walked away.

CHAPTER SIXTEEN

Pauline found herself alone, wandering the streets of Pamplona. It was not long before she realized she had gone in a full circle and was back in front of the façade of their *pensión*.

She had not intentionally wandered back this way, but when she found herself in front of the carved oak door, she paused, checked herself, then made a decision. She unhesitatingly went inside, strode past the registry desk and walked upstairs to the room Ernest shared with Hadley and the baby. Pauline knocked.

Ernest quickly answered the door, flushed and out of breath. Pauline scanned the room, looking for Hadley; she was nowhere to be seen, nor was the baby. Pauline took a deep breath.

"Come in, come in," he urged, excitedly. "Come over here and see *this*." Ernest yanked her into the room, slammed the door behind her and pulled her toward the open window. "You're not going to believe this, Pauline – it's *amazing*." His face shone with excitement and vigor. Pauline walked closer to the window and stood slightly behind him. Then she moved to his side, and followed his gaze down into the narrow street below.

The room overlooked a small city square, a dusty open space with a diamond-shaped fountain in the middle. People had filled up the streets, so that an enclosed place had formed next to the fountain. At one edge of the diamond stood a bull, tethered to a post, pawing at the hard stone paving of the street. The crowd was growing.

Ernest turned to her, face aglow with excitement.

"This is one of the *real* Pamplona bullfights, Pauline," he grinned. "This is it, a *tourada ã corda*. Here it is, right underneath our noses." He turned back to the window.

"Oh," Pauline replied, composing herself. "This what you were telling me about last night?" She tried to sound calm, conversational. Ernest glanced sideways at her, irritated at what he deemed an insipid comment.

"Just watch, for Pete's sake," he spat. "It's a bullfight, a real bullfight." She leaned forward beside him, and watched.

The crowd below began catcalling; a few young men were being pushed forward, into the open space near the bull. Some of the young men held back, showing either trepidation or feigned bravado. Finally, one youth stepped forward, confident and smiling, and the crowd surged inward, roaring. Someone threw the young man a dingy scrap of cloth.

An older man warily made his way to the diamond, and, with a quick hand and an even quicker retreat, unleashed the bull's tether from the post. The crowd roared and moved back, forming a circle next to the fountain. The young man, brandishing the small cloth, waved it over his head, and then swept it with a brave flourish out to his side. He waved his makeshift *capote* in a faultless *verónica*, and the crowd yelled and pulsed again. The bull seemed oblivious.

The young man moved closer. He waved the cloth again. Eventually, the bull seemed to be aware that there was a bothersome presence, something that needed tending to. It turned its massive head and stared at the young man.

Pauline cringed. Although Ernest had explained it to her, she could not believe this was going on, in a public street, in broad daylight. Surely that boy would be gored, or at least thrown and trampled. She looked up at Ernest's face, and was astounded at the look of pure joy in his eyes. He felt her stare

96

and gave her a brief, indifferent glance before turning back to the spectacle.

"It's almost magical, isn't it, Pauline?" He put his arm around her and without hesitation, pulled her close; Ernest never took his eyes from the street. The brave young man faced off with the angry bull; he danced in front of the beast, taunting him. Pauline felt the muscles of Ernest's chest and arm rhythmically tensing, and smelled more than felt the wetness of his sweat. He was clearly stimulated by the scene and his excitement was contagious. She let herself be held.

"I can't believe what I'm seeing," she whispered. Bull and man and crowd, a fiery, blistering entanglement, alive and poignant. Part of Pauline was repelled by the thirst for violence reflected in the faces of the crowd, but she could not look away. Ernest continued to hold her under his arm, pulling her into his side.

As they watched the fight ensue, Ernest hands moved to her waist and, not speaking, he pulled Pauline around in front of him, still facing the window. He put his arms on either side of her, placing his hands on the windowsill. Then he slowly bent his head over her shoulder and, cheek to cheek, they continued watching the fight below. Pauline felt his chest press against her back. She was encircled, unable to pull away, even if she had wanted to.

They watched, unmoving. Their eyes never left the man, the bull, the crowd. Pauline had no idea how it was going to end.

In the arena, the finale was the bull's bloody death and the toreador's beaming acceptance of the crowd's adulation. It seemed, however, that in a street bullfight it was a more even match between man and beast. They continued to watch, captivated by the surging crowd, the dancing man, and the darting bull.

The fight ended when the old man who had untethered the bull stepped into the makeshift arena. The single rope still in his hand was not enough now to subdue the angered bull. With the other hand, he began to swing a *bolo* in tight circles by his side. Expertly, he flung the lasso, and its spinning balls lashed around the bull's horns. Quickly, the old man leaned back, pulling on the *bolo's* rope against the sharp yanks of the beast's craggy head. He spoke sharply, and the bull stopped, and stared at the man.

The old man continued in a soft, seductive patter, and began to lead the bull back to the tether post. The crowd parted and let man and bull pass through. The amateur toreador melted into the appreciative crowd, and, as suddenly as it had begun, the impromptu bullfight was over.

Pauline felt Ernest's arms loosen from around her and felt him move away. She turned, and saw him walk toward the bed, the bed he shared with Hadley. He picked up a coverlet that was lying, unfolded, at the foot of the bed.

Ernest grasped two corners, one in each hand, and held it out to his side. Then, smiling broadly, he waved it over his head in a perfectly executed *verónica*. With a final flourish, he returned to a neutral stance, the coverlet held tauntingly out to his side.

He stared at Pauline, a smile barely perceptible on his face. Pauline stood frozen. He roared with laughter and stamped his foot.

"Come on, little bull, come fight with Papa." He swirled the coverlet again and took a step toward her. She moved sideways, trying to figure out what to do. Ernest had, not for the first or last time, caught her completely off guard. He began to advance toward her.

"Little bull," Ernest goaded. "I'm going to catch you." He stamped his foot again and shook the coverlet, taunting; "You had better put up a fight." Pauline sidled toward the door, but stopped when Ernest switched his orbit to cut off any possible exit. They began circling each other, and the grin on his face widened.

"That's it, little bull, see if you can get away," Ernest hounded her. Through the open window, a sudden roar from the street indicated that another *tourada* was about to begin. But Ernest and Pauline were so intent on their own skirmish that neither of them even glanced toward the window. They glared at each other, prey and hunter, and continued circling the room.

In one swift move, Ernest lunged at Pauline and wrapped the coverlet tightly around her. He wove it around and around, her arms pinned at her sides. He pulled it tight, then stared down at Pauline where he had imprisoned her, their faces inches apart.

His smile was contemptuous. He pulled her closer, and kissed her. His kiss was rough, and he smelled of the liquor he had drunk that morning. He kissed her again, searching and insistent. Pauline could not move, tied up in his arms.

He picked her up and tossed her, still wrapped in the coverlet, onto his bed. Then, with one sharp pull he extricated her from his improvised *capote de brega*. The increasing clamor from the crowd outside seemed to egg him on.

The bullfight in the street was quickly over. Pauline assumed no blood had been spilled, and that it had been another draw. It had not been loud enough, protracted enough or anguished enough for another type of outcome. But there had been a conquest, and she lay beneath him, barely able to breathe.

At length, he lay beside her, his breath coming slower and more regular. Pauline did not move. Although uncovered beside him on the bed, she felt just as she had when he had wrapped her tightly in the coverlet: she could not escape now.

CHAPTER SEVENTEEN

It did not take long for Hadley to realize what was happening. She could not ignore Ernest's long absences or Pauline's discomfiture in her presence. Hadley may have been shy and quiet, but she was not stupid. She confronted her rival in a small café, near the bar where Ernest had first kissed Pauline.

"You're *fornicating* with him, aren't you?" Pauline was shocked by Hadley's forthrightness, and choice of words. She supposed she had hoped Hadley might ignore the developing affair. In retrospect, however, that had been an expedient fantasy. Hadley was a woman with a marriage and a baby to protect, and she was going to fight for both.

"I don't know what to say, Hadley. It just happened," Pauline responded. She did not offer any denials or explanations. She simply let her words hang in the air. Pauline saw, beneath Hadley's gaze, a kind of hatred. She had never been the subject of that kind of look before; it was overwhelming.

"I am disgusted by both of you," Hadley said. "But I particularly loath *you.*"

Her tone was steely, her anger palpable. This was not the shy, malleable girl Pauline was used to; this was fury and fear and disgust, and it was all aimed at her. She thought, *if Hadley has a gun right now, she just might use it.*

"I'm sorry, Hadley." Pauline knew the words, as soon as they left her lips, were wrong – insipid, useless, even goading.

"How I *hate* you right now," Hadley continued, "I hate both of you. I cannot believe you would be this low, this crude, this revolting, to sleep together right in front of me." Hadley's face was red with fury. "I have a child, you know. A child – *his* child. You have inserted yourself into a family, for heaven sakes. What a *disgusting* thing to do." Hadley spat her words, then closed her eyes and breathed in sharply, as if composing herself for battle.

Pauline was speechless. There was nothing to say, nothing to do in the face of such anger. And she had no defense. Saying that she loved Ernest – for she had decided that she did – was an insufficient justification: Hadley loved him as well. And Hadley was right – they had a child. All of Pauline's Catholic upbringing pressed down upon her shoulders, with its judgment and condemnation.

And yet, even in the face of such blunt abhorrence and self-criticism, Pauline was certain that neither she nor Ernest would stop on the path they had chosen.

It was as if, in the face of this colossal sin, Ernest and Pauline would continue to defy gravity, to choose each other in spite of what they both knew to be a great wrong. They had reached the point of being unable to judge themselves dispassionately; they were acting solely in response to their emotions, not to reason or common sense. And, Pauline thought, neither she nor Ernest had any intention of turning back.

As Hadley continued to rant at her, Pauline found that she had nothing more to say.

CHAPTER EIGHTEEN

Hadley left the confrontation with Pauline in a swirl of anger and invective. Pauline had never heard her speak so harshly or so coarsely. But then, Pauline reflected, Hadley had more than enough tutelage in Ernest's rough language to replicate it when necessary.

And she obviously had felt it necessary.

The festival was almost over. The atmosphere in town was sluggish, fatigued by the incessant revelry. Another confrontation was almost too much to contemplate, but Hadley had insisted. She requested that both Ernest and Pauline appear to receive her ultimatum. Like chastised school children, both complied.

They planned to meet at a café near their *pensión*. Pauline arrived to find the uncomfortable couple already seated– Hadley clearly angry and Ernest clearly heart-worn – at a table in the back. It was barely nine o'clock. The morning sun had not yet reached the dark corner where they waited. Pauline moved slowly toward them, like a bull with one sword already hanging from its neck. She sat down. Hadley glared at her.

"Right now, the sight of you two disgusts me." Hadley looked down at the grimy table's surface, then placed two clenched fists on the wood. Without looking up, she slew condemnation at Pauline and Ernest. "I do not have words to express my repugnance, my disgust at you," she spat. She continued to stare at her hands, knuckles white against the dark surface; her anger seethed like a volcano. Neither Ernest nor Pauline spoke, afraid that a single word from either would cause an eruption. Hadley, continuing to berate them, began to explain what she considered a fitting response to their transgression.

She had decided to impose a one-hundred-day moratorium. After a separation of one hundred days, if Ernest and Pauline were still bent on this folly, she would consent and give him a divorce. If that were the outcome, however, she would have her pound of flesh: they would live with their guilt until it either reformed them, or became a permanent part of them. Ernest and Pauline sat quietly as they were confronted with Hadley's demand.

Hadley laid out her terms, without hesitation or interruption. Ernest agreed, with no objection. He too stared down at his hands, they seemed large and impotent, lying in his lap. He did not speak his assent; he merely nodded his head.

Pauline realized that Hadley had moved a chess piece into a seriously threatening position. Although she did not immediately move to counterattack, Pauline resolved that she would not be checkmated. She stood, took one last look at Ernest, and without saying a word, turned and left the dark corner of the café, moving out into the sunshine of the square.

Pauline flexed her shoulders and began to walk briskly along the dusty sidewalks. Once she was out of sight of the café, she slowed her pace. Head down, hands clasped behind her back, she strolled pensively through the quiet streets, pondering her next move. It was early in the game, and she could still plan her castle kingside.

CHAPTER NINETEEN

L ater that day, in a dim bar on Pamplona's *plaza de la ciudad*, Pauline found Ernest seated at a small round table. A pitcher of sangria and a half-full glass sat at his elbow. Condensation ran down the sides of both pitcher and glass, making circular puddles on the wooden table. Pauline paused at the end of the bar and watched him.

Ernest was bent over a sheet of paper, scratching at it in his acute, angular handwriting. He had not noticed her entrance. Pauline stood for several minutes, watching him. She thought about Hadley's ultimatum and Ernest's immediate acquiescence; she realized she did not know when – or if – she would see him again. She continued to watch him write, line after thin, wavering line, in his pressing, crabbed script.

Pauline wondered what he was writing. A letter, perhaps? Part of a new novel? She mused again as to whether she would ever appear in one of his books. It occurred to her how narcissistic it was to stand there, waiting to say goodbye to her lover, whose marriage she had perhaps destroyed, but thinking about whether he would someday write about her. She held her hand to her mouth and coughed, pointedly.

Ernest glanced up, startled. He did not look pleased to find her standing at the wooden bar. He often told her that he hated to see anyone watch him write.

"You're leaving, then?" he said. Pauline detected a bit of impatience, as well as sadness in his voice. She knew that he wanted her to leave, just as she knew that he wanted her to stay.

Pauline acknowledged the immediate relief from stress that their parting would provide. Hadley's rage, their guilt, and yet their continued desire for each other despite causing so much pain—it was almost too much to bear. The weight of contradictory passions was tremendous.

"Jinny and I rented a car," Pauline said softly. "We'll be leaving in a couple days." Ernest stared at her, then slowly rose from the small table, dropping his pen by the drafting paper. At times like these, he reminded Pauline of a bear: he moved toward her, grunted loudly, and lowered his lumbering head. He rested his cheek heavily on top of her head. After a moment, he burrowed his nose into her hair, and inhaled, moving his face back and forth, back and forth on her scalp, as if to try and decide between the conflicting emotions of sadness and desire.

"By gad, I love the smell of you," he growled. "I love the smell of your skin, the scent of your hair, the oil of your skin." He nuzzled her again, and said, smiling, "You smell like making love." Ernest did not speak softly; the entire bar heard him. Pauline did not know how many of them understood English, but it was clear from the several smiles and quickly turned heads that at least a few did. She was surprised that she did not blush, or flinch.

She wanted more. She wrapped her arms around him.

"I want you now more than ever," she said quietly. "I will wait, and I will wait, and I will wait, and when this is over, I will be your wife."

It was the first time Pauline had spoken these words, but certainly not the first time she had thought them. She left her kisses on his lips, with promises that she would give him anything he wanted, if he would make her his wife. At the time, she gave no thought whatsoever to what those promises might cost her. They stood together silently for a long time, embracing in the crowded bar, intent only upon each other.

CHAPTER TWENTY

Pauline and Jinny's departure date was set, and after the scene in the bar, both Ernest and Pauline found it far easier to simply avoid each other. But the fact that they were in the same small inn made it impossible to completely evade all contact. Pauline, knowing that Ernest tended to sleep late, got up early the next two mornings and out of the *pensión* – she spent the days with Jinny, playing tourist. On the last day, she accidentally – but unavoidably – ran into Ernest.

They were both checking out of the *pensión*, and both had had difficulty locating the desk clerk to settle their accounts. Pauline walked into the dingy lobby for the third time in an hour to scan the reception desk and collided with Ernest, waiting there for the same reason.

The tension was immediate and palpable. The cloud of conflicting passions was a pall between them, massive and heavy. Ernest stared at her; he seemed to be straining not to speak. Pauline gazed up at him, and her face flushed. The two said nothing; in truth, they did not need to. Their contract was already a bond, and an anchor.

The silence was broken when the *pensión* desk clerk, obviously hungover, lurched into the reception area from the back anteroom. He stared at them, bleary-eyed, and belched. They were both grateful for his arrival.

Ernest gestured to Pauline, and she slipped in front of him to the desk, and quickly finished the business of paying her bill. She felt Ernest watching her, felt his gaze on her back, appraising her. It electrified her. She felt herself more alive, just being in his presence, even though no word had passed between them. After she finished with the desk clerk, she snapped her purse shut, turned, and allowed the smallest of smiles to purse her lips. She glided past him, her hand barely touching his as she left. He needed no more consideration.

When Pauline and Jinny left Pamplona, Pauline believed nothing could eradicate that undeniably powerful attachment. She held firmly to the beliefs that she would become Mrs. Ernest Hemingway, and that their lives together would become a blissful, unending sojourn of mutual regard and satisfaction.

Pauline would find out that, in at least the latter respect, she was wrong.

* * * * *

PART TWO

~Summer~

CHAPTER ONE

Paris, May 1927

Soon after the divorce was final, Ernest and Pauline began to make plans for their wedding. Ernest planned to be in Pamplona for the running of the bulls in July, so they needed to get all their affairs in order quickly. They decided it would be easiest to marry in Paris, rather than travel back to the states. Pauline knew her mother would be upset but was unconcerned; they made plans for a small service in a Paris church.

Pauline and Jinny were still in their *cinquiéme arrondisement* apartment, and Ernest had rented a flat nearby. Pauline's days, and nights, with Ernest were an intoxicating delirium of happiness. They spent every moment they could together, walking, eating, making love, sleeping. As they talked about their wedding plans, however, the issue of Pauline's Catholicism became unavoidable. Although she was daily engaging in sin with Ernest, she knew it would be necessary to stop, repent, confess, and receive the Eucharist before she could marry. In addition, she knew that Ernest would have to convert.

It occurred to Pauline, not without some amusement, that she should be focusing on these transactional issues. She felt as if she had become a diplomat, putting blinders on past blunders and transgressions, to focus solely on preliminary negotiations prior to engaging in the final consular settlement.

"You know," Pauline said, as they lay in bed late one afternoon, the sun shining lazily through the curtains, "you will have to convert." It was the first time she had used that word, but she could see from his reaction it was not the first time he had thought of it. Ernest did not flinch, move away, react negatively in any way. He simply lay, passively, his large chest moving rhythmically with his breathing. She put her hand out, and caressed his hair, his shoulders, his face. After a few moments, he spoke.

"You know, my little Pilar, as I told you before, I think if I am anything, I am Catholic." Pauline lay silently, pondering what he meant by this. Soon, Ernest spoke again. "I've talked to one of your priests – it won't take much." Again, he was one step ahead of her. "He's already agreed to take care of my stained, sinful divorced status. And I understand the process I must go through to repent and confess. So in fact," he concluded, "the problem really isn't me." Ernest paused for effect. "It's *you*." Pauline sat up and pulled the bed linen up to her chest.

"What do you mean, the problem is *me*?" She felt a frisson of fear.

"Well, my dear, "it seems you've been continually and, clearly, without firm purpose of amendment engaging in what your ilk calls a 'venal sin.' Pretty big issue, don't you think?" He flashed a small, almost imperceptible smile; Pauline could not divine whether it was malignant or benign. She responded tartly.

"OK, so you've learned enough to know about the Catholic hierarchy of sinful behavior. Why does that make *me* the problem?" Ernest shifted onto his side, and his smile widened. He reached over to the bedside stand, pulled a cigarette out of its box and lit it, slowly drawing smoke into his lungs. He blew the smoke out in a long gray plume.

"Well, here's how I see it." Ernest took another drag. "After I go through this little circus of converting, as I understand it, and assuming I do and say all the correct rituals according to Hoyle, and believe them with all my heart when

I say them, well, then, my love, I've been given to understand that, at that precise moment of conversion, after receiving the body and blood of Christ, blessed and anointed by one of your holy order, I shall be a completely, utterly, truly clean soul, ready to enter the kingdom of heaven." He pulled on his cigarette. Pauline lay beside him, waiting for further explication.

"But," Ernest continued, "to answer your question, little bird, it seems that, although I shall have achieved the status of being pure and white as the driven snow," he blew out another plume, "the problem remains that, in the eyes of your church, you will still be little more than a common *putaha*."

His words stung; they were meant to be unkind, but Pauline did not respond.

"So you see, unless you do something to correct that problem, a good Catholic boy like me will not be able to marry a trollop like you."

He finished his cigarette, stubbed it out in the glass tray, and turned toward Pauline. He ran his hand casually over the top of her head. His fingers fell to her nape, and he entwined them in her hair; he tipped her head back slightly to expose her neck.

"So, my bad girl, what are you going to do?" His mouth found the tenderest spot of her neck where Pauline felt his teeth graze her. He continued to whisper, "Answer me, little bird," lining her neck with harsh kisses, "how are you going to make yourself proper enough for me?"

Pauline knew he expected no answer other than her submission. His contorted theological reasoning was not up for debate. She realized at that moment she could no more have spoken to rebut him than she could have gotten up and walked out.

CHAPTER TWO

Ernest's conversion was undertaken swiftly and without fanfare. Pauline had known of other adult converts, all of whom had become zealots. But Ernest's conversion had a different genesis: his was part of a game-plan, a scheme, not necessarily a true discovery of faith. She listened to him castigate the Catholic church in one breath and ostensibly embrace it with the next. His two-facedness alarmed her, not just for herself, but for him. Pauline was enough of a Catholic that this sentiment was deeply ingrained: Do not trifle with *The Church*. Do not blaspheme or belittle. Hell was a real place to her; she was scared by Ernest's insouciance.

After a brief ceremony in a dismal parish church in which the priest blessed Ernest's new-found denomination, they began in earnest to make wedding plans. They both, however, continued in their sin of intimacy. Despite Ernest's earlier proclamation, final repentance and confession would have to wait until closer to the wedding day. They justified this cognitive dissonance with the determination and skill of diplomats; however messy the negotiations, the final treaty was what mattered.

Pauline met with a priest at *St. Julien le Pauvre*, a small, reclusive church on an unprepossessing Paris street. They scheduled the date, and wrote to their circle of friends in Paris, a few in England, Germany, and Italy, and sent notes back to the States, giving dates and details. They did not expect many people to attend, and Pauline's terse communications indicated as much; they were announcing, in effect, the fact of their marriage. There was almost a defiance in sending out the invitations: they knew that many of their acquaintances were

115

displeased with their callous treatment of Hadley; Ernest and Pauline did not care.

The week before the wedding was cloudy and humid. The air was heavy, the skies threatening but withholding rain, making it hard to breathe. Ernest, with his usual offhanded casualness, informed Pauline he would not be seeing her for the few days left before their wedding. Pauline wondered at his decision to remove himself. She did not think it was because of any sensitivity to her feelings or a nod to decorum, and she said as much.

"There, my dear, you are quite wrong," Ernest replied. They were sitting at a sidewalk café, sipping turgid, lemon-scented espresso. Pauline fumbled with her napkin, and refolded it in her lap. Ernest continued. "It is not merely a 'nod to decorum' as you so prosaically put it. I am leaving my bride in chaste abandonment for the days before her marriage, and I will make my repentance and confession. I suggest you do the same. You should be able to understand that." He looked, not at Pauline, but down into his demitasse cup, then sipped the coal-like liquid silently. She was frozen by the chill of his tone.

In the past few days, Ernest had developed a trace of nastiness toward Pauline. She was afraid it might have become his default mode. He had begun to find it all too easy to speak down to her, to chastise her in supercilious tones, and make derisive comments toward her. Pauline chalked it up to pre-wedding jitters.

Despite her internal insistence that she would not become another Hadley, that she would find ways to stand up to him, Pauline realized she had already accepted the very treatment she abhorred. She had not told him to stop, nor had she protested. She was too close to the goal line—of becoming Mrs. Ernest Hemingway—and she was taking hits that a few months earlier would have made her throw a glass of whiskey in his face. She shifted in her chair and changed the subject.

"Ernest," Pauline said, with a determined air, "I've been thinking about something." She paused, watching his face for any sign of emotion. "I want a dog." She leaned back and waited tensely for his response. Ernest stared at her. He appeared stunned by this announcement.

Pauline smiled inwardly with the satisfaction of having temporarily flummoxed him. Of all things he might have expected her to say, the very last, she believed, was a desire for a canine presence in their lives. Ernest was nonplussed. Pauline enjoyed watching him try to recover. He sipped his coffee.

"Really." Ernest stared at her. "A dog." He was working to find some equilibrium, some balance of what he knew of her, some sense of what this latest gambit might represent. It was hard to stay ahead of him in any game, but Pauline was determined to try. "Why the hell do you want a dog?" he said. "You grew up on a farm – didn't you get enough of animals?" It seemed to Pauline he was reaching for something to put her off her pins. Pauline squared her shoulders.

"I don't mean a farm dog. I mean a little, sweet lap dog – one that is all mine, who will sit in my lap and love me always and best, and perhaps despise you."

Ernest glared at her. She could tell something excited him when she challenged him. It was an odd balancing act: he dominated, she stood up to him, and he would be moved to exhibit his dominance in the most atavistic of ways. Pauline intuited that this pattern was inherently maladaptive, possibly destructive, but she felt unsure how to stop it. Ernest finished drinking his coffee and frowned.

"A little, yappy dog. That's what you want, eh, my sweet? Something that will irritate me, and pee on all the carpets, and bite any guests who are brave enough to enter our abode?" He smirked at her. She sipped her espresso slowly and deliberately, until she drained the small cup.

"Yep, you've got it," Pauline said. "That is precisely what I want. Somehow you nailed it on the head." She signaled to the *garçon* to refill her cup. "And after my new little dog has irritated, and peed, and bitten, he will top off the day by spending the night in bed with me, and pushing you out."

Ernest sat perfectly still, taking in her rebuttal. Then he slowly turned his massive frame toward her, reached out a hand, and circled his fingers around her forearm. His grip was tight enough to hurt.

"Let me make something perfectly clear, my angel." Ernest's eyes glittered with anger. "You may purchase any type of little animal you choose. You may lay with it, and coddle it, and make yourself a fool over it." He paused, and glared at Pauline. "But you will never, never," he tightened the painful pressure on her arm, "you will never be free from me in your bed. There, I own you. I will not let anything interfere with that."

Pauline was stunned. She tried to pull her arm away. He held on tightly, squeezing even more painfully.

"You do understand, my sweet, that you are entering into a contract with me?" This was the first time he had spoken explicitly of their "contract." Pauline sat perfectly still, wondering what his next revelation would be. She had upped the ante, after all. Ernest continued, "And that contract entails certain requirements from you." He let go of her arm, sat back; the atmosphere seemed to coalesce around him. "You have already given yourself totally to me, and I will continue to require that. What I am looking for now is a more complete gift of yourself." His words were threatening; he intended them to be. Pauline felt herself curling inward.

"I don't understand, Ernest, I'm sorry," she said. "Why does my asking for a dog make a difference to you? I'm just joking with you." She sat back in her chair and rubbed her arm where his grip hurt her, and she realized her voice sounded pleading, almost scared. She was certain it was obvious to Ernest as well.

She began to understand that she would never best him in ordinary, everyday encounters; to do that would necessitate an unending series of apocalyptic fights; she would have to choose her battles. Pauline lowered her head.

She was aware that she did not understand his demands completely, but she knew he was asking for more than she had originally bargained for. Even though the contours of the bargain were unclear, she knew that he wanted to control her.

She was hesitant, even frightened, to say yes. At the same time, she knew it was too late to say no; she was determined to get her prize, her legal right to be called his wife.

Pauline looked up at him, her eyes steady, then she closed them. She slowly leaned forward until her cheek fell upon his forearm. They sat still, in their respective postures, until he spoke.

"Alright, little girl, you've made your point." Ernest hesitated. "But you must understand you will never *win* with me. You will never best me. You will never take away my ability to chastise you when you deserve it."

She looked up into his eyes, then lay her forehead back down on his arm. She kissed the back of his hand.

His forearm was flat on the tabletop; his hand felt warm to her skin. As she rested her forehead against him, she felt his pulse.

Slowly he turned his arm until his palm cradled her cheek. Pauline's lips grazed him. Without moving her position,

Ernest began to stroke beneath her chin, as if hoping to conjure a purr from her.

"Well, my little one, well, what have you done?" he purred. "What has my little Catholic girl gotten herself into?" Pauline's eyes were closed, her lips still on his palm. Her head was reeling under his spell. "Do you want me to pet you, *mmmm*? Is that what you want?" His fingers continued to stroke her neck; the rest of his body remained immobile. He was waiting for her to answer.

Pauline had no verbal response to give him. She had stopped thinking, evaluating, she only reacted to her need to touch him, to feel him touch her.

"Keeping doing that," he said. Pauline realized, then, that she had continued kissing his palm, drugged by the saltiness of his skin. "Keep doing that, and we will be fine, my dear little one."

If Pauline had been able to distance herself at that moment, she might have responded differently. She might have been offended—even given him the back of her hand. But she was in the quicksand, hip-deep; she could not retreat. She lifted her head and looked into his eyes. Ernest read the acceptance on her face and smiled. He had succeeded.

CHAPTER THREE

The days prior to the wedding were an unpleasant round of last-minute planning and quarrelling. Pauline argued with Jinny, the priest, and with Ernest. True to his word, Ernest only spoke with her over the telephone, and only when she called him. But on the afternoon before the wedding, he inexplicably relented and permitted Pauline to see him in the lobby of his hotel.

She found him seated in an armchair at a small writing table in the front parlor. The room was crammed with several pieces of dusty, overstuffed Victorian furniture. Ticking and clanging pendulum clocks clung to every wall, and a taxidermied owl leered censoriously at the room's occupants. Ernest sat looking down at a manuscript, oblivious to her entrance.

"Yes, that's right, that's right," he muttered, shuffling papers, re-reading, shaking his head, rearranging, and making sharp-slashed line-throughs with his pen on the yellow paper. Pauline touched him lightly on the shoulder, and he flinched. He glanced up at her, then back at the writing. Pauline wanted to grab the yellow papers and pen and hurl them into the fireplace. Ernest stared gloomily downward at his writing.

"Darling, please, don't go all down in the mouth on me, please," Pauline said. "I'm just asking for a little attention. I just wanted to see you once before tomorrow morning." She hated to sound as if she were begging, but indeed, she was. She could not stand any more unhappiness or anxiety or strain. She just wanted some reassurance and comfort.

Still standing beside him, she looked down at this mammoth man who was to become her husband. She gazed at the back of his head and squeezed his shoulder. She knew that his was an oversized personality, a man for whom one woman, one pleasure, had not previously been enough. Pauline was determined that she would show him, she would be more than enough for him. Pauline had watched Hadley as she had devolved, descended into a domestic mess, totally and completely dependent on Ernest's opinion of her, her only enduring accomplishment being the production of a son. Pauline was determined to be more, and to give Ernest a run for his money.

What did not occur to her, at the time, was how dependent she had already become on his assessment of her. She was blind to that, in her overwhelming desire to become his wife. The past two days had been miserable, and Pauline yearned for some rapprochement between them. Ernest finally raised his head, mute, and stared blankly at her. Pauline looked at the papers still scattered in front of him, his large hands lying palms down, protectively on top of his writing. She moved to the front bay window, pulled the chintz curtains to the side, and looked out into the darkening street. She spoke quietly.

"Do you still want to marry me?" Pauline turned, slowly, aware that the late-afternoon light through the windows framed her silhouette. The silence was heavy between them. She had opened the keyhole, and she waited, her stomach in a knot, for his response. The expression in his eyes gave her no comfort; they were blank. "Ernest, do you realize what I am asking?" Pauline's voice cracked as she spoke. "We have been through fire to get to this place, and the past few days it seems as if you don't want me around. If you don't want to marry me, for heaven's sake, say so now." Her heart was in her throat, waiting for his answer. Finally, he spoke.

"My dearest one, I'm sorry." Ernest said, still staring at the papers under his hands. Pauline felt as if her knees would give out beneath her, as if the floor were melting under her. She did not know if she could bear what she felt was coming next, a rejection of her, of a life with her. "Come here." Ernest leaned against the wing of his armchair and patted his lap.

Pauline felt like a dog being called to the master's seat. But she answered, and moved slowly toward him. She sat down on the great expanse of his broad legs and turned toward him. Pauline felt as if she were a little girl on her uncle's lap. Her head began to swim. She could not speak.

"Please," Pauline said, "this is misery. Please, either let me go, or say you're going to marry me tomorrow and I'll smile again and be happy. Please." He shook his head and put his arm around her waist. To Pauline's amazement, he began to laugh.

"Oh, my little bird," Ernest chuckled, "my little Pilar, my sweet, scared, childish, impudent, engaging little girl." He looked at her and grinned. "You'll get what you want, little one – you will get your Catholic marriage, in your Catholic church, blessed over by some delicate Catholic priest. You'll get it all." He continued to chortle to himself. "You'll get it, you'll get it all my dear." His soft, derisive laughter disconcerted her.

Then, as abruptly as he had started, Ernest stopped laughing. His expression slowly became stony. "But, my darling," Ernest continued, his voice now low and still, "my dearest one, it will not always be an easy ride. You have taken up with a magician, a maverick. I am part of a strange tribe."

Pauline sat still on his lap, and felt her body begin to sway. She felt as if she did not find something to hold onto, she would fall. She lifted one slim arm around the back of his neck, and slowly sank her head onto his chest.

"Yes," she said, "yes, I see that." Her thoughts were tumbling, her breath coming fast, her pulse racing; she wondered for a moment if she would faint. Ernest continued.

"And you will always be, my dear, just what you are now. Difficult." Ernest paused. "As will I." One arm lay around her waist, his other on the arm of the chair, his hand hanging heavily over the edge. Pauline sat motionless, and Ernest gazed out into the street, watching the afternoon shoppers on the sidewalks as they passed hurriedly by, laden with packages. Neither one of them spoke.

Without words passing between them, another pact was entered. A new phase of their contract, one that would bind them irrevocably. She was taking him as he was, and he, her. The deal Pauline was striking was not precisely what she had imagined, but she would take it. And she would get the most she could out of it.

In that moment they silently acknowledged a joint truth: they both had uncommonly faulty hearts. They were both guilty of sin, and chary of what actual repentance might lead to. They were entering this contract not as giddy lovers, not as starry-eyed fiancés, but as equally guilty bargainers, culpable bettors on what they both imagined would be a worthier hand dealt to them. Ernest and Pauline were each wagering that they could win. At that point, however, neither understood that it was to be a zero-sum game.

CHAPTER FOUR

After she left the portentous session with Ernest, Pauline went to confession. She was determined to enter her marriage in as close to a state of grace as she possibly could. She would prepare herself as the church required for her wedding day.

She chose not to go to St. Julien's for absolution – she did not want to run into the priest who would be performing the wedding, or worse, draw him as her confessor. Instead, she walked around the fifth *arrondisement*, looking for a church with an open door and an empty confessional. She wanted her declaration and supplication to be anonymous: every Catholic knows that, in your own parish, in your own church, the screen between the penitent and confessor is a slim, and usually non-existent, pretense of anonymity. Priests usually know precisely who is sitting on the other side.

Pauline expected that she would be able to find a church far enough away that it would be impossible for the priest to identify her. And she had enough to confess that she wanted to be truly nameless.

She soon found what she was looking for: a non-descript Catholic church with a little sign on the front wrought-iron gate, *Notre Dame de la Victoire* – "Our Lady of Victory." It occurred to her, as it had before, that Catholics used the most unwieldy names for their places of worship, and that their veneration for The Virgin sometimes verged on the risible. Pauline banished her usual cynicism quickly – she was trying to remain as pure in heart as possible prior to the wedding. She did not need something more to confess, such as blasphemy; she had plenty on her list already.

Pauline walked through the heavy wooden door, into the apse of the church. She made her way into the cool, dark interior, and her hand immediately found the holy water font, a gray stone appurtenance stuck to an even grayer stone wall.

She paused and looked at the font. It seemed almost droll, a nonsensical thing: enter the church, and touch a bit of water, probably straight out of the church kitchen spigot, blessed by the brief over-passage of a priest's hand, then dotted quickly onto forehead, chest, and shoulders in genuflection. Somehow, this secret password allowed the penitent's feet to keep moving forward. All good Catholics know this feeling; entering a church without the ritual ablution creates a sense of nakedness, awkwardness. That day the procedural act struck Pauline as merely expedient.

She walked slowly back through the nave of the church until she saw the cloistered wooden confessional booths, the openings hung with heavy burgundy drapes. Pauline stopped. She had not been to confession in years. She found it hard to walk forward toward the cubicles, but was compelled by the ancient necessity of the ritual. She walked carefully, trying to step as silently as possible on the stone-flagged floor.

She looked down for a minute, just to appreciate the beauty of the tiling. It looked like coal black slate, and Pauline wondered what expense the church had incurred to install such a lavish foundation for a small parish church. Perhaps some guilty parishioner had donated it; guilt was a powerful motivator, as she was experiencing.

She reached the confessional and, after a brief pause, pulled aside the heavy drape and stepped inside. The deep red cloth fell closed behind her almost soundlessly. She sat down tentatively on the narrow wooden bench opposite the confessional screen. A dank, musty smell enveloped her, and she held her breath for a moment. She looked around her and exhaled. Pauline squinted in the dim light, and inhaled sharply at the astonishing interior of the compartment.

Usually, confessionals are barren little cubicles, but this one was remarkable. Heavy, intricate carvings deeply etched into the dark wood surrounded her, resembling nothing so much as a Hieronymus Bosch painting. All manner of human sin was depicted, floor to ceiling in the heavily sculpted wood; Pauline was fascinated. She wondered, briefly, if the carvings had been completed during the Northern Renaissance, or if this was simply an exceptionally good later replication of the famous master's painterly work. She wiggled on her narrow perch, and then heard movement on the other side. The small solid inset panel door slid open; dim points of light came thought the carved wooden screen. Pauline took a deep breath.

"Bless me, Father, for I have sinned," she recited. "It's been several years since my last confession." Pauline spoke in broken French, and was immediately grateful when the priest responded in English, thankful for his immediate assessment of her native language.

"Bless you, my child. What have you to confess?" The priest's heavily accented words were spoken with the voice of a young man, his timbre soft and fluid. Pauline wondered, for a fleeting moment, what he looked like. She had seen some handsome priests, and it had always seemed to her such a waste. Pauline quickly shook her head, chastised herself for letting her mind wander, and redirected her thoughts to the purpose of her visit.

"Well, Father, I'm not really sure where to start." She paused and breathed in the cloying air of the tiny chamber.

"Take your time," he said in lilting English. Pauline wondered briefly as to the sufficiency of his command of her language; then she thought, sin is apprehendable in any tongue.

"Well, it's been years since I sat in a confessional," Pauline continued, "and in that time I've committed a whole lot of minor sins, but I'm here because I'm getting married, and I want to confess something big." The atmosphere on the other side of the grid was expectant; the priest waited for her to continue. "I committed fornication," Pauline felt awkward, saying the archaic word out loud, "with a married man."

At this last revelation, she heard a sharp, sudden intake of breath; he probably thought he had heard the worst of it after the first clause. "And that's the man I am marrying." As she sat and waited for the priest to respond, it occurred to her that she had been silly to be so trepidatious about this, the actual confessing of her sin had taken surprisingly little effort. She hesitated, waiting for a response.

"So," the priest began, drawing out the word as if he were a teacher writing on a chalk board, "so, you committed this sin – a big one – and now you are going to marry him." He paused. "Is he a Catholic?" Of course, this would be his first question; it would be of paramount concern to a priest. Although lapsed, Pauline had been initiated into the bosom of the lodge; she understood that sinning with an outsider would make it that much worse.

"Well, he just converted. So that he could marry me." She waited for this bit of information to process.

"Hmmm, I see. He's converted. And you believe this to be a true conversion?" Suddenly, Pauline wondered why, even in the privacy of the confessional, Ernest had become the focal point. Could she not even have a confession all to herself?

"Well, hell, I guess so." Pauline realized that she had just sworn to, and possibly at, a priest. Her stomach convulsed with a puerile reaction – she remembered the nuns of her youth, and their strict reverence for and obeisance to anything uttered by a priest. Pauline wondered if he would stick a ruler through the wooden grid and rap her knuckles. She was surprised to hear a soft chuckle on the other side of the wood.

"Well," he said in a youthful, humored voice, "you know, you've just given yourself something else to confess." There was a silence, and then they both started to laugh. Pauline wondered, again, what this young priest looked like.

"I'm sorry, Father, forgive me." Pauline paused, then continued. "Okay, in addition to fornication, I swear." Again, quiet laughter emerged from both sides of the confessional. Priest and penitent, absolver and confessor were bound together, in a moment of mutual appreciation for the peculiar Kabuki performance of a Catholic confession.

They let their humor roll between them until it stopped naturally. The ensuing silence was brief, and welcome. After a pause, Pauline spoke. "Father, have I just done it yet again? Given myself another sin to add to my list? Something like, violating the probity and sanctity of the confessional?"

Her words seemed to have an unexpected effect. It was as if the young prelate had recovered himself, and there was a stony silence from the other side of the grated opening.

"I am sorry, my child, I should not have done that." The priest's words were somber. Now Pauline truly did feel guilty – she had tempted and somehow corrupted a priest into unholy laughter, provided an occasion for sin by a minister of God. *Dear Heavenly Father*, she thought, *what is wrong with me?*

"I'm sorry, Father." Her voice was subdued, and now truly penitent. For some reason, she momentarily felt sorrier for having engaged in this odd exchange with the priest than she did about her illicit affair with Ernest. The next words from the other side were abrupt.

"You will recite the prayer of contrition." Pauline struggled to remember the ancient words. She began, stumblingly.

"Oh, my God, I am heartily sorry for having offended Thee . . . ." Pauline paused, she could remember no more of the rite, and she suddenly felt beads of sweat on her forehead. Her heart pounded in the silence. Finally, the priest spoke.

"I will say it with you, we will recite together." The priest firmly began again, "*Oh, my God*," and Pauline mumbled along with his words, relieved and grateful when they finally reached "*I firmly purpose by Thy holy grace never more to offend Thee.*" There was a heavy silence on both sides of the confessional. The priest spoke.

"Five Hail Mary's and Five Our Father's. And watch that you keep yourself from sin in the future." The small panel door slid closed. Pauline breathed in deeply, and sank back onto the small hard seat.

Surprised at the leniency of the penance, Pauline continued to sit in the cloistered confines of the confessional and waited. Soon she heard the movement of the heavy draperies on the other side; the young priest had left the confessional. What had she done? she worried and wondered to herself. Was her mere presence enough to unnerve a confirmed Catholic priest? To cause him to unveil some heavy weather in his own heart? She bowed her head, and deeply breathed in the dank air.

After a few minutes, Pauline got up and left behind the lurid phantasms of the enclosure's walls. She went into the main well of the church, stepped toward an empty pew, turned, genuflected, and slid onto the smooth oak pew, polished over the years by innumerable Catholic bottoms. She pulled the kneeler down, slid forward onto her knees, clasped her hands, elbows resting on the pew in front of her, and bowed her head yet again. This time, in real and earnest expectation of forgiveness, Pauline repeated the prayers of the rosary that she had been given for her penance.

After a couple Our Father's and Hail Mary's, however, she found her mind beginning to drift. Pauline looked up and surveyed the other occupants of the church. Most of those pious few who were there in mid-day, during the week, clearly were comfortable with the ritual. They were mainly older ladies, heads covered in dark lace scarves, and a couple of older men who looked to be laborers, judging by their utilitarian garb. There was one young girl, a teenager, who was weeping silently, her shoulders moving shakily with hushed, sharp intakes of breath. Pauline wondered what had caused her to be in this place, at this time of day. Family troubles, boy troubles, school troubles? Hard to tell with a teenage girl.

She jerked herself back to her penitential act and recovered the track of her prayers. She could not remember precisely how many of each she had said, and suddenly she felt she did not really care. *Enough*, she thought. Pauline sat back, lifted the kneeler, rose, and exited the pew. By innate reflex, she knelt and genuflected, then she quickly walked back down the aisle, and out into the mid-day Paris sunshine.

It had been a confession, of sorts, she supposed. But whatever it had been, it would have to be good enough. There were to be no more. Pauline was ready to be married.

CHAPTER FIVE

Pauline wakened the next morning in their little apartment and wondered briefly where she was. It took a moment to remember: in Paris, the day of her wedding day, with her sister sleeping in the next bedroom. Pauline did not want to move out from under the duvet. She felt a heavy, sodden dread and tried to rouse herself. When Pauline opened her eyes, however, it was still the same, sour feeling. *This is no way to start a wedding day,* she thought.

Jinny had been in a bad mood for days. Pauline wondered if her sister would be able to muster any sort of good will, for either Pauline or for her new brother-in-law. Given Jinny's intense antipathy toward Ernest, and Ernest's complete indifference to Jinny's criticisms or opinions, Pauline doubted that was going to happen.

She sat up in bed and contemplated what she needed to do first. Her wedding dress – a simple sheath of white *moiré* silk with an overlay of Valencia lace, the neckline and hem studded with innumerable tiny pearls – was draped over a padded hanger on the front of the wardrobe. Her make-up and veil were laid out, just so, on her dressing table. Her small white satin shoes were tucked under her bedside chair. They were to be at the church at ten o'clock. Pauline shoved back the covers and called to Jinny in the other room.

"You awake?" she called. "Today's the day. Rise and shine." She heard nothing but the irritated rustling of bed sheets. Pauline imagined Jinny had pulled the blankets over her head. Pauline rose and walked out into the little kitchenette to make the first pot of coffee.

She had always loved the ritual of making coffee. She thought she might even have a slight addiction to it. Pauline had never had a problem with drugs, alcohol, gambling, but coffee was a different thing. The pleasure she derived from the first cup, the first sip, was so intense that she craved it just as an addict craves his drug. And she had, like an addict, all manner of paraphernalia to prepare and serve her preferred obsession: demitasse cups for espresso, tiny copper pots for swirling and brewing Turkish coffee, a hand grinder for milling roasted whole beans. As she stood in the kitchen, waiting for the water to boil, Pauline pondered the addict's curse.

What is an addict? Wanting something that is not necessarily good for you, and not being able to stop the wanting? Her thoughts turned to Ernest: *Am I addicted to him?* She had dated many men before him, but none had affected her the way Ernest had. Irritated that she could not even have her morning coffee without intrusive thoughts of Ernest, Pauline scowled and poured her first cup.

Pauline sipped the scalding liquid and stared out the window at the hazy sunshine. *Here it is*, she thought, *my wedding morning, and I'm consumed with doubt.* Pauline wondered, why is this so difficult? Why can't Ernest make this easy for me?

Pauline continued to drink and ponder. *Can enough love overcome what may be insurmountable problems?* Pauline wondered. Ernest's intense appetites for food, drink, women – could she satisfy all of them? She entertained the thought that, if she could not, it meant a great deal of heartache and suffering, for both of them. And, as independent as she had liked to think of herself, Pauline could not, at this point, disengage. She needed Ernest, like she needed coffee.

Pauline looked up when Jinny walked into the kitchenette. Jinny sleepily padded toward Pauline, and then laid her head on her sister's shoulder.

"So, today is your last day as a Pfeiffer, huh?" Jinny sighed. Pauline knew that Jinny disliked Ernest, that she did not think him a suitable life partner, and that she earnestly desired something would break the hold he had on Pauline. She turned and put her arms around Jinny. Pauline stroked the back of Jinny's head and felt the nape cropping of her sister's short blond hair.

"Yep, today's the day," Pauline responded. "You get a brother-in-law." Jinny sighed again.

"*Arggh*, yes, I know." Jinny did not bother to hide her antipathy toward Ernest. She knew her dislike would not make any difference in Pauline's conduct, and Ernest had made it abundantly clear that he did not care one whit about Jinny. Pauline doubted that this dual antagonism would ever abate, no matter how much time passed.

They drank their coffee, and Jinny toasted some bread, but Pauline felt too agitated to eat anything. They had decided that they would dress at the apartment, take a cab to the church, and meet Ernest and their few attending friends there. Pauline took a small sip of her coffee, set her cup down on the counter, and walked into her bedroom. She stared at her wedding dress.

Suddenly, Pauline felt inordinately tired, wanting only to go back to bed, pull the covers over her head, and go to sleep. She closed her eyes and wrapped her arms around her shoulders. *Stop this*, she thought, chastising herself. She opened her eyes, turned away from the wardrobe, and headed toward the bathroom. She had to begin to get herself ready.

"Take your time, it's your wedding day," Jinny called to her. It was the first time this morning she had said something that was not derisive. But Jinny's forced solicitude was somehow painful to hear: it made Pauline feel pitiable.

Leaning against the bathroom sink, eyes downcast, not wanting to investigate the mirror, Pauline felt desperate and trapped, and unable to fix precisely upon what was wrong. She shook herself, lifted her right hand, and slapped herself sharply across the face. Whether or not Jinny heard her, there was no comment from the other side of the door. Pauline finished washing, then walked into Jinny's room.

"Please," Pauline pleaded, "I know you don't like him, but it would be really helpful if you didn't make this day harder for me." Pauline looked at her sister, seated on the thin quilted coverlet of her bed. Pauline wished she could snap her fingers and make all this discord and apprehension go away.

"Darling," Jinny said, "I can't fix this for you now. If you want to walk away, do that, and believe me, I would be ecstatic. But I don't believe at this point you are capable of leaving him." They stared at each other for a long moment, and Pauline sensed the heavy weight of all the years between them and of their present division. Jinny knew and loved Pauline like no other, but at this moment she despised what her sister was about to do. Pauline sat down beside her on the bed.

"I'm going to go through with this, Jinny." She felt Jinny stiffen, and pull away ever so slightly. "I'm going to marry him, and I know you don't like him, and more than that you think he is bad for me. But I'm going to marry him. You don't know him like I do. His writing will change the world, he's going to be famous and I'm going to be there, right beside him." She sat still, looking down at her hands. Pauline watched the pulse of her blood in the veins on her wrists.

"I know." Jinny stared down at her own pale hands. "I know you are going to do this, and I think I probably understand why, but that doesn't mean I don't hate it." Hate was a strong word, and Jinny didn't use words lightly or unintentionally. Pauline thought briefly, what a terrible way to begin a wedding day, to begin a marriage. If their mother had been here, there would at least have been the lightness of frivolity, a feigned unawareness of any tension, and the simple delight at the gaiety of a wedding. But neither Jinny nor Pauline could produce those distractions. They were burdened with their solid, separate truths, which sat like heavy stones between them. Pauline decided there was no benefit in continuing the discussion.

"I'm going to go get dressed." She stood, looked down at Jinny, who was still staring at her hands, and left her room. Pauline felt as if she might as well have been preparing for a wake. In a way, she was: this was the death of their girlhoods together, the end of their easy acceptance of each other. But even at the cost of losing her sister, Pauline was determined to marry Ernest.

And so she did.

CHAPTER SIX

Pamplona, Spain, July 1927

Pauline continually daydreamed about how different it would be, to be in Pamplona with Ernest as his wife and not as his mistress. She remembered the secretive afternoons they had spent loving each other in the small bed in her *pensión* bedroom, clandestine moments stolen while Jinny was out and Hadley was tending to their baby in the room across the hall. Pauline knew that many of the same friends who had witnessed the disastrous smash-up of his marriage at the last Pamplona gathering would also be present this year to witness Ernest's introduction of his new wife. She had no idea what her welcome, or unwelcome, would be like.

The arrangements for the trip to Spain ended up being uncannily like those of the previous year. Pauline noticed, with slight apprehension, that even the train times and numbers were the same; they were even staying in the same *pensión*. It occurred to her that this might portend other reenactments – what was the possibility that Ernest might cheat on her as well? Pauline quickly pushed that thought from her mind; this marriage would be different. Pauline was not the meek, mild, domestic mouse that Hadley had been. Pauline was determined, it was necessary to the image she had constructed for this marriage that she would be able satisfactorily to keep Ernest as her husband.

Once they arrived in Pamplona for the San Fermin festival, Pauline was disappointed to find that the town proved to be just as unpalatable to her as it had been the previous year. Apart from Ernest, Pauline found no intrinsic enjoyment in the fights, the noise, the revelry, but this time, at least, she had her prize. She was Mrs. Ernest Hemingway.

And Ernest was in his element. He loved the excitement and danger of the fights and the runnings, he enjoyed the machismo of sitting in a steamy bar in the afternoon after the bulls had barreled through the town, hot and sweat-stained in a once-white shirt and tilted red beret. He would sit for hours, his new wife beside him, and down glass after glass of raw red wine. Pauline would try to keep up with him, but usually ended up sleepily dosing in a corner of their *pensión's* bar, until Ernest wakened her at the end of a long evening, to go upstairs and to bed.

Every afternoon Ernest would trek down to *Las Tres Damas*, the same pub in which he had seduced Pauline the year before. He chatted with locals and tourists, with anyone he found interesting or engaging, anyone he might later be able to write about. Ernest was, as always, bigger than life; he attracted a crowd wherever he went. Sometimes Pauline refused to go with him, and would spend quiet afternoons sleeping in the still, hot air of their room.

On these days, Ernest would stay out alone all day, seeing the fights or drinking in the bars, and would not return to their *pensión* until late evening. Those evenings, out of boredom and loneliness, Pauline would walk sulkily down to the *pensión's* pub to find her husband. Ernest would often as not be able to entice her to stay, to drink and listen, and to linger in the bar far longer than she wanted to.

On a hot, uncomfortable afternoon, on the day before the end of the festival, Pauline walked to *Las Tres Damas*, and entered quietly. She heard boisterous laughter and catcalls coming from one of the back rooms. She did not see Ernest in the main bar area; she made her way toward the source of the noise. A doorway in the back led into a smaller room. Pauline slowly paced to it and stood in the opening.

Ernest held a black-haired woman – more of a girl, really – firmly on his lap. They were engaged in a kind of game that included alternatively petting and slapping each other. The audience of men, accompanied by a few sour-looking women, were enjoying the competition. Ernest slid his fingers along the girl's neck and under her hair; he moved his fingers like a corn reaper up the back of her head. He squeezed a hank of hair, causing the girl to yelp, then tipped her head back. He slapped her thigh, and the girl responded with a fast back of her hand to his chest. Ernest jostled the girl like a toy doll, and put his mouth on her neck. He executed a series of mock chewing bites, gnawing at her dusky skin. The men howled and slapped their tables; their attendant women sat moodily and swirled the wine in their glasses. Pauline stared, mesmerized, at the vulgar scene.

One of the men turned and saw Pauline in the doorway. He pointed at her, and threw his head back in a drunken, laughing *hi-yi-yi*. Other men followed his pointed laughter; they smiled tipsily, and rolled their eyes. The women kept their gaze downcast, staring into their wine.

Ernest turned in his seat and saw his wife standing in the entryway. His body froze for a moment, then he squeezed his arm more tightly around the girl on his lap and tossed his head back in unruly laughter.

Some of the men, surprised, stopped smiling. They had expected Ernest to show some embarrassment at being caught, to exhibit perhaps some slight remorse at his wife's distress, and they were discomfited by the blunt callousness. One of the women shook her head. She glanced up at Pauline, briefly, then turned away. Ernest finished his drawling, noisy guffaw, and it seemed to Pauline that he had to exert effort to hang onto his smile.

"Well, my little bird, you left the cage. Are you sure this is where you should be?" His comment was meant to be heard by his audience, but also to carry a deeper meaning, an oblique threat. He was challenging her.

Pauline felt her gorge rise. She walked over to the nearest table where two men and a woman sat. She did not know which man the woman belonged to; she sat equidistant between the two, head down, acknowledging nothing. The woman's glass held a half-pint of beer. Pauline picked it up and twirled it, so that the brown liquid sloshed up the sides of the glass, almost to spilling over the sides. Pauline stopped twirling and turned toward Ernest. With one swift motion, she threw the liquid in his face.

The silence in the bar was complete. The woman whose beer Pauline had taken lifted her head slightly and stared at her with veiled admiration. Slowly, the woman got up from her chair, looked at the men on either side of her, and spat forcefully on the floor. She pushed her chair back and walked out the door.

"Oh no, my angry little bird, look what you have done now," Ernest mocked. Pauline glared at him, then she too turned and left. Pauline walked heavily back upstairs to their room; she felt hot, dirty, tired. She went into the bathroom, but the effort of taking a shower seemed too much. She splashed water on her face, dropped her clothes in a heap on the floor, and walked naked back to the bed. She crawled in between the coarse sheets and, thrusting away thoughts of the painful scene in the bar, she closed her eyes.

It was hours later, just before daylight, when Ernest woke her, dropping heavily into bed beside her. Pauline lay still, hoping he would ignore her and fall asleep. She listened to his heavy breathing, to the sounds of dogs and drunken men in the courtyard, and prayed Ernest would not speak.

Her back was toward him, and, after he had lain quietly for a quarter hour or so, she felt him pull the sheet down slowly, until her long spine was exposed. She shivered in the cool pre-dawn air. Pauline felt the palm of his hand come to rest on her shoulder. He pressed, then squeezed, then pulled his hand, flat-palmed on her skin, down the length of her back.

Later, as the early dawn sun pushed pink strands of light through the slats of the window blinds, Pauline lay still beside her now-sleeping husband. So this was not going to be, Pauline thought, the starry-eyed idyll that she had envisioned. Nor was her marriage to be what she had dreamed about in those few happy weeks in Paris after their wedding.

In the preceding months, Ernest had made it clear that, whatever happened, he would oversee their plans, their ventures, their happiness. Their original contract, forged the day before they married, was the basis from which they had started. And none of it was going to be easy.

She lay on the clammy sheets, the coverlet pulled lightly over her, and watched the pale ribbons of pink light creep down the wall. Pauline reminded herself that she had gotten what she wanted. She lay there quietly, wondering, what costs she would be required to pay? Pauline stared at the gray expanse of the ceiling, her mind also gray, blank.

The depression of the night before pressed her downward into the sweat-damp sheets. Wanting the oblivion of sleep, she found that it escaped her. She felt her tears slide down her face. She lay motionless, staring at the grainy plaster above her. She would not speak of this night again.

CHAPTER SEVEN

On the last day of the San Fermin festival, Ernest wakened early, hot and heavy beside his wife. The sun was up over the rooftops of Pamplona, and its light shone purple and orange on the pale, scudding clouds. Although there were runnings every morning, Ernest was particularly excited about the largest run that always took place on the last day. He was also looking forward to the evening's final bullfight in Pamplona's main arena, lavishly decorated for the grand end to the festival. The arena would be packed tonight, and the atmosphere would be electric and charged with anticipation.

Ernest rolled over and jostled Pauline awake, wordlessly. They lay silently together in the small bed, the sweaty sheets uncomfortable against their skin. Finally, he spoke.

"Well, today's the day we come for, my darling. Excited?" He placed a hand on her belly and sat up, leaning straight-armed on his other hand. She stiffened but did not turn from him.

"Yes, oddly, I am," she said. Pauline felt, suddenly, that she was in the mood to bargain. She would not descend to speak to him about the humiliation of the previous evening; she would not give him the power of knowing that he had hurt her. Pauline forced a smile. "And I've decided what I'm going to wear." Ernest flopped heavily back onto the sheets and began to laugh.

"What you're going to wear? *What you're going to wear?*" He repeated, derisively, "Oh dear girl, how ridiculous you are. I don't care, nor does anyone else, if you are wearing a burlap potato sack." He sat up again and swung his legs over the side of the bed.

"I'm fully aware of that, Ernest, which is why I *do* care," Pauline responded. "So, go on, go get dusty. You'll see me later and think, who is that vision in red?" He placed his hands on the mattress, firmly on either side of his thighs; he bowed forward, bending low from his hips, and let out a long, low sigh.

"Yes, love, you do that, and that's exactly what I'll be thinking." Ernest's sarcasm made it obvious she had not made him happy by this little exchange – Pauline knew that she was going to have to work hard to get his attention, and his approval.

Ernest stood, pulled on his trousers and leather boots, and left the bedroom. She heard his heavy footsteps as he walked down the hallway. She was sure he was going to the café, for the first dark coffee of the morning, to be followed shortly by his first whiskey of the day. Pauline got up and walked to the tall, open casement window. She looked down into the square, and watched the early morning activities of the locals, already well underway.

There was a little boy in the middle of the square, sitting on the limestone wall surrounding the center fountain. He had a goat on the end of a short rope and was just sitting, still as a statue. The goat cropped little tufts of grass that grew between the stones of the fountain. It was almost like a painting, still and clear, except for the occasional bobbing of the goat's head. The boy sat; the goat chewed.

After a little while, an old man in dirty brown pants and an open-necked coarse flax shirt walked over to the boy. The boy seemed to have been expecting the man. A few clipped sentences passed between them, then the man reached behind to the back pocket of his trousers and pulled out an ancient leather wallet. He carefully opened it, inspected it, as if re-surveying the contents; he stuck bony thumb and fingers into the slit, and pulled out some paper money. He handed the money to the boy.

The boy, without looking at the goat, stared at the paper in his hand, and then passed the end of rope to the old man. He stood and moved quickly with short, bouncing steps, away from the fountain and the limestone wall. The boy did not look back at the goat.

The old man stared at the goat and tugged at the hank of rope in his hand. He reached forward and ran his hand around the ring of rope circling the goat's neck, ensuring that it was tight enough. The old man slowly stood upright and pressed his hand into the middle of his back. He arched backward in a slow, painful stretch, letting out a low moan. Then he bent slightly forward, releasing the stretch, and stared up at the morning sky.

Pauline knew the fate of the goat. Tonight, the last night of the festival, there would be drinking, dancing, and eating all through the sultry Spanish dusk and on into the next morning. The goat would be the centerpiece of the evening's feast, roasted whole and *en esada*, turned on a spit over an open-air fire pit.

Pauline had seen this once before, the previous year in Pamplona. The local men would kill and butcher the animal and then tend to it over the fire, while the women made all the other dishes for the meal. Once the men got drunk enough, they abandoned their duties over the pit and left the *carne asada* for the women to finish. For the men, it was a night of pleasure and fun; for the women, it was just another meal to prepare, but one requiring a great deal more effort.

Pauline remembered her mother and her aunts complaining when they hosted the annual holiday gatherings at the farm in Piggott. Her mother had often complained that large family holiday gatherings were "a treatment, more than a treat." The women would spend days cooking and assembling all the expected dishes: platters of country ham and turkey and roasts of beef, sides of potatoes – white and sweet, salads – green and jellied, huge pots of green beans with salt pork, and roasters of collards swimming in savory pot liquor. There were assorted pickles – cucumber and tomato and melon rind, piccalilli, and chow-chow, which had been prepared weeks before. Coconut cake required a full day's worth of labor, beginning with transforming the strange, hairy tropical fruit, hammering a nail in one of the "eyes, draining the milk, splitting the husk with a hammer, peeling away the hard-brown outer layer, and finally grating the tough, white shards.

The meals were always concluded with pies, the usual apple, cherry, and peach, but also rhubarb and raisin and green tomato, as well as shoofly and chocolate custard; the sideboard groaned with so many desserts. Later in the evening the women would bring out the pecan tassies and cheese straws and coffee. Watching the Spanish women carry and heave and load and stir, Pauline was reminded just how much effort those gatherings back home had been.

The goat would be killed, usually with one swift knife-blade slash to the throat. Someone would carefully hold a pan underneath the gash to catch the blood: that would be used as well, in *fauces de cerdo* – meat trimmings and blood, stuffed in the animal's stomach and boiled in broth. After the initial kill, there would be the ritualistic knifing down the belly, splitting the animal open, the scent of entrails acrid and pungent under the hot sun. With goats, unlike the pig butcherings of her youth, the innards were removed and thrown to the other goats to eat. This was the part Pauline could not stand to watch; she had found the cannibalistic feast nauseating.

Then the goat's carcass would be skinned and skewered on iron spit stakes. It was a crucifixion of sorts, the backbone of the butchered goat wired through the meat to a spit rod on which it would rotate, and the feet, front and behind, tied together and bound to the long rod. Once the carcass was affixed taut and rigid on the black metal, the men would suspend the skewered animal over a fire in a three-sided concrete block pit, with grooves in top of the two opposing walls to hold the spit rod. A curved handle stuck outside the firepit on one end of the rod, and the men, and later the women, would take turns slowly spinning the carcass as it roasted over the fire.

The men enjoyed themselves, drinking, dancing, singing as they alternated their turns at the spit. Later, when they drunkenly abandoned the *asada*, the women would take over. Already tired with the day's efforts, they would mutely take turns rotating the spit in the early evening sun, refreshing the fire, then by turn retreat to the shade to continue their other cooking and serving.

Pauline pulled herself from the window. Today was the last run, the last bullfight, the last day of unbridled excess. She looked around the room and imagined the hours ahead of her. She would put on her red dress and stand at the window to watch Ernest and the other men in the running of the bulls. Then she would walk to the square to find Ernest, sweating and proud. Ernest would drink, and drink some more, and Pauline would sit, just as mute as the cooking and serving women in the square, and watch him drink through the afternoon until they made their way to the arena.

There, she would sit again, mutely, and watch the red and gold pageantry preceding the fight. The entry of the toreador, the ritual throwing of flowers and candy, then the fight itself. The swirling *verónicas*, the facing off of beast and man, the crimson arcs of blood as the swords plunged into the bull. The final sensational lauding of the conqueror, the clamoring crowd tossing roses onto the red dust at the toreador's feet.

Despite her attempted *bravura*, Pauline felt despondent; she felt she had been conquered as well. She had entered the arena, and Ernest had swirled his *capote de brega* in front of her, beguiling her, enticing her. She had run toward him, and he pulled out his *muleta* and had inserted the swords, one by one. She had succumbed.

Pauline wanted nothing more than to leave Pamplona, immediately. But she would endure this last day, this last bullfight, and then they would be on their way back to Paris. She prayed that she had not sold herself too cheaply.

CHAPTER EIGHT

Ernest and Pauline arose late the next morning. The hot sun beat into the room, and they roused themselves grumpily. They had both drunk too much the night before, and had wakened with heavy heads, dry and swollen tongues, sandy eyes. They were to drive to Bordeaux later in the day and take the midnight train on to Paris. The had the afternoon to pack and get ready to leave Pamplona.

"Hey," Ernest barked, "get your fancy city girl clothes on and let's get something to eat, Pauline. And I need a hair of the dog." Ernest was sitting on the side of the bed, elbows on knees, forehead cradled in cupped palms. He spoke to the floor.

"I'm coming, but I'm not hurrying," she replied. "If you want to go without me, go." Pauline's tone was cool, and she made it clear that he could leave with or without her, it didn't really matter. Pauline was tired, sick of Pamplona, and ready to get back to Paris.

Ernest sat slumped, unmoving, on the side of the bed. He slowly got up and dressed himself, then sat back down and waited. When Pauline finally presented herself to him, he looked at her and grunted. He stood and walked out the door, and Pauline followed him, down the stairs and out into the uncomfortable sunlight of the summer morning. Ernest groaned.

"Gad, let's get inside. I need a beer." He pulled Pauline into the first bar they encountered off the piazza, and immediately ordered a pint of Spanish ale. Pauline raised her two fingers to the bartender, who nodded in comprehension. Ernest noticed her order, his head still sagging, but grinned up at her. "You going to try and keep up with me today, little bird?" he snorted. They both felt ill and bilious; Pauline made no response. The bartender pushed two glasses toward them across the wooden counter of the bar. They reached for their drinks, and each lowered their mouths to the rims, rather than risk lifting the glasses. They drank in silence.

They finished their first round and ordered a second. Ernest requested some bread and cheese, and they managed to get some food, as well as beer, into their protesting stomachs. Church bells chimed, children outside in the street squalled, and chickens squawked; Ernest and Pauline did not speak. They sat silently, glumly working through the beer and the bread and the cheese.

As they continued to drink, the haze from the night before began to lift. The nasty pall of the week's continual drunkenness was eventually replaced with a new buzz, a new lightening of the head, and easing of the stomach. They ordered more beer. They soon began to talk to each other a bit, and to a few of the other bar patrons. The boozy, banal banter helped to drown the ill effects of the previous week's bad decisions with the erasure effect of this day's bad decision. For the moment, it sufficed.

And then the ambiance changed. Ernest straightened his spine, his eyes widened, he grunted. He swung his arm in a wide circle, slapping at his back pocket. He looked dizzily around him, right and left, as if trying to catch sight of a jokester moving from side to side behind him. He turned back to stare angrily at Pauline.

"My wallet!" He bawled. "Where's my wallet?" Pauline did not respond immediately, trying to comprehend what he meant. The alcohol had slowed her understanding.

"Your wallet? Your wallet is missing?" Pauline was dimly aware through the beery haze that she sounded like she was playing catch-up in a game, and that she was not on the winning side.

"You saw me get my wallet, right?" Ernest glared at her. She felt like there was a spotlight on her; she screwed up her forehead and tried to think. Yes, yes, she had seen him pick up his wallet a hundred times. Hundreds of times. Yes, absolutely. Hundreds of times.

"Yes, I saw you pick up your wallet." Pauline was dimly aware that something might have been lost in her translation, some vital bit of accuracy, but she knew she was incapable of putting her finger precisely on what it might be. She felt that she had contributed as much as she probably could to the conversation; she shut up.

"Barkeep, call *les gendarmes*!" Ernest seemed to forget he was in Spain; the French phrase, however, did as well. After several repetitions, the bartender reluctantly picked up the phone behind the bar and made a call.

Very soon, a Pamplona *policía* appeared, dressed in the casual uniform of the Spanish constabulary. The policeman stood in the doorway, his dark blue shirt silhouetted by the yellow sunshine.

"Ah, there you are, about time!" Ernest bellowed, and motioned the policeman to the bar. It was obvious that Ernest was tight, and that Pauline was trying vainly to pull herself together. With increasingly loud bluster, Ernest continued to accuse, and Pauline tried to focus: Ernest had lost his wallet, a policeman was here, and now something else would happen. She watched, wordlessly.

"Sir, may I help you?" The policeman spoke very respectfully to Ernest in lightly accented English; he seemed to have some idea who the man was, even perhaps of his growing celebrity status. Ernest bellowed his response.

"Someone has stolen my wallet – what are you going to do about it?" The policeman hesitated, and formed his response carefully. He was well-practiced in dealing with drunks.

"Are you sure that you had it with you sir? Perhaps you left it at your hotel?" Pauline could see the anger roil over Ernest's face; she knew this kind of questioning enraged him. She jumped in immediately, in an attempt to circumvent what she knew would be Ernest's volcanic response.

"Officer, I saw him with his wallet, he had it with him." Pauline strove, in her own drunkenness, to appear as clear and sober as she possibly could. She decided that her schoolteacher imitation was probably the best course to effect this. Her voice and demeanor changed. "Yes," she began, somewhat condescendingly, "Yes, officer, please understand, I was there, I saw it, and he had it with him." She smiled the smile her third-grade teacher had used when speaking to a particularly obtuse student. Pauline thought, beerily, *I hope this is working*. She could feel Ernest smiling at her. Or perhaps laughing. She dared not look at him. The policeman continued.

"Ah, well, if madam saw him with his wallet, and you're sure he had it when he came in here . . . ," the policeman raised his eyebrows at Pauline, and she nodded to him in what she hoped was a knowing, scholarly fashion, pursing her lips. The officer continued, "Well, then it is clear that someone has stolen it. You wish to file a complaint then?"

"Yes, we wish to file a complaint," Pauline quickly responded. She got enough nerve to glance up at Ernest and was gratified to see him smiling broadly at her. It emboldened her. "I'm so glad to see you take these things seriously, young man." Her schoolmarm pose was in full blossom, and Ernest snorted. The policeman looked up from the small ticket sheet he was writing and glanced briefly back and forth between the

154

two of them. They stopped laughing and composed their faces as best they could. The policemen went back to writing.

With little administrative fuss, the *policía* finished getting names and pertinent information, and left the bar, saying that he would file all necessary forms at the station house. Ernest slapped the policeman on the back, his jolliness belying his assertion of a lost wallet. The policeman left, and they ordered another round.

After several more beers, Pauline began to feel that she needed to lie down. She told Ernest that she was going back to their room, and asked him to come get her when it was time to leave. She staggered through the sultry afternoon square toward the inn.

Once inside their room, she fell on the bed and was almost immediately asleep. An angry rapping on the door fifteen minutes later wakened her; it took her some time to shake herself from the alcoholic fog to get up from the bed and answer the knock. It was the front desk clerk, saying she had an urgent phone call. She followed him downstairs.

At the lobby desk, the clerk gestured to the upright telephone speaker sitting on the desk in front of him. He proffered the earpiece, connected to the speaker with a dirty, cloth-covered wire. Pauling gingerly accepted it, noticing that it needed a good cleaning. She held the earpiece slightly away from the side of her head, then leaned over the speaker.

"Yes, who is this?" Her voice sounded rough, raspy. She closed her eyes, wishing she had never gotten out of bed that morning.

"It's me, Pauline. It's Ernest." She opened her eyes. Whatever this was, it would not be good. On the other end of the line, Pauline could hear raucous noise, a lot of loud voices tumbling over each other. She could not make out any specific words.

"The police came back, Paulie," Ernest said breathily, "and here's the thing – they arrested me for making a false statement and I'm in jail. And not just that, for being drunk in public. I'm in jail, and I need you to come bail me out." She closed her eyes again. Her stomach lurched.

"I'll come, Ernest. I'll be there." She looked at her watch and calculated the hours until they needed to leave Pamplona. She thought she heard laughter in the background.

"I'll be right there Ernest. Where are you?" Now she was sure she heard laughter, then the crash of the receiver falling to the floor. More laughter. And then she heard, unmistakably, Ernest's laugh. The phone went dead.

She stood quietly in front of the hotel desk with the telephone earpiece in her hand, then she silently handed it back to the clerk. The clerk softly settled it back in its cradle, and stared at Pauline, wondering what message could have caused a look of such overwhelming pain.

Her head was pounding, and she was still fighting the vicious remains of her hangover. But suddenly Pauline had a clarity, an intuition. She gazed limpidly at the desk clerk, and realized with solid certainty that she had just been made the butt of a joke. She pressed her palm to her forehead and screwed her eyes tightly shut. Her pain gave way to anger.

Pauline made her way back to the bar she had left just a half-hour before. She walked through the open door, and saw what she had expected to see.

Ernest was sitting at the bar, with a girl on his lap. He was surrounded by people, laughing, drinking, singing. They did not notice her at first. She had been right – he had made a prank call to her, betting with the whole bar that he could get his wife to come bail him out. He had made fun of her, and everyone in the bar had had a good laugh at her expense, including the heavily made-up girl on his lap.

Pauline's head began to reel in anger. Very slowly, she walked toward the bar. Once there, she reached for a half-full glass, sitting on the bar just next to a man's elbow. The stranger's back was to her, he did not see her pick up his glass.

In one swift, swirling motion, Pauline hurled the glass at the mirrored wall behind the bar, and watched with satisfaction as both glass and mirror shattered. Oblivious to the shocked stares around her, she focused on a circle of used glasses at the end of the bar, picked one up, and threw it. And another. And another.

It was so remarkable, so unexpected, no one stopped her. When Pauline had thrown the first glass, Ernest had abruptly stood up, unceremoniously dumping the girl on his lap to the floor. He stood, silently, watching, as Pauline broke glass after glass. In the face of Ernest's inability to stop his own wife's demolition, no one else seemed able to move.

Finally, it was the girl who came to Pauline's aid. She had been watching the astonishing scene from the floor, mouth gaping open, and finally moved herself to her feet. She stood, adjusted her skirt, looked at Ernest and shook her head in disgust. She muttered under her breath. The girl walked toward Pauline, who was reaching again toward the bar for yet another glass. The girl gently put a hand on Pauline's arm. In heavily accented English, she spoke softly to Pauline.

"Stop. He is not worth it." She looked at Pauline, and Pauline turned to her, trying to focus on what was being said to her. It was as if an otherworldly event was happening to her, as if an alien were trying to speak to her. The girl spoke again. "He is not worth you." Pauline stared at her. The room was still, and no one moved.

"He is not worth you." The words echoed in her head. If that were the case, then what was she worth? Her head ached, swam, the interior of the dank bar seemed to be tilting on its axis. Pauline slowly turned and walked outside, into the dying sunset.

CHAPTER NINE

They drive to Bordeaux was silent and unpleasant, and the long night's train ride to Paris was equally disagreeable. They returned to their apartment tired and dispirited. After this decidedly ignominious start to their marriage, after only a few weeks of happiness, Pamplona had hardly been the honeymoon Pauline had desired or anticipated.

She was glad to be back in Paris, to be home in their familiar neighborhood. She had moved into Ernest's flat after they married, and now, back in their home together, she was looking forward to perhaps getting on a more even footing with her husband. She thought that maybe they could resume the late-night strolls and cocktails, the early morning coffees and caresses, and they might heal the scars they had inflicted upon each other in Pamplona. The more she thought about it, the more she convinced herself that their path would even out now that they were back in their beautiful adopted city. Pauline hoped and expected that Paris would work its magic on both of them.

They soon resumed a comfortable, if somewhat uncertain détente. Ernest returned to his regular routine of morning writing. He rented a small atelier, and he would leave their apartment every morning to write. Pauline spent her mornings cleaning, shopping, browsing the stores. And in the evenings, they easily slid back into the routine of parties, rounds of evening drinks in local *boîtes*, circles upon circles of gossip and diversion. The truce was comfortable, if tentative.

The summer ran on and as the weather heated up, so did the emotional thermometer of their little crowd. At every party now, there were histrionic scenes, glasses of wine thrown, and every night seemed to end with theatrical drama. Being part of it was interesting, but exhausting.

Ernest was sketching the outlines of a book about his time in Italy, during the war. Prior to their marriage, he had often been the center of these evening imbroglios, but now that he had a new manuscript to focus on, he was more staid, more apt to sit on the sidelines and watch others make fools of themselves. The emotional outbursts they witnessed every night began to irritate rather than entertain him.

Pauline remembered how, the previous year, after much coquetry on her part, she had managed to get him to let her read drafts of *The Sun Also Rises*. She had offered her edits, and he had even taken some of them. He seemed surprised that she knew her way around the English language.

This new work, however, Ernest kept close to his vest. She had seen nothing of it, and only knew the vaguest outlines of the subject matter. There was to be a female protagonist based on someone he had known in Italy. From his few vague comments, Pauline surmised it was someone he met after he had been wounded and was recovering in a hospital.

While he would not talk about the book, he spoke freely about his recovery time. He had been shot in the leg, and his knee was severely wounded. There were other injuries – to his head, his arm, his side – but the leg and knee wounds were the most critical. He told Pauline about the morphine dreams, about the nurses, about the lush green hillsides of the Italian countryside, framed like a painting in the open window beside his hospital bed.

There was one special nurse he talked about often. It was clear to Pauline that Ernest had fallen in love with her – and it was she that Pauline believed was to be the woman in this new book. One evening, sitting at their dining table over a second bottle of wine, she asked him specifically about his female protagonist.

"She's the nurse who cared for you, isn't she," Pauline ventured. "The one you talk about so often. Tell me, did you ever kiss her?" Ernest paused and stared down into his glass. He stuck his finger into the wine, then began running his finger around the rim of the glass. He repeated this, over and over, until the glass began to ring. He continued the shrill noise for a minute or so, then stopped. Without looking up at Pauline, still staring into his glass, he began to speak, low and soft.

"Her name was Agnes. She was lovely." He paused and dipped his finger again. This time, he raised it to his mouth, and sucked the wine off it. "I was very young, and very ill. She took care of me, she evened bathed. She was so gentle. Those were some of the most evocative experiences I've ever had."

Pauline held her breath; she had never heard Ernest speak of this. "When she gave me a bath," he continued, "I couldn't hide my affection for her. I tried, but that was futile. I supposed nurses were used to things like that, but Agnes was disconcerted by it. She could deal with blood and puke, but she couldn't deal with my being stirred. It became mortifying." Pauline was embarrassed, and she was sorry she had asked him about it. Ernest was revealing a very personal, private humiliation, and Pauline did not want to be privy to it. She did not want to hear any more, but Ernest continued.

"When it became clear that I liked her more than she liked me," he said softly, "I began to ignore her, to request other nurses be assigned to me. Weirdly, it was then she began to try and seek me out. But I had had too much of it by then, I suppose." He dipped his finger again and went back to rimming the glass. The sound, piercing and sharp, began to make Pauline feel sick to her stomach. She reached over, gently took his hand and pulled it away from the glass. For the first time, he looked up at her, and his soft, slightly drunken eyes focused first on her forehead, then shifted downward to the lower half of her face.

"I love your mouth, Pauline. You have the most beautiful lips." He dipped his finger in the wine again, and this time raised his wet finger to her lips. She rose slightly and leaned toward him across the table; the hard edge pushed against her ribcage. He pulled his chair around closer to her and kissed her.

The wine made him slow, and he took a long time to finish the kiss. At length, he stopped, breathing heavily, and she slowly eased back into her chair. "I do love you, Pauline, you know I have to love you." He leaned forward and breathed into her ear. He kissed her lightly on the neck. "You will always, always be only mine, no matter what." Pauline thought his words sounded more like a threat than a promise, but she did not care; she leaned toward him, and took his hand.

"Yes, I will always be yours, no matter what." She relaxed slightly, pleased that she been able to distract him from the beloved woman in this new novel. She felt she had broken through a hazy barrier in their mutual entrapment. While relieved to have succeeded in attracting Ernest's full attention, Pauline knew that this accomplishment would not be easily replicated. *I am going to have to work awfully hard at this,* she thought. *Awfully hard indeed.*

CHAPTER TEN

As the heat of summer turned into the languor of a cool Paris autumn, Ernest suggested that they plan a trip to Schruns, to go skiing. Pauline did not hesitate to say yes; Austria seemed the perfect anodyne to the continuing tension in their marriage.

It didn't seem fair to her. She had waited so long for this, and now, for some reason, what should be her perfect happiness was marred by persistent anxiety. Pauline tried to pinpoint the precise genesis but could not capture it. They both felt it, and it made them snap at each other. The strain between them was increasing, and Pauline thought that perhaps the physical exercise and the cool, clean air of the Austrian Alps might help remove the pall over their relationship.

Pauline did not care that Schruns had been a favorite vacation spot for Ernest and Hadley; indeed, she was anxious to make it her own with Ernest, to obliterate Hadley from his memories there.

Ernest quickly made their train and hotel reservations and within a few weeks they were in the mountains of western Austria. On the first day there, Pauline breathed in the clear, icy air and was sure that this wintry vacation spot would lighten the mood for both of them.

They had arrived at the resort outside of Schruns late on a mid-November afternoon. The first several snows of the season had already fallen, and the alpine lodge looked like a fairy tale – rustic, warm, and charming, with a sugary icing of white powder covering the roof and edging the windowsills.

The innkeeper greeted them with delight, so happy to see *Herr Hemingway* again. If he felt any surprise that a different wife now accompanied his increasingly famous guest, the innkeeper did not show it.

The Hemingways were ushered to a snug room on the second floor and soon settled into a habitual schedule of early rising, hearty German breakfasts, and long days of skiing and hiking in the refreshing mountain air. They seemed to have reached a mutually suitable truce and were able to avoid any harsh words or arguments for the first few days they were there.

On the fourth day, however, they awoke tired and sore and irritable. They were unused to continually exercising the muscles they had put in play on the slopes and trails, and fatigue had finally caught up with them. Ernest had slept fitfully, and so had kept Pauline up most of the night. The morning sun seeped in the window in a grayish haze, and Pauline closed her eyes, wishing to go back to sleep for a while and start the morning over.

"Let's get out of here today," Ernest intervened. "Let's rest our bones, and go find some good food, some shops, something a little different." Pauline was surprised to hear Ernest mention shopping – that was a first. He generally scorned what he called "your little world," meaning fashion, magazines, advertising, merchandising. He generally elevated his *gestalt* over hers; his was the life of the mind, of the artist, of the aesthete, while he considered was the pedestrian world of the tradesman. It was another unspoken area of disagreement, evanescent but palpable. Nonetheless, she was pleased that he had made this overture.

"I'd love to, sounds perfect." Pauline got out of bed and groggily started to dress. She took her time, thinking Ernest might pull her back into bed, but he did not. So she continued dressing, and then waited for him to finish putting on his clothes. When he was finally ready, he took her hand and pulled her through the door of their room and out into the cold hallway.

Once down in the lobby, they found the innkeeper, and asked him for suggestions. The innkeeper was a short, round, florid man, bespectacled and graying and eager to please. He smiled warmly as the two approached.

"What can I do for the lovebirds this morning?" he said, in thickly accented English. Ernest responded quickly.

"I think we'd like to find an art gallery," he said firmly. This further surprised Pauline; she did not know Ernest had that kind of shopping in mind. The innkeeper reached down and pulled a small tourist's guidebook from the recesses of his desk. After perusing and flipping pages, he located a few places to recommend. He wrote down their addresses and handed the slip of paper to Ernest.

"Perhaps you buy some beautiful painting today for the lady," he said, ingratiatingly. Ernest smiled and replied distractedly.

"Yes, I might." Ernest stuffed the paper in his jacket pocket. They silently buttoned up their coats, pulled on gloves and hats, and walked down the snowy trail into town.

The first shop on the list was interesting, but not what Ernest was looking for. It was less an art gallery than a collection of artifacts: old chess boards, fraying wall tapestries, chipped netsukes from Japan. Ernest stood still in the middle of the shop floor, looked around for just a minute or two, then wordlessly grabbed Pauline's hand and pulled her out the door.

"Guess that wasn't the shop for you?" She tried to make conversation, but he was silent. They walked on through the dull sunshine until they found the second address the innkeeper had given them.

The shop door was made of dark wood inset with cylinder glass panes. The door handle was an odd brass ornament: it took Pauline a minute to realize that the knob was fashioned in the shape of a human head. A woman's head, hair pulled back from the crown smoothly, forming a ball. It felt cold and smooth in Pauline's hand as she grasped it and pulled open the door; there was a weirdly amatory feeling to the metal. Pauline looked up, wanting to show Ernest the bizarre handle, but he had already swept past her and into the shop. Pauline shrugged, followed him into the shop, and closed the door behind her.

Inside, there was an overpowering musty smell. Pauline imagined dead mice and old clothes that had been put away without being washed. She wanted to leave, immediately. Ernest, on the other hand, visibly relaxed. His facial muscles smoothed, and Pauline watched him become calmer as he began to look around.

"This is what I was looking for," he said. "Someplace to find a hidden treasure." He turned to her and smiled wickedly. "You think there's a treasure in here, darling?" Ernest was taunting her.

Pauline's expression was transparent: she wanted to leave. Ernest knew she was uncomfortable, but it somehow pleased him to keep her there.

"Not sure," she replied guardedly, "depends upon what kind of treasure you are looking for." Pauline turned from him as she spoke, so that he could not see her unease. Ernest began to look around and pick up little things – a dog statuette, a cast brass ship's bell, a miniature Delft clog. Pauline tried to make herself invisible. Minutes passed, and they made their separate ways around the tiny, claustrophobic space. Pauline heard Ernest make a small noise.

166

"Ha, come look at this." He was standing in front of a large painting, staring. Pauline moved beside him and gazed at it. The painting was entitled *The Farm*, by a Spanish artist named Miro. Pauline had heard of him, and had a vague recollection that he was becoming more and more well-regarded for his surrealist art. She had heard Picasso speak warmly of him at one of Gertrude Stein's salon evenings. Pauline was surprised to find one of his paintings cloistered here in this dim little place.

"What do you think this is doing here?" she asked. "Miro is getting a good name for himself." Ernest turned away from the picture, for the first time, and looked at her.

"You know of Miro?" He seemed surprised.

"Well, yes," Pauline responded, hesitantly. "Pablo spoke of him, quite nicely, and I've seen others of his paintings, at someone's home in Paris. I can't remember who just now." She studied the painting. *The Farm* was clearly one of Miro's better works. A cerulean sky hovered over a painterly, stylized homestead vignette: an impossibly tall stone barn, the rear end of a horse visible in the byre doorway, a tree – with oddly feather-like black leaves – erupting phoenix-like out of a black hole in the ground, geometrically-hoed rows with a few stylized plants, a Dada-esque version of a chicken coop. At the sight of the last, Pauline stiffened.

It was clear this was a fine work of art, but suddenly all Pauline could think of was Piggott, her family's farm back in Arkansas, the workers, the livestock. That was what she had been trying to escape, and this painting filled her with uncomfortable resonances. Ernest was oblivious to her discomfiture.

"Hadley saw this painting once, in Paris," he said. "Must have passed through a few hands to end up here." Ernest continued to gaze at the painting. "Hadley loved it. I couldn't afford it then." His tone was soft and reminiscent and nostalgic; Pauline flinched at his bringing up Hadley in such a tender way. Clearly, the painting reminded Ernest of a pleasant memory.

She turned away from him and was struck with the depth of her discomfort: she did not want to be reminded of her family's agricultural roots. And it seemed to her almost as if Ernest's interest in this painting was an intentional provocation, a goading.

As she stood and watched Ernest gaze at the Miro, she remembered the last time she had been back in Arkansas. She began to feel angry. Ernest was supposed to take her away from all that, and yet here he was, gazing at a painting of a farm as if it were Nirvana, and bringing up his ex-wife fondly in the process. Pauline suddenly wished she had a brush laden with black paint, so that she could spatter it all over *The Farm,* or perhaps all over Ernest.

"I'm going to ask him what he wants for this," Ernest said, looking around for the shopkeeper. Pauline's anger melted into fear. Ernest was going to purchase this thing, this monstrosity that would become an insistent reminder of her old life and of his first wife. "I'd like to hang it above our bed." Pauline could not believe what she was hearing.

And then she knew, in a sudden burst of insight, that Ernest knew precisely what he was doing. He knew the effect this was having on her; he could be diabolical in his calculations and actions. Pauline wondered why he was visiting this new cruelty on her. She turned her face away from him, so that he could not see her pain and anxiety. If he wanted to hurt her, he was succeeding admirably. But to allow him to be aware of it would be far worse.

Ernest walked back to the shopkeeper, sitting behind his cash register. Ernest glanced back two or three times at the painting, and once at Pauline. Pauline watched him walk toward the back of the shop and thought, he's like a chess master, he anticipates and controls opponents by carefully planning his moves on the board. She sat down quietly on a brocade-covered stool, and closed her eyes.

"That painting back there," Ernest said loudly, directing a glare at the shopkeeper and pointing over his shoulder at the Miro. "What do you want for that?" The shopkeeper jumped with alacrity from his little perch and scurried around his desk, maneuvering around stacks of books and yellowing newspapers.

"Oh, *Herr Professor*," he said, ingratiatingly awarding Ernest the title, "you have found my prize, my best piece in the shop. You have a good eye, *jah?* The eye of a master. And you are interested, *hein?*" Ernest swelled; he liked being complimented, even if the accolade was tendered in anticipation of a sale.

"Well, I'm thinking about it," Ernest countered. "I'm wondering, particularly, what this painting is doing here?" Ernest continued, with the air of a *connoisseur*. "I saw it in Paris a couple years ago – I assume this is a private sale?" Pauline didn't know where he came up with all his knowledge about so many things: fishing, hunting, writing, and now he was playing the part of an art aficionado. And doing it well. Ernest was maddening in his capabilities. The shopkeeper looked at Pauline.

"Your wife, she likes the painting, *jah?*" Something had made the shopkeeper turn toward Pauline, but the look on her face told him that it would not help his sale for her to respond. He turned back to Ernest.

"She doesn't have much of a choice," Ernest answered. He began to laugh, a broad, deep laugh that was more appropriate for a bar than an art gallery. "If I like it, she'll have to like it.

Jah?" Ernest's big hand swung toward the smaller man in a smooth arc, a manly gesture, and clapped the innkeeper on the shoulder. Then he repeated his declaration. "If you like something, your wife *has* to like it, *jah?*"

Ernest was clearly enjoying himself, fomenting tension with each utterance. The shopkeeper's expression clouded over, he cast his eyes downward and he murmured, "Ach, whatever you say, *Herr Doktor Professor.*" Pauline watched the uncomfortable interchange and sullenly thought to herself, if that little man keeps on as he is going, Ernest would soon be receiving the title of Prime Minister.

"Well, what do you say? Name a price, *Herr Ladenbesitzer.*" Ernest's mockery was lost on the shopkeeper; Ernest glared at him, defiantly. It occurred to Pauline, not for the first time, that Ernest got a kick out of another person's discomfiture. There was a word for that in German – *schadenfreude* – and Ernest was a master of dispensing it. She wondered what thrill, what advantage, what pleasure it gave him, to put others at such unease. The little shopkeeper stood quietly, eyes clouded, and did not answer for a moment. Then he looked up at Ernest and spoke defiantly.

"I will take fifteen-hundred *deutschemarks*. That is the price." There was a finality, a flatness in his manner. Pauline had no idea whether the price named was ridiculously high, ridiculously low, or somewhere safely in between. She only knew that Ernest's chess match had become a bull fight, in a German shopkeeper's tiny arena. As it had in Pamplona, the face-off between the toreador and the bull drew her and repelled her at the same time. She couldn't keep from watching.

For some reason, her mind cast back to Hadley. Pauline remembered Hadley talking about the bullfights in Pamplona, and she remembered how shocked she had been that this little modest woman, this subordinate to Ernest, had been able to stomach such an event. But watching Ernest and the shopkeeper, Pauline had a glimmer of insight. The tension was exciting, if brutish. She hated and loved him, all at the same time. This was a man who could fascinate her, entice her, intrigue her, excite her, and at the same time repel her, anger her, frustrate her, and hurt her.

Pauline watched Ernest glare at the little Austrian, challenging him. Ernest glanced back over his shoulder for a moment, at the painting. The object at issue had become secondary to the fight at hand, which necessitated dickering over the price of the underlying commodity. Pauline saw the veins in Ernest's forehead pulse – he wanted to win this bullfight.

"I will give you half that." The insult in the counteroffer was apparent; Ernest had spat out his words. The little man jerked his head and glared back at Ernest.

"Half, *Herr Doctor Professor*? Half? You do not know what you are buying."

"On the contrary, I know exactly what I am buying," replied Ernest, executing his *verónica*. He paused, and glared at the shopkeeper, then pulled the figurative sword from his belt. "You, on the other hand, don't understand to whom you are selling." The sword entered and had found its crucial mark. The shopkeeper, wounded but still circling, gamely tried to continue.

"I cannot sell it to you for half, *Herr Professor*," the little man said, trying to gather his confidence. "I will sell it for a little less, but not that. You insult me." Ernest's deep *basso profundo* laughter plunged in like another sword. The shopkeeper's chest curled inward, defeated.

"Good grief man," Ernest bellowed, "of course I'm insulting you. And I'd be a fool to pay you what you ask."

Ernest reached into his back pocket and pulled out his wallet. Pauline watched as he pulled a wad of bills from it. "Here you are." He threw the money on the counter. "Cash, on the barrelhead. Take it or leave it." It was disturbing to watch the shopkeeper cower as he stared at the paper money on the counter. He reached toward the money tentatively, as if to count it.

"No," Ernest said coldly. "Take it or leave it I said." The little man seemed to shrink even more. Pauline felt sorry for the shopkeeper, and suddenly wished she were back in Pamplona, watching a bullfight. This scene, with such unevenly matched opponents, was worse than what she had witnessed there.

It was over and done in a second. The money was scraped off the counter into an apron, the apron was clutched to the belly, and a limp swipe of the arm indicated that the offer had been accepted.

"It is yours. But you don't know what you have gotten for this," said the shopkeeper, his final effort in the fight. Ernest laughed again.

"I know precisely what I've gotten, and I'll thank you to wrap it for me." This ignominy was almost too much; Pauline wondered if the shopkeeper would, at last, become belligerent. But he meekly took the painting off the wall and began to wrap it in brown butcher paper.

The defeated man was wordless, eyes blank as he finished his task. He brought the wrapped package around the counter and handed it to Ernest. For the first time during their encounter, he looked as if he had recovered some *bravour*; he tried one last attack.

"She does not like this painting, your wife." The shopkeeper cocked his head at Pauline. "You have paid cheaply in *deutschemarks* for this, but you will pay dearly otherwise." Ernest stared back at him, disconcerted. Pauline wondered which part of the little diatribe had bothered him, the implied threat, or the reference to her. Ernest brusquely snapped the package out of the shopkeeper's hands and turned toward Pauline.

"Come on," he growled, "you've caused enough trouble for one day." He pulled her out of the shop, wordlessly, out into the darkening, cold air.

CHAPTER ELEVEN

"**O**h look, Ernest, look at the cats." Pauline and Ernest were bundled up, scarves, gloves, hats, taking an early evening walk through the Paris streets. It was late December, and the light faded early behind the cantered rooflines on these shortest days of the year. Their return from the turbulent Schruns trip had brought about another tentative rapprochement. Their relationship had become a series of low valleys and high peaks, and it was exhausting for both of them.

They walked up to a small stone church, which was, inexplicably, covered with crouching, creeping, caterwauling felines. They were everywhere. In the doorways, on the eaves, prowling along the roofline. Pauline did not remember seeing anything quite like it before. "Look at them, Ernest, they are everywhere." Ernest glanced idly up at the church's slate-shingled roof.

"Good grief, they're all over. I bet the whole place smells like cat pee." That had not occurred to Pauline, but as they came to a stop in front of the church, watching the cats crawl from one corner of the edifice to another, she could not help but notice that he was correct.

"You're right, Ernest. My heavens, that's an unpleasant odor." She wrinkled her nose, and Ernest laughed.

"You know, my sweet, sometimes you sound just like an aging spinster. *'My heavens,'* indeed," he mocked, and suddenly his manner became abrupt. "Good grief, Pauline, why do you attempt to put on those airs with me." Ernest glowered at her. "Who the hell do you think you are?"

Pauline stared at him, dumbfounded. They had certainly had cross words during their marriage, but it remained a

175

continual surprise when Ernest erupted spontaneously like this, particularly because she had no inkling of the genesis of his animosity. Usually Pauline shrugged it off or tried to placate him, but it had begun to happen all too often, and this time she was not prepared to let it slide.

"What do you mean, *'who the hell do I think I am?'*" Pauline shot back. "Who the hell do you think *you* are?" They were both tired from the cold walk, but Pauline had upped the ante by repeating his profanity. She wanted to hit back, to goad him, bait him, get some reaction, even if negative. Pauline was ready to show Ernest she could fight. He abruptly turned and started walking away from her, back toward their apartment.

Pauline had become acutely aware of the independence she had given up in entering this marriage, and these frequent altercations with her husband made her sensitive and irritable. When they had been in Pamplona the previous year Ernest had been married to Hadley, and Pauline had been an intensely interesting distraction. Back then, he had spoken to her only in endearments and enticements. Now, a year and a half later, he seemed to default all to easily to argument and belittlement. Pauline was hurt, and she rebelled.

"You are a selfish pig." Pauline yelled after him down the street as he stalked away. She waited for him to respond, but he did not. Ernest paused only momentarily at her additional insult, but did not look back, and kept on walking down the street, away from her. At length, Pauline began to follow, and found herself scurrying after him on the cold sidewalks until they finally reached their apartment house.

In silence, he opened the front door and walked inside. She trailed behind him up the stairs and followed him into the chill air of their apartment. Peeling off gloves and hats and coats, their breath still steaming, they faced off in the frigid living room.

"Pauline," he said to her in a clipped manner, "Pauline, I am very unhappy to hear you speak to me that way." He stood, straight as a statue, and stared angrily at her. "You need to apologize."

He roughly took her arm and frog-marched her into the bedroom. He pushed her down onto the bed, seated, then continued to force her shoulders back onto the bed. He put his hands on either side of her, effectively pinning her in place. Pauline felt like a butterfly stuck on a cork board. She gazed mutely at him. She refused to speak.

"I will tell you again." He straightened up, and his gaze felt hot to her. "You need to apologize." Pauline's mind was swirling with emotions: regret, anger, confusion. She continued to lie there, still, and silent. "Alright," he said, "I told you what to do. Don't say you had no warning."

In one swift motion Ernest pulled Pauline to her feet, twisted her sideways, and brought his hand down in a heavy blow on the back of her skirt. He paused and tightened his grip on her arm. "Are you ready to apologize now?"

Pauline found she had no voice; she was unable to utter a word. She was not sure if this was a game or not; she remained silent. Ernest's hand came down again. "Now? Are you ready to apologize now? Pauline, I'm telling you once again, apologize."

She realized she had to speak, she had to verbalize, or he would continue. Pauline was stunned and confused; it was difficult to make anything other than a guttural noise. She grunted, then said, weakly, "Yes." She did not know whether that was the right thing to say in this weird competition.

"Yes, what?" he demanded, and Pauline spoke quickly, to fend off further blows.

"Yes. Please." She was not sure why she was supplicating, but she hoped her submission would move him to release her. Ernest paused, and Pauline felt his tension relax somewhat, but not completely.

"Please, what else?" He waited, and Pauline searched for her voice. He repeated himself, more stridently. "Please, and what else?" She knew she had to find, somewhere inside of here, the strength to answer him, and the sensibility to answer correctly. In a small voice, she said, "I apologize."

When Ernest made love to her, she did not think, she only felt. Most of the time he was raw, forceful, violent in his movements. This time, however, he was slow, deliberate, like a machine. After he had finished, Pauline lay quiet beneath him, unmoving. When he recovered his breath, Ernest spoke.

"That was productive, I think, my little bird." Pauline did not respond, she continued to breathe underneath him, shallow and silent. "You understand what I am telling you?" He pulled back and looked in her eyes. "You understand, little bird?" Pauline, unsure, felt momentarily scared.

"What do you mean?" Her voice was small, and weak, compared to his. Ernest laughed.

"I mean precisely what I said," he growled. "That was productive. Figure it out." He rolled off her, got up and walked into the bathroom. Pauline began to shake.

Yet another phase of their contract had pulsed into effect. Pauline knew that, if this were true, Ernest had put a yoke on her shoulders, and she felt the suffocation of its weight. She would never again be without the constancy of his power over her. She knew that bearing his child would not be an easy task, for either of them, but she was sure it would be harder for her.

And although it did not occur to her at the time, if she had been able to consider other actors she would have also realized that any child born to Ernest and Pauline Hemingway would not have an easy time in this life.

CHAPTER TWELVE

By February, it was clear that Ernest had been correct in his prognostication: Pauline was pregnant. She felt nauseated, bloated, and moved like a sick animal. She wondered about women who talked of pregnancy as a divine and exalted state; Pauline felt awful. Every morning she would waken and remember, dully, that this new and unpleasant event was happening to her, that she had not desired it, and that there was no way out. At least, no way out for a Catholic.

Ernest decided the baby would be born in the states, and so he began planning for their return. Pauline did not think of it as returning home; home was Piggott, and she certainly was not going to have the baby there. She dreaded the thought of travel, feeling as she did, but she liked the idea of American doctors and of an American hospital. That was fortuitous, since Ernest had already made up his mind.

Pauline had not been able to keep up with the rounds of evening parties during their last weeks in Paris, which was just as well; in her constant state of fatigue, the revelries that had entertained her a few months ago now only annoyed her.

Pauline was not the archetype of a glowing pregnant woman. She was tired and sick and generally unhappy, longing for the days of putting on thin sheath dresses and circling her neck with beads. Anything around her neck right now would only increase the nausea. She wanted time to pass, for these months to magically be over. She did not think about actually having an infant, a son or a daughter; the prospect gave her no pleasure.

Ernest was irritable as well because Pauline was not responsive to him, in any way, and was not particularly interested in doing anything. She felt miserable, and she did not try to hide her misery from him. Soon he was going out most evenings alone, returning after Pauline had fallen asleep and before she wakened. In the early mornings, no matter how late he had returned home, he would get up and almost immediately leave for his atelier, to write. Pauline sometimes saw him after lunch, often during the hours when she most longed for the oblivion of sleep. On occasion Ernest might try to engage her in conversation or, more rarely now, a caress, but she had no stomach for either. She would lie in the bedroom during the long afternoons, listening to him get ready to go out for the evening.

Ernest was not a man who paid much attention to his personal toilette; Pauline would hear the sound of a few brief strokes of the pig-bristle hairbrush, the spitting after hastily brushing his teeth, the quick turning on and off of the tap as he wetted a cloth to swipe at his face and neck. Pauline would listen from her bed, eyes closed, seeing his movements in her imagination, and waiting for him to leave. Waiting for sleep.

And so their last days in Paris passed. Again, not as she had imagined they would, together in the city of lights. But she endured, and she liked to imagine that perhaps she was forcing Ernest to endure as well.

CHAPTER THIRTEEN

Cherbourg, France, March 1928

Ernest and Pauline left Paris one morning in late March out of the familiar port, aboard an ocean liner that pushed its way almost imperceptibly away from the dock in Cherbourg. Pauline had not eaten before they boarded, knowing it would be a futile effort. She moved like an automaton, dully going through the process of embarkation until she could get to their stateroom and lie down.

Once aboard and ensconced, she felt just as bad as she had back in their apartment, except for an added dread that ocean waves were going to make things worse. On this crossing, she expected their entrenched patterns to continue: Pauline would lie in the cramped stateroom bed and listen to Ernest in the tiny head, noisily going through his ablutions. The only difference would the Lilliputian surroundings. She assumed that this voyage would be much like their past few weeks, Ernest enjoying his evenings, and she, alone, in their stateroom.

After their first full day on board, Pauline wakened the next morning in their room, in the narrow berth across from Ernest. He was lying on the truncated, hard bed, snoring, with his shirt off but his dress trousers still on. She thought to herself, *Well, at least he kept his pants on last night.* Before they left Paris, Pauline had begun to wonder whether Ernest was seeking satisfaction elsewhere. She had no specific evidence of that; her intuition, however, kept niggling at her. And after all, Pauline reminded herself, he had a history of infidelity.

She lay in bed with her eyes closed and waited for the familiar nausea to descend. She had expected it to be even worse on-board ship. But nothing happened. This morning, she was not feeling like she wanted to drown her head in the sink. She did not feel her stomach plummet. This morning, something was different. Pauline wondered briefly if, please God, she was no longer pregnant. She lifted the sheet and saw the small rise in her belly. So that was not it. She slowly moved back the sheet and thin blanket, and swung her legs out, gingerly, over the side of the bed.

The berth was built up on a little platform, with drawers underneath it, to increase the efficient use of space in the cramped compartments. It made the bed somewhat high, and Pauline had to point her toes downward to find the floor. She made her way into the tiny bath, and stared at the mirror, examining her face under the unforgiving fluorescent lights.

For the first morning in months, although tired, Pauline felt no nausea. If she was still pregnant, and the nascent lump in her belly indicated that was the case, why was she not feeling sick? Pauline braced her hands on the basin counter and leaned closer to the mirror, as if peering into her own reflection would provide some answer. None came.

Ernest was still sleeping. Pauline found that, amazingly, she wanted breakfast. She washed, quickly and quietly, and stepped back into their stateroom to find something suitable to wear. She moved silently, cat-like; she did not want to waken, speak to, or breakfast with Ernest. She simply wanted to get out of that claustrophobic space, by herself, and find something decent to eat.

Having accomplished this – Ernest still lay unconscious, snoring, on the platform bed – Pauline crept out into the hallway and closed the stateroom door with infinite care. The corridors were long and narrow, and she imagined the sleeping, snoring, scratching passengers behind each cabin door. It was still early morning; Pauline thought again about breakfast.

She turned when she came to the first juncture in the hallway and headed toward the elevator lobby. She was uncertain which deck the early breakfast service would be on; she knew, from previous crossings, that each boat's schedules were different. She got into the first elevator that appeared and stared at the bank of buttons to see if there was a designation for the dining floors. There was none. Exasperated, Pauline breathed out a quiet expletive.

But not quietly enough. A small, stooped old woman with a translucent complexion and an angelic aura of silver hair stood behind her in the small compartment, and she trilled out a gentle laugh, bird-like and happy. The several silver spangles on her thin wrist jingled in a pleasant counterpoint to her laughter. She seemed delighted at Pauline's miniature outburst.

"Tryin' to figure out where to go, honey?" The voice was lovely – soft and Southern, the American South – a voice from Pauline's youth.

"I'm so sorry, ma'am, excuse me." Pauline's innate politeness was even more ingrained than her Catholicism. The "ma'am" was automatic. "Please, excuse me," Pauline continued, "I'm just a bit frustrated. Trying to figure out where to get breakfast, and I don't seem to be able to find the right floor here." She searched the elevator buttons again. The older woman gleamed at Pauline through rheumy blue eyes. Her hair was pulled up and back in a halo of softly waved silver, a white mohair sweater rested on her shoulders. Her gentle smile was incandescent.

"Follow me, honey, I always know where to find the food. I'm a Southern gal – we've got a nose for that!" She laughed, a gentle titter, at her own joke.

185

"Where you from?" Pauline smiled at herself, at the automatic truncating of language, the *sine qua non* of the American Southerner.

"Mobile, Alabama," the little woman responded, "and I think I hear a little of the South in you, my dear – where you from?" The elevator opened, and they stepped out. She hooked her arm in Pauline's and began walking purposefully toward open glass doors.

Pauline smiled down at her, walking carefully beside her, and surprised herself by responding that she was originally from Arkansas. Since her arrival in Paris two years before, she had disdained her rural background, but somehow, in this safe discourse with this angelic woman, Pauline's accent came back on like an old glove, smooth and lilting.

"I thought so!" The old lady beamed. "Well, let's these two Southern gals go see if the chef on this little ol' boat knows how to make biscuits – I bet he don't!" They laughed together, easily – this was one source of the immediate common bond between Southern women: biscuits. It was like a French girl's instruction on a good baguette, good wine, good cheese. In the American South, just the five or so states from Louisiana to North Carolina, a woman's culinary prowess – indeed, her worth – was often judged by her biscuit-making. The conversation was so blithe, and so refreshingly easy, Pauline laughed out loud.

"What's makin' you so happy this mornin', honey? You got a good man waitin' for you?" The old lady was pleased with herself, pleased to have found a fellow traveler, and pleased to be able to make a genteel risqué remark.

The introduction of Ernest into the conversation momentarily put a slight damper on Pauline's mood. She cast it off. Without responding, Pauline looked up at the entrance to the dining room.

She forgot the old woman's question, she forgot about Ernest: there was *food*. It was like Christmas morning, food abounding on heaping tables, spread out in a glorious bacchanalia all around them. Remembering her manners, Pauline replied.

"Well, to be frank, this is the first morning in months I've wakened and not felt like being sick." Pauline used the Southern euphemism. "I'm feeling this morning, for the first time in a long while, like I could devour a plate of ham and eggs and grits and gravy. I just want to get at it." Pauline beamed at the over-laden tables of food. The old lady threw back her head and laughed. Again, the sound fell in the air bell-like, sweet and sincere.

"Oh honey, you sound like you just hit three-month – that what's goin' on?" She gazed at Pauline's belly. Pauline did not respond. She was not familiar with the term the old woman had used.

"I'm sorry, 'three-month?'" Pauline tilted her head, questioning. The woman leaned forward, and patted Pauline's stomach.

"You goin' on three-month? That's what it sounds like. Like a switch goin' off." Pauline stared at her wonderingly. The old woman continued into the dining room, then stopped and turned to Pauline. "First three months, you feel like death on a cracker. Just want to close your eyes and let the world spin around and leave you alone. Then, bingo, three months to the day, you wake up and could eat a horse." She turned a little glimmer toward Pauline. "That what's goin' on, honey?"

Pauline paused, and thought. She had been so miserable; she had not kept track of the duration of her pregnancy. She thought back to that December day, the day Ernest had told her it had been a "productive" jointure. She looked at the old woman and said, "Well, I guess it was December, so what does

187

that make it?" The old lady clearly enjoyed the sound of her own laughter. It was delightful, and Pauline appreciated it as well.

"December? Well, honey, I don't know how much math you took in school, but if you start with December, then January, February, March – that makes three-month to me!" Pauline stared at her and thought. Yes, it was three months. Pauline realized that she had never been much interested in, or educated about, human pregnancy.

"You might be right," Pauline said. "Do you have children?" This elicited the loudest laughter of all.

"Do I have children?" the old woman said sparkling. "Laws, honey, I've gone through this twelve times, and thirteen children. One set of twins." She paused. "And one died, at four." Her face, which had shown nothing but brightness, was momentarily gray. She shook herself, a small, almost imperceptible movement, and then looked up at Pauline again, eyes shining. "So, I've raised a dozen children, to adults. And only one set of twins! And only ever one husband, by the way, God rest his soul. Believe me, honey, I know all about three-month!"

They had been talking just inside the entrance to the dining hall, and Pauline felt an overwhelming gratitude toward this sweet little old lady. At the same time, she felt an overpowering hunger: all she wanted was to sit and eat a gargantuan meal, and continue talking with her silver-haired angel.

"Come on, let's go eat," Pauline urged. "I'm so glad I met you this morning." Pauline smiled at down at the old woman, who hooked her arm through Pauline's.

"Honey, that's what we're goin' to do, eat and eat and eat, to our heart's content!" She pulled Pauline toward the first bountiful table of splendid food.

They seated themselves at an empty table and were soon devouring plate after plate of an exquisitely executed breakfast. Ham, eggs, salmon, baguettes with French butter, they ate appreciatively and a lot. And when attentive white-jacketed waiters noticed a near-empty plate, fresh dishes would obligingly appear. After finishing off some delectable cinnamon buns and drinking even more pungent hot coffee, they sat back in their seats, paused, and looked at each other.

Pauline glanced at her watch and laughed: they had been in the dining hall for well over an hour. The ice swan sculptures in the centers of the food tables were beginning to show signs of melting, the plates of salmon and fruit and cheeses and breads had been picked over by several waves of hungry morning passengers. They had been well into their feast before the women exchanged names.

"Thank you, Sylvia," Pauline smiled glowingly at her companion. "I don't know when I've had a better meal, better company, or a better appetite." She sat back on the dark leather settee and cradled her stomach in her hands. It seemed to her it had grown, visibly, since the day before. She laughed.

"Look at me!" Pauline said, "I'm getting so fat." Sylvia laughed, and gazed affectionately at the swell under Pauline's dress.

"Yes, and it will get to a point where you don't think you can stretch any farther. And then you do." Sylvia sighed, and tilted her head back. "So long ago, *so long ago*," she murmured. The older woman leaned forward, reached across the table, and placed her hand on Pauline's slim forearm.

"There's somethin' I want to say to you, Pauline." She peered into Pauline's face, then paused. "Here's somethin' to remember, honey, always: *It's only the days that are long, the years are short.*" Sylvia looked searchingly into Pauline's face, and repeated her words. "Please remember, it's only the days that are long. The years are short."

Sylvia closed her eyes briefly, and then slid effortfully to the end of her banquette. "Time for me to be going, honey." Pauline leaned forward and reached for her, as if to keep her longer. Pauline realized she looked like a little girl reaching for something she wanted to hang onto, a dandelion, a hair ribbon, a piece of candy. Suddenly, desperately, Pauline did not want her angel to leave.

"You don't have to go now, Sylvia," she pleaded. "Please, stay, stay with me." Sylvia leaned forward, and kissed Pauline on the top of the head.

"Yes, I do, child, yes I do." She looked into Pauline's eyes. "And you will be alright, you will have a fine, healthy baby." Sylvia patted her shoulder. "Life's not easy, but you will survive."

Survive. Pauline was suddenly reminded of her French lessons back in high school and remembered being lectured on the Latin roots of the French words: *sur vive,* to "over live." *What can that mean,* she thought, *to "over live?"* Was the meaning related to husband, family, friends, children? And if so, did she want that, whatever it meant?

Pauline shook herself out of her musing and looked up. Sylvia was gone. Pauline stood and walked swiftly to the entrance of the dining room. She searched the hallway, but Sylvia was nowhere to be seen. Pauline turned and scanned the dining hall: it was now silent. She had been one of the first patrons, and now she was one of the last. A few staff were wordlessly cleaning the tables and sweeping the floors. They studiously ignored her.

Pauline left the dining room and began to wander about the ship, searching in the well-appointed lobbies, brilliant with chandeliers, and down the winding staircases adorned with heavily carved wooden banisters. She could not find Sylvia. Perhaps she would show up again. Suddenly, Pauline felt immeasurably tired. All she wanted to do was lie down. She made her way back to the elevator and pushed the button.

When Pauline got back to the small stateroom, she was not surprised to find it empty. She lay down on the small, hard bed. Her last thoughts before falling asleep were of the kind old lady who had given her such sweet advice. And although she searched for Sylvia during the rest of the voyage, she was never able to find her again. All Pauline had were her words, echoing with her silvery laughter.

CHAPTER FOURTEEN

Pauline did not find out until halfway through the trip that their first port of call was not in the United States. It was their fourth day at sea, soon after she had started to eat again, to feel an appetite and not constant nausea, just a few days after her visit from the angelic Sylvia, that Ernest casually broke the news.

"You have never been to Havana, have you my dear?" They were reclining on side-by-side chaises on one of the upper decks, covered in lap blankets against the chill, salty wind, soaking in the thin morning sun.

"No, I haven't. Why do you ask?" Ernest emitted one of his deep, resonant laughs.

"Well, since that's where you are going, I thought you might evince some interest in learning about the city and about Cuba, my sweetheart." Pauline started, and sat up rigidly in her chair.

"What do you mean, 'that's where I'm going'?" She stared at him, uncomprehending.

"The boat we are on, my sweet, this boat, this big ship, is docking in Havana, Cuba in three days. Were you not aware of that?" Pauline's mind reeled; momentarily, she had no words.

"Cuba? What are you talking about? I thought we were landing in New York!" Pauline could hear the shrillness in her voice, and how utterly silly she sounded. She knew it was ridiculous, to have boarded a ship and not to have known the destination, but her reliance on Ernest in planning the trip had been so complete, it never occurred to her to question, or to ask about the particulars. All she knew was that the final destination was the U.S. But here she was, a grown woman, married, getting ready to be a mother, and she had boarded a ship as if she were boarding a city tram. Pauline felt foolish and frightened. She shook her head, attempting to recover some equanimity.

"What on earth do you mean, Cuba?" She repeated and stared at him, her anger and fear threatened to overwhelm her. She felt dizzy. She leaned slightly forward in her chair and put her hands to her face; she needed to still herself. Pauline dropped her hands and, staring at her lap, once again repeated her question to Ernest. He seemed unperturbed, or at least he was doing an extremely good imitation of imperturbability.

"Darling, the manifest and course are public, available to all, even the lowest press." Ernest did not demur, even in the face of her distress, from sticking in a dig. "We dock in Cuba," he continued, "and from there we go on to Key West." Pauline could not believe what she was hearing. Cuba. Key West. The city names reverberated in her ears.

Her head swam. What had she done? What Faustian bargain had she undertaken? Pauline knew that she had connived to become Mrs. Ernest Hemingway. But at what price? Now, she was pregnant, not by choice. She was on board a ship to destinations she had no desire to reach. And Ernest seemed so far removed, so distant a figure from the man she had flirted with in Pamplona only a couple years earlier, slept with illicitly under the gaze of disapproving eyes, danced with during all those hazy, swirling Paris nights. Now he was her husband, and he made decisions without concerning or including her.

Pauline began to cry. She had never cried in front of Ernest, ever. She had been raised to consider tears a weakness, something embarrassing, something to hide. Strong emotions were to be channeled into productivity, not wasted on useless and ugly sentiment. Pauline felt the tears fall down her face, and she was ashamed. She did not think that she had ever felt so low.

Ernest gazed at her, at first dispassionately. When she managed to stop weeping, she folded her blanket to one side and swung her legs to the other side of the lounge, facing away from him. She was appalled that she had let him see her emotion.

But something in her tears affected him. She first heard, then felt him get up out of his chaise and come sit down beside her.

"I'm sorry, little bird, I'm sorry." He placed his hand on her back, and Pauline could feel the warmth of it through her jacket. "I didn't know you would feel this bad. I'm sorry." He began to move his hand slowly, in a small circle between her shoulder blades. "It won't be bad, I promise. It won't be bad, little bird." He continued circling with his hand, large and warm.

Pauline sat, hunched forward, silent. "Please, Pauline, look at me," Ernest entreated, and reached his other hand toward her and cupped her chin. She did not move. He gently pulled; she resisted, then let him turn her face. He continued to pull, softly but insistently, until she was facing him. Then he moved his other hand up to the nape of her neck and cradled the back of her head. Pauline kept her eyes downcast.

"Look at me." Pauline closed her eyes completely. "I said, look at me," Ernest repeated. With his hand still on the back of her head, he gave her a small shake. Pauline opened her eyes and looked at him forlornly. "I am telling you, little one, it won't be bad. You must trust me, and you must believe in me." He let his hand fall down her back and began rubbing in circles again. Pauline felt herself falling over some emotional precipice, into a space she had not previously occupied. "I need for you to trust me," Ernest continued.

Pauline remained silent, and his hand fell from her back and he stood up. Then he turned abruptly and walked away.

Pauline felt torn: should she get up and go after him, or should she stay in her chair, alone and waiting? She straightened and wiped the tears off her face. This was part of the continuing bargain. She rose heavily from the chaise and followed him.

CHAPTER FIFTEEN

Havana, Cuba, March 1928

Unlike Pamplona, Pauline immediately liked the swirling, decadent ambience of Havana. From the moment they arrived she was captivated by the lush tropical greenery, the coconut palms and banana trees swaying along every street, the sabals and aurelias lining the sidewalks. They had driven from the boat docks to a small *pensión* on a cobblestone square in the center of town, and her senses were saturated with the sweetness in every exotic sight and sound and smell. She had never been to the Caribbean, and she was enthralled.

Their hotel room was small, and held only a bed, a bureau, and a miniature sink. There was a mirror above the sink, with tiny etchings of frangipani flowers around the border, and Pauline reached up to find that it fronted a small medicine cabinet. She pulled on the mirrored door and looked behind it.

A lone razor lay, its rusted blade beside it, on the lowest shelf. The two glass shelves above it were bare but showed evidence of wet bathroom implements having been put away on them. There was the clear outline of a toothbrush that had been stored there, the wet paste residue having dripped and dried around it. Pauline thought, *it looks like a chalk outline of a little murder victim.* Somehow this prosaic, benign evidence of previous occupants reassured her.

"I like this place. I'm glad we came." Her statement was meant as an overture, as well as a stab at some independence. She may not have chosen to be here, but she could choose whether or not to like it.

"I'm glad to hear that, darling. I'd hate to think that you were doing something you didn't want to do." Ernest's tone was slightly mocking, challenging. Pauline wondered, briefly, would she ever win an argument with him? She doubted it.

The following thought was more sobering: how could she survive being this man's wife? She did not have an answer. On the passage to Havana, after the revelation of their destination and her resignation to it, Pauline had made a decision.

She would bow to him, but she would control how far. It was a gamble: she did not know how he would react to calculated submission on her part, nor did she know how she would react to being subservient, even ostensibly on her own terms. But she felt she was in a complex emotional corner, as if they were on an irrevocable, inevitable path and she needed a survivable way to negotiate it.

Pauline was still trying to convince herself that she would never end up like Hadley – a meek, self-less, invisible wife. That was not what she was contemplating. Her plan was to submit to Ernest, *and to see how much she could get from him by doing that.* She decided this was her only option to attempt to have self-determination: to control the gift of herself to him.

Soon after they had gotten to their room, they had lain down to rest. It was hot, and the process of disembarking from the ship and getting into their room had been tiring. They had both fallen asleep almost immediately and had wakened several hours later in the steamy room to a setting sun. Pauline got up and went to the tall, narrow window to pull back the curtain sheers.

"My goodness, Ernest, we've slept the day away." He rolled over and grunted, but she knew he was not awake. She left the window and walked out onto the miniscule balcony. She surveyed the early evening traffic, human and animal.

It seemed to her that Havana was more civilized, more urbane than Pamplona. She watched the car traffic speed through the wide thoroughfares and heard the *musica campesina* drift upwards from the street.

This was a tropical city, but still a city, to be sure. Well-dressed women in colorful, stylish dresses, high-heeled shoes, and designer handbags hurried along the busy sidewalks, where village men in from the farms stacked cages of squawking chickens. Stray dogs ambled, nose down, hunting for scraps outside the bustling corner *bodegas*. The leather shoes of businessmen in neat *cubaveras* and *fedoras* tapped on the sidewalks, quickly passing stooped women in loose cotton *vestidos* who sold peeled mangoes out of wooden crates. City buses rolled past dusty vacant lots, where little boys, dressed only in ragged shorts, played stickball with rolled-up socks.

And there was the descant of urban, electric sounds – radios playing music from Miami, phonographs, car horns. It was not the provincial place that was Pamplona, and Pauline could feel the beat of city life. She turned and went back into the room. Pauline crossed to the bed, stood beside it, and gazed at Ernest. She thought to herself, *Now is as good a time as any to start.*

She pulled the white ribbon at the top of her cotton nightgown and loosened the neck. She quickly glanced in the mirror, running a hand over her hair. She stood beside the bed, mute and calculating. Pauline stared at her opponent.

"Ernest, wake up," Pauline said purposefully, her voice low and silky. "Come look at the evening sky with me, it's beautiful." She intended to control this seduction, and garner Ernest's gratitude in return.

Ernest sleepily turned and looked at her, evaluating. Then he slid his large body backward in the bed and pointed to the jurisdiction of the sheet he had just vacated.

"Here. Come lie right here," he commanded. Ernest slapped the bed sheets where he had lain. With his barked directive, he had stood her invitation on its head, and turned it into his demand. He had ignored her offer, and had put himself in the role of seducer.

Pauline sighed. This was not how she had planned this to enfold, but she couldn't back out now. She had started it. Pauline responded to Ernest's directive by sitting, not where he had instructed, but on the side of the bed. She then slowly reclined, as far to the edge of the bed as she could.

Ernest looked down the length of her body. Then with one quick yank on her torso, he corrected Pauline's position, pulling her onto the place he had originally indicated.

It crossed Pauline's mind, briefly, that perhaps Ernest was clairvoyant. She had intended that she would have the upper hand in this overture, at least in her mind, but once again he had done an end-run on her. He was besting her in this mental game she had started. "Don't say a word," he breathed.

This was not what Pauline had imagined, not how she had envisioned her controlled, subversive submission to Ernest to unfold. She had imagined her seductive offer and eventual planned acquiescence, with ensuing appreciation from him. That was not at all what was happening. "Don't speak, and don't move," Ernest, continued. "I want to look at you."

Later, the sun had fully set, and Ernest was again snoring beside her. She lay still, hot and unhappy on the white sheets, her nightgown rumpled around her hips. She stared at the ceiling, and her thoughts roiled. She lay rigid, unable to decide what to do. Eventually, Ernest wakened, and rolled over to kiss her.

"You, my dear, are an angel." He kissed her neck. She lay, diffident, keeping her eyes closed. "And tonight, I am a lucky man." He kissed her again, on her lips. He stroked her hair and turned her head to face him. "Hey there, open your eyes, I know you are awake," Ernest jostled her head.

Pauline felt caught, and opened her eyes to his clever, smiling face. "You just keep doing exactly what you are doing, my little bird." He kissed her again. "Exactly what you are doing." She felt tears well up in her eyes.

She rolled over and turned her back to him. Pauline wondered if Ernest could also see the sadness that she felt. He stroked her back through the thin nightgown, and she waited. "Gad, I love that long back," he whispered, and stroked her again.

She felt defeated, bereft. And it was she who had started this. With effort, she rose, walked to the sink, and splashed her face with cold water. She turned and composed her expression.

"Thank you, Ernest. That was nice." Pauline calculated her words, intending them to be innocuous, sweet, gauged to not engender retribution, and at the same time, implicitly cutting. It did not work.

Ernest laughed. He lay with his head on the rumpled pillow and laughed at her. She was immediately embarrassed, at herself, at her thin nightgown, at her vulnerability. He rose and walked slowly over to her. He put his arms around her, in an iron-lock embrace.

"I will give you nice, and I will give you nasty, and I will give you everything in between," Ernest said quietly. He kissed the top of her head. "And you will keep wanting it." He released her and moved over to open his suitcase. Without speaking or looking at his wife, Ernest pulled out a pair of trousers and a shirt and began to dress. Finally, he turned to her.

"You had better put something on, Pauline," Ernest said breezily. "I'm not going out to dinner with a woman in a flimsy nightgown." He moved to the frangipani-etched mirror and began to wash his face in the tiny sink.

Pauline knew she had lost another round. She had thought that she would be able maneuver, to be in control of something in this strange competition between them. But he had called her cards.

He had won the hand and acted as though he was well on his way to winning the game. She moved forward and bent to reach her clothes. In the act of bending, she felt the swelling of her belly, something new and difficult to bear, something further to contend with. She stood and rubbed her hand over the round of her stomach, slowly circling.

Pauline had a sudden thought: here was something she held over him. She would be giving him a child, and he was certain, a son. This was something he could not do. This was hers, from inside her, and he could no more control it than he could control the moon. Pauline straightened up and closed her eyes.

This was hers, this pregnancy. This was something she could manage, use, gain from. Pauline picked up a dress and slipped it casually over her head. She would find a way to capitalize on this advantage.

CHAPTER SIXTEEN

That first night, they walked out into the still-hot evening air, and Ernest took her hand. They strolled, unspeaking, down narrow streets, lights blinking in the windows, radios blaring competing *cancións* as they passed. They made their way to a district of outdoor restaurants and cafés. Ernest chose one, they found a table, and sat down under a warm tropical evening sky.

Ernest ordered champagne. Their small table sat unsteadily on the uneven cobblestone patio, and Ernest laughed as they grabbed their glasses to keep them from toppling. The food was succulent and hot, and the sea breeze was scented with night-blooming jasmine.

In the foreign, sensual environment, Pauline decided that it would not be difficult to put on the outward patina of a happy, loving wife. Pauline was determined that she would not be overcome, that she would not allow Ernest to make her miserable. She would put on a smile, and enjoy this exotic island. She would make Ernest work for control over her.

They finished their dinner and strolled to the promenade next to the *Almendares*. The river was blue-black in the moonlight, flowing imperceptibly to the bay and lazily sending its tendrils into the Straits of Florida. Pauline and Ernest held hands as they walked, and people all around them smiled, nodded in welcome, and spoke sweetly. Pauline briefly imagined that it was as if Ernest had spun a charm around them.

The next three weeks in Havana were spent exploring the city, resting in the warm little room on the square, and refining their newly adopted marital roles: she the calculating supplicant, and he the cunning opportunist. And as they tested out their respective personas, they amused themselves by hiking in the countryside, visiting vineyards in the mountains, swimming in the warm Caribbean waters, and sunbathing on Cuba's crystalline beaches. Pauline continued to try and enjoy the romantic landscape, and at the same time to try and find some sense of control in her submission to her husband. Ernest, for his part, seemed cannily aware of her endeavors, and continued blithely to thwart her.

In their brief sojourn in Cuba, Pauline and Ernest began to become proficient in their dueling characters: she watchful, careful, scheming, and he shrewd, deft, and confident. And overlaying this, they continued public their display of mutual regard. The face they presented to others became the shell in which their relationship was defining itself.

They were both caught, spun in their jointly fashioned web. It was not what either of them had expected or planned, but they were ensnared in each other's hold. One way or another, for better or for worse, they were both entrapped in this new compact.

CHAPTER SEVENTEEN

Key West, Florida, April 1928

They finally reached Key West on a blustery morning in early April. By mid-spring on the island, the cooling trade winds had slowed, and the days were already becoming too hot for comfort. Pauline prayed that they would be quickly in and out of this little Caribbean island, and on their way to Missouri.

Ernest had decided that the baby should be born close to their families, and he thought that St. Louis was a good split of the difference. His family's home in Chicago, and hers in Arkansas, were both equidistant from the good hospital in St. Louis. Each day, Pauline surveyed her growing belly; it had become a game of hers, to think of her pregnancy not only as her trump card but also as her ticket back to civilization. Perhaps she could not sway her new husband completely with her subterfuges, but she felt confident that she could influence him with fear.

Fear was an uncommon emotion to Ernest, but Pauline had been pleased to note that the pregnancy at times clearly scared him. Unlike Pauline, he already knew what it was like to have a child, but he had no idea of what giving birth was like. Pauline imagined his mother had instilled in him, through her efforts to further her own martyrdom, the horrors and mess of childbirth, and the idea seemed to terrify him. Getting Pauline to the best hospital possible was his first goal, and letting someone else take over until she had given birth was his second.

Pauline had not known that Ernest's plan included the purchase, through an agent, of a Model A Ford roadster, and that he intended to take delivery of the car in Key West. As he explained, his plan was for the car to be there upon their arrival, to spend a few days in the Florida Keys, and then to drive, just the two of them, across country to Arkansas and then on to St. Louis.

Again, she was mystified as to why he had not spoken of this earlier, but continued with her mute submission. She focused instead on trying to relax and enjoy herself, as much as that was possible, concentrating on the enhanced status that her ensuing motherhood would, she hoped, bring in his eyes. Having a baby had not done much for Hadley as far as keeping her husband, but Pauline planned on handling it differently. For one thing, she would not get fat and dumpy and clingy, as Hadley had. She would not let having a baby harm either her figure or her dignity.

Pauline was dismayed when Ernest explained that delivery of the Model A was delayed. Some paperwork had gotten misplaced at the Miami car dealer, and the owner of the small Ford dealership in Key West told them that it would be at least three weeks before the car would be delivered to the island. Pauline hated the Model A before she ever set eyes on it – its delay was keeping her from getting back to the mainland.

The Ford dealership, located on the first floor of a tall, blocky building on Simonton Street, was a mom-and-pop affair, as was just about everything else in what Pauline considered a backward little town.

The "southernmost city" – although Pauline hardly thought it qualified as a city – was an odd admixture. There was a white upper-class stratum, its wealth garnered primarily from the wrecking industry, a middle class comprised mostly of Cuban workers' households supported by the cigar and pineapple factories, and a vibrant population of Bahamians on the south side of the island, mostly poor and working as laborers and house servants. Key Westers were a jumble of cultural and ethnic heritages: in addition to the British and Caribbean, there were French, Spanish, and East African, and though there was an ever-present entrenched racism, almost everyone seemed to be able to exhibit a patina of tolerance. Pauline thought it was the most unusual place she had ever visited.

Oddly, it was the Key West Ford dealer who offered them a place to stay, in a spacious apartment above the car showroom, to wait for the Model A to be delivered. Ernest accepted the offer immediately, and they soon found themselves ensconced in the second-story flat. Pauline could not understand why there was an unoccupied, furnished apartment above a car dealership, but, like so many things in Key West, the inexplicable was the common place. People did not question things there, they just accepted them.

Days passed into weeks, waiting for the delivery of the car, and they fell into a rhythm. Ernest, as was his wont, wrote in the early mornings, and Pauline slept as late as she possibly could, accommodating her growing pregnancy.

It was usually the late morning sun that wakened her, hot and sweating in their tousled bed. Ernest had not rented a separate writing office, as he usually did, but instead wrote in the apartment, often carrying his Royal typewriter out onto the small wrought iron balcony. He would write early in the morning, only stopping when the tropical sun forced him inside.

Sometimes after Ernest had finished writing the couple would walk down to the marina for breakfast at one of the shack-like eating establishments favored by the locals. Those locals, islanders who had been born in Key West, called themselves "conchs," referring to the beautiful Queen Conch sea mollusks found lying on the ocean floor surrounding the island. The weird pride they took in this delighted Pauline; she had never been to a place, anywhere in the world, where there was such a strange mixture of erudition and rusticism, of intellect and ignorance, of acceptance and chauvinism.

And something in the Key West atmosphere began to affect Pauline. Despite her initial contempt, she was finding herself fascinated by the tiny island. She encountered things every day that delighted her, appalled her, intrigued her, humored her. After a while, she found a certain freedom on the island and felt, as many others before her had, that she had found a singular place, a place simply to be herself.

At length, the car was delivered – an ugly green monstrosity with black fenders and, to Pauline, an inscrutable method of locomotion. Ernest tried to teach her what "double clutching" meant and how to do it, but she found it irritatingly difficult, furthering her antipathy toward the rickety car.

But however much she disliked it, the car was to be their means of transport up the Florida Keys. They would travel east and north on the overseas highway, not yet twenty years old, then on through the long state of Florida and west, toward America's heartland.

Up to this point, she had not thought about where they would eventually make their home. But after three weeks in Key West, Pauline had been bitten. As odd as the tiny island was, and in contradiction to her initial appraisal, Pauline somehow had come to feel that Key West was where she wanted to be. It was a singular emotion she would come to recognize as understandable only to those whose hearts were captured by this unique island.

Surprisingly, it also occurred to her that she could live comfortably in Key West, with or without Ernest. But her immediate future, of course, required a leave of absence: she had a baby to produce.

Their last days in Key West were hot and hurried. On their final morning, they packed their luggage in the rumble seat of the Model A, and headed north, crossing the causeway out of Key West. Pauline looked to her right, over her shoulder, and kept her face resolutely turned so that Ernest would not see her sadness at their departure. She did not want to leave the intermission of peace that she had found on the island. Imperceptibly, little by little, Key West had captured her heart.

She knew that this pregnancy that had trapped her required that she return to the mainland; Ernest would not allow his child to be born in this tropical hinterland. She was, in a sense, executing a penance: returning to St. Louis to endure what she now regarded as an unpleasant but necessary duty to be weathered. She was paying a price for her alliance with Ernest.

Pauline could not change the fact of her pregnancy, but she could try and use it to her advantage. As they drove through the early heat of the South Florida spring, she stared down at her bulging belly. She thought, this is what is taking me away from Key West, this is what I am leaving for.

She massaged her wide stomach and made a promise to herself, looking out at the Atlantic Ocean, that she would be back. As improbable and inexplicable as it was, Pauline determined that, with or without husband or children, family or friends, someday she would return to Key West.

CHAPTER EIGHTEEN

Piggott, Arkansas, May 1928

Ernest insisted that they drive straight through from Key West to Arkansas. They stopped only at small car camps late each day and left early each morning on the drive north and west. The trip was exhausting.

When they finally arrived at her family's home in Piggott, the homecoming was muted. Pauline was fatigued and miserable; Ernest was antsy and unpleasant. Pauline's parents accepted the arrival of the hapless couple with bewilderment.

Their second day at the farm, Ernest announced his intention to drive north to Illinois to spend time with his family. Although surprised, Pauline was not displeased at the prospect of finishing the last months of her pregnancy alone with her family, without the incessant enervation of negotiating constantly with Ernest. She acquiesced easily to his plan.

On the morning that he was to leave, Pauline accompanied Ernest to the car. He had parked on the sloping hill of the bank barn, and as he climbed into the Model A to leave, he turned to her.

"Look," Ernest said gruffly, "I'll be back soon, when it's time. I'll get you to St. Louis." His words were not comforting; they were said with the resignation of one burdened with a required chore. Pauline did not answer. She watched him pull the car door shut, start the motor, and pull away, down the gravel track to the highway.

And so Pauline was left on the farm in Piggott, to gestate and to deal with the tedium of talk about pigs and chickens and silage, and the incessant murmur of farm noise. Her parents crept quietly around her, as if she were a fragile bomb, about to burst.

Their treatment of her irritated Pauline; she was exasperated by their trepidation and solicitude. As time passed, she also became increasingly anxious, as her fear of the upcoming delivery escalated. She had heard horror stories of what could go wrong in giving birth; she did not want to think about it. She retreated into sullen waiting.

One morning Pauline left the breakfast table and walked out to the large shaded front porch. She lowered herself ponderously into a whitewashed oak rocker, and stretched forward her swollen ankles, gently rocking herself back and forth. The slats of the rocker massaged her back and legs as she moved, and she closed her eyes and felt grateful for the pressure of the wood, for the gentle gift of its comfort. Her calves felt leaden, her legs too heavy to move, and she felt nothing so much as wanting to be anywhere else, to not be carrying an unwanted burden in her belly.

Pauline was rocking, eyes closed, when she was surprised by the sound of the rocker next to her, moving back and forth. She opened her eyes.

It was JerHenry. He had come up onto the porch. This was a bold intrusion, since the servants rarely occupied this space unless providing lemonade or conveying a message. JerHenry looked at Pauline, and continued his slight movement. His only deference was to perch at the very front edge of the seat.

JerHenry was always the first person up every morning, starting his day by carrying the last evening's table scraps out to the sty for the pigs' morning slops. He was little more than a child, perhaps fifteen at most, but he worked like a man, day in and day out. His skin was the color of weak coffee, and he had born on the farm; his people were bound to it by heritage, if no longer by law. He was not a slave on this farm as his grandfather had been, and he tentatively explored the freedom his place in the working hierarchy afforded.

"You lookin' mighty uncomfortable, if you don't mind my saying so, ma'am," JerHenry said quietly. He rocked with quick, small thrusts of his bony ankles, back and forth. Pauline's initial reaction was that, yes, she did mind. She was forming a suitably condescending retort to shoo him away, but something stopped her.

Suddenly she felt hungry for companionship, not facile, surface interaction, but real communion with another human being. Pauline stared at the young man, struggling to form an appropriate response. Talking with JerHenry would be an easy, if uncommon, conversation. She hesitated, then with deliberate care, she spoke.

"Well, JerHenry, I suppose you are right. I suppose I am uncomfortable. Even though it's expected, I still hate it." Pauline did not look at JerHenry, but gazed out over the manicured front lawn. She continued to rock.

"Yes'm, I know all 'bout that," JerHenry responded quickly. "I know you don' feel so good right now, and you jes wan' it all to be over." He did not elaborate, and Pauline wondered how he had gained the extent of his knowledge in this area. She sent a small, swift prayer upward that this was not going to turn into a conversation likening her gestation to that of his littering sows. She heard herself let out a subtle but unladylike snort of laughter. "What, ma'am, you all right?" JerHenry leaned forward solicitously; he looked genuinely concerned.

"No, JerHenry," Pauline responded. "No, I'm not all right, but it will be okay." She smiled and emitted another small laugh. "I was just hoping that you weren't thinking about telling me how your sows give birth to their piglets." Her moment of humorous honesty between them hung pleasantly

213

in the air. They looked at each other mutely, straight-faced, then both chuckled quietly. After a few moments, he spoke.

"No, ma'am, I ain' never thought 'bout you like that. When I said I knew all 'bout this, I meant from my mama and my sisters. Thas what I meant." They were both still smiling, and the laughter felt good in Pauline's chest.

"Well, JerHenry, the truth is, I feel a bit like a pig." JerHenry frowned at her comment, and Pauline continued, quickly, to explain what she meant. Pauline felt a strange and sudden urge that she not offend this young man. "What I mean is, I know that pigs are good mothers. I'm not sure I'm going to be that good. Not sure I'll be as good as a pig momma." JerHenry stared back at Pauline and stopped rocking. He looked at the ground.

"You gonna be a good momma, ma'am." He continued to stare forward, at the gray-painted porch floor in front of him. "You gonna be the best, the best momma." He gripped the sides of the rocker, and pushed himself forward, like an airplane readying for take-off. For the first time, he looked directly into her eyes. "You gonna be the best momma, better than any pig ever was."

Pauline sat, transfixed, staring at this earnest young man. Their eyes locked, and Pauline felt an odd connection to him, something she had not felt to many other people. He had just given her a benediction, more profound than she had ever received from any priest.

"Thank you, JerHenry." Now it was her turn to cast her eyes downward. She felt it impossible to raise her head to look at him. "Thank you, and I can't tell you how much that means to me, to hear you say that." The improbability of this conversation struck Pauline, even as it was occurring. And she did not care.

"It gon get better, ma'am. And you may not think 'bout how it will be, but things allus change, and I allus say, things gon' change for the better." Pauline rocked, and stared at the gray floor in front of her. She could not lift her head. Then she spoke, quietly, and earnestly.

"Yes, JerHenry, I believe you. I hope that things get better, too. And if they don't, well, I guess we can just say, that's all we have. We have what we have now." JerHenry nodded, and tentatively reached forward and touched the back of her hand.

"Yes'm, thas true, thas true what you say. We have what we have now." And then he pulled his hand away, turned quickly and scurried down the front porch steps.

It occurred to Pauline that this was the most honest, straightforward interaction she had had with another human being in an exceedingly long time. And the upshot of had been, someone thought Pauline would be a better mother than a pig.

CHAPTER NINETEEN

St. Louis, Missouri, September 1928

Patrick's birth, in the hot, humid days of a mid-west summer, was for Pauline a thing to be endured. Ernest had, as promised, returned to the farm just in time to transport his heavily pregnant wife to St. Louis. The day-long drive was excruciating for Pauline: she kept her eyes closed most of the way, and tried to ignore the bouncing and heaving of the small car as they drove north on the dusty highway.

When they reached St. Louis, Ernest did not offer to take her to a hotel: he drove straight to the hospital. He walked her inside, found a nurse, and watched as Pauline was wheeled in a chair down the hallway and through doors that swung closed behind her. Then Ernest fled.

Pauline was an uncooperative obstetrical patient: she did not breathe or relax or sit or stand in all the helpful ways the doctors and nurses instructed. Each new directive was intended to ease the birthing process along, but when the time came, she didn't push as instructed, she simply willed herself to be elsewhere. Finally, the doctors decided to take the baby by Caesarian, letting her know that this was, in large part, a result of her failure. They gave her a full anesthetic, and Pauline smiled as she slipped under.

When Pauline woke, she was tired, and wanted nothing but to sleep. She did not care to do anything, even to roll over to see the little being in the bassinet beside her bed. She just wanted the oblivion of slumber.

Ernest, on the other hand, had reappeared once the trauma of the actual birth was over, and was ecstatic. He came to her room bearing an armful of roses, a box full of cigars, and a triumphant smile. When he first saw Pauline, lying wan and tired in the maternity bed, Ernest was solicitous. He bent and kissed her forehead.

"Good job, little bird," he said quietly, with a warm grin. "You did a magnificent job." Pauline gazed out the window and pointed weakly to the small bassinet beside her bed.

"Take a look, Ernest." The big man leaned over the infant and stared with clear amusement. The baby was red-faced, bloated, and as his father looked at him, he scrunched up his tiny face, showing evidence of a great internal effort. Ernest laughed.

"He's ugly, Paulie, but he'll get better." He turned back toward Pauline and kissed her again. Seeing that she was unresponsive, he murmured again softly, "You did a good job, little bird." Pauline didn't respond.

The baby was boy, just as Ernest had predicted. He was good enough, Pauline supposed, as babies go. He seemed to her to be quite unattractive, and when she first saw him all she wanted to do was roll over and go back to sleep. The nurses had insisted on putting him to her breast and trying to get him to nurse – this effort was helped not at all by Pauline's complete disinterest. The whole process reminded her of what she had seen in JerHenry's piggery; she wanted no part of it.

She lay there in the hospital bed, as a body dispossessed. She did not want to participate but she did nothing, on the other hand, to stop the revolving staff from trying to get her to take part. If they wanted to attempt to get this little alien body to find some nourishment from her, fine – she would neither help nor hinder.

When the nurses eventually realized that Pauline would not actively participate in attempting to feed her child, they finally gave up. They hung a little sign at the bottom of her bed: "Bottle Feeding Only." Pauline had seen it when she had finally gotten out of bed to go to the bathroom; she knew this branded her either as a mother who was inadequate or who did not care. And truly, at that point, Pauline did not care. Either way fine with her.

CHAPTER TWENTY

Piggott, Arkansas, Fall 1928

Ernest and Pauline returned to Piggott with the baby and
spent their child's first few months navigating the
difficult territory of new parenthood. Pauline was not, in any
sense of the word, a natural mother; everything about caring
for an infant was foreign to her. She did not like it and made
little effort to hide the fact of her disinterest and antipathy.
Ernest had at first evinced sporadic interest in the child, but
his curiosity had dulled as the weeks passed. He was obviously
more inclined to spend his time writing in their bedroom,
hunting in the nearby hills, or fishing in the stream that ran
through the farm meadow. The baby's care was left almost
entirely to the hired nanny and to his bewildered
grandmother.

Ernest had named the boy Patrick, a solid name for a boy.
Ernest insisted that no one was ever to use any diminutive,
but always the full name, always Patrick. Sometimes, after
they had first arrived back in Piggott, Pauline would creep into
the nursery to see the baby sleeping, and would try to conjure
up what she imagined were maternal feelings. Nothing
happened. Soon, she stopped trying.

Pauline didn't feel blue or depressed; she just didn't feel
anything. If the proper thing were to have been to wonder
what was wrong with her, she did not do that either. The baby
gave her nothing, and, in retrospect, she supposed she gave
nothing back. If pressed, she might have admitted that she felt
she had done enough, just giving birth to him.

Unlike babies, Pauline understood cats. Cat mothers give
birth to a litter, they feed the kittens for the short period of
time required by nature, and then they soon return to being

what they were before: just a cat. That's what Pauline wanted, to return to what she had been before.

Ernest and Pauline continued their uncharted road, each trying to figure out the bargaining balance between them. Every day was a challenge. She wanted to be with him, to continue to feel him out and test him, to see if she could derive some pleasure from his company. She did not know what the outcome would be, but she struggled to figure out how to move forward with Ernest, how to get what she wanted from their relationship. Ernest's path was primarily to ignore his wife and son and in-laws, and to do as he pleased with his days. It was a rocky path to navigate, for both of them.

The one bright spot for Pauline were her daily interactions with JerHenry. They had quickly resumed the friendship they had begun before Patrick's birth, but unlike Pauline, JerHenry was excited about the new baby. He took every opportunity to come up to the kitchen of the big house and watch the nanny feed the baby, pat him, rock him in the bassinette they had moved in beside the old cookstove.

JerHenry often asked if he could rock little Patrick, and the diffident nurse always assented. Soon she allowed JerHenry to feed the baby and pat his little back after a bottle. JerHenry's broad smile showed deep satisfaction when he could elicit a reassuring burp from the tiny body.

Pauline soon found herself headed toward the kitchen on late afternoons, hoping she might see JerHenry there. She was usually rewarded in her search. JerHenry's day started before dawn, and most late afternoons he chose to end his workday in the kitchen with the nanny and Patrick. The overworked nanny, grateful for the respite from constant baby-tending, would offer JerHenry a comfortable seat by the stove, place the baby in his capable arms, and set a mug of cider on the table beside him. She would then retreat gratefully to the adjoining parlor and lie down on the day bed for a rest.

On these quiet afternoons, Pauline and JerHenry soon fell into the same easy, pleasant conversations they had had in the spring. JerHenry could neither read nor write, but his sharp eyes shone with keen intelligence, and he was an admirable companion. He could name every bird trill, every leaf fall, every flower blossom on the farm, and he could foretell the minutest alterations in weather and season, he seemed to be able to remember all the myriad, mysterious indications of coming changes.

JerHenry could also read faces, as quickly and accurately as if the expressions were spelled out on the printed page. Pauline's moods were transparent to JerHenry; he was an astute and compassionate listener.

One cold afternoon in early December, Pauline went to the kitchen to find some company, and found JerHenry there as usual, gently rocking and cooing to Patrick. JerHenry looked up and smiled when she came in. He was as happy for her company as she was for his. In fact, to an outsider it would have been obvious that JerHenry's affection for Patrick was simply a transference of his fondness for Pauline. It would have been unseemly for JerHenry to show any type of regard or fondness for Pauline, but he could, without fear of disquiet, dote on her child.

"This baby gettin' big, ma'am. I can feel he weighin' more and more each day." JerHenry grinned at Pauline and bounced the infant up and down on his chest. JerHenry was a slight young man, but his shoulders and arms were already broadened from years of labor, and he held the baby with the easy grace of a natural athlete. Pauline watched him jostle Patrick up and down and smiled.

"Thank you so much, JerHenry, for giving nanny a bit of a rest. It's truly kind of you." She continued to smile at him, and JerHenry blushed under her gaze.

"It alright ma'am," he said. "I enjoy it. Really I do. Ain' no trouble for me a 'tall." JerHenry paused, then emboldened by curiosity and concern, turned his face up to Pauline. "Ma'am, you don' mine my aksin' you, but I hear you and Mister plannin' on a trip." He faltered, then continued, "I hear you plannin' on takin' a trip, and leavin' this baby here." JerHenry looked down at the floor and held Patrick tighter. He waited for a response.

Pauline felt left-footed by the question. She did not want to engage in any unpleasantness with JerHenry. She did not want to admit to him that she wanted desperately to get away from Piggott, from her baby, from the cloistering care of her family. Although he was just a hired hand, he had become her only friend on the farm, and she did not want to engender his disapproval.

But JerHenry was correct: the Hemingways were indeed planning a trip. Pauline did not want to disclose to this guileless young man that she thought perhaps by going away alone with her husband, she might be able to recapture his attention, perhaps even his love. The baby did not figure into her calculations. She hesitated, forming her answer.

"It's complicated, JerHenry." She considered how best to proceed. "You see, Mr. Ernest is not happy here." She paused and tried to formulate a further explanation.

"He not happy here on the farm, ma'am, or he unhappy with somethin' else? What he unhappy about?" JerHenry stared up at Pauline, confounded. Pauline struggled to find an appropriate response.

"Well, JerHenry, I suppose he's unhappy about a lot of things." Pauline walked to the window, looking out over the frozen yard.

Twigs of young fruit trees stuck up through the snow, bare and vulnerable and defenseless in the cold. The fencepost heads were dark smudges of black against the white landscape, the connecting wires almost invisible in the darkening afternoon light. A cardinal flew across the yard and landed on a snowy branch of a loblolly pine. Pauline, still staring out the window. continued.

"I guess he's unhappy with Arkansas, and with his work." She paused, then turned around to look at JerHenry. "And if I'm honest, I suppose he's unhappy with me." JerHenry stared at her; he stopped rocking. His face clouded with consternation and then, with an unexpected insight, JerHenry looked up at Pauline and sighed.

"So, you think he unhappy 'bout this baby too?" Pauline did not try to dissemble.

"Yes, I think so," she said. "I think he probably is unhappy with the baby, too." The kitchen was now dark with the fallen light of late afternoon, and Pauline walked over to the small brass wall lamp and switched it on. Its meagre light did little to lift the heaviness of the moment. Slowly, JerHenry stood and walked toward Pauline. He held the tiny bundle in his arms out toward her.

"Here, you take him ma'am. Imma go and fetch nanny." He handed over the baby and walked into the parlor; Pauline could hear him gently talking to the nanny, shaking her awake.

Pauline stood stiffly, her baby in her arms. She was grateful when nanny reappeared and Pauline quickly dropped the bundle into waiting, proficient arms. She watched the nanny slide Patrick to one hip and go about the business of warming a bottle for him. Pauline fled the kitchen and ran upstairs.

JerHenry walked out the back door of the big house, and automatically made his way to the piggery. All his chores for the day were done, the hogs had been slopped and fed, and were now bedding down for the night. The mother sows were resting on their sides, waiting for sleep, and the new stoats of last spring, growing rapidly now, were carefully bedded on abundant straw lining the floor of the loose boxes. The piggery was quiet, calm, and comforting. JerHenry peered over the box gates at the animals; he wished he could forget what he had just heard back in the kitchen.

JerHenry had already known that the big man was difficult and unkind; he had, several times, heard him shouting at his wife, and had sometimes seen her leave the house in a hurry, as if to get away from her husband. JerHenry also knew that the big man drank too much; he had seen him get sloppy drunk and roar around the farmyard, sometimes late at night, wakening and frightening the pigs. More than once, JerHenry had had to come out to the piggery to calm them down after one of the big man's tirades.

And he knew that the big man liked to shoot guns. But not like the other men JerHenry knew, who hunted for food. The big man seemed to like to shoot guns just to make himself bigger; JerHenry had seen him scatter shot at little birds in the trees, nothing you could eat, the man just wanted to kill them.

But how could a man not like his own baby? JerHenry shook his head. He gazed down at the young stoats, now fast asleep and nestled into the hay. *That man a mystery,* JerHenry thought to himself and shook his head, *a pure mystery.*

CHAPTER TWENTY-ONE

Ernest had decided that he wanted to leave by Christmastime. As he explained to Pauline, he needed to leave the stifling atmosphere of the farm, and he wanted to go west. His justification was that he was going to make a trip to Wyoming to finally finish his novel. Pauline, surprising her family, had quickly announced that she would accompany him. Her mother was aghast that Pauline would choose to leave the baby and follow Ernest across the country; to Pauline, it was an obvious decision. She wanted to be with Ernest; she did not want to be with the child. Going to Wyoming with Ernest was part of regaining her former self, the woman who could still entice and interest her husband.

They arranged for the baby to stay in Arkansas. Pauline negotiated with the nanny to retain her services, and busied herself making whatever purchases she thought they might need for the trip. The daily grind of diapers and feedings, she left to others to handle.

Pauline and Ernest left Piggott on New Year's Day. The incision from the Caesarian had fully healed, and Pauline could not wait to be on the road with Ernest, to get away from the farm and the baby and her family. She wanted to be alone with Ernest, headed to an opportunity for a fresh start, a chance to rekindle Ernest's interest in her.

The morning they left, her parents followed them out into the frosty yard, the thin ice on the grass crunching under their shoes. Pauline's mother held the bundled Patrick. Her father had insisted on purchasing a larger car for their trip, a 1928 Ford Model A sedan, with a comfortably heated interior and a new engine capable enough to weather the snowy drive out west. Pauline was grateful for the upgrade; long winter travel in their Florida roadster, which had no windows or heater, would have been unimaginably unpleasant.

JerHenry was loading the last of their suitcases into the back of the car and Ernest was standing at the driver's door, impatient and stamping his feet on the frozen ground.

"Say your goodbyes now, Pauline, time to hit the road." She was grateful for his abruptness and his instruction; she wanted to get out of there as much as he did. Pauline's mother moved toward her and proffered Patrick; Pauline reached forward and quickly patted the baby's head, fending off her mother's advance.

"He'll be fine with you, thank you, mother. And he's too young even to miss us. Nanny knows everything to do, you won't be bothered." Her mother stepped back, still holding the baby, and gazed at her daughter, trying to hide her sadness and disappointment.

Ernest turned the key in the electric ignition but was rewarded with only a small clicking sound. He slammed his hand against the steering wheel and cursed.

"I'm going to have to crank the bloody thing," he bellowed. Ernest fished the crank out from the leather pocket inside the front door, got out of the car, and slammed the door shut. Pauline, her parents, and JerHenry all stood mutely watching him. Pauline prayed the crank would work.

Ernest moved around to the front of the car, inserted the crank into the small hole below the radiator, and with a grunting snarl, began to turn the rod. He had made a few revolutions of the iron bar when his gloves slipped off the cold metal; the crank immediately recoiled and clouted him on the shoulder.

Ernest yelled and jumped backwards, cursing at the car, the crank, the cold, at everything. He spun around in a circle, jumping, holding his shoulder, and groaning in pain. Pauline watched with growing fear, first that Ernest had been hurt, and second that perhaps he would not be able to get the car started. The latter would be far worse to her than the former. The others stood by mutely, not wanted to say anything to further anger or irritate Ernest.

When he had finally exhausted himself with spitting and cursing, he bent over and took a long, deep breath. He stood and exhaled fast into the freezing air; his breath made a little rising cloud in front of him. He walked over and picked up the crank from the ground where he had thrown it, walked back to the car, and began again.

This time, to Pauline's rush of grateful relief, he was able to get the engine to turn over. He motioned to her abruptly to get in the car and Pauline quickly complied. She rolled down the window and smiled at her parents, her mother still clinging to Patrick.

"Goodbye, mother. We will see you later." Pauline had purposefully not given her any return date; frankly, no return at all would have been fine with her. Her mother wiped her eyes and raised Patrick's tiny arm in a forced wave. Pauline could not muster any tears. She felt nothing but impatience and the desire to flee.

As they pulled away, a spray of icy gravel spattering behind them, Pauline caught a glimpse of JerHenry as he stood still beside her mother and the baby. JerHenry did not wave, he did not call out goodbye, he stood motionless as a statue.

Pauline thought, as they sped down the driveway, that JerHenry looked like she had never seen him before. In that moment his face, usually placid and complacent, was contorted somehow. JerHenry's expression, she thought to herself, was one she had never seen on him before; it was of raw, unadulterated rage.

Pauline slowly rolled up her window and turned to look out the windshield at the road in front of them. She stared ahead and reached over to touch Ernest's thigh. Her shoulders were tense, and she tried to relax them, to push them down and adjust her face to a relaxed bearing. She thought about JerHenry, and then pushed him out of her mind. She did not need to worry about him, and or about anything in Piggott anymore. She looked at the black ribbon of road in front of them.

"Somethin' got to be turrible wrong with a man like that," JerHenry muttered to himself as he watched the car drive away. He spat at the ground, his spittle freezing as it hit the ground. "Somethin' got to be far, far wrong." JerHenry turned and began to make his way back to the piggery. He stopped and breathed in the sharp, cold air. He looked up at the hazy winter sun, and felt a fierce, overweening fury harden in the pit of his chest.

JerHenry was unused to such strong, negative emotion, and it almost made him sick to his stomach. He stooped and picked up a stick lying on the frozen ground. He stood, shaking, and forcefully threw the stick as far and as hard as he could, with a sudden rageful ferocity.

"I know the Good Book say it wrong," he whispered to himself as he turned to walk back to his small living quarters beside the piggery, "But I swear," he muttered into the freezing air, "I swear I hate that man."

CHAPTER TWENTY-TWO

Jackson Hole, Wyoming, January 1929

The drive across the western countryside, even in their more commodious vehicle, was difficult and exhausting for Pauline. Ernest, on the other hand, despite the physical effort of long days of driving on snow-blown roads, seemed invigorated. As they drove further west, Ernest was entranced by the strange, extraordinary landscape unfolding in front of him through the flat glass screen of the windshield.

Ernest liked to drive fast, and the Model A was a car built more for endurance than for speed. He pushed it to its limit. It had blessedly been a mild winter so far, so fair that on some days, the red mercury line in the radiator cap thermometer would rise into the "too hot" zone. At those times, they would have to pull over, wait for the car to cool, and then carefully pour water into the radiator from a jug they kept in the back seat for the purpose. The first time the car had overheated, Ernest had made the mistake of trying to refill the radiator immediately and without any protection against the spouting hot water, and had gotten splatter burns on his hands. Pauline had turned away to hide her laughter.

When they finally arrived in Wyoming, both the car and Pauline were well on their way to worn out. Ernest chided her and said he felt like he did after a good, long hike, or a vigorous day of skiing. In the end, Pauline fared better than the car did; her body could regenerate, the car needed professional help.

Their first stop was Jackson Hole, where they purchased food, more warm clothes, oil lamps and oil, as well as hunting and fishing gear. They found a garage to look at the car, and after a timing adjustment and one new tire, they were ready to continue.

The couple loaded their provisions and drove east toward the Wind River Indian Reservation. Ernest located a rustic hunting camp, with log cabins by a lake. It looked like a picture on the cover of *Field and Stream*. They unloaded all their luggage and gear, and moved into one of the cabins.

The air in the Wind River Valley was uncomprehendingly clear, and the nights were so cold that they could not find enough blankets to keep them warm. Their cabin had a pot-bellied stove, and the first evening Ernest built a fire and they sat beside it, drinking wine and relaxing. After enough wine and small talk, Ernest put woolen blankets down on the floor as a pallet, slid back the grate in the door of the stove, and they lay down in front of the gently dancing flames. There were no distractions, no family, friends, overbearing concerns or worries – they had decided that they both simply wanted to try and enjoy themselves, and perhaps even each other.

Ernest and Pauline fell asleep on their pallet, and by midnight the fire had died down to just a few struggling embers. They woke up shivering, laughing, and hurriedly got up and wrapped themselves in all the clothing, blankets, hats, and gloves that were available. They moved quickly on cold stockinged feet into the bed in the corner, burrowed under the duvet, heavy with extra wool blankets. Sleep came easily, and was long.

Ernest was still working on his novel, but Pauline saw there was an ease in him that meant the book was almost completed. *A Farewell to Arms*, the book he had substantially written in the little apartment above the Ford dealership in Key West, was nearing its end. This was when Ernest was at his best: when he had produced, in final, a work that he knew was good. He exuded happiness and, strangely for him, a rare kind of contentment.

After a few days at the cabin, Ernest decided to hire some help. He did not want to spend his free time chopping and hauling wood, and he did not want to go through another night with a dying fire. He wanted to make sure there was at least a cord beside the house, and a smaller daily store inside to keep the stove going.

Ernest drove into Jackson Hole, where the manager of the hardware store suggested that a young Arapaho, Sam Blackmoon, might be of help. Ernest wrote down the name and directions, thanked the manager, and got in his car to drive out to the Wind River Reservation.

Ernest was fascinated by the Wyoming landscape. He drove slowly, drinking in the enormity of the red mountains peaked with snow, the strangeness of the buttes and mesas, the immense expanse of the grassy plains dotted with snowy rifts, and the astonishing grandeur of the Rocky Mountains. As he drove, he occasionally glanced at the written directions on the seat beside him, and soon was at the entry road to the reservation.

It was marked by only a small sign, but the arrow pointed down the road that the hardware store manager had described; Ernest was sure he was in the right place. The manager had told him that he would not be able to drive back into the reservation; even though the winter had been mild, enough snow had already fallen to make the unplowed reservation roads impassable. He had instructed Ernest to leave a note for Sam in the small wooden box nailed high on a post at the reservation entrance; the box served as the tribe's only post office.

Looking at the dilapidated, weathered cubicle, Ernest was doubtful that he would get any response from his note. And even if he did, he wondered, how was anybody supposed to get out of this snow-bound expanse? The manager had assured him, however, that the note would be delivered, and that Sam would get it and would respond. Just give him a couple days, he had said. Ernest lifted the slanted lid on the mailbox, its rusty hinges creaking, and slid the note to Sam Blackmoon in the box.

As promised, two days after leaving the note, a rider on a dappled white and gray horse rode up to the front of their cabin. Pauline heard the thud of hooves on the ice-hard ground, and opened the door to peer out at the visitor. As the horse and rider got closer, Pauline squinted into the sun directly behind them.

The bright sunlight shone through the horse's standing-cut mane in small silvery slashes. The rider wore a large-brimmed Western hat, the crown ringed with silver medallions. The glint of the medallions in the dazzling sun rays hurt Pauline's eyes. She raised a forearm to her brow, and stared, squinting, up at the rider.

"May I help you?" Pauline asked. She continued to peer up at the visitor, blinded by the strong sunlight. The rider swung a leg easily out of the saddle, and hopped down onto the hard ground. Pauline stared: it was a young woman.

The woman's face was angular, the skin pulled tightly over high cheekbones. Her long leather gloves were fringed along the forearm, and fringe circled the yoke of her deep-brown leather jacket. The woman lifted the bridle reins over the horse's head, and tied them around a low-hanging tree limb. She walked slowly toward Pauline.

"Good morning, ma'am, my name is Anita. Anita Blackmoon. I am Sam's sister." She spoke softly, precisely. "Your husband left a note, he said you could use some help." Pauline stared mutely at the young woman's weathered, pleasant features; she had not known that Ernest already hired someone, and she certainly didn't know he had hired a woman. She recovered from her momentary fluster and responded.

"Let me go get my husband, he's just inside." She turned and walked into the cabin, calling for Ernest as she entered. *Nice-looking lady*, Anita thought to herself.

Ernest appeared at the front door and strode over to Anita. Warily, he stretched out his hand.

"Yes?" Ernest said cautiously. "Who are you?" Anita looked evenly at the big man. As he spoke, his foggy breath carried a stale scent of alcohol. She proffered her hand.

"I am Anita, Sam Blackmoon's sister. Responding to your note." Ernest looked at her blankly, then laughed.

"Well," he grinned, "I guess if your brother isn't interested in the job, you'll have to do. Can you chop wood?" Anita did not respond immediately, but the corners of her mouth twitched imperceptibly.

"Yes," she said evenly, "I can chop wood. And I can do any other chores you need." Ernest hesitated, and then began to prattle loudly.

"Over there," he stammered, pointing imperiously at the side of the cabin. "I want a lot of wood stacked over there." Ernest seemed to be struggling with his instructions. "And inside, make sure there's a pile of wood just inside the front door. I don't want to have to go out at night."

He sounded irritated, petulant; his condescension toward the young woman was palpable, and the pitch of his voice increased as he continued to speak. Anita listened silently as Ernest superciliously reeled off a list of other chores.

Anita Blackmoon was accustomed to letting other people talk; with sharp-edged acumen, she had long ago learned that she found out much more about folks that way. She let the big man natter uninterrupted.

Ernest finally got to the end of his speech, which included an offer of an hourly rate. There was silence; Anita did not feel the need to respond immediately.

Ernest was discomfited. He expected new acquaintances to fawn over him, and this slight little woman, by her silence, had managed to set him off his balance. Finally, Anita spoke.

"That sounds fine to me," she said evenly. "When do you want me to start?" Ernest had expected some haggling and was again put off by the straightforward response. He blustered, attempting to assert control.

"Today, right now, in fact," he said brusquely. "The ax is leaning against the shed, over there, you can start right away." Ernest paused and searched for another directive, but he was at a loss, and found he could only reprise his earlier request. "Stack at least a cord outside this door, and put another stack just inside the door," he continued his rambling, pugnacious instructions. "Enough to keep the fire going through the night – I don't want to have to walk outside in the middle of the night to get more wood. And make sure there's always enough, I don't want to run out." His voice trailed off, rambling, repetitive. Anita waited.

Anita noted that the man had made no effort to be polite. Then she noticed the woman, still standing behind the belligerent man, squinting uncomfortably in the glaring sun. The woman was obviously embarrassed at her husband's barked orders.

Anita felt an urge to make the woman feel better. *Do not worry*, Anita thought, *I have met men like this before. They are big and full of bluster and fight, but I am not bothered by any of it.* Anita looked at Pauline and smiled. She continued her kind expression as she responded to Ernest.

"That sounds good. I will make sure you and your wife have enough wood. You can pay me at the end of each week.

And I will keep you with enough wood for as long as you are here." Without waiting for a response, Anita walked over the side of the shed, picked up the ax, and walked off into the woods.

Ernest walked gruffly past Pauline, back into the cabin. She stood out in the glistening cold for a while, feeling the incessant thud of her own heartbeat. She watched Anita disappear into the woods, and stood alone in the snow, not wanting to go back inside.

Anita was as good as her word: a neat cord of wood was stacked by the side of the house at the end of the day, and a smaller stack was piled in the wooden bin just inside the front door. That evening, Anita had smiled at Pauline as she climbed back up on her horse. She spoke evenly to Pauline.

"I will be back tomorrow, to make sure you have whatever you need." Anita turned in the saddle and rode away.

Pauline went back into the cabin and approached Ernest. He was bent over a roughhewn writing table, working on final edits to his novel. The table was placed in front of a four-paned wooden sash window; Pauline looked out through the crown glass panes at the snowy winter woods. She put her hands on Ernest's shoulders and began to massage them.

"Hey," she said softly, "we've got enough wood to get through the night, and probably several nights, easily. But Anita said she would be back again tomorrow anyway, just to see if we need anything else." Ernest shrugged off her hands and turned swiftly around in his chair. He glared at Pauline.

"Look," he growled, "that redskin is lucky to be making a few bucks from me. I'll have plenty for her to do." Pauline was surprised and dismayed at his sudden anger, his ugly epithet; she had not seen him erupt like that since they had been in Wyoming.

"Of course," she responded placidly, placatingly. "She'll do whatever chores we've got, so that you can finish the book and so that we can enjoy ourselves." She reached out to put her hands on his shoulders again; this time he let her gently rub them. He turned back to his editing, and Pauline looked out blankly at the darkening forest, and continued – slowly, passively – massaging the big man's shoulders.

CHAPTER TWENTY-THREE

Weeks passed in their small cabin with a predictable routine. Ernest spent his days editing and his solitary afternoons hiking or hunting in the woods. Pauline enjoyed the solitude of their idyll, knowing that she would have Ernest to herself on their quiet evenings in front of the fire. Anita Blackmoon was a constant reassuring presence, taking care of the never-ending need for wood, and doing whatever other chores Ernest might have for her. Anita kept herself to herself, never intruding on the couple's privacy.

Anita wondered often about the strangeness of the man and his wife: the wife seemed to dote on him, but the man was usually actively ignoring her or chastising her for something. Anita thought the wife was a pretty, pleasant woman, and it was a shame that she was saddled with such an unkind, useless husband. *But*, Anita concluded, *that is often the way: a good woman gets stuck like glue to a bad man and she cannot unstick herself. It takes some strong dynamite to break up that kind of glue.*

One morning at the end of their first month in the woods, Pauline got up early to make breakfast. She stoked the stove with wood from the box, and when it was hot, she put a cast-iron pan on top of the stove. She brought in some thick-cut bacon and several eggs out of the cold larder in the back room, and fried the bacon first, then the eggs. Pauline moved the eggs and bacon to the side, then buttered two thick slices of bread and dropped them into the vacant half of the hot pan. She flipped them, then filled two plates with the hot eggs, bacon, and fried bread.

She put the plates on the folding dining table, one plate in front of Ernest, who had sat silently watching her prepare the

239

meal, and one at her own place. She sat down in her chair and looked at him. He began to eat, slowly, appreciatively.

"Gad, this is good, Paulie." She smiled slightly at the compliment and began to eat her breakfast. "Eat up, my dear, we've got a big day ahead of us." Pauline looked up from her plate.

"What do you have planned, Ernest?" She had expected him to spend the day at his desk, editing. Ernest finished eating, and let his fork fall with a clatter onto his plate.

"Today, my wife, we are going fishing," Ernest announced. "You are going to clean and gut whatever fish you catch, and then you're going to cook it for our dinner." Pauline stared at him but did not respond. For the first time since they had arrived in Wyoming, he was inviting her to go on one of his outings. She was pleased, and at the same time, trepidatious.

Silently Pauline rose from her chair and began to clear away the dishes and put them in the aluminum washing bowl. She poured cold water from the pitcher over the dishes and sprinkled soap powder over the surface of the dirty plates. She would not wash them now, she decided; she needed to go get dressed.

They drove to a campsite near a wide bend in the Snake River. They hiked about a mile from their parked car to the riverbank. Pauline looked at the rushing water; it was so clear, a sparkling silvery blue, not like the brown, muddy Mississippi or Missouri Rivers Pauline knew from her childhood. She pulled the cold air into her lungs, and smiled. *Impossible*, Pauline thought to herself, *impossible not to feel good in this beautiful place.* She felt herself begin to relax.

Ernest set down his boxes and creels, and dropped several rods on the hard ground, along with two long cylindrical cases. Ernest had also carried from the car two sets of waders, which he deposited beside the rods. Smiling, Ernest cocked his head and grinned at Pauline.

"I'll tell you now, my dear," Ernest said, "I've tricked you a bit." Pauline turned away from the river and looked at him; she suddenly felt frightened. "Yes," Ernest continued, "you are still going to gut and clean fish, but I've decided that today you will not be a lowly baiter, but a real fisherman." Pauline stared blankly at him.

He walked over to the cases lying on the ground, opened them, pulled out the thin bamboo sections, and carefully pieced the long rods together. He attached the wide, thin reels, and handed one of the rods to Pauline. She accepted it gingerly.

The rod seemed go Pauline to have an unnecessarily oversized reel, and an odd mix of coloration and thickness to the lines; it felt deceptively light in her hands. Pauline looked at Ernest, questioningly.

"Yep," he said smugly, "Today, I'm going to teach you how to fly fish."

Ernest opened his tackle box, and took out two small flies. He handed one to Pauline. She watched him expertly tie the small fly to the end of the heavier dark green line, using a miniature pair of needle-nosed pliers to finish the knot. Ernest completed his task, then noticed Pauline still standing there with the fly in her hand.

With an impatient grunt, he pulled Pauline's rod away from her, grabbed the fly from her hand, and repeated the tying on. He handed her rod back to her, without looking at her. Then they both set down their rods and began to pull on the heavy, oiled cloth waders.

Pauline struggled with the too-long suspenders; Ernest turned her around and pulled roughly on the straps, constricting them over her shoulders. He picked up his rod and began to walk down the shallow bank.

Pauline followed him into frigid water. She felt the cold, swiftly moving current pull heavily at her legs as she tried to move forward in the cumbersome waders; she struggled to find her footing as she followed him further into the river. She hoped she would not fall. Ernest turned and brusquely told her to stop where she was. She watched while he waded thirty feet further downstream from her.

"Okay Pauline, this is what I want you to do," Ernest called back to her. He began deftly to let out line with his left hand, while beginning to slowly arc the slim rod back and forth a few feet above the surface of the water. Pauline watched, fascinated.

As Ernest's flowing movement with the rod moved higher and the long, thin rod carved increasing large swaths in the air, the line obediently crescented out further and further. Then, at the apogee of the highest swing, Ernest made a flicking movement with his wrist, and the fly flew in a graceful arc and splashed quietly onto the water's surface. He quickly began to reel in the line, his movements fluid and graceful.

As she watched him cast repeatedly, Pauline was reminded of the beautiful toreadors in Pamplona, swirling their red *capotes* with practiced ease in front of the massive bulls. Though she felt an intrinsic dislike for bullfighting generally, the toreadors had been mesmerizing to watch, and she felt the same captivation as she looked at her husband, moving his fly rod balletically back and forth over the top of the water. After several casts, Ernest turned back to Pauline.

"Come on!" he barked, "go ahead and cast, Pauline!" Startled, she stumbled slightly in the fast current, then replanted her feet on the uncertain river bottom, struggling to maintain her balance. She raised the rod slowly in her right hand and began to hesitantly move it forward and back in small, twitchy strokes. "No, no!" Ernest roared, shattering the silence of the river. "Feed out your line! Move your rod! Stop fluttering about like a cripple!" Pauline flinched at his distasteful invective.

She pulled hard on the leader line with her left hand, and began a series of ungainly, shuddering whips of her rod. The fly was soon tangled in the icy reeds at the edge of the riverbank.

Pauline stared helplessly back at Ernest. He angrily reeled in his line and began to slosh, with long furious strides, back to the bank. He pulled on Pauline's line, and snapped the fly out of the reeds.

"Get back up here," he snapped, and walked quickly back up the shallow bank to the place they had laid their gear. He put down his rod and reel and picked up one of the shorter rods. "Here!" he hissed, as he shoved the bait rod toward Pauline. She was only halfway up the bank, struggling in the heavy, cold waders. She hurried toward him. "Use this, you obviously aren't going to be able to do any kind of decent fishing." She took the rod from him sullenly, and he pointed toward the bait box. "The worms are in there. You're on your own."

Ernest marched back to the river, leaving her standing among the scattered boxes and creels. She watched him move well far down the bank before he entered the water, far away from her. She sat down on the frigid ground and contemplated the bait box.

She sighed and opened the small tin. She saw nothing but dirt. Then she stuck her finger down into the soil and began to wiggle it around. Soon she felt small, slimy wriggling, and quickly hooked an earthworm up on the joint of her finger. The worm tried to pull away, but she pinched it with her thumb. The fishhook was snagged tautly into the lowest guide hole of the bait rod; she pulled it out and poised the hook next to the worm.

Without thinking, she pushed the barb of the hook through the middle of the slippery body and watched as the worm began immediately to twist and writhe. She wondered if it felt pain, or if it felt anything at all. She pulled on the worm, straightening it, and then skewered another section onto the hook. The worm wriggled even more. She impaled a third section, then stood, the worm still struggling on the end of the dangling line. She walked to the edge of the water.

Pauline clicked the bail on the reel, raised it back over her shoulder, and cast forward overhead, as hard as she could. She heard the worm plunk loudly into the water; it was a satisfying sound. She clicked the reel handle, engaged the line, and began, slowly, to reel in.

Pauline liked the paraphernalia of bait fishing. She remembered when Ernest had first taught her to fish, back in Arkansas in the late autumn after Patrick was born, a rare moment of compatibility. She liked the simple, short rod, and the sinker attached just above the leader line of the hook, and sometimes, when the river was running slowly enough, a red-and-white bobber, placed judiciously a few feet upwards of the lead. Ernest had taught her how to look at moving water, how to figure out where to cast.

"See that, see the white-ish line on the top of the water?" He had stood behind her, left hand on her hip and right arm over her shoulder, his hand pointing at a barely discernible color shift on the water's surface. "That's where I want you to cast. There is a bridge of rocks underwater there – imagine a waterfall, but completely underwater. That's where the fish are."

He had taken her rod and had shown her where to pinch the lead sinker, and how to calculate how far above the sinker she should wind the fishing line around the top and bottom of the bobber.

Pauline had loved watching the motion of the pulsing bobber, the twitch of the minute bites on her bait. She had become proficient at waiting until the right moment, when she felt the line pulling hard away from her, pulling swiftly up on the rod, and setting the hook. She had loved the feeling of reeling in the fish, and watching it thrash and pull as she reeled in. The feeling of triumph pleased her.

Back in Arkansas, Ernest would go out early in the morning to the utility shed behind her parents' barn. He would survey the ground and then with a fierce push of his foot on the rim of a spade, he would pierce the ground, waggle the spade, and uplift a mound of earth. After doing this two or three times, he would take his big boot and kicked at the wet-brown earth, breaking it apart.

The earthworms, newly exposed, would try to escape, to wriggle back into the safety of the dank earth. Ernest would have an empty coffee can ready, into which he would have already thrown some handfuls of dirt. He would hand Pauline the can, and then begin to point.

"There, there's one, get that one, get that one." He would continue to point, and she would scramble to pick the worms out of the dirt. Ernest's eyes would dart back and forth, finding the small prey that would, just a little later, lead to bigger prey. The worms would form a wriggling layer on top of the soil in the can.

Ernest had also taught her how to bait a hook. That first time, back in Arkansas, he had circled her with his arms, moving them forward around waist. He had held the worm in the right hand, hook in the left. He had started the piercing, then said, "Here, take it, you finish." Pauline had taken the hook and worm in her hands. Ernest hadn't removed his arms from around her; he had stood behind her, hands on her hips. Ernest had watched her, corrected and commented, and eventually, the worm was skewered onto the hook in the way he had instructed.

"You want to hide the hook, all but the very end point, that's what's needed to 'set' the hook in the fish's mouth." He would examine her baiting technique, praise her, and tell her she had done it "just right." Other times he would frown, shake his head, pull the worm off and toss it aside, then tell her to start again.

Pauline had felt bad for those worms, the ones that were thrown away, because she had not baited them properly. She had wasted them. But it was only a brief thought; back then, she had been much more consumed with pleasing Ernest than with the squandering of a worm.

Now Pauline stood in the cold, alone on the Wyoming riverbank. She started, something was pulling on her hook. Warm memories of fishing back in Arkansas vanished, and she stared at the icy waters of The Snake, feeling the insistent pull on her line. She quickly jerked the reel upward and began frantically to reel in the line.

Pauline wound in the fishing line until the insistent, thrashing movement just beneath the water's surface was directly in front of her. She continued to reel and pulled the fish up out of the water.

It was small. A young brown trout, too little to keep, too little to eat. A disappointment. Pauline swung the rod to vertical and grabbed the wriggling fish tightly in her hand. She removed the hook gently from the parabola of the fibrous mouth, then tossed the little body back into the river. She sighed. She knew that her disappointment in her inconsequential catch would be overshadowed by Ernest's disillusionment with her.

CHAPTER TWENTY-FOUR

They returned to the cabin late that afternoon, just as the red ball of the sun was beginning to skim the treetops. Anita Blackmoon was there, picking up pieces of freshly chopped wood, one in each hand, and tossing them onto the chest-high woodpile, neatly stacked against the side of the house. As they pulled up in front of the cabin, Anita stopped stacking. She stood with two pieces of wood, one in each hand, and watched the car come to a skidding stop. Ernest got quickly out of the car, and slammed the door shut.

"Get the things out of the back!" he shouted, and sullenly stomped into the cabin. Anita watched him slam the wooden front door. Pauline was still sitting in the car. She looked at Anita through the windscreen; Anita stared back at Pauline, unmoving.

Pauline slowly got out of the car; Anita dropped the wood on the ground and walked toward her. Neither was sure whether Ernest had been speaking to one or the other or both in his dour directive to empty the car. Pauline hoped he had been speaking to Anita; Anita felt certain that Ernest had yelled his imperious instructions at his wife.

Anita made her way around the back of the car and twisted the cold handle of the trunk. The metal lid slid slowly back on its hinges. Anita began to remove tackle boxes, creels, waders. She pulled on the bait rods, curved to fit in the trunk. Her arms full, she carried the load toward the small shed beside the house.

Pauline felt for the flyrods in the front seat. They had ridden back with the butt ends on the floor at her feet, the tip ends sticking out of her slightly open side window; Ernest had been in such a foul humor he hadn't bothered to break them

249

down. Pauline pulled them from the car and followed Anita into the shed. Anita silently put the tackle on the wooden shelves, and leaned the bait rods in the corner. Pauline hurriedly dropped the flyrods against them. The two women did not speak. Pauline left the shed and walked, brooding, back into the cabin.

Anita looked at the corner where Pauline had dropped the flyrods. She gently extricated the two bamboo rods from the now-tangled mess. Then she walked back out to the car and located the empty half-cylinders in the recesses of the trunk, and carried them back into the shed. She broke down the fly rods, wiped them clean, and carefully replaced them in their cylindrical cases. At least, she thought, she could spare Pauline the certain wrath of her husband at her improper storage of the rods.

Anita left the shed, and quickly threw the few remaining pieces of wood on the more than fully stacked cord. She walked over to her horse, patiently waiting in the waning sunlight. The horse drew a forefoot against the cold ground and nudged her head against Anita's shoulder; she was impatient to get moving, to ride home. Anita untied the reins, and quickly mounted. Horse and rider moved down the snowy path, and Anita, uncharacteristically tense, shook her head and blew out her breath quickly in an exasperated huff.

"That man," Anita said quietly to herself as she rode away, "that man is one easy bastard to hate."

CHAPTER TWENTY-FIVE

Pauline felt a tangible transformation in Ernest. He had finished his novel, and had become more casual and relaxed in his demeanor. While she welcomed the change, Pauline remained wary: she did not want to do anything to incur Ernest's anger. She became increasingly passive toward her husband. She did not initiate conversation, and responded with quiet reticence to Ernest's words or touch.

One evening, after they were well into a second bottle of wine, they sat at the small dining table, eating their supper. Ernest had gone out by himself fishing that day – he no longer tried to engage Pauline in these outings – and they were finishing the last of the trout that he had caught. After his last bite, Ernest half-stood, reached across the table and pulled Pauline up out of her chair. He sat back down and pulled her onto his lap.

She sat inert as he put his arms around her, then he nestled his face into her hair. He raised his hand to her face, and she smelled the day on his fingers, wood and smoke and fish. She did not respond as he continued to embrace her.

"Gad, I love the smell of you. I love the smell of your scalp." He rubbed his face back and forth on the top of her head.

"I have a new shampoo." Her voice was soft, her head downcast. He continued to stroke her.

"No, that's not what I mean," he said, tersely. He rubbed his face back and forth again, rough against her scalp. "That's not what I mean at all. It's the smell of your scalp, the oils in your hair. From you – not from a bottle. That's the smell that I love." He pulled her to her feet. She stood, passive and unresponsive as he embraced her.

Later, as she lay beside him under the duvet, Pauline listened to the increasingly regular breathing that indicated he was finally asleep. She assessed the metamorphosis of their marriage. Despite all her efforts, out here in this wilderness alone with Ernest, she had become a compliant, uncomplaining wife.

In the cool dark of the cabin, Pauline tried to think of way in which she remained distinct from Hadley, but could find none. Isolated in the Wyoming mountains, she had become the submissive companion, never assertive or aggressive or demanding, only adapting, and trying to please. She had expended so much effort to get what she had wanted, and now, somehow during their time in Wyoming, she had become completely subservient, consumed with giving Ernest what he wanted. She wasn't sure how it had happened, but it had. Acknowledging the change depressed her.

Pauline had a sudden, unwelcome thought: what if Ernest, now that he would be gaining even more notoriety and income with this new book, what if he decided that he no longer wanted her? She felt cold and scared, and immediately pushed the thought away. Having moved so this far into his world, under his control, she could not contemplate that. That, she was sure, would destroy her.

Ernest moved beside her and grunted; he rolled toward her and pulled her next to him. She felt his breath on her back. Quietly, he whispered into her ear.

"It's going to be hard to leave here." Pauline stiffened, and pulled away. Although she knew that, at some point, they would have to go back, she had not asked him when or to where. And for some reason, she suddenly felt cold, and anxious.

"Do you have plans in mind, Ernest?" Her voice sounded timid, childlike. She did not like it. She cleared her throat, and spoke again, trying to put some firmness into her voice. "I hadn't thought about leaving yet." Ernest sighed, and rolled onto his back.

"Well, my dear, you are certainly welcome to stay. I need to get back to New York and work with Scribners on the new book." He paused, then continued. "In fact, I think it would be good for you to extend your stay here. Or simply to go on ahead to Key West without me. You can pick up Patrick along the way." Pauline's mind reeled. He was so lucid in his meaning; he clearly had been thinking about this for a while. Her thoughts raced to catch up.

"Key West? What are you talking about?" Her voice, while louder, now had the timorous sound of a scared child. She felt loathing for her own speech.

"Dos Passos always said the fishing there is the best in the world and, from what I remember, he's right," Ernest responded. "That's my plan, to finish what I need to do in New York, then to head south. You can meet me there after I finish in New York, or you can go on ahead by yourself. Your choice."

Her choice. He was telling her she had a choice when she realized dully that she had little. He had decided they were leaving, where they were going, and left her to the single narrow decision only as to whether she would make her move before or behind him.

Pauline felt hot and sick, and defeated. She could not put the words together to say what she was feeling or thinking. With the passage of just a few words between them, he had again overcome her. She struggled to right herself, to find a way to keep afloat through this, but she was completely at sea. Pauline hugged her knees to her chest and put her arms around them. Ernest lightly touched her thigh, but she shrugged him off.

"Let me think, Ernest, let me think." He pulled his hand away. The silence was deep, and heavy.

"Alright, Pauline." He got out of bed and walked to the table. She heard him uncork the bottle and pour a glass of wine. He sat down at the table in the dark, and drank. He did not offer to pour her a glass; indeed, he offered nothing. He was not going to provide her any comfort or solace; he had made his cast and had set his hook.

Pauline lay in the bed, silent. She was captive on the end of his line. Whether she fought and pulled and struggled, or whether she let herself be reeled along, she knew she would end up in the same place. She was to be on his boat, or in his wake, always.

CHAPTER TWENTY-SIX

It was a cold March day that Ernest left Wyoming for New York. Pauline was to drop him at the train station, then head south in the Model A sedan, driving alone, back to Piggott. Anita was at the cabin to assist with their departure and helped Pauline load the car. She offered her a quiet goodbye as Ernest loudly slammed and locked the cabin door. Ernest ignored both of them as he walked briskly to the car and climbed into the driver's seat.

"Get in!" Ernest yelled through the closed windows, and the engine strained as he revved the throttle. Pauline and Anita looked at each other and shared a brief smile before Ernest pulled on the throttle again and honked the horn.

Pauline jumped at the sound, and quickly walked around the back of the car and got in the passenger's seat. Anita watched as the car roared away, spewing ice and gravel behind it. *I am sorry for her,* thought Anita, *but I sure as hell will not miss him.* She strode over to her dappled horse, and swung herself into the saddle.

"Time to go home," Anita clicked to the horse, and they followed slowly on the snowy gravel, riding in the car's snowy-gray tracks.

On the long ride back to the reservation, Anita mused about men and women, love and hate, happiness and regret. As horse and rider turned onto the snow-covered path leading off the highway and back to the reservation, Anita spoke quietly to her horse. "One thing I am sure of," she said softly, "the woman would be much better off without that son-of-a-bitch. He is like a horse with a broken leg, it is better if you put a bullet in him." Anita shook her head, and continued the ride home in silence.

Pauline dropped Ernest off at the train station in Jackson Hole; they parted with a taciturn hug. The experience of driving by herself, she had decided, would be invigorating and fun. Since this journey had been forced upon her, she would at the very least be in charge of herself for once, even if it meant driving alone across the country.

The first leg of her trip was to St. Louis. After two long days on the road, she was tired, and wanted the comfort of a decent hotel. She got a suite at the Mayfair and decided to rest for a few days before getting back out on the road.

She called her parents and let them know where she was staying; it had been one of her father's strident requests that she at least let them know where she was on this long solo drive. After the quick phone call, and a reassurance that she was fine, Pauline made a request to room service, pulled a nightgown out of her suitcase and put it on, then gratefully lay down on the satin comforter. She closed her eyes.

Thirty minutes later, a discrete knock at the door wakened her. She sat up quickly, unsure of where she was. She looked around and remembered, *yes, the Mayfair, St. Louis, a rest from the drive*. She padded to the doorway, opened it, and gestured the bellboy inside. She found herself feeling grateful for his kind smile, his careful lifting of the food domes, and his gentle explanations of the dishes. She signed for the meal, tipped the bellboy generously, and pulled the food trolley to the side of her bed. She sat at the edge and devoured her food. It was good, and she was hungry. It was not long before she lay back down on the white satin spread and was again quickly asleep.

The shrill ringing of the phone wakened her. The room was dark; the sun had set hours ago. The detritus of her meal littered her plate, cold and solidified on the food tray beside her. Pauline sat up and turned on the bedside light, pushed the trolley away with her foot and at the same time picked up the phone.

"Hello?" Pauline answered sleepily. The windows shone black in the darkness, and the bedside clock indicated that it was three o'clock. The front desk clerk informed her that she had a transatlantic call. Pauline struggled to orient herself; Ernest was in New York, why was she getting an overseas call? she wondered.

It was Uncle Gus, calling from Paris. Pauline had heard nothing of her uncle since his enjoyable, if turbulent, visit to Paris. His ensuing silence was unusual, but she had been so consumed with the roller coaster of her marriage, she had not given him much thought. She was thrilled to get his call.

"My dear girl," the familiar voice boomed over the crackling line, "I am so glad finally to be able to hear your voice! I tracked you down to this hotel after a series of almost incomprehensible conversations with your mother. What are you doing in St. Louis? And what's this I hear about your driving, alone, across the wild, wide country? What on earth is going on?" He paused long enough for Pauline to get a word in.

"Well, I left Wyoming two days ago," she responded, "and I'm leaving in a few days for Arkansas. I'm picking up Patrick, and he and the nanny and I are going to drive to Florida."

"By yourself? You must be joking, dear girl. That's too much!" Uncle Gus sounded genuinely concerned. Pauline had become used to this during her trip. At every rest stop, every diner, she had received the same solicitous queries, and had received consistently surprised and anxious reactions to her explanation.

"Well, first, I'm not going to be by myself. We made some accommodations to address those concerns, Uncle Gus." Pauline explained that her father had already arranged for one of his workers to accompany Pauline, Patrick, and the nanny to Florida. Pauline explained that they would be traveling in two vehicles: her father's hired driver in the Model A, and the nanny, Pauline, and the baby in another newer and even more commodious vehicle, again generously provided by her father. Pauline elided over the fact that she had already driven quite a distance by herself, and still had many more solitary miles to drive.

When Pauline's father had offered help, and inasmuch demanded that she accept it, Pauline had found that it was not hard for her to acquiesce. The thought of having people take care of her, and having someone to take care of Patrick, was too attractive to reject.

Pauline and Uncle Gus chatted for a bit, and then a thought occurred to her. While she remembered how much she had liked Key West, she really did not know anyone on the island, and it suddenly seemed like a wonderful idea to invite Uncle Gus for a visit. He did not hesitate to accept.

"That's a thrilling idea, dear girl! Of course, I'll come visit you in Key West. It's one of my favorite places on the planet." Pauline was surprised to hear this; she did not know Uncle Gus had ever been to the Florida Keys. He had never spoken of it. He began to chatter about ship departure and arrival dates, and how soon he might join her in the Southernmost City.

"And, dare I ask," he interjected, "what about Ernest?" Pauline felt he had been dancing around that subject. She responded with an oblique question.

"What about Ernest?"

"Well," Uncle Gus hesitated, "I'm assuming from what you have just said that he will not be accompanying you any time soon. Will he be expected, at any future date, to present himself?" Something in his tone made Pauline think that he would be pleased if she answered in the negative.

"He'll be joining me after he visits his publisher in New York." Gus said nothing for a long minute. The disappointment in his silence was palpable.

"Well then," Gus continued, "perhaps we will have some time to visit alone together before he arrives." It was the most diplomatic comment he could make. Pauline knew that an announcement of their separation would have pleased him tremendously. And although she was not happy about Ernest's recent treatment of her, she still wanted to try to recapture his attention, to find some even keel on which they could co-exist. She hoped she would be able to do that when they were eventually together in Key West.

"Well, let me ponder on the details of this, my dear," Uncle Gus responded. "I'm not sure when I'll be able to make it, but it would be delightful to see you, and at some point, I suppose I could use a vacation." Pauline intuited that her uncle's only hesitancy was the possibility of having to deal with Ernest. The conversation ended with mutual endearments, and they rang off.

Pauline walked over to the window and looked out over the twinkling lights of St. Louis, the city where she had once been a college girl. So many parts of her had changed since then, but one had not. The acquisitive drive, the overweening desire to get what she wanted, was still deeply ingrained. In his final dismissal of her in Wyoming, she had felt that she had lost a game in her latest set with Ernest, but she was determined that the match was not over.

CHAPTER TWENTY-SEVEN

Piggott, Arkansas, March 1929

Pauline arrived in Piggott just after the vernal equinox. The first signs of spring were just beginning to show: redbud trees flushed with tiny bursts of brilliant purple at the tips of their slim branches, yellow jonquils flamed in the hedgerows, and burgundy peonies sported their first, tight buds that would soon blossom into shaggy, showy pom poms.

Pauline's reception at the farm was warm, if awkward. She pulled into the driveway, and her parents hurried down the front steps to greet her. They had been watching for her.

Pauline was struck at the similarity of the scene to that of last December: her mother smiling hesitantly, holding little Patrick forward toward her, her father standing slightly behind, apprehensive and tentative. Pauline got out of the car walked toward them. After reaching around the baby to briefly hug her mother, she looked down into the small, bright face of her son.

Pauline stared at him, self-conscious and embarrassed. She knew she was supposed to hold him, to coddle him, but she did not. Instead, she reached out timidly and patted the little infant on his head. Her mother stared at her daughter, dismayed.

"Don't you want to hold him, Pauline?" Her mother's voice was plaintive, supplicating. Pauline felt a sudden aversion to this unwanted intimacy.

"I just want to go upstairs now, Mother. I'm extremely tired." Her father looked at his daughter with disappointment. Pauline avoided any further discomfiture by quickly walking up the stairs to the front porch, inside and up to her bedroom.

At the farm, Pauline soon established a routine. She became adept at absenting herself from the family, ignoring Patrick's cries as well as her parents' overtures. Pauline found that she could, more and more easily, shut out her family; Patrick's care she entrusted completely to the nanny. Her mother was shocked but said nothing about her daughter's lack of any maternal inclination. Pauline kept to herself, waiting, until she could see Ernest again.

Pauline went down early every morning and sat along the back edge of the cool front porch, watching the pale morning sun stipple the budding trees. She would sink gratefully into a rocking chair, and let her gaze settle on the blue-painted porch ceiling. Some said the blue kept the wasps away, some said it fended off ghosts, some said it was a bit of heaven brought into the home. To Pauline, it just looked like a small portion of sky. She would sit in her rocker and wait for the sun to rise higher with the advancing morning, only moving when the sunshine hurt her eyes.

After mid-day, she would come back to the porch again, and watch the flies buzz in the hazy light as she waited for the mailman. It was not as pleasant as it was in the mornings; and Pauline would sit, irritable and impatient, waiting for word from Ernest.

Pauline was waiting for Ernest to forward his itinerary; she would schedule her departure from Piggott in accordance with his plans. If the post did not include a letter from Ernest, as it rarely did, she grew more and more restless.

Growing up, Pauline had not paid much attention to her homestead, nor had she done so on her infrequent visits back to it in her adulthood. It was, as she supposed just as a home is for most children, simply a given. It was just *there*.

Now, as Pauline sat daily on the front porch, waiting for one of the infrequent, terse letters from Ernest, she found herself with time to look around her at the surroundings she had always taken for granted.

The Pfeiffers lived in a traditional Southern home, antebellum Colonial architecture in the classic plantation style. Almost one hundred feet long, but only twenty feet wide, a large two-story central structure with long wings on either end. If Pauline stood on the walkway leading up to the grand house, she could look in the elegant double-wide front door straight through the center hallway and out the back to the garden doors that gave onto the lilac-lined veranda. The open center hall was wide and cool, and let the breezes through.

On the front of the house, broad green shutters partnered all the tall, six-over-six paned windows. A Palladian fanlight spanned the front door, with dozens of small panes that would glint in early evening sunlight. Pauline wondered about the craftsman who had built it; she thought it looked like nothing so much as a woman's splayed hands, joined thumb to thumb, a subtle feminine touch to the stately façade.

One unusually warm morning, Pauline glanced at two of the several dogs that were sleeping in the shade of the porch, already escaping the heat of the rising day. She had found herself habitually keeping company with the dogs, waiting, just as were they, for something good to come along. She had few interactions with her family or the household staff, virtually none with her baby, and she was pleased that everyone left her, for the most part, alone. She stared at the dogs and wondered if they were as bored as she was.

JerHenry came around the corner of the piggery, on his way to the henhouse. He did not look up to see Pauline on the front porch. He knew she was there, but he had found it difficult to talk with her since her return. She was different now, distant, and did not even seem to want to have anything to do with her baby. JerHenry wondered, *what that husband done to her to make her so mis'rable?* He continued his way to the chicken coop.

Pauline watched him, and then quickly descended the short set of wide steps off the front porch. She followed JerHenry's footsteps around to the back of the house. As she approached, Pauline could see him bending over, picking up several wire baskets out of a lidded metal storage bin just outside the coop. She knew the baskets would soon be filled with eggs.

"Good morning, JerHenry. How are you this morning?" Her words had an electric effect on him; he dropped a couple of the wire baskets back into the metal bin, and the sharp, loud clatter of their dropping disconcerted them both.

"Pardon me, JerHenry, I didn't mean to startle you. I just thought . . .," Pauline's voice trailed off; she didn't know what to say. She was simply relieving her boredom, finding a bit of distraction. JerHenry stared silently at her, confused and bothered. "Please," she continued, "don't let me interfere, I don't want to bother you. I'm just . . . here." Her presence embarrassed them both.

Pauline walked to the metal bin and picked up the baskets he had dropped. She handed them to him, silently, and he hesitated before reaching out to take them. He glanced shyly at her. The ease the two had had in each other's presence the previous year had evaporated, and they stood together, awkwardly.

"Thank you, ma'am. Sorry I dropped those."

"Don't be sorry at all," Pauline responded. "Totally my fault. What are you doing out here this morning?" It was an inane question; clearly, he was gathering eggs. JerHenry looked at her with the benevolence.

"Just gatherin' eggs ma'am," he said patiently. "Just like ever' mornin'." JerHenry paused, and then said, "Do you want to help?"

Pauline was suddenly overcome by the solicitude in the young man's voice; and she was disconcerted to feel tears begin to prickle behind her eyes. So few of the family or servants now even attempted to engage with her, JerHenry's offer seemed a great gift. She wondered, as she wiped quickly at her eyes with the back of her hand, what state had she come to that the trivial kindness of this young farm worker could bring her to tears?

"Well, yes, JerHenry, thank you. I'd like to help." Pauline was surprised by the softness in her own voice, and by the sincerity. At that moment, she truly wanted nothing more than to gather hen eggs. He turned and began to move casually through his usual routine, occasionally glancing sideways at his companion.

As a young girl, Pauline had hated gathering eggs on the few times she had been given the task. She had detested the unfamiliar, intrusive feeling, sticking her hand beneath the prickly-hot feathers of the pecking hens. It had felt like an almost indecent thievery.

Sometimes, Pauline would take a little stick and prod the hens up off their nests so that she could pick up the eggs without having to touch the broodies. The hens would squawk at the unceremonious removal from their roosts. When she would return to the kitchen, her little basket filled with warm eggs, her grandmother would query her, "What you doin' to those hens, child?" Pauline would ignore the question and plop the basket of eggs down on the kitchen table hard enough to express her displeasure at having been asked to get them, but not hard enough to break any. After a few of these episodes, no one bothered to ask Pauline to gather eggs.

JerHenry went about his egg-collecting with practiced ease. He carefully lifted the latch to the wood-framed wire door to the coop yard, as if he were acknowledging that he was entering another's territory. He padded up the slanted board leading from the ground up into the henhouse.

Pauline followed, bending her head as she entered the low-ceilinged coop. She watched JerHenry as he slowly, methodically gathered the eggs from the double rows of roosts. His hands were quick, and he barely disturbed the sitting hens. Pauline picked up a few eggs that were laying in already vacant roosts, and carefully deposited them into one of the baskets.

When there were no more eggs to gather, she helped him carry the wire baskets, now full, into the kitchen. They walked wordlessly, but companionably, together. It was the first time since Pauline had returned home that she felt calm, at a relative peace.

JerHenry brought out the large aluminum-lined wooden egg storage box from the side pantry, and began transferring the eggs gently into it, one-by-one. The box was used to keep the contents cool and fresh, and JerHenry positioned each one just so, inter-layering them with handfuls of hay pulled from a basket under the sideboard. Pauline watched as he performed this mundane task and was touched by the care he took with each small oval.

After he finished storing the eggs and the storage bin had been safely put back in the pantry, Pauline followed JerHenry out to the piggery. JerHenry took the same kind of care and interest with the hogs. He fed and watered them twice, sometimes three times a day, depending on when the slops were produced from the kitchen. Pauline often saw him leaning against the sty fence, softly talking to the pigs. He treated these large, phlegmatic animals with great dignity, and his demeanor with them was always calm and kind.

Pauline watched JerHenry pour out aluminum pails, heavy with slop from last evening's cooking, into the trough. JerHenry ducked into the piggery and walked over to the boiler. He stirred the bubbling pig mash with a long stick. Then he tipped the boiler on its hinges and carefully poured the swill into several of the aluminum buckets. JerHenry hauled the steaming mash over to the trough and poured it out onto the cold slops. Then he stirred the trough thoroughly with his long stick.

"Don' want them pigs to burn they snouts." He offered, continuing his stirring, shooing away the waiting pigs with gentle nudges of his foot. When he was satisfied the mixture was cool enough, he moved away, and the pigs hurried to bury their muzzles in the mash. Pauline watched, fascinated. As with the chickens, she had never bothered to understand much about the animals on the farm, and she found herself entranced with the pigs' obvious noisy gusto as they ate. They silently watched the pigs, admiring the speed and enjoyment with which they ate.

"Nothin' puts on fat like a pig, ma'am. It's good to watch 'em. Good to think about they gettin' fat, makin' some good pork pies.' He smiled at the pigs, evincing a farm hand's ingrained acceptance of the inherent dissonance: careful fostering life with the goal of ending it. They watched the pigs feed, and when the trough had been licked clean JerHenry picked up the empty pails, rinsed them out at the yard pump, and stacked them upside down outside the sty fence. He leaned over the top fence rail and began talking softly to the milling pigs.

"What are you all talking about?" Pauline asked. JerHenry stared at her self-consciously. "Uh, I'm sorry," she stammered, "I didn't mean to interrupt you." JerHenry's silence unnerved her.

It surprised Pauline that, after having felt some measure of ease over the past half hour, she suddenly felt once again so out of place, so ill at ease. She was afraid that she had embarrassed JerHenry, and she did not want the morning's pleasant companionship to end. It was clear to her that JerHenry sensed her discomfiture. "I'm sorry," she repeated, and felt ridiculous. Her continued apologies made them both even more uncomfortable. Pauline began to feel that she was even disconcerting the hogs with her stammering apologies.

She turned to walk away, and heard a small sound, not a cough, not an actual word, just an outflow of breath. Pauline was not sure if it was human or animal. She turned back and saw JerHenry looking at her.

"You want to touch one?" he said, almost inaudibly, staring stolidly down at her feet. She looked at him, startled by this offer. Pauline hesitated, and then slowly walked over to the sty fence, and stood quietly beside JerHenry.

"Thank you, JerHenry, yes, I do. I do want to touch one." Pauline's voice sounded stilted and strange, but JerHenry did not seem to notice. His attention was on the pigs and he turned to cush softly to one of the large Poland China sows, the one nearest to him. The sow looked up, and gently began to sway and lumber toward him.

JerHenry turned his head toward Pauline and without ceasing his quiet whispers to the sow, cocked his head, indicating that she could come closer.

The smell of pig was strong, dank, earthy. The sow looked up at JerHenry, and he reached his long brown arm over the top fence board and scratched the animal's large ears; the sow rolled her eyes at him and moved her head appreciatively under his hand. For a moment, Pauline was entranced at this palpable bond – they *knew* each other.

"Go ahead," he said, "You can give her a scratch." Pauline didn't move, scared that she might cause either the sow or the boy to move away. She slowly bent over the fence and stretched out her arm toward the sow's head.

Pauline was surprised at the feeling. The sow's hair was bristly and short, and the skin underneath the coarse hair was pleasantly warm. The pig jerked her head upward at Pauline's first touch, then allowed her to continue scratching, just as she had with JerHenry. Pauline felt like an interloper who had been given a rare and special privilege. It crossed her mind, *What would Ernest think of this?* but she pushed the intrusive thought away quickly. Right now, Pauline just wanted to be alone with JerHenry and the China sow.

"Thank you, JerHenry. I've never done that before."

"You grew up on this farm, and you ain' never touched a pig?" he said, and turned his face fully toward her. His tone was sorrowful, and somehow discouraged.

"No, I never did, not until just now. And I thank you for that." Again, she was embarrassed, and sad. JerHenry, had, unwittingly, shown her a bit of herself she did not want to look at too closely.

She had always been so self-absorbed, so unconcerned about those around her, and so set on looking at what she might achieve in the future, what she might be able to attain for herself, that she had missed out on much of the daily pleasantness of life and of the companionship of other people. She did not like this feeling; she wanted it to stop.

Pulling her arm away from the sow, she quickly crossed her arms in front of her chest. She took a few halting steps away from the railing, then turned and looked frostily at JerHenry. Her eyes were cold, her tone curt. JerHenry had drawn her into this scene, and its unpleasant revelation of her self-centeredness was his fault.

"Thank you," she said, and brusquely turned away. JerHenry stared sadly at her slim back as she walked back up to the big house.

"Poor woman," he muttered, "that man o' hers done really made her sad." He turned back to the China sow and addressed the softly grunting animal. "Anyways I could do it," JerHenry told the pig despondently, "I'd find a way to git her free o' that bad man."

PART THREE

~Autumn~

CHAPTER ONE

Key West, Florida, September 1930

Over a year had passed, and the Hemingways were provisionally settled in a one-story clapboard rental on upper Duval Street. Soon after her arrival on the island, Pauline had located the house with the help of a real estate agent. Although it was small, the house was near the Atlantic, and the view of the evening sunsets from the front porch was magnificent.

The car trip to Florida the previous spring, even with her father's generous assistance of a comfortable car and ample help, had been grueling for Pauline. She was exhausted by the time they had crossed the Overseas Highway and had finally arrived in Key West.

The last leg of the drive, down the narrow ribbon of coral highway, had been undeniably beautiful. But Pauline was enervated by the long trip, and had barely taken notice of the deep blue Atlantic sparkling on their right and the placid Gulf of Mexico reaching out to the western horizon. She had only stared ahead as they drove, waiting for the trip to be over. She was tired not only from the journey, but also from the incessant worries about Ernest.

Ernest had reneged on his promise to meet her on her arrival in Key West. He had explained that needed to stay in New York and negotiate the final publication details of *A Farewell to Arms* with Scribners. He had told Pauline that she should go ahead and leave Piggott with her entourage, set up a suitable living arrangement in Key West, and he would get there when he could.

Pauline had complied, and her long trip to Florida was further weighted by continuing concerns about her marriage.

When she had finally arrived, Pauline had wanted nothing more than sleep, solitude, and respite from relentless worries.

After she had moved her small family into the rental house, Pauline –as she had in Arkansas – left Patrick's care and tending completely to the nanny; she simply could not bring herself to raise a hand to care for him. And besides, once she had gotten over her traveler's fatigue, the island had offered too many delights to be distracted by the boredom of caring for a baby. In the pleasant warmth of the tropical winter, Pauline loved walking around the island, enjoying the healing sunshine, and pulling the salty air deep into her lungs. The abundant, lush tropical plants continually reminded Pauline of their time in Havana and of her first, engaging visit to Key West.

She took long, solitary walks on the island's narrow streets, and drank in the beauty and the strangeness; it was intoxicating. She walked along crooked sidewalks, asking strangers the names of all the gaudy, glorious flora she encountered – heliconia, bougainvillea, jasmine, Spanish lime, mango, tabebuia, alligator pear. She was fascinated, and enthralled.

Although Key West called itself a city, it still seemed to Pauline to be no more than a fishing village. A village that, to be sure, had its share of riches borne from the scavenging and wrecking industry, but it was small and provincial nonetheless. One obvious evidence of the wrecking wealth was the remarkable and varied architecture of the private homes on the island: the ornate Victorians iced with gingerbread and the grand Bahama-style houses were stunning. Pauline loved walking the brick-paved streets and lanes, marveling at the magnificent properties.

At the other end of the architectural spectrum, many of the houses were tiny and cramped, built in an odd style

Pauline had never seen before. The locals called them "shotgun houses," ostensibly because you could stand at the front door and shoot a shotgun straight through to the back yard, down the long side corridors off of which all rooms of these small houses ran. It seemed such an odd architectural quirk, and even stranger that the islanders seemed so proud of it.

A real estate agent had explained the zig-zagging shiny tin roofs on many of these peculiar houses: the metal roofs were required by town ordinance, the regulatory legacy of a massive fire in 1886 that had burned over sixty percent of the town. The undulating rooflines were the result of successive additions onto the back of the small homes as the occupants' families grew. Pauline thought the roofs looked like long metal snakes, baking atop the little houses in the tropical sun.

The larger two-story homes also were required to have metal roofs, and the agent had explained that some of these more elaborate homes were adorned with "eyebrows," windows peeking out from under the over-hanging second-story eaves. These overshadowing eaves were intended to keep out the intense sub-tropical sun. Although the efficacy of the design was questionable, Pauline was charmed by the look of the second story windows, winking at her as she walked the sidewalks of Key West.

Pauline also learned about "Dade County pine"; the locals were enormously proud of the use of this heart pine wood in their frame houses. It was hard, resinous, and impervious to termites, which were a constant plague in the subtropical climate. The agent had boasted about the mortise and tenon joinings in these Key West wood homes; this type of fastening, he said, was used in place of nails.

"The houses are built like ships," the agent had informed Pauline on one of her first house-hunting trips on the island.

"Ships' carpenters constructed them, and so when the tropicals come, the houses just sway with the hurricane winds, they don't splinter, and they don't collapse."

"Hurricanes," she had asked. "How often does that happen?" The agent had laughed and shaken his head.

"Well, we have our share, June through October, August and September bein' the most likely, but as you can see, these houses keep on weathering them." He was right; many of the grand Victorian and Bahamian-style homes had been built in the 1800s, and those that were well-tended looked none the worse for wear.

When Ernest had finally arrived in Key West the previous December, his appearance had been predictably stormy. He had immediately dismissed the servants who had accompanied Pauline on the long trip south. He also abruptly, and without consultation with Pauline, located a new nanny for Patrick, a local named Ada. Pauline did not complain; she was glad to have Ernest back and did not want to begin a disagreement with him over something so unimportant to her as a domestic help.

Ada was overbearing, complaining, but Pauline was unbothered by the nanny's obvious enjoyment of her authority over the baby and the running of the small household. Under Ada's critical eye, Ernest and Pauline settled into a strained domesticity.

Now, six months later, the couple struggled to deal not only with the barely concealed tension in their relationship, but also with the uncompromising, unforgiving heat of a Caribbean summer. Each day they woke to the sticky-hot air, the oppressive, unrelenting humidity. Passing relief was sometimes attainable in the shade of a front porch, a lazily moving fan, a sweating glass of sweet tea. More often than not, Ernest found respite on a bar stool at Sloppy Joe's.

Sometimes, when the mugginess of the air was momentarily relieved by a cooling Atlantic trade wind, Pauline continued with her long, rambling late-afternoon walks. She investigated the smaller avenues off well-traveled Duval and Whitehead Streets, continuing to marvel at the concatenation of architectural styles. Exploring these quiet neighborhoods, switching sidewalks to ensure she took advantage of the shade, Pauline was able to relax, to enjoy being alone, to escape from the daily strain of trying to deal with Ernest's presence.

One of these afternoons, after having left Patrick again in Ada's capable hands, Pauline went out for another solitary exploratory walk. Ernest was absent again, *probably sitting on a bar stool somewhere*, she thought. Pauline had the afternoon to herself.

She strolled down Duval Street, turned onto Catherine Street, and headed toward the small business district on White Street. She walked by colorful storefronts – a jeweler, a hardware store, a bakery – all were painted and furnished with the gaudy colors of the tropics. Pauline paused in front of a large shop window.

The colors in the extravagant storefront display were striking: bolt after bolt of brightly colored silks and cottons, piled in dazzling pyramids, in all manner of patterns. It looked like something one might find in a Middle Eastern bazaar, or in New York's garment district, or in a cramped designer's workroom in Paris. Pauline was surprised to see such a rich display of beautiful materials in this sleepy little Southern town. She must have been staring quite a while, because a woman finally appeared at the front door and beckoned her in.

"Come on in out the heat, honey," the woman drawled in the distinctive *patois* of the Key West native. She ushered

Pauline into the cool of her shop. The wooden floorboards were dark and tracked with years of service, and a large wide-bladed fan turned lazily at the ceiling. The fan moved so slowly Pauline wondered if it had been turned off and was gradually coming to a stop. But the fan just kept going at an unhurried, deliberate pace, as if it couldn't muster the energy to move any faster.

"You like fabric?" The woman smiled at Pauline, gently, kindly. It was like a drink of cool water to Pauline, after the constant latent tension with her family and servants. To have someone treat her sweetly, even a stranger, was a welcome change.

"Heavens, yes," Pauline replied, "and these are lovely," she said, pointing at the bolts of fabric. "Are you a seamstress?" She looked around the room at the numerous display tables piled high with the colorful textiles.

"*Un hunh*, when I'm not cookin' whatever fish that man o' mine brings into my kitchen ever' durn day." The woman smiled. "I'd always rather be sewin' but seems like I have to do more of everythin' else before I kin git to that. Lemme show you some more nice fabrics – I like it when someone enjoys 'em with me." She led Pauline to the back of the store, and the air was cooler and stiller back there. On long, low narrow tables there were dozens of bolts, neatly laid out and stacked. It was a treasure trove.

"My name's Lorine," the woman pronounced it "*Low-rine*," elongating the first syllable of her name into an extended, drawling "*o*." "Lorine Thompson. You new here, or you visitin'?"

Pauline hesitated, thinking about how to answer the question. She was a relative newcomer, having been on the island just over a year, but whether she was "just visiting," or whether Ernest planned for this to be their permanent home, those were questions Pauline did not have a ready answer for.

It was embarrassing not to be able to answer such a simple question. That was another thing Ernest had taken away from her: any certainty about her own future. Pauline had grown to love the island, and would be happy to stay there, but she was unsure what Ernest had planned. She had become so dependent on him, on his decision making, on pleasing his whims to avoid another fight; she felt a familiar dismay with having allowed herself to get into this position.

Lorine, graciously, did not take notice of her failure to respond to her question. She merely smiled again, and spoke companionably to Pauline.

"Let's have some tea." That was the ubiquitous balm in The South: sweet tea. And whatever else Key West was, it was southern. Pauline envisioned a tall cold glass, filled with ice cubes swimming in the cool, sweet liquid.

"Thank you, that sounds wonderful," she answered. Lorine left the shop floor and returned shortly with a tray holding two tall pretty glasses, mint leaves overhanging the edges, and a small plate of powdered sugar cookies. Two dainty white linen napkins with lacy borders hung over the edge of the tray. She led Pauline to the back corner of the shop, where there was a low coffee table and two wicker chairs covered with lively tropical print cushions. Lorine set the tray down on the coffee table.

"Please, set down honey." Lorine was so gracious, and the scene so inviting, Pauline almost wanted to cry. She had not experienced this kind of hospitality in a long time.

"Somethin' wrong honey?" Lorine bent her head toward Pauline, inquisitively.

"No, no not at all. Forgive me, I think it's just the heat," Pauline stammered, embarrassed by her maudlin reverie.

"Well, set yourself, and let's cool down," Lorine said kindly. Pauline sat down on the cool wicker settee, picked up a glass, and drank. It was heavenly. She sipped again before speaking. The glass was cool and sweating, pleasantly chilly in her hand.

"Oh, golly this is good." She sounded like a child, and indeed, felt like a child, happy in the receipt of a gift. Pauline relaxed, and looked up at the slowly-spinning fan overhead. She smiled at Lorine. "Tell me about your shop," Pauline asked, and drank some more of the cool tea. Lorine smiled and laughed.

"Well, I have fun here; it's my 'musement. And it makes a little money 'long the way. My husband and I, we both lived in Key West all our lives, and I needed somethin' more to do than be a fishwife." Pauline leaned back against the soft cushions of the wicker.

"So," Pauline continued, "you meant what you said at first, your husband is a fisherman?"

"Yes, life-long, and his father was, and our son is. Cain't get away from the *wahtuh*." Lorine emphasized the last word, pronounced in the peculiar, clipped fashion heard only in Key West. She chuckled, and the two women sipped in companionable silence. Then Lorine interjected, "Where you from honey?"

Since Pauline had not been able to tell her about her future, Lorine thought perhaps she might inquire about her past. Lorine was an acute and accurate judge of human character, and she had already determined that her guest was someone to handle gently.

"Well, originally Arkansas," Pauline responded, happy to be on a more comfortable subject. "That's where my people are, but I haven't lived there in a long time. Went to school in St. Louis, then lived in New York, and worked for a while. In

Paris I had a job, before I met my husband." Pauline paused. She supposed it sounded, to Lorine, like a glamorous life, but at that moment it did not feel like that to her. In recounting her path to this place, Pauline felt as if she had taken some as yet unidentifiable wrong turn.

"You two have children?" Lorine continued, politely.

"One. A baby boy. And Ernest has a boy from a previous marriage, but he doesn't live with us."

"Your husband name is Ernest? What's your last name, honey?" Lorine looked at Pauline, searchingly.

"It's Hemingway. My husband is Ernest Hemingway." Lorine laughed loudly at this, catching Pauline by surprise.

"Honey," Lorine laughed, "I already met him! I didn't know he was so lucky to have such a pretty lil' wife. He didn't mention that." As soon as she said this, Lorine stopped short. "What I mean is, when I met him, he wasn't in much of a condition to mention anythin'. It was just the other night, and I was retrievin' my own man from Sloppy Joe's. I caught yours in my net as well – brought them both here to sleep it off."

As each word spilled out Lorine looked more and more uncomfortable, but she was clearly not a person for whom dissembling came naturally. If Lorine said something, it was undoubtedly true. In Key West, Ernest had quickly returned to his habit of staying out late, often not returning until dawn. Now Pauline knew where he had spent at least one of those nights.

"Please, it's all right," Pauline said, trying to make Lorine feel better about her revelation. "I guess all good men drink a little too much, at one time or another." Lorine visibly relaxed, relieved that this disclosure was not news to Pauline, and that she would not make a scene about it. "It seems as if our husbands were intended to be friends," Pauline continued, "they seem to have a lot in common. Two things, at least, fishing and drinking." Lorine smiled, relieved.

"Un hunh, we call it the "Key West disease" – some people mean just the drinkin', but I mean both, fishin' *and* drinkin'. Some days I think if I told my man to choose 'tween me and the wahtuh, the wahtuh would win."

"I have no doubt about that, as far as Ernest is concerned." Pauline grinned conspiratorially at Lorine over their mutual misfortune. Then she changed the subject. "That ceiling fan up front moves so slowly, I thought it was turning off, but I notice how cool it keeps it in here. Very nice."

"Yep," Lorine answered, glad to be off the topic of husbands and their foibles. "Fans are a necessity. Don' know how they lived without 'em a hundred years ago. Perhaps the slaves fanned them." She glanced quickly at Pauline, to see if she had said something offensive to her.

"I grew up in the South, Lorine." Again, they acknowledged a mutual understanding, there really was no need to speak of their shared heritage. They were two southern-raised white women, with the mutual bond of having difficult husbands. In the privileged fact of their race, problems with husbands were more central to them than any issues of past or present social injustices. Pauline decided to like this woman.

"Say, Lorine, would you and your husband like to have dinner with us one evening?" Pauline suggested. "We haven't settled into a permanent home as yet, we're just in a small rental, but perhaps we could go down to one of the restaurants at the pier and get to know each other better?" As soon as she finished speaking, Pauline knew that she sounded over-eager; she lowered her head over her glass to hide her embarrassment. Lorine quickly relieved her discomfort.

"I'd love that!" Lorine responded. "I don' get to go out much with the old man, and I know he'd say yes to an evenin' with Ernest and you. What a lovely idea." Pauline smiled gratefully, then sipped the last of her tea and stood.

"I won't take any more of your time today," Pauline said. "This has been delightful. And I'll be in touch with you about dinner." To Pauline's surprise, Lorine stood and hugged her.

"You make sure it's not too long, girl. You've made my day. Somethin' nice for both of us to look forward to."

CHAPTER TWO

By the time the early winter had reached the tropics, Ernest and Pauline were well set in their patterns of barely tolerant co-existence. They grudgingly presented themselves as a couple, and visited often with the Thompsons. Ernest found a new set of friends, mostly fishermen, with whom he spent the better part of his days. This group referred to him as "*Papa*," as it was Ernest who usually coordinated the day-long fishing charters. Sometimes the men headed west out to the Marquesas, returning with wells of snapper, tilefish, wahoo, and Jewfish. Sometimes Ernest arranged for multi-day charters, and the group would sail out to the east to fish the waters around Bimini, in search of the big marlin and sailfish that swam the warm waters of the Florida Straits. Pauline suspected during this trips that the draw was not just the big game fish, but also the easy company of local island girls who waited on them in the dockside bars.

Ernest's periodic absences were a relief for Pauline; she could spend her time as she preferred, exploring the island. She imagined that he as well was similarly pleased to be away from wife and child. Still, on his returns home, salty sea spray crusting his clothes and hair, they both managed a strained deference toward each other, and even succeeded in producing a semblance of companionable affection to the public, if not actual tenderness.

And so it was a surprise to Pauline one February morning when she awoke with familiar feelings of nausea. *Oh no*, she thought to herself, *please God, not again*. She rose and walked heavily to the bathroom, and immediately bent over the toilet in a draining wave of biliousness. After she was sick, she rinsed her mouth and face at the cool tap and stared at herself in the grainy mirror of the medicine cabinet.

"God help me, please," she breathed. "Please, don't let this be happening again." She padded back to the dark cool of their bedroom and lay down again beside her sleeping husband. She melted into the depression in the bed, feeling desperately alone. She closed her eyes and prayed for the nothingness of sleep.

The next day, Pauline decided to take an afternoon walk, to distract herself from thoughts of a possible pregnancy. She left their house on Duval and walked toward Front Street, down toward the docks. She thought that perhaps she could divert herself by watching the funny pelicans, ever-present at the daily return of the fishing boats.

They were ungainly birds, and she liked to watch them swoop clumsily down to the water and return, often as not, empty-beaked to the pier pilings. She had almost reached the edge of the pier when a wave of nausea overcame her, so forceful that she had to lean against a fence post and put her head down. She felt faint and clammy, ready to be sick. She stood for several minutes, leaning over, waiting for the feeling to pass.

"Are you alright, ma'am?" An older tourist couple had stopped behind her, and the gentleman spoke solicitously while his wife looked on, concerned.

"Yes, yes, I'll be alright in a minute, just got a bit lightheaded." Pauline did not raise her head, and the effort of speaking had brought back the nausea. She was afraid she was going to be sick in front of them.

"It's this humidity dear, difficult to bear." It was the wife who spoke. "Can we help get you to your hotel?"

"No thank you, I live here, just back down the road." Pauline pointed vaguely over her shoulder.

"Well, we'll walk with you, make sure you get home safely." The woman took her arm, gently, and began to lead her down the sidewalk. Pauline was grateful for the support of the woman's arm.

They walked slowly, until they found themselves passing in front of a dilapidated old house. Crumbling stonework was falling down around the unkempt yard, broken windows scarred the front façade. Pauline stopped, and the older couple looked at her questioningly.

"I'm so sorry, I made a mistake," she stuttered. "This isn't my house. I mean, this isn't my house, I don't know why I stopped here." Pauline knew she sounded like a drunk; the older couple looked doubtfully at her, their expressions confirming Pauline's thought. "Really, thank you, I feel much better now, I can make my way from here." Pauline wanted to get away from them and from the embarrassment she had caused all of them. They were silent for a bit, then the old man spoke.

"If you're sure, young lady, then alright. We hope you feel better soon." She could tell that the nice old man wanted to get away from her too – *just another Key West drunk*, he was probably thinking. Pauline managed a wan smile and thanked them; the couple turned and walked back down the road the way they had come.

Pauline saw them whispering to each other after they had reached a discrete distance away from her. She tried to shake off her embarrassment and concentrated on standing up, walking straight, and getting back to her home without being sick in the street.

She finally made it back to the little house and slipped softly into an easy chair in the living room. She closed her eyes, and the dizziness returned. She opened them, and focused on one spot on the far wall, and breathed in deeply.

She blew out slowly, through pursed lips. After a while, her head cleared a bit, and the nausea abated. She closed her eyes finally, and slept, slumping in the armchair in the evening heat.

When she woke, she felt hungry and thirsty. Ernest was not at home, and there were no sounds from Ada or Patrick; Pauline wondered briefly where they might be. She went to the little kitchenette and made herself a sandwich and a glass of iced tea. She ate half the sandwich, then went back to the rumpled cushions of the easy chair.

Pauline leaned back, wiggled herself further into the softness of the chair, and closed her eyes. She was soon asleep again, and glided into dreamless, if fitful, slumber.

CHAPTER THREE

Pauline soon confirmed she was again, indeed, pregnant. She told Ernest over breakfast early one tropical spring morning, and he received the news with the stony silence. He stared at her over their breakfast dishes.

"So, you've done it again," he muttered, picking up the newspaper beside his plate and unfolding it noisily. He buttered a piece of toast, and chewed loudly as he perused the paper. He did not look at his wife.

"Well, Ernest, I can hardly say it was a sole operation," she goaded, but he did not stop chewing and reading. When she realized that he was not going to respond, she got up and left the table.

Pauline's second pregnancy, in the hot, humid climate, was more difficult than the first. She had gotten over the morning sickness with Patrick after the first three months; this time the nausea never abated. It was, at times, almost intolerable; all she wanted to do was be somewhere else, and not pregnant. She had not terribly minded the intense heat so much before; now, it was unbearable. Pauline could do nothing but sit. Any effort at all was unthinkable.

Ernest was indifferent about the pregnancy. They sat together one evening on their small lanai over cocktails, and she watched him sullenly regard her gin and tonic. Pauline had found that the tonic and lime helped to settle her stomach, and the gin provided some relief from the constant tension, irritation, and unhappiness.

"You know," Ernest said, "you had better lay off that stuff." He pointed to her glass, then tossed back the last of a large mojito. He poured yet another from a sweating glass pitcher, clinking with ice cubes and dripping with condensation in the evening heat. Pauline responded by raising her gin and tonic to her lips.

"Women in Italy and France and Greece and Spain drink all the time, all through their pregnancies," she said, and continued sipping. He responded with a grunt.

"Well, I can't stop you." He still had not expressed any comfort or support about the fact of her pregnancy, and Pauline refused to ask him for any; it was just too demeaning. If he was not going to extend any solicitude to her, so be it. She would not beg for it.

Pauline wondered again how they happened to come to this state. They had been so madly in love in Pamplona that first year. They carried the joint guilt of having broken up a marriage and deprived a son of his father's presence, they had risked public and family censure and disapprobation, and it had been, all of it, not an easy undertaking.

Once they had been so wildly passionate, now they could barely tolerate each other's presence. And in the face of what most couples would view as wonderful news, they barely had any conversation about the upcoming birth of their second child. Ernest took a long drink of his mojito. He looked around the back yard, then focused on Pauline.

"There is certainly a carousel of situations going on here," he said. She wondered what he meant, and he did not explain. Pauline pondered, briefly, if the same bug that had bitten him when they had first were together in Pamplona had bitten him again. A jealous bilge rose in her throat. If Ernest had found another woman, there would be much regret, on all their parts, and she would not endure it as diplomatically as Hadley had done. If that were indeed the case, she would find a way to make it very costly for Ernest.

Pauline continued sipping her gin and tonic, reached the bottom of the glass, and rose to mix another. Yes, *"a carousel of situations"* could certainly encompass another woman. She would have to watch and wait to see what was circling.

"Well, if you're going to get drunk Pauline, I'm going out," Ernest spat. He did not give her time to respond, just stood, put down his glass, and walked back into the house. She could hear him through the open windows, opening and closing drawers, getting dressed for the evening. Pauline knew that she would not see him again until morning. Feelings of sadness and weakness and vulnerability overcame her. She put her head down and cried.

Pauline had not wept like that since the scene on the ship, when Ernest had surprised her with the news of their Havana docking. She sobbed distractedly and unreservedly. She cried for the love that was lost between them, for the anxiety of a possible betrayal, for the pure childlike dread that came from the expectations of hurt, uncertainty, loneliness, and unfaithfulness.

Pauline finally came to the end of her tears and pulled out a handkerchief. She wiped her eyes and blew her nose. She looked up at the swaying coconut palm fronds overhead, now dark gray against the evening sky. As she watched the palms move gently in the trade winds, she suddenly felt a stab of panic. She realized with a deadening, still dullness in her chest that with Ernest, she had been all too often right in her expectations.

CHAPTER FOUR

The tropical spring turned into blazing summer, and the island was getting ready to celebrate the Fourth of July. Pauline was heavy and uncomfortable, well into the middle of her pregnancy. Although she would have been happy to stay home and rest, Ernest had decided that they would watch the fireworks that evening from the south end of the island.

There was a little restaurant – really, nothing more than a lobster shack – on Dog Beach, with a rough plank bar and an accommodating bartender; Ernest had decided they would walk down there to find a spot to watch the display. They left the house around nine o'clock and walked down Duval Street. Pauline moved slowly, heavily. Suddenly she stopped in front of a house along the way and buried her face in a trellis full of night-blooming jasmine; the smell was intoxicating.

"Ernest, stop a minute." He had continued to walk ahead of her but came back at this request. "Put your head down here – smell this." She pointed to the small white flowers. He looked at her, and she thought perhaps for a minute he was irritated at her, at the interruption in getting to their destination.

Ernest prolonged his gaze for one more second, then dropped his head not to the flowers as she had requested, but to the back of her neck. He lifted his head and placed his hands at the juncture of her neck and shoulders and squeezed roughly. He ran his fingers through the back of her hair. Then just as quickly, he released her, withdrew his hand, and put his fingers to his nose.

"Yes," he said, "it smells delightful," and began to walk quickly away down the street. She was disconcerted, but not unsurprised, at Ernest's antics. She paused, and then hurried as best she could to catch up with him.

Ernest had a habit of reaching an arm behind him, without looking back, to grab her hand as they walked. He did not have to look; he knew she would be there. Ernest reached and grabbed, and, as always, Pauline's hand was there. They proceeded down the street, toward the ocean.

They turned left onto United Street and walked along the small, shaded lanes toward Dog Beach. At the lobster shack, they moved through the patrons already seated at tables and went to the bar window the back of the lean-to restaurant. Jimmy, the bartender, looked out through the window and greeted Ernest with his usual gusto.

"What'll it be tonight, Ernesto?" Jimmy smiled at Pauline and reached out to shake Ernest's hand. After the usual pleasantries, ordering and negotiations – Ernest always made a production out of ordering drinks – they picked up their glasses and walked down to the beach.

They walked north a bit, toward some empty chaise lounge chairs, abandoned by sunbathers earlier in the day. Technically, this spit of sand was not public – it belonged to Henry Flagler's famous Casa Marina hotel, but Ernest was not one to care much about respecting another's private property. And they had the beach to themselves; the Casa Marina guests were all congregated in the resort's ocean-side atrium, enjoying the pool, the bar, and a lavish holiday banquet. Ernest and Pauline could barely hear the party: the murmur of the hotel guests' revelry was dimmed by the waves and wind.

Ernest led Pauline over to the two empty chaises, turned them toward the western sky, and swept his arm over the nearest chair, indicating that she should sit. Pauline wondered whether they would get kicked off the beach, but did not care.

It did not matter to her if some hotel staffer wandered out onto the beach and tried to take on Ernest. It would never be a fair fight.

They sipped and watched the sky and waited for the residual sunlight to leave the horizon. Ernest left at one point to procure a couple more drinks. She lay on the chaise, drew in the sand with the fingers, and lazily felt the calm presence of the ocean slide over her.

Pauline did not think about much of anything: not her child, her pregnancy, not even Ernest. She focused on the ocean breeze on her skin, the sea-salt smell in her nostrils. She pressed her back against the canvas of the chair, and eased her muscles into relaxation. Ernest reappeared with the drinks and stood over Pauline, staring down at her.

"Gad, you are still beautiful, Pauline." Even when he made it clear that, in the moment he might detest her, he still indulged himself in her unusual beauty. He did not hand her the drink, just continued to stand and stare at her. She looked up and smiled at him, but he was not smiling back, just staring at her, inspecting her. She looked back out over the ocean; she had grown used to his unusual habits. She knew simply to remain silent and wait for him to act on whatever was on his mind.

Ernest ran his eyes over the entire length of her body, pausing to look at her swollen belly. He bent over and set both their glasses down in the sand, screwing the bottoms hard into pressed little circles to ensure they did not fall over. She set her empty glass down beside her. Ernest reached down and put his hands under her arms, high up on her ribcage. He lifted her, rather than waiting for her to stand, and then he put his arms around her.

"Ernest," she started to protest, but he silenced her with a kiss. He pulled her gently toward the shoreline. At his urging, soon all their clothes were on the sand, and they walked slowly into the ocean, warm as bath water, gently lapping around their legs. He pulled her out further so that they were chest-deep, and embraced her tightly.

It was easier for her to walk in the buoyant water. They stood swaying in the ocean waves, and soon they saw the fireworks bursting directly overhead. They watched from the warm, salty surf until the last fiery chrysanthemum exploded.

When the fireworks were over, Ernest took her hand and pulled her back up to the beach. They walked back to the place where their clothes lay in a heap on the wet sand. Ernest motioned for her to stand still. She watched him walk several feet away to a small dark pile on the beach – a towel abandoned by a tourist earlier in the day. He picked it up and flapped it harshly in the wind several times, sending sand spray into the gentle shore wind. He came back and wrapped it around her. While she dried and dressed herself, Ernest put on his own clothing. He kissed her again, and they made their way back to the stolen chairs. Ernest reached down and picked up their now-warm drinks and handed Pauline her glass.

"Let's make a toast, Mrs. Hemingway," he said, smiling. Pauline smiled back, wondering what he would choose to celebrate: the beautiful evening, the romantic sunset, the ocean swim, the upcoming birth of their second child. Perhaps, she dared hope, he might even toast her, her beauty, his love for her.

Ernest leaned over and pecked her briefly on the cheek, and she held her breath, waiting. Ernest then quickly pulled away and clinked his glass on hers.

"Chin, Mrs. Hemingway. Here's to the Fourth of July."

CHAPTER FIVE

For Pauline, the only respite from the physical and emotional weight of her unwanted condition was the upcoming arrival of Uncle Gus. His trip had been much delayed, and Pauline wondered whether his business had detained him, or whether he had simply demurred at the thought of having to spend time with Ernest. Either way, it did not matter. He was coming, and she could look forward to his affection and his pleasant company.

On the day of his arrival, a windy fall morning, Pauline walked down the narrow brick streets of Key West to Garrison Bight. She remembered Uncle Gus' arrival in Cherbourg and mused as to whether he would be hungry when he arrived this time, as he had been then.

It was a pleasant September day, and Pauline sat at a dock bar, drinking gin and tonics, heavy in the later months of her pregnancy. She watched the dolphins breach the surface of the water and show their backs to the morning sun. Pauline thought, for just a moment, that Uncle Gus would probably disapprove of her drinking so early in the day, particularly since she was pregnant, and she briefly considered finding peppermints to conceal the alcohol on her breath. She quickly abandoned the idea.

Drinking had become a habit, even while she was pregnant, and she did not think that hiding it would be either useful or successful. Gin took the edge off everything, and she welcomed the relief. Of course, it also dampened any happiness she might feel, but she easily accepted that trade-off.

Pauline had seen the large ship drop anchor out in the deep harbor in the Gulf earlier in the morning, and had watched the deck hands run around like ants as they readied the passengers and their trunks for off-loading. The bight was too small for a ship this large; several smaller ferries would transport the passengers to shore. It was a daily, entertaining event, and the locals often spent their mornings watching the ships come in, whether or not they were waiting for an arrival.

On this bright, warm morning, the sea gulls and pelicans were fighting for turf over a school of mutton snapper. Pauline enjoyed watching the birds plummet to the sea and rise again, sometimes with the wriggling fishes in their beaks. She wondered if they ate in flight or settled somewhere to ingest the meal. She guessed that sea birds did not really care whether they enjoyed a meal or not; they just wanted food.

Then she wondered, ever so briefly, *do I care if I enjoy what I get, or do I just enjoy getting it?* She had gotten a child, was soon to have another, and she had an increasingly famous husband, but she certainly had found little joy. Perhaps, she thought as she tossed some bread out to the birds, she only enjoyed the getting, not the having.

Soon a flat-bottomed john boat carrying passengers appeared around the end of the weather-grayed pier; their luggage was in a second john following close behind. Uncle Gus was sitting in the bow of the first boat, smiling broadly and looking straight at Pauline. He had spotted her before she had seen him. He raised his hand and waggled a few fingers – a feminine gesture that would have made Ernest scoff. Pauline waved her arm in the air like a semaphore flag; she was happy to see him.

Watching Gus disembark from the rocking boat was funny and engaging. He stood precariously, moving erratically from one foot to another and looking as though, at any moment, he might tumble into the sea. At the same time, he seemed as if he did not really care. He kept on giving instructions to the ladesmen, who studiously ignored him. He waved intermittently at Pauline, and gestured at the swooping birds, which seemed to fascinate him. She almost broke out in laughter, but she was afraid he might hear and be offended. Uncle Gus was one of the few people who could pull her better angels to the fore; Pauline genuinely wanted to be kind to him and make him feel welcomed.

After numerous attempts, they finally got Uncle Gus and all his expensive, tooled-leather luggage loaded onto the dock; more than his fair share of the lade in the second john turned out to belong to him. Uncle Gus looked at Pauline, hands on hips, and then grasped her in a bear hug.

"You look marvelous!" he said softly into her ear as he swayed her back in forth in a warm embrace. He let go of her, and surveyed her, head to toe.

"I have to admit, I didn't hold out much hope for this marriage, but it is clearly agreeing with you – and I see you've gained some weight, *Ha!*" He smiled and patted the side of her bulging belly. Pauline was pleased with his comments and was awfully glad that he was not starting out the visit with the expected negativity toward Ernest. Remembering the horrid boxing scene back in Paris, Pauline wondered how much of his warranted antipathy toward Ernest might possibly have faded with time. She realized with a pang that hers had only increased.

They finally got all of Gus' belongings off the dock and into a waiting taxi. Pauline had reserved a room for him at the La Concha hotel, and she told the cabbie to head there.

"I think you'll like this hotel, Uncle Gus, it's the tallest building on the island, and there's a delightful bar on the roof. We can watch the sunset from there." They drove through the dockside lanes, and quickly found themselves on Duval Street. The cab pulled into the shaded, iron-gated entranceway beside the hotel. They moved slowly in the increasing heat, disembarking the cab and paying the driver, who began carrying all of Uncle Gus' many bags and parcels into the hotel lobby.

"Good heavens, Uncle Gus, you look like you brought half of Arkansas, New York, and Berlin with you," she chided him, gently. He grinned sheepishly, and they followed the taxi driver into the lobby.

"Well, I do have a few little things for you," he murmured in justification. The bellhop appeared and began the process of getting Gus' bags loaded onto a brass trolley, which he then wheeled across the high-ceilinged lobby to the elevator hallway. The bellhop stood beside the trolley and waited. Uncle Gus' handsome leather shoes tapped on the white marble floor as they walked over to the registration desk.

"First thing we're going to do is get you some island shoes," Pauline said. "You can't wear Oxfords here – too hot, and you look like a German tourist with those heavy shoes and black socks."

"Well, I guess I am a German tourist," Gus laughed. "I spent quite a while in Berlin this past year. And I do have an awful lot of black socks." He paused and pointed toward a tourist relaxing in a wicker lounge. "Not sure I can wear those flippy floppy things," he said, pointing at the man's open-back *huaraches*, "but perhaps I could attempt something a trifle less formal. And maybe some colored socks."

They were both laughing now, the desk clerk smiled at them. It made Pauline feel good to banter with Uncle Gus like this, without the hidden agendas or double meanings that had become ubiquitous in her conversations with Ernest. She felt, for just a moment, like she was a young girl back in Arkansas, beloved by her favorite uncle. What surprised her was the

300

momentary sadness that feeling caused. She checked herself and turned toward the desk clerk.

"My Uncle is checking in," she said briskly to the clerk. "Perhaps you could help him; I'm going to go take care of a few things." Uncle Gus stared at her, wondering at this change of expression in her. "I'll come back and pick you up in a couple hours," Pauline said to her uncle, "and after you've settled in, and we'll look around the town, and find someplace nice to have lunch." Gus remained silent, then nodded his head.

"Okay, sugar, whatever you'd like. I'll see you in a little while." Pauline turned, and left the cool marble lobby, staring sadly at the sleek white floor as a she left.

CHAPTER SIX

Gus was an engaging man, and people were naturally drawn to him. Pauline certainly had an awareness of his sexuality, but it did not matter to her. Although the Catholic church's teachings were unequivocal – and harsh – on the subject, she had grown up with enough kindness toward her uncle not to have cared much about that sort of thing.

And in Key West, it simply did not matter. There was an acceptance, a freedom, a feeling that it was just alright to be whatever, whoever you were or wanted to be. Pauline thought that was why the island drew so many artists, writers, and iconoclasts. It was a wonderful place to be accepted, and a wonderful place to be yourself.

Pauline was grateful that, even though Uncle Gus was not enamored of Ernest, still he had made the effort to come to Key West. Despite his first encounter with Ernest in Paris, when he had rescued Man Ray from being beaten to a pulp in one of Ernest's ridiculous living room boxing matches, Uncle Gus still would endure him to be with her.

And while she was happy for his visit, she suspected that her uncle might have other motives than familial loyalty. She had an idea that Gus was perhaps searching for a refuge, a haven where he could be himself, and enjoy friends with similar appetites.

Shortly after his arrival, Uncle Gus became her tour guide. Pauline was surprised to find out how many friends he already had on the island. It was a ready-made social circuit for them, a lively, entertaining, and welcoming group.

While Ernest wrote every morning, and drank away most of the afternoons, Pauline and Gus slowly wandered the sidewalks of Key West, stopping often so that she could catch her breath. She was heavily pregnant and uncomfortable, but she still enjoyed exploring odd little shops with her uncle and drinking afternoon cocktails with his friends at the local cafés. They talked about locating a permanent home for the family, and explored the varied Key West architecture, looking for a suitable property.

One evening, just after Ernest had left them to make his habitual appearance at Sloppy Joe's bar, Pauline and Gus decided to take a stroll to watch the dusk fall over the island. The streets of Key West at twilight were beautiful. There were pretty homes to look at – the old Victorians and Bahamian-style houses built with wrecking money, edged with elaborate gingerbread and adorned with fresh paint against the tropical storms. There were always new and different plants to wonder at; the abundant plant life was like nothing that grew in temperate zones, and it was always delightfully surprising to Pauline to find a new flower or tree. They walked along a tiny lane, and Pauline suddenly looked up.

"Look," she pointed, "a Spanish lime tree." Pauline reached down and picked up several of the small, round green fruits and offered one to Uncle Gus. "Break it open, like this," she demonstrated, "and then pop the inside part into your mouth." Uncle Gus warily complied, and the two stood in the lane, sucking the tart, sweet, soft inner fruit around the marble-sized pit. Pauline was pleased at the response: Uncle Gus' face broke into a wide grin as he rolled the large ball around inside his mouth.

"It'th good," he lisped, and they both laughed. They spat out the pits on the ground and continued their stroll. Pauline was quietly proud to be able to show her uncle various trees and flowers on the island, and speak knowledgably about them. As they walked by a tall, weeping tree, heavy with pendulous orange fruit, she explained that it was a "stink fruit" tree, the plum-sized orange *tiesa* that dropped its heavy brown fruit to the sidewalk. The fruit would get squashed underfoot to bake and then stink in the tropical winter sun. She explained to Gus that the locals made a creditable facsimile of pumpkin pies with it. They passed Barbados cherry trees with sour blood-red fruit, tiny bright red cherries that puckered the mouth. They were almost all pit, but delightful when boiled and made into sweet teas or jellies. They continued their walk, entranced by new vistas at every turn.

They turned onto Whitehead Street and headed toward Mallory Square. They had started their walk on upper Duval, on the Atlantic, and they were headed down to the other end of the island to see the sunset.

Key West sunsets were like nothing Pauline had ever seen, and she never tired of watching them, the brilliant reds and oranges splaying upward across the southern sky, the semi-circle sliver of the sun becoming brighter and smaller as it lowered over the horizon. Some evenings, the last rays of the sunset even set off an incandescent green glow. It was unspeakably beautiful.

Suddenly, Pauline looked up at a derelict house on her right. She paused and stared: it was the same house that she had stopped at the afternoon the older couple had tried to walk her home, thinking she was just another island drunkard. Pauline ignored the memory in her excitement at seeing the aging mansion.

"Look!" she said excitedly, pointing at the house. "Look at that Uncle Gus!" Gus stared into the yard, at the tumbling down, dilapidated, ancient two-story limestone house, paint peeling, windows broken, shutters hanging askew. The vegetation was overgrown and ragged, and the yard looked, from the residue of trash she could see, as if it had hosted a few squatters. Indeed, there were small black circles in the grass where itinerants had built fires, for cooking or for warmth. To Uncle Gus, it looked as if it were the perfect setting for a ghost story, but other than that, he was not impressed.

"Not sure what you're excited about, my dear, unless you think you've found a haunted house," he said. Pauline stared at the stately, if dilapidated mansion, not sure what precisely about it intrigued her.

"You're right, I guess," she said, still staring up at the broken-down ruin. "It's a mess." They slowly walked away. Pauline glanced back over her shoulder several times to look again at the ramshackle property.

That night, she dreamed of Piggott.

CHAPTER SEVEN

The baby came in early November. Pauline welcomed not so much the new child as she did freedom from the physical burden of pregnancy. She was relieved to quickly hand off the care of the new infant to Ada. Then, as soon as she had recovered from the delivery, she renewed her search for an island home. She wanted to try and persuade Ernest to live on the island permanently. She contacted the land agent who had helped her locate the rental house and asked for a list of suitable properties.

Pauline worked assiduously to narrow down the choices, and soon settled on a likely possibility. She could not wait to show Uncle Gus her discovery; he was planning on going back to Arkansas soon, and she wanted to show him her diamond-in-the-rough before he left.

"Surely, you don't mean this is your surprise?" Uncle Gus gazed incredulously at Pauline as they stood one sunny morning in front of the old house at 907 Whitehead Street. It was the same broken-down house that had captivated Pauline on their earlier walk.

"I talked to the house agent last week, Uncle Gus," Pauline smiled broadly, excited to show her uncle her find. "The agent that's listing this house. I told him I wanted to surprise you and show it to you, it's amazing. I've already gone inside and looked around," Pauline paused to catch her breath. She beamed. "Wait until you get inside, Uncle, you'll see what I mean."

The words spilled out of her as she pushed open a creaking wire fence gate. Gus followed her gingerly, stepping carefully over gravel and broken concrete, as they walked up the crumbling path to the front porch.

The porch was wooden, and had been, at one time, painted dark green. Now the paint, what was left of it, was peeling, and there were gaping holes in the floorboards, weeds sprouting up through them. Uncle Gus stood, mute.

"This is it? The haunted house?" he asked, bewildered. "I must admit, I was expecting a better surprise than this." Pauline grinned at him.

"Wait until you get inside, Uncle Gus," she repeated. "You're going to be amazed!" Pauline took a large skeleton key out of her purse and began to work at the ancient door lock. "It's a little sticky, just needs some oil, I think," Pauline muttered as she struggled with the key.

"I think it needs some dynamite," Uncle Gus said softly, under his breath. "How are we supposed to get inside without breaking our legs?" Pauline smiled, and laughed as she heard the lock click. She turned the knob and pushed the heavy door open into the dark foyer. Pauline turned and took her uncle's hand.

"Just step where I step, you'll be fine." They navigated their way into the dusky interior, Uncle Gus stepping tentatively on pointed toes behind her. Once they were inside, they both turned around and gazed back at the huge front door. The wood surrounding the lovely fanlight window at the top was moldy and rotting. The channel windows on either side of the door were cracked or missing. Pauline was unfazed, she turned around and pointed excitedly upward.

"Look!" she said, "Look at this!" she laughed. An elegant, narrow staircase rose directly in front of them, piercing through the falling plaster ceiling to the second-floor hallway above them. The entire entryway was open a full two stories, and the beautiful, if battered staircase pulled the eyes upward.

The antique wooden moldings, floor and ceiling, were heavy, ornate. They had suffered from years of over-painting, and more recently neglect, but their original elegance was still evident. Pauline felt her uncle staring, intrigued, at the soaring stairs.

"It gets even better," Pauline said, pulling on his hand. "Come this way." She led him through a large, high doorway to the right, into the front parlor. The room was girded with four huge arched windows, almost floor to ceiling, each of which was surrounded with the same heavy, ornate molding. Plaster had fallen off the walls and ceiling in large chunks. Shards of the horsehair sheathing had dropped in jagged pieces, and were scattered all over the heart pine floor. Even so, it was obvious that the room, while decaying and dilapidated, had once been a grand salon. The high, soaring ceilings, though now crumbling and falling down, were evidence of a gracious and opulent past.

"There's more," she said, pulling him through a large pocket doorway into yet another room. They continued around the first floor, each room reminiscent of a former elegance. The house was in a decrepit state, but Pauline was entranced, imagining the splendor of the once-grand home. Her enthusiasm began to affect Uncle Gus.

"OK, I see what you mean," he said. "This must have been quite a mansion at one time, Pauline." She smiled.

"Yes, it was. It was built in 1851, and the walls are constructed with the limestone dug from the foundation – sort of like turning a sock inside out." She turned in a circle, staring, eyes alight. "There's a huge basement – not something they do here, because it's like digging through solid rock," she continued, raptly. "Can you imagine the labor – probably slave – that went into tunneling out that stone, then lifting each huge limestone block into place to make the walls? Two stories of it. Gorgeous." Pauline seemed lost in time, staring at the moldering walls, deep in enjoyment of the idea of this majestic estate.

"It was built by a wrecker, a very prominent man," she continued. "This is, by all that I can see, one of the finest homes on the island – or once was. No hurricane is ever going to blow this place down – it will be here when all of us are dead and gone."

Pauline's enthusiasm was infectious, and she could tell something about the house had begun to capture Uncle Gus; as they continued to explore, his expression began slowly to transform from skepticism to charmed enchantment. They walked through the first floor again, then made their way up the towering staircase.

"Watch where you walk, Uncle – the floors are mostly solid, but there are lots of boards that will need to be replaced. Come this way, and be very careful." Pauline led him cautiously up the stairs, into one of the upstairs bedrooms, and finally out a double French door onto a wide, sloping upper-level porch. They looked out over the iron railing, and Uncle Gus gasped.

The yard, which at eye level seemed to be a mass of overgrown weeds, was a hidden tropical beauty. From this vantage point, it was possible to envision the lush oasis that this garden had once been. They stood silently looking at the overgrown grounds.

Pauline looked past the drowning pothos that strangled even the largest trees, the Royal Poinciana, African tulip, mahogany, tamarind. She had become familiar enough with the island flora that she could pick out crimson splashes of heliconia, orange bursts of hibiscus, and pink, lavender and burgundy sprays of bougainvillea. It was a joyous riot of colors and scents.

"There's a full acre of this, Uncle – the largest residential lot on the island. This could be made into a paradise." Pauline took his hand and they stood, silently, just staring, taking it in. "This is a house I could live in for the rest of my life," she said quietly.

"Is that what you're thinking?" he asked. "You want to buy this house for yourself? For you, and Ernest, and the little ones?" Pauline nodded. He looked around at the peeling paint and falling plaster. He turned slowly toward her and smiled at his niece.

"Well," he said softly, shifting his gaze in a smooth arc over the garden, "if that's your intent, and you clearly seem set upon this, then let me help you." Pauline stared at him, stunned. He continued. "I know it will be a huge effort, but really, Pauline, I can see that once you have gotten your grit into this, there could be no finer house on the island." Gus stopped talking, but kept turning and gazing downward. "Yes," he said finally, almost to himself, "with enough money and expertise, you and I could make this into a paradise." Pauline stared at him intently.

"You mean you want to live here with us?" she asked. The sharply focused question jerked him out of his reverie.

"No, no . . . of course not," Gus stammered. "I'm just thinking out loud. Once properly renovated, it's a house I could live in, so I know that you would be happy here as well. And it has stood for over eight decades. I believe it will stand for many, many more." He turned and looked at her. "Please let me do this for you Pauline. It would make me very, very happy to give you this. And to know that you will be safe and secure in this beautiful place, for the rest of your life."

For the rest of her life. She had not been able to answer Lorine's question about what their plans were, but Uncle Gus' incredible offer provided a pathway to a response. They made their way slowly back downstairs, and out onto the ragged front lawn.

As they walked, Pauline wondered, briefly and ungenerously, if her uncle's lavish investment also carried with it a benefit to himself. Pauline knew that he didn't care for Ernest, and it fleetingly crossed her mind that Gus might be imagining Ernest could one day out of the picture, so that Gus could enjoy this home as well, in a city that he loved. The climate in all ways suited him, and the scheming part of her brain made this easy for her to imagine.

But Pauline pocketed the thought away; Uncle Gus was sincerely offering something supremely generous, big-hearted. It was not right of her to ascribe ulterior motives to his actions. He simply loved her and wanted to give her an elegant home. They stood together in front of the house, and Pauline put her arms around him and embraced him firmly.

"I can't believe you are being so generous, and yes, if you'll help me, of course I could make this into a grand home again. But it will take a lot of work, and a lot of time. How will we manage that, practically?" Uncle Gus smiled at her, appreciating that she seemed to be seriously entertaining his offer.

"Well," he began, "I've got a business to run, so I won't be able to be here with you as you do the renovations. I'll take care of the initial investment and provide you with the funds you're going to need to fix this place up." He glanced appraisingly around him again. "And I will leave all the particular choices as to how things should look in the end to you. You have impeccable taste, my dear, and I trust you implicitly." Again, he was speaking of the house in a dual fashion, both as a gift and proprietarily. Gus seemed to intuit Pauline's thoughts. "This will be your house," he said reassuringly, "and yours alone, Pauline. If you agree to take this on, I would plan to title it solely in your name."

"Uncle Gus, I don't know what to say," she stammered, and looked up at him.

"Just say yes, my dear. Just say yes." He held both her hands in his, brought one of them to his lips and kissed the back of her hand." She hugged him, then stepped back and surveyed her uncle. Pauline made a decision.

"Yes!" she said excitedly. "Yes, yes, and yes!" They embraced again, then turned to survey the dank walls of the house behind them.

"You will turn this place into a mansion of light and beauty and elegance, Pauline. Nothing could make me happier than to help you do this."

"Thank you, Uncle Gus," she said, softly. "Thank you. No one has ever done anything this kind, this generous for me, ever. Thank you." She felt tears spring into her eyes, and she quickly brushed them away.

It struck her with the force of certainty that this was absolutely the right house for her, and then, a nanosecond later, Pauline wondered if perhaps she had not chosen the house, but rather –like the island itself – it had chosen her.

313

CHAPTER EIGHT

When Pauline had finally worked up the nerve to tell Ernest that she had found a house, that it was badly in need of restoration, and that it was going to be purchased as a gift from Uncle Gus, she had expected fireworks. Instead, as he often did, he surprised her.

"Well, quite a development," he said, over the top of his evening Negroni. The clear red drink swilled in the glass, and he stirred it with the tip of his finger. "Sounds like something just up your alley. You and Gus will have a fine time playing at fixing up a dollhouse." He managed, with just a few words, to convey his condescension toward Gus, toward her, and toward the undertaking of renovating the old house. But neither was he fighting it, or her. Pauline did not tell him that the house was to be titled in her name only; she did not want to pull the tiger's tail. That bit of information could be revealed later, if ever.

"We can stay in this rental until I get the basics done," she responded. "I'm thinking that will be about a month. Then, once we're in, I can do the rest of the renovations, well, sort of around us." Pauline continued, briskly. "We'll need the essentials – bedroom, kitchen, common living area, the plumbing and electricity will eventually all have to be re-done, as well as complete plastering and painting. And I have some ideas about removing a pocket-door wall between the first-floor parlor and back sitting room, making one large, elegant room." Ernest continued stirring his drink, staring into the top of it.

"Sounds like you're fairly well on your way to doing this. Let me know when I can move in." He stood, threw back the rest of his drink, and turned toward the doorway. "I'm going

315

down to Sloppy Joe's. I'll see you later." He turned and, without a further word, left.

Pauline had recovered quickly after the new baby's birth, and over the next few weeks she threw herself into overseeing the minimally necessary renovations required to move into the dilapidated mansion. As usual, she left all responsibilities for care of Patrick and the baby to Ada.

Pauline was consumed with a new passion: she promised herself that, eventually, she would turn this crumbling estate not into just a livable, but a notable dwelling, destined to become one of the finest private homes in America. She didn't have time to think about her children, or her husband.

Just before Christmas, when enough of the first-floor interior was habitable—sufficient for camping out—the Hemingways, Ada, and a newly hired caretaker, Toby, moved into 907 Whitehead Street. The complete renovation would take another two years. There would be rebuilding floors and walls and staircases, refinishing and re-hanging the antique doors, re-glazing and painting the numerous tall delicate windows. But by late December enough had been accomplished – a temporary bathroom, a small kitchen, and cot beds spread out on the living room floor – so that at least they were inside, living in their new home.

Surprisingly, Ernest's demeanor toward Pauline seemed to soften slightly after they moved into the house. Whether due to her now-concluded pregnancy, or to all the effort she was putting into the renovations, he seemed to moderate his words and actions toward her. She noted it and responded with gentler reactions to him.

The first night in the house, Ernest woke Pauline from a sound sleep, and jostled her until she was fully awake. "Come with me," he said, and pulled her by the arm out of her cot bed.

He led her carefully up the staircase and pulled her toward a small closed door in the second-floor hallway.

The door led to the rooftop. It took a minute or so of wrangling with the old lock before he could get the door open; finally it swung creakily out into the hallway, and Ernest started up the ladder stairs. Pauline hesitated, and then followed him. He turned around, halfway up, and said entreatingly, "Come on." He urged her upward.

Ernest climbed the narrow wooden steps, and she followed with effort, careful not to hit her head on the low rise of the roof. He turned around to offer his hand as she ascended, and when she emerged through the roof door, she caught her breath. She knew why he had brought her here.

The moon was a huge, glowing disc in the midnight blue sky. Pauline stared at it, enraptured. From their rooftop vantage, it seemed like the moon was just a few feet away; she felt almost as if she could reach out and touch its silvery, cool burn. Ernest encircled her with his arms, and she leaned into his chest. They stared silently at the lustrous night sky.

He separated from her and walked over to the south edge of the flat roof. Pauline smiled when she saw what he was doing: Ernest had, sometime earlier in the evening, set up a little table on the rooftop, covered it with a silk scarf, and set out two glasses and bottle of champagne on ice. She watched as Ernest uncorked the champagne, sent the cork flying over the lawn, and poured two bowls. Ernest walked back to Pauline, and handed her a glass. She smiled at him.

Ernest tipped his champagne bowl, and poured a trickle of the bubbly liquid into the small crevasse between the delicate bones on top of her shoulder. Some champagne spilled down Pauline's chest; he steadied her with his other hand, then poured a little more into the dimple. He leaned forward, put his lips in the small pool, and sipped.

"Here's to the moon," he whispered in her ear. He lifted his glass to his lips, and drank deeply. "Money spent on champagne is money well spent." He smiled as he said this, and tipped his glass again, this time onto her lips. They turned together and looked at the moon.

Pauline stared at the silver circle, surrounded by a reddish haze. She finished her champagne, and started to ask for another, when she felt a chill. She shivered.

Suddenly, Ernest's uncommon solicitude, under the too-bright moon, made her feel wary. The unusual luminosity, which had beguiled her only a few moments ago, now seemed a portent, an ill omen. She stood silently beside him. Ernest finished the champagne.

They went back down to their cots in the living room, the children asleep on their pallets. Once back inside, in the familiar soft artificial light, Pauline thought for a brief moment that perhaps the pall of the full moon could be lifted, that the separation and anger between them could be fully cured, and that they could find a way back to what they had felt that first year in Pamplona. Back in their neighboring cots, they soon fell asleep, not touching each other, breathing separately and unevenly in the cooling night.

Just before dawn, Ernest rolled over in the cot next to her, and reached out to touch her back. He sighed in his sleep. Pauline wondered, as she lay beside him, if whether last evening on the roof Ernest had been celebrating her, the children, or the house. Then she began to wonder if he had been thinking of someone else.

CHAPTER NINE

Even though the days were now cool and comfortable in the late island winter, Pauline could not bear to hold the warm little bundle of her second child. Just as she had with Patrick, she handed off the baby entirely to the nanny for his care. She had her new house to focus on.

Ernest, on the other hand, initially showed an avid interest in the new baby, whom he had named Gregory. It seemed to Pauline there were inverse primal pulls between the four of them: the more time Ernest wanted to spend with the boys, the less she was interested in them, and the more time he spent with the children, the less he was interested in her.

Ernest's writing continued well. He was working on a non-fiction book about bullfighting, tentatively entitled *Death in the Afternoon*. As he became more engrossed in his manuscript, however, he found he had less time for or interest in his sons. Patrick and Gregory were soon left solely in Ada's irascible and temperamental care.

They settled into a pattern in their increasingly gentrified home. Ernest wrote in the mornings in a second-floor writing studio, a room set above a guest house in the back yard. His studio was connected to the house by an iron catwalk, which he traversed early every morning to start his workday. Pauline was busily and happily occupied with their continuing renovations. The Hemingways had negotiated an unspoken détente, and they were occasionally even able to spend some time alone together without obvious disagreement.

One evening, Ernest decided that they needed to go out, just the two of them, and have a drink down in one of the bars on Duval. He liked it when Pauline put on something risqué and went out in public with him; he seemed to enjoy it when she defied her Catholic upbringing to dress a bit indelicately for him.

Even more so, he liked to take her to bars, particularly the bars along Duval Street that drew the sailors and the tourists and the habitual drunkards. He enjoyed sporting his well-bred wife on his arm as they went into seedy dives and ordered drinks. Pauline felt she understood the contradictory pleasure this gave him and tolerated it. *Let him have his bit of fun*, she thought, *at least it keeps him companionable.*

Pauline found a black dress with a low neckline that she knew he liked, and when he met her at the front door he smiled approvingly. They walked out onto Whitehead, and he guided her around the corner onto Olivia Street.

"We're walking down Duval tonight," he said. "I want to show you off." She was not surprised by this; it was not the first time. They strolled past guesthouses and homes, little shops and small restaurants. When they reached the northwest end of the street, they came even with the door of Ernest's favorite bar, Sloppy Joe's, and she was surprised when he did not turn in. She did not ask where they were going, she just kept up her pace with him.

This was their custom. Ernest would not tell her where they were going or what they were doing; he liked for her to follow him, and he liked her ignorance of the destination. She could tell by the swagger in his shoulders, the proprietary cupping of his hand over hers, the unquestioning assurance that he knew she would follow him. He seemed to revel in that, and it had become one of the few minimal pleasures she seemed still to be able to provide him.

They walked west until they came to the harbor, where Ernest turned toward a wharf warehouse. At this point, Pauline was truly mystified. She knew that he had wanted to go out for a drink, yet they had passed a dozen bars. They came to the side wall of the long stucco building. He stopped and stared down the length of it.

The warehouse had been built during the first World War, and had been used to house munitions, food, and men if necessary. The walls were thick, white concrete, covered in a yellowing stucco that had cracked and broken in the tropical heat. There were several deep insets in the walls at intervals; Ernest pulled her into one of these depressions and turned her to face him.

He pushed her back against the unyielding stucco. He kissed her, pressing her head back into the jagged edges of the wall. She writhed and tried to push away but he kept her pinned against the rough stone. After a minute, he stopped abruptly, then turned away and began to walk back toward the quiet street. She quickly followed.

After they had walked a few blocks, Ernest stopped next to a coconut palm. He turned to her again, gazed into her face, then pushed her up against the palm. Like the stucco, its bark was rough her back. The embrace was swift, and he again left her abruptly and walked away down the sidewalk.

Finally, without ever having stopped for a drink, they had circled back until they were at their own front gate. Ernest paused one last time and smiled coolly at Pauline. She did not know what had prompted this strange evening promenade, and she knew that she would not get an explanation. Ernest kissed her one more time, then pulled away, turned in a business-like fashion, opened the iron gate and walked up the flagstone path. Pauline trailed behind him. Before they reached the front door of the house, Ernest turned around and faced Pauline. He had one hand on the doorknob and gripped it lightly as he spoke.

"You know, Pauline, you really must be more careful about public displays of affection. You might get caught one of these days." He then turned and walked, alone, through the front door, leaving it open behind him.

Pauline stood watching him as he mounted the stairs to the second floor. It was yet another enigmatic, inexplicable moment, yet another time that she did not protest. She followed Ernest through the front door, closing it softly behind her, and slid into their silent house.

CHAPTER TEN

Ada irritated Pauline, but she knew that the nanny was necessary. Ada was incredibly efficient and seemed to anticipate the need to keep the children out of the way. Pauline knew that Ada did not like or esteem her either, but Ada took adequate, if unloving care of Patrick and kept him and the new baby quietly out of Pauline's way. Patrick did not seem to like Ada very much either, but he did not have a choice in the matter.

Patrick loved the grounds around the magnificent home, the garden was still wild and jungle-like, and certainly not the carefully manicured arboretum it would become in later years. Pauline purposely left as many native plants in place as possible; she wanted to keep the island feel of the lawn and garden. The last thing she wanted was for this special place to look like something it was not, with an artificially green lawn or clipped hedges. This was not Arkansas or Missouri or New York; it was Florida, wild and exotic, and she wanted to keep it that way.

As winter turned to spring and then to summer, Pauline continued to oversee the ongoing interior and exterior renovations of the home. Ernest seemed removed from the painting and decorating and remodeling. It was as if he had washed his hands of the project. He had started to complain about the inconvenience, and about the expense. When he argued with her about how much money she was spending, she would casually remind him that it was not his money that was turning the house into a tropical island mansion.

That infuriated him further, and it reached a point where they simply did not discuss it. It was sad, and difficult, to be living in the same house together, going through what should have been an enjoyable joint effort. Instead the house had become just another fissure between them, another point of contention. Their communications became noteworthy for their exercise of anger, blame, and silence. Feelings of compassion or love seemed only part of the remote past.

Pauline was standing in the front foyer one August morning, overseeing the carpet men trim in a Persian paisley runner up the long, narrow front staircase. She bent over, and ran her hand over the beautiful wool rug, blue and purple and gold. She could not wait to see it cascading down the steps, magnificent in its opulence. Caught up in her excitement about the rug, she was only vaguely aware that Patrick was playing upstairs in his room, making low, unobtrusive sounds.

In an unusual moment of maternal care, however, it occurred to her that once the workmen began tacking in the runner, Patrick would not be able to come down the front stairs. If he waited, he would have to use the door from the master bedroom that led onto the upper front porch and come down the outdoor staircase, a route they rarely used. Ernest did not like Patrick in their bedroom, at any time, and Patrick was still little enough that the high porch, fifteen feet off the ground, scared him. Pauline called up to him from the foyer.

"Patrick, if you want to come down the front stairs, you need to come now – they are going to start laying carpet in a minute or two." She heard his play sounds stop, and then resume after a few seconds of silence. She shrugged and left him to his own world – he would just have to use the outdoor staircase. Her maternal effort was concluded.

The carpet installers started at the top and began carefully to lay the gorgeous wool tightly and neatly down each step, securing the falls to each riser with a thin brass rail. Pauline watched, delighted, as the runner made its way down the long staircase. After watching the installation of five or six steps, she went back the narrow hallway to the kitchen and poured herself a glass of tea.

Pauline had imported hundreds of painted tiles from Cuba, and she watched the workers as they lay the tiles in the courtyard, the brilliant colors enhanced by the sun. She glanced up at Ernest's studio. She could hear his intermittent typing and knew that at least he was momentarily content. Ada had left to do the morning shopping, and so she had the house and lawn to herself.

Pauline walked out the back door and looked at the huge concrete pit that would soon be an in-ground pool. It was to become her favorite part of the entire estate, a salt-water sanctuary she would enjoy almost always alone.

Ernest had previously used the space where the pool had been dug for an impromptu boxing ring. He had roped it off, and would carry on messy, drunken boxing bouts with his friends after a long night at Sloppy Joe's. The grass had become completely worn down, and when it rained the area was one large mud puddle. *Suitable for pigs*, Pauline mused, *but not much else*. Pauline had decided that this was the spot where she would put her pool.

The islanders thought she was either foolish or stupid to attempt to dig into solid limestone for an in-ground pool, but she forged ahead with her plan. Bahamian labor was cheap, and Pauline rationalized that they were grateful to have the work, as backbreaking as it was.

She had drafted an immense sixty by twenty-four-foot rectangle for her pool. It would be filled not with precious fresh water – there would never be enough cistern water to fill such a large space – but rather with salt water. The pumping system was designed by a local plumber, who clearly thought she had lost her mind. But she persevered, and now the almost-finished result lay in front of her.

Pauline sat and watched the several Bahamian workers down in the empty concrete depression, struggling with heavy buckets of blue marine paint. Their dark skin glistened with sweat as they slowly covered every inch of cement.

The men had started at the deep end of the pool, ten feet down, and were painstakingly making their way to the shallow end. Pauline had installed underwater lights around the sides of the pool, and she was impatient to see it filled, lit up under the warm night sky. She stood, daydreaming, not thinking of anything else but her lovely pool.

She heard Ada's rummaging in the kitchen; she had returned from her morning's shopping. Pauline wondered vaguely what she might be preparing for her lunch. And then, Pauline heard a thump, followed by a child's yelp. She turned around, irritated at the disruption of her reverie. She did not see anything unusual at first, so she walked back across the lawn and turned around the far corner of the house.

Patrick was at the bottom of the outside staircase, lying on the ground. She rushed over to him. Ada came quickly out of the back door and bent down over the child.

"What happened, Patrick, are you alright?" Ada queried. The child's scared eyes looked up at her, then at Pauline; he was silent. Their handyman Toby had appeared behind Pauline, and chirped, in his odd, creaky voice.

"Looks like he fell." Toby continued to peer over her shoulder at Patrick, still lying on the half-tiled courtyard.

"I can see that, Toby, thank you," Pauline spat at him. She was trying hard to focus and keep the irritation out of her voice. She knew that was not the proper emotion right now. She tried to summon up what she thought was a motherly tone of voice.

"Patrick, are you alright?" It was clear that he had not lost consciousness, his eyes were open and staring intently, if fearfully. He sat up, and crossed his arms in front of him, cradling his chest. Pauline wondered if he had hurt his ribcage. "Where did you fall?" she continued, and the little boy pointed to the stairs. Pauline felt the uncomfortable irritation arise again. She realized he had misinterpreted her question.

"I know that, Patrick. I'm asking you where on your body you fell. What did you hurt?" The little boy stared at her, silent. She stood up. "Well, it looks like you're alright now. Be more careful, Patrick." He continued to stare up at her, still silent, wide eyes fixed on her. His quiet, needy gaze made Pauline uncomfortable.

"I'm going to go check on the carpeting," she said. Something prickled her that this was not the right response for a mother to make; she tried to compensate with another aloof response. "You can come with me, if you want." Pauline knew that interior decorating held absolutely no interest for a little boy, but it was the only offer she could muster. When he did not respond, she turned and walked back inside the house.

Pauline started to unpack the groceries, a small task that felt like a kind of penance. When Ada returned to the kitchen, Pauline asked what was planned for dinner. Ada silently pointed at a beef roast wrapped in butcher paper, sitting in a reddish, watery puddle on the counter. The sight of the bloody parcel made Pauline nauseated; she left the kitchen.

Pauline decided to check on the carpeting. Just as she turned into the front hallway, she heard Ernest walking across the upstairs catwalk. As she reached the foyer, she heard an upstairs bedroom door slam open against the wall, and Ernest's booming, angry voice reverberated through the house.

"Pauline, where the hell are you?" she could hear, and feel, his footsteps in the floorboards; whatever was going on, he was terribly angry. Pauline looked up to the second-floor landing, and saw Ernest cradling Patrick in his arms.

"Where the hell have you been? Did you not know that Patrick fell down the steps?" Pauline stood mute in the face of his anger, staring at the little boy in his arms. She felt distant, removed, as if she were looking at a painting.

"I knew he had bumped himself," Pauline stammered. "I thought he was alright." Ernest hurried down the steps, carrying Patrick in his arms. She felt a groaning sense of inadequacy. It was clear from looking at the boy that he was not alright. At the bottom of the steps, Ernest turned angrily toward Pauline.

"It looks like his arm is broken!" Ernest yelled at her. "What is wrong with you? Don't you have eyes in your head?" He swore again, sharply, and Pauline made a step toward them. Ernest turned, as if to shield Patrick from her. "Get out of my way, I'm taking him to the doctor."

Ernest's voice was low and menacing. Pauline stepped to the side of the narrow hallway, and Ernest passed by angrily as he carried Patrick down the hall and out the front door. She watched them exit the front gate and turn swiftly down Whitehead. She walked slowly back into the kitchen.

Ada stared at Pauline, and smirked. Pauline felt alien, unwanted, unnecessary. She did not know what else to do but walk away.

Several hours later, Ernest returned with Patrick. The little boy had a thin white plaster cast on his right arm. Ernest carried him up the stairs and took him into his bedroom. Pauline followed. When she got to the door of the room, Ernest was tucking the child in bed, tenderly, quietly. The early evening light shone softly through the open curtains. When Ernest saw Pauline standing in the doorway, he glared at her.

"Get out, Pauline. I'm taking care of him." The icy anger in his voice cut through her; here was another turning point in their relationship. She had given him a son, but it was clear that he thought she was unfit to be a mother. Another battle lost.

Pauline turned in the bedroom doorway, and walked back down the stairs. She did not know where to go, she could not go back upstairs, and she did not want to see Ada in the kitchen, still gloating over Pauline's inadequacies. Pauline went out the back door and walked across the thick grass to her pool.

Immediately, she felt calmer. She watched as the workers finished packing up brushes and covering tubs of paint. A couple of them stopped and stared at her, mute, and then turned away. It seemed to her they wanted to avoid her gaze.

She was alone. Surrounded by human beings all around her, but she was alone. And she had done that to herself. She stood still, thinking. Then she sat down on the grass and stared quietly at the empty pool.

CHAPTER ELEVEN

The pool was finally finished, and Pauline delighted in the buoyancy of the salt water, at the extravagance of her invention. One evening, shortly after they had filled it for the first time, all four of them sat eating a late dinner in the dining room, Ernest, Pauline, Patrick, and little Gregory in his highchair. Pauline looked at Ernest and could tell that he was agitated. Not displaying his usual anger, just preoccupied, his mind somewhere else. He kept looking out the window at the Royal Poinciana tree, and then moving his gaze back to his plate, but not giving his food his usual full attention. At one point, he got up and left the table without a word.

Pauline heard the back screen door swing shut. Patrick, Gregory, and Pauline continued their meal in silence. She wondered what Ernest was doing. Their relationship had been very strained since Patrick's fall, but this evening Pauline felt Ernest was laboring under some different emotion.

After a little while, the dining room door swung open, and there he was, dripping wet and wild-eyed. He had obviously been in the pool. He circled the table, and then came around the back of Pauline's chair, and leaned down behind her. He whispered in her ear.

"Don't you get it? It's a full moon." He turned on his heel and quickly walked back outside. Patrick looked at his mother, frightened, his lower lip trembling.

"What's wrong?" he said, "did I do something wrong, Mama?" Pauline blithely reassured him that no, he had done nothing. She then focused on what she knew was expected of her.

She tersely explained to Patrick that Papa simply wanted her out at the pool, and that she had better go. She rose from the table, and boy stood up immediately, with an almost military reaction. It vaguely troubled Pauline to see the effect of Ernest's behavior on the child. Patrick left the table quickly, not finishing his meal. It was as if he were trying, with his precipitous retreat, to spare himself, and perhaps his mother, further agita.

Pauline left the dining room and began to walk down the hallway toward the back door, vaguely concerned as to what Ernest might be planning. He had not touched her, in any way, since Patrick's accident, and she was frightened of the anger she knew was simmering just under the surface. Gregory was left alone in the dining room with Ada to finish the family dinner.

Pauline walked out to the back yard. She stepped onto the flagstone lanai at the narrow end of the pool and paused underneath the awning.

The full moon was an unholy silver, and uncommonly bright. Ernest's moods were hard to predict at the full moon: he could be amorous or angry, or sullen or charming. But whatever his mood, the full moon amplified it. And after the accident, she was sure that his overwhelming feeling was anger.

Pauline stood quietly under the awning and looked out over the shimmering water, trying to locate Ernest. He had turned on the underwater lights, and the combination of the reflected moonlight and the pool's glowing lights made it difficult for her to focus. She called out his name, softly, and disliked hearing the tentativeness and fear in her own voice. She did not like it that Ernest could make her so unsure of herself.

He answered her almost immediately, from the far end of the pool. Thankfully, he did not try and make her come to him, but began to swim languidly toward her. He stopped halfway across and stared at her.

Pauline pulled off her overshirt and moved toward the edge of the pool, wearing only her camisole and shorts. She stepped down onto the pool ledge, and stood in the inch of water surrounding the entire circumference of the pool. She waited for him to come nearer.

Ernest swam toward her, and when he reached the edge, he grasped her ankles. She was not sure if he was going to pull her off her feet and into the water; she felt he could just as easily pull her completely under. Pauline did not give him the opportunity: she leaned forward quickly and dived over his head into the water, her ankles slipping out of his grasp.

The pool always had a magical effect on her. The salt water was so buoyant, and she felt as though she had left the earth momentarily, had left the force of gravity behind. She swam to the middle of the pool, with only a few feet of water under her, and turned onto her back. She wanted to avoid the deep end when Ernest was in the pool.

Soon she felt his hands under her back, pushing her halfway up out of the water. He stood beside her, leveling her out on her back. He used one hand to hold her up, and the other hand to direct her head: he wanted her to look at the moon. He sank down beside until his head was level with hers, still holding her body face up, half out of the water. His voice was menacing.

"Look up," he said, "Look right there." He pointed to the moon slivered between the fronds of a tall coconut palm. The night was completely still, and the palm leaves did not move. "Watch this," he said. Ernest continued to hold her up with one hand and raised his other arm up into the night air. He began to move his upheld hand slowly back and forth across the evening sky. "Watch it move," he whispered.

Just then, the palm leaves began to sway against the moon, in tandem motion with his hand, in perfect timing with his fingers. He stayed beside her in the water, but pulled his hand out from underneath her, letting her float alone. "Now you do it," he said. "Raise your arm. Make it move."

Pauline hesitated; she felt frozen in the warm water. His spoke again, hissing angrily in her ear, "I said raise your hand. Make it move." She raised her arm; she felt powerless to disobey him, even in this weird, fantastical game. Her imagination sped ahead of her thoughts; she would not have been surprised to see Ernest as a faunus in the water beside her. Stiffly, she moved her hand as he had instructed, but the palm fronds didn't move; they remained still, etched against the night sky. Pauline's legs began to sink down in the water, finally resting on the concrete bottom of the pool.

She was embarrassed, defeated, and slowly lowered her arm. Ernest stared at her, as if gauging her abilities or competence. He watched as she clumsily righted herself, standing in the waist-high water, her soggy camisole clinging to her skin. Then Ernest turned and walked to the edge of the pool. He pulled himself up out of the water and walked back into the house. He left Pauline alone, in her moonlit pool.

PART FOUR

~Winter~

CHAPTER ONE

Key West, Florida, January 1935

Over the years, Ernest often recounted to Pauline a previous marital calamity. Agitated at each retelling, he repeatedly relayed to Pauline how Hadley had once lost one of his manuscripts. With each repetition, Ernest description of Hadley's culpability was more conclusive.

As Ernest told it, Hadley had been travelling alone by train from Paris to Austria, bringing with her some of Ernest's writing to deliver to him in Schruns. She was carrying the manuscript in a small satchel that she stored underneath her seat. At some point, she left the compartment momentarily, and when she returned, the satchel was gone. As Ernest repeated this story over time, it was clear that he had never gotten over his fury at Hadley.

As the story was embellished, Hadley became an intentional actor, somehow conniving to lose the document. Ernest made it clear that it had been a pivotal point in their relationship: Hadley never regained her previous standing with him.

Pauline wondered about the contention that this had been a deliberate act on Hadley's part. At first Pauline had not believed that was possible, but now, after several increasingly antagonistic years of living with Ernest, she was beginning to look at the incident in a different light. Hadley had been upstaged by Ernest's writing, and Pauline imagined that, after the birth of their son, Ernest might have reacted to Hadley then as he was to Pauline now: making it clear that his wife was not his first priority. As hard as it was for Pauline to imagine Hadley, sweet, meek Hadley, doing something that disastrously vengeful, she now wondered at the possibility.

One evening, in their fourth year of living in their palatial home, Ernest and Pauline had a particularly nasty argument. Their fights had become more and more frequent over the years, but this one had been exceptionally vitriolic. She became so embroiled in anger she forgot the genesis of the disagreement. It ended with Ernest stomping out, slamming the door, and heading off to Sloppy Joe's, and with Pauline fuming volcanically by her pool. The children were quiet upstairs in their room, and Pauline had no doubt that they had heard every bit of the row. She did not, however, have the energy or inclination to go see if they needed comforting. She needed comfort herself.

She left their bedroom and walked out onto the wooden boards of the second-story porch. They wood felt smooth and pleasantly cool under her feet. A bracing wind was blowing in off the Atlantic. Pauline leaned heavily on the wrought-iron handrail, then looked across at Ernest's writing studio. She stepped gingerly across the catwalk, and walked into the room.

Ernest's studio was a place she rarely ventured, and certainly not ever when Ernest was *in situ*. She looked around the dim room, the last of the evening sunlight coming through the rampart windows. She saw several mounds of papers strewn messily about his desk and copy table. She saw that he had carefully organized his current manuscript, however, scaling it chapter by chapter along the edge of the table.

Pauline looked at his pipe, tobacco tin, and several boxes of unopened Cuban cigars on his credenza. All the paraphernalia of his tobacco addiction were strewn about: the cigar cutters, the large ashtrays, the boxes of long wooden matches. She picked up one of the boxes.

She slid back the thin balsa lid, took out one match, and slid the box back together. Without giving herself time to think, she struck at the match paper on the side of the box, and the small blue and orange flame erupted. The brief sulfur smell was oddly pleasant. She held the match until the black char almost reached her finger, then she dropped it. It made a small round burn hole in the carpet, and then it flamed out.

She pulled out another match and struck it. This time, Pauline thought about what she could do with that little fire, and a brief thought of Hadley came to her mind. Had Hadley felt like this? Had she thought purposefully about what might happen when she left the satchel containing Ernest's writing under the seat on the train? Had it pleased her to contemplate, as Pauline now was, the destruction of the idol that had displaced her in his eyes?

Pauline looked at the manuscript, full of Ernest's precious words, lying on the desk. He was working on a book entitled *To Have and Have Not*, about a supposedly corruptible fishing boat captain who shows his nobility at the end. *Hunh*, thought Pauline, Ernest liked to imagine himself as the noble one, the hero in every story. She fumed inwardly. She'd like to let him know she considered him an amoral fraud.

Pauline had been so deep in thought she had forgotten to watch the match, and she flinched as it burned her – she dropped the second match to the floor. She watched it make another burn hole in the carpet. She took out a third match.

It would not take much to drop the match onto the paper, Pauline thought. It wouldn't take much at all. She held the match to the red striking paper, and then stopped.

There was no way she would be able to avoid blame for this; it would be apparent that the fire had not started spontaneously. Particularly after their fight, she would be immediately suspect, and that was not a position in which she wanted to place herself. She wanted to hurt him, but she even more strongly wanted to protect herself.

339

Elizabeth Ritter

Pauline put the match back in the box and picked up what she could of the first two charred match-ends. She scuffed at the carpet with the toe of her shoe; the burn holes were small, barely noticeable. Ernest might think, if he noticed them at all, that he had accidentally made them himself. Pauline turned and walked back over the catwalk into the main house.

She did not go into the bedroom, instead she walked around the upstairs porch to the front of the house, still holding in her hand the little charred bits of two match-ends. Pauline looked down at Whitehead Street, now dark in the late twilight. She threw the small char over the railing, and watched the little pieces float down and settle into the St. Augustine grass. Then she went to bed, alone.

CHAPTER TWO

A few mornings later Pauline overheard Ernest, sitting on an upturned fruit crate, talking with the yard man, Toby. They were discussing a fishing trip. She had become used to finding out his plans this way – Ernest did not talk with her directly anymore, she learned what he was planning by listening in on his conversations with others.

The fishing trip was planned for a Saturday, two weeks away. The men were intending to make it an all-day affair. As Pauline listened to Ernest and Toby discuss the excursion, her anger and despair increased. He was going on another trip, another exclusion of her from his plans. Pauline walked out into the yard to confront him. Toby, watching her stalk angrily toward them, made a hasty retreat to the garage.

"So, you're going out on the water again, huh?," she hissed at Ernest, "and you'll come back drunk, stinking of fish, and probably try to touch me with dirty hands and a dirtier mouth. Lovely, Ernest, *just lovely.*" She glared at him, her sarcasm hanging heavily between them. She waited for his retort.

Ernest did not respond immediately, but continued to sit and fiddle with a small pocketknife and a block of wood he had in his hands. He flicked his wrist, and a little shaving flew. He flicked again; another shaving fell. And another and another. But he did not speak. It was maddening to Pauline; she stood, mute and fuming, waiting for his response. Finally, after a little pile of wood bits had accumulated around his shoes, he looked up at her.

"You seem to have great confidence in your ability to attract me, Pauline," Ernest said quietly. "I wonder if perhaps your confidence is misplaced." Ernest continued the flicking of his knife. Pauline's anger spilled over.

"Really?" she spat furiously at him. "Perhaps it's you who are overconfident. You're not the only one who knows how to drink and carouse and lie." Pauline knew she had stung him; she had meant to. He paused his whittling and looked up at her.

"My girl, please don't threaten me." Ernest's voice was cool, menacing. He pointed the tip of his knife at her. "If you have any thoughts of being unfaithful to me, I suggest you think again." He continued to flick his knife against the narrowing block of wood.

Pauline had intended to threaten Ernest, but now it was she who was being threatened. Ernest had a way of doing that, of turning the tables so quickly and so effectively that Pauline did not have time to formulate a thought, much less a response. She only knew that, once again, he had defeated her. Pauline walked back into the house, shaking with rage. She mumbled to herself as she walked up the stairs, "This cannot go on forever."

CHAPTER THREE

As always, Pauline found her most reliable solace when she was alone in her pool. She was often out swimming in the pre-dawn, before anyone else was awake, and again in the late evenings, when Ernest was out at the bars. She enjoyed her solitary respites in the pool, swimming endless laps back and forth in her sanctuary, the jewel in her tropical garden.

Pauline had gotten up early one morning and had gone down to the pool to enjoy the quiet solitude and comfort of the cool water, of her private time away from children or servants or husband. This morning Pauline was unaware, however, that she was not alone.

The boy stood motionless just on the other side of the fence, staring through the close wooden slats, watching the woman in the pool. Didi lived with his grandparents in the shotgun house next door to the big mansion, and he had watched with fascination as the new neighbors had worked month after month on the falling-down house, and had turned it into a magical castle.

Didi was even more fascinated when he watched the beautiful woman in the huge blue pool. He had learned her habits and would sometimes creep out of bed in the early morning, just to watch her. He had to be careful not to waken his grandparents, sleeping head to foot in the bed in the next room.

His grandma slept with her head at the bottom end of the bed so that she could see out the bedroom door. This way, she could make sure Didi was not sneaking out or getting into trouble. But most nights his grandma slept soundly after a long day of housekeeping, and he could often tiptoe quietly past the door without rousing either one of them.

If they did happen to waken, Didi was sure to get a thrashing. His mother was long gone, and his grandparents were fiercely protective of the little boy they were now raising by themselves. They felt that lashing him with a tamarind twig was the best way to keep him safe, to keep him from doing anything dangerous. And the world, to them, was a dangerous place. Didi was used being yelled at in his grandpa's broken English, *"Don' do that, you get kilt!"* The refrain was repeated many times a day, week after week. Didi soon became inured to it.

Just before the turn of the century, Didi's grandpa, at eighteen, had made the precarious crossing from Cuba. It was not uncommon for Cubans to travel the ninety miles over the Florida Straits to the little island, but the immigrants often found that life was only marginally easier in Key West than it had been in Havana.

Grandpa was lucky: he had found work as a gardener at the Key West Naval Yard. Soon after his arrival, he had married a fourteen-year-old Dutch Bahamian girl whose family had emigrated from Abaco. He spoke no English; the girl spoke no Spanish. But soon they had a daughter, and the man struggled to provide a meagre living for his new wife and child.

He borrowed three hundred dollars to purchase a rickety little house on a dead-end lane. He liked the property because it was on *suelo elevado* –high ground. They lived quietly and simply in the little house, and raised their only child there.

The daughter was gone now, but the grandson, Didi, remained. They used the switch and fearful admonitions to try and keep Didi safe, but it did not stop the little boy from getting up before they wakened to peer through the fence whenever he could, to watch the beautiful woman.

Didi had seen other people at the big mansion as well. He knew there were little boys in the house, but they were both too young to be of any interest to him. There was also the big man: he strode around the back yard, yelling at workers, and sometimes at his wife. Didi knew the beautiful woman was his wife, because of the way she acted around him. She seemed like she wanted to try and do what the big man wanted, but, Didi thought, it didn't matter how hard she tried, that big man just wouldn't be nice to her.

Day after day, Didi watched the beautiful woman in the pool whenever he could, whenever he could safely sneak away from the cloistering confines of his grandparents' house. But even when they caught him and took to him with a tamarind switch, Didi didn't mind; watching the beautiful woman was his secret joy.

The woman had become an idol to Didi, a reprieve from his loneliness and solitude, a lovely icon he could worship, all to himself. She was his private treasure.

That morning, Didi watched the woman swim endlessly back and forth in the pool. He watched for as long as he could, aware that the lightening sky would soon be waking his grandparents. He turned and made his way quietly back into the house.

As he walked across the small back yard, he suddenly heard the big man crossing the black metal catwalk that connected the big house to the smaller building in the back yard. The man was standing in the middle of the catwalk, yelling at something. Didi looked up over the fence to see what he was yelling at. The big man was yelling a lot, pacing back and forth on the iron walkway. Every time he yelled, he aimed his angry words down at the woman in the pool.

Didi turned and walked in the back door of his house. He slipped into his bedroom, got back under the covers, and waited for his grandma's call to get up and get dressed.

Didi felt sad. He felt sad for that beautiful woman, and he was very angry at that bad man. He felt the unfamiliar burn of hostility wrench his stomach. Didi sat up and clenched his fists tightly. He pushed them into the mattress, making sharp little indentations in the sheets. Didi shook his head and punched the bed with his small fists.

"I ever get big enough," Didi squinted his eyes, "I ever get big enough, I'm gonna kill that man."

CHAPTER FOUR

As time passed, Pauline was forced to acknowledge the irremediable downward twists in her relationship with Ernest. As Ernest's confidence in his writing increased, he became more detached from Pauline, more patronizing. Their lives were becoming more separate, their interests progressively divergent.

And so Pauline was surprised one evening at the dinner table when Ernest asked her to take an evening walk. She had finished her meal, and had risen from the table warily, staring at him from the corner of her eye. She wondered whether she should assent, but decided that non-compliance held too many risks. She found a shawl, threw it around her shoulders, and followed him down the front sidewalk to the street.

They walked slowly around the block, the tamarind and mahogany leaves rustling underneath their feet. She had lost more confidence with each passing day, trying to figure out how to please him. Compliance was the last refuge she had, and it sickened her that she was reduced to this: pleasing him to find some way to bridge the widening gulf between them.

It was strange to her to think about the woman she had once been with him – confident, gay, able to poke fun at him, to teasingly rile him. Now she was as meek as Hadley had been, even if her meekness was manipulative. She knew that he disliked it, and she did not like seeing it in herself. And it was becoming more and more ineffective.

But something about Ernest had reduced her to that. His brooding, his emotional bullying, the long silences, the blunt insults – they all had their effect. Pauline longed for the days when they had been good together. She wanted nothing more than to be that girl again, that girl who fell willingly into his arms and gazed lovingly into his eyes.

But it had recently occurred to her that even back then, she had needed and wanted him more than he had ever needed or wanted her. It was a nasty realization, and she couldn't quite work out how she had not seen it. She was tired of the fighting and the machinations. It had become pellucidly clear to her that it was impossible to win with Ernest. He would outwit her always.

They continued their walk in brooding silence. His insouciance made things even worse for her. They were both aware of the changed dynamics in their relationship; he refused to acknowledge it, as if it were simply not important to him. She had been important to him at one time, Pauline thought, years ago when he had been pursuing her, when she satisfied a desire that Hadley could not meet. But now Pauline had to acknowledge that she was no longer enough.

Ernest used his calculated silences with her as a weapon, one that she did not know how to combat. The long wordless pauses, staring at her without speaking, his real or feigned deafness to her words, it was becoming more than Pauline could bear.

Worse than that, sometimes when he did speak to her now, it was as if he were being painfully kind to Pauline, generous enough to throw her a bone. He doled out deliberately gentle comments, calculated to give her just enough attention to keep her silent and on the leash. But the humiliation she felt in being treated like a wounded dog was overwhelming. How had she lost so much status?

The years of scheming to get what she wanted had worked, for a time. She had gotten – as Ernest Hemingway's wife –fame and money and notoriety and respect. She had her precious house, so lovingly restored and decorated, but it had begun to feel more like a tomb to her. And the boys, she had managed through her own missteps and miscalculations and mistakes to completely alienate them. She doubted they would ever be close to her, in any sense. She had lost friends, again through her own devices and misdirected desires; even the dozen cats that lived in and around the mansion seemed to avoid her. And Ernest's presence was a constant open wound now; Pauline felt powerless.

Once, years earlier, when she had thought Ernest was infatuated with a blonde actress, she had dyed her hair blond. When she had seen him flirting with a young barmaid with short-cropped hair, she had cut hers short. When he mentioned liking a certain style of dress on another woman, she had bought several. Over time, she had developed the habit of acting on the smallest indication he gave of what might please him to prompt an imitative response on her part.

But they were vain attempts, and humiliating. Now, his comments were almost always terse and uncomplimentary, acknowledging, as perfunctorily as possible, whatever change Pauline would come up with. And usually the comments were punctuated by criticisms. "I don't blow smoke up your skirt," he would say, after delivering a left-handed compliment or an outright insult. This statement was now almost always accompanied by a malignant stare, as if it were a challenge.

And it was. He was challenging Pauline, in any way, to react to his negativity. But she knew that if she responded in kind, things would only get worse. In addition to his dismissiveness, Ernest had over time developed a stable of comments to shut her up – that she was too emotional, that she was "over-thinking," that whatever she was feeling was not justified. More than that, if Pauline managed to let him know he had hurt her feelings in some way, within seconds he would turn things around so that she was in the wrong. So that

349

whatever they had been discussing, he was right, and Pauline had erred. It had become intolerable.

Pauline thought about the times, years ago, when he had written love poems to her. When he had used his magnificent words to thrill her and delight her. When he had spoken to her every day, all day, and deep into the night. When she could lay her head on his chest and hear him whisper to her. Just to her. Loving words. But Ernest had slowly taken all but the most mundane of his words away from her.

Pauline had tried responding to his silence with silence of her own. Aside from being extremely hard, it only served to increase the loneliness. And it was clear, even in this, that Ernest would win – he would always be able to outdistance her, overpower her, in anything. Including the silence game.

Their walk ended, as it had begun, in silence. They had made a circle of the blocks around their palatial Key West home and were back where they started. Ernest dropped her hand, and without looking at Pauline, left her at the gate and walked on down the street, alone.

CHAPTER FIVE

Ernest particularly did not like it when Pauline drank to keep up with him. At the same time, he did not like it if she tee-totaled. As their marriage deteriorated, she began to ignore his signals about how and when she should imbibe, and drank whenever and wherever she felt like it. In Key West, that became a dangerous game.

One evening after dinner Pauline sat alone by the poolside, sipping a cocktail. She was surprised when Ernest came down the iron steps from his studio and joined her. He had a glass of whiskey in his hand and sat down beside her on one of the comfortable cloth chairs near the pool. They did not acknowledge each other.

As the sun was setting, Ada came out to say that some guests had arrived. Pauline had not been expecting anyone, but Ernest had been in a foul mood all evening and any distraction at that point was welcome. Ada had made sure the children were secured away someplace and would not bother them for the rest of the evening. Pauline asked Ada who the new arrivals were, and when she told her, Pauline told Ada to bring them back.

Pauline liked Tennessee and was always interested to meet any young man he happened to have in tow. Tennessee Williams had not, by the mid-1930s, achieved any particular amount of fame or notoriety as a writer. He was still a young man, and his *Streetcar* and *Rose Tattoo* and *Glass Menagerie* were all yet to be written. To Pauline, he was simply a neighbor, a close friend, and a delightful dilettante.

Ernest, on the other hand, could not abide him, which made him even more attractive to Pauline. And Tennessee was

351

always entertaining, with a different young man in hand – she never saw him with the same companion twice.

Ada, unsmiling, brought the guests back to the swimming pool, then went abruptly back into the house. Tennessee strode toward his hosts, holding hands with a young, handsome Cuban; Pauline could see Ernest bristle at their entrance. She jumped up and embraced her friend.

"Tennie, you've been absent too long! And who is this delightful child?" Ernest hated it when Pauline talked like this; he called it her "fairy talk." Pauline, in turn, despised it when Ernest reverted to vulgar and boorish idioms about homosexuals; she wondered at times why he was so hateful about them, but she never had the courage to confront him directly. She ignored Ernest's irritated scowl.

"This is Frederico, my dear little Freddie," Tennessee crooned, running his hand, in one long stroke, over the top of the young man's head and down his slim back. Pauline smiled and motioned to the nearest chairs.

"Sit down, sit down," she said, and smiled indulgently at her guests. "We'll open some champagne; we need to celebrate tonight." She could see that Ernest chafed at this. He was probably calculating how long it would take to get rid of them, or when he could get out of the house. This made Pauline determined to keep their guests in attendance as long as possible.

"Freddie, where are you from, dear?" Pauline was certain that, if he could not understand English, the answer would be Cuba. And after a several-second pause and a chortle from Tennessee, it was clear that the language barrier, while present, was not an issue for him.

"He doesn't understand a blessed word you say," Tennessee said, gleefully. "And I find that utterly delightful." Tennessee smiled like a ten-year-old in a candy store, and

Frederico looked at him adoringly. Ernest glared at the two men, then pounded his sandaled feet across the flagstones and over to the poolside bar. He poured himself another whiskey.

"Aren't you going to offer our guests a little something, my dearest love?" Pauline's voice was mocking. Ernest glared back at her. She responded by raising an eyebrow at him.

"*Oooh,* so that's how it is," said Tennessee, watching the interaction. "I see. Well, well, well. So what games are we going to play tonight?" He smacked little Freddie on the thigh, causing the young man to yelp gleefully and leap from his chair. Tennessee seemed to enjoy fomenting the discord between Pauline and Ernest, and at the same time teasing the oblivious but obliging Freddie.

"Please, Ernest," Pauline asked, "Would you open a bottle of champagne? I'd like to celebrate tonight." Ernest remained silent, continuing to glare at Pauline. She wondered if this would turn into one of his violent brawls, one of his angry verbal outbursts, or one of his nasty, slamming departures. He surprised her. It was none of those.

"Whatever you say, *Madame.*" Ernest's voice was icy. He cocked his head and stared at her. "I'll be right back." He walked through the back kitchen door and Pauline heard him searching through the refrigerator, looking for the bottles. She was more disconcerted by this than she would have been by an angry response. She was not sure where he was headed.

Ernest returned quickly, with a childlike, almost idiotic grin on his face. "This what you wanted, dearest heart?" He had five bottles of champagne cradled in his bear-like arms, sticking this way and that and threatening at any moment to escape and crash onto the flagstone slate. "Is this it, darling?" he simpered.

Ernest's caricature of a doting husband scared her – this was something new, and she did not like it at all. Pauline had not seen this particular performance before, but she knew that Ernest never acted casually or unintentionally.

Ernest did not wait for her response, but roughly dropped the bottles into the deep seat of one of the canvas pool chairs.

"Just a moment, dearest, let me get the proper glasses." Ernest gave her a simpering smile, and walked back into the house. She heard him banging pantry doors.

Tennessee knew enough of Ernest's behavior to recognize that something was seriously amiss but, unlike Pauline, it did not seem to bother him. On the contrary, Tennessee seem relaxed, completely at peace, and expectant at what was probably going to be for him an enjoyable evening with a new, undemanding, and doting Cuban boyfriend. When Ernest returned, Tennessee swiveled a charming smile on him.

"Ernie, pour me the second biggest one you have, and give her the biggest," pointing his thumb at Pauline. "Don't give him much," he said, nodding toward Frederico, "I'm not sure little Freddie can handle it." Tennessee laughed, and pulled Frederico out of his seat and onto his lap.

Pauline watched the muscles in Ernest's neck tense. He stood completely still for a moment; she wondered if the dam were going to burst, if he would turn and lambast Tennessee with a machismo blast, either verbal or physical.

But Ernest did nothing. He stood motionless for another few seconds, then began, with his back turned to all of them, to carefully to unwrap the champagne lead and liberate the cork.

The sound of the bottle popping seemed to release some tension, and Freddie let out a girlish scream and clapped his hands. Ernest poured carefully, slowly, deliberately. He balefully eyed the top of each champagne glass to ensure they were all filled to the maximum amount, so that the glass could be held without spilling, but just barely. He delivered the champagne all around, then abruptly turned to Pauline with a malicious smile.

"Just a minute, darling," he purred, "I forgot the most important part." Ernest went for a third time back into the kitchen. Pauline wondered, with some trepidation, what he had in mind. Ernest soon returned with a bowl of strawberries.

Pauline had a fondness for strawberries floating in the bubbles in a glass of champagne, and while momentarily pleased, she was deeply suspicious. Ernest approached her with the bowl of fruit, and she furrowed her brow at him.

"Here you are, my sweet. Hold up your glass." Pauline gingerly proffered her champagne, and Ernest picked the biggest strawberry out of the bowl. Then he leaned forward and, dramatically and from a height, dropped it into her champagne glass.

The amber liquid splashed upwards onto her face and neck, and Pauline could feel it dripping down the front of her dress. She sat stunned, motionless, taking several seconds to process what he had just done. "Oops." Ernest said quietly, and smirked. He turned and walked back toward the edge of the pool.

There was a long silence. Tennessee and Freddie stared, noting the darkening spots on the front of Pauline's dress. She could feel Ernest turn and watch the tableau, taking it in, another brilliantly sardonic scene he had created. For a moment, she wondered if he would put this in one of his books.

"Dear me, aren't we violent tonight." Tennessee smiled, trying to break the tension; he leaned back on the chaise. Tennessee feigned not to be disturbed by Ernest's behavior; indeed, he thought, this was probably tame compared to his usual evening escapades. Freddie, however, not understanding anything that was being said but clearly comprehending that the strawberry incident had been an insult, looked up hesitatingly at his date, wondering whether this was the ending, or just the beginning, of a very long evening. Pauline's heart was racing, but she would not let Ernest see her discomfiture.

"Thank you, dearest one," Pauline crooned to Ernest. "You know how much I love it when you are *fruity*." She put as much emphasis as she dared on the last word, just enough to cut, but not overtly insulting. Pauline could tell that Ernest had been expecting anger, tears, perhaps a glass thrown and shattered on the pavement. He got none of that. She tipped what remained of the champagne into her throat and emptied the glass in a single draught.

"While you're up, my love," Pauline continued, smilingly caustic, "please fill me again. And certainly, add all the flora you choose." She was challenging him, and he knew it. Ernest refused to play on anyone else's turf or by others' rules, and he could pivot on a dime. He smiled at her, and she knew the game was changing.

"Certainly, angel, let me refill you." This time, Ernest poured her glass with excruciating slowness, but again filled it to the brim. "Here you go, my love, let me know when you need another." He put the bottle down into the ice chafer, crossed his arms on his broad chest, and glared at her. She knew a challenge when she saw one. Pauline tilted the glass to her lips, and, once more, drained it.

"Again," she demanded. Ernest and Pauline glowered at each other. He poured, she drank, he poured, she drank. Their guests were no longer in the penumbra of their sight or thought; they saw only each other, the matador and the bull, the hunter and the prey, the soldier and the enemy. They were consumed with each other.

"Oh my, my, perhaps little Paulie is going a tad overboard this evening," Tennessee said softly as the evening wore on. Pauline usually loved her friend's idiomatic expressions; tonight, she was irritated by them. Tennessee and Freddie had become a distraction from the main event, the bullfight in the arena. She was determined that she would not end this match a loser.

"Oh, Tennie, do be quiet," she said, not looking at him. She continued to stare at Ernest, and he at her. Neither one of them knew precisely where this was going, and each wanted to outwit the other. But if their history was any instructor, the result was going to be ugly.

CHAPTER SIX

The four of them continued their tense tightrope walk of a party by the pool, and soon two hours had passed. All five bottles of champagne had been opened and emptied; Pauline had, by far, consumed more than either of their guests or her husband. She stood to walk to the bathroom and reeled. Ernest reflexively leaned to catch her; he had been exceptionally restrained in his drinking and moved with alacrity.

"Let me help you, darling," he said magnanimously, extending his broad hand. His endearments and his touch, in her drunken state, enraged her. Pauline spun around drunkenly.

"*Get. Your. Hands. Off. Me.*" Her voice was low, liquid, on fire. Ernest merely smiled, which further enraged her. She pulled herself up to her full height, working hard not to topple or fall, and slitted her eyes at him. "I want to go for a drive. In the car." The tension between them was immense, like a rubber band pulled to the point that it is sure to snap back and sting. Pauline was overwhelmed by a feeling of simply wanting to leave, as quickly as possible. With as much dignity as she could muster, Pauline walked away. She could hear Ernest's derisive laughter follow her.

Unsteadily, Pauline strode back to the house and walked into the kitchen. Inside, she lay her head for a moment on the cool blue and white tiles of the countertop. Then she stood and shook her head. She looked around the room for the car keys. Pauline had a vague idea of driving the car up the Keys toward Boca Chica beach.

After a rambling search, Pauline located the keys in their bedroom, where Ernest had casually thrown them on the dresser. She looked around the room – at their massive bed with the monastery headboard, adorned at the foot with the primal decorations of an African birthing chair and midwife's bench. She hesitated, considered lying down on the bed and going to sleep, where she would cause no more trouble for the evening, but she stopped herself. She straightened her back, ran a hand over her hair to tame it, or imagined that she did so, left the bedroom, and went down the stairs. She walked out the front door, rather than leaving through the back and facing them all again, and went around to the garage, just underneath Toby's apartment. She walked across the back terrace and entered the garage through the back door.

The car was in the garage, challenging her to take it wherever her fancies desired. She stood, keys in hand, and shook her head to clear it. Open the garage doors. That was the first order of business. Pauline walked around the back of the car and fumbled with the throwbolt lock until it finally banged open. She pushed the large green doors open into the sultry Key West night. She walked out, peered up and down Olivia Street, and walked back to her quarry. The car was now a thing to be tamed, overcome, taken by force, and shot for display if necessary.

It took Pauline a few minutes to remember what to do with the convertible top; with one hand she fumbled with the large wing nuts that held it fast to the front window frame. After a few tries, the top finally came free and she awkwardly pushed it backwards, folding it in upon itself on the top of the front seat and forming kind of a shelf. She realized only then that she had been carrying a glass of champagne throughout her tour of the house searching for the keys, and that it was, amazingly, still in her hand.

Pauline gazed at the glass, congratulating herself that it still contained some champagne. She looked around, then decided that the convertible top "shelf" was an appropriate place to deposit her glass.

The glass immediately tipped over, and champagne ran freely over the black material of the top and spilled down onto the front seat. Pauline swore. Then, as if flipping a switch, she attempted to be dignified – as if she had an audience watching her. She was dimly aware that spilling her drink sloppily down the seat of her car didn't qualify as particularly decorous or fine.

She stood for a moment, trying to figure out how to proceed. She had, she noted with some surprise, seemingly forgotten how to start a car. Or even how to get into it. She stood and stared at it, as if at a wild beast. She squinted her eyes at the door handle, challenging it.

The next thing she knew, Pauline heard short, staccato footsteps behind her. She wondered, briefly, if one of the cats was wearing shoes. She turned and saw Tennessee grinning at her from the garage doorway.

"Oh heavens, you silly girl, what on earth do you think you are doing?" Tennessee strode forward, with considerably more vigor than she usually witnessed in him and grabbed the keys from her hand. "You are certainly in no condition to drive a car, if indeed you actually know how to operate this contraption." He waved his hand back and forth in a dismissive gesture at the car, and Pauline found herself, inexplicably infuriated, so angry that she wanted to hit or bite or curse or hurl a stony object at someone.

"Leave me alone, I'm fine and I'm going for a drive." She glared at him. Tennessee merely looked at her; she felt as defiant as a little girl when told she cannot sit with the grown-ups.

"I have your keys, sweetie," Tennessee responded. "You're not going anywhere tonight." He jostled the keys in front of his chest, which only further enraged her. Pauline got in the car, laboriously and awkwardly slid into the driver's seat, and stepped on the brake – it was the only pedal with which she could associate an action. She seemed surprised that nothing happened.

"Give me the keys, I'm leaving." She frowned at him. Tennessee continued his half smile at her, and Pauline noted briefly that he seemed to be barely controlling his laughter. His condescension chafed. She started to fumble with the throttle, the spark advance, anything she could find to turn or twist. Finally, she blew the horn. She heard Tennessee's laughter billow up and around her, and then she felt a bilious wave of nausea.

"Good grief, you are as green as a turtle, my dear," he said. He opened the driver's door and reached in to grab her around her waist. Pauline's immediate, and violent, response was to turn toward the passenger side seat and be sick, copiously and loudly.

The air felt thick and heavy around her, and Pauline's head reeled. She was sick again and again, until finally she stopped, bent over sideways with her forehead resting on the back of the seat. The smell was wretched. She wanted to be anywhere but there. She wanted to be lifted up, out of the car, into a bath, and then left to sleep for a day.

"Gad, she's a messy little girl, isn't she?" Pauline's head was foggy, and she was not sure where the voice was coming from. She opened her eyes, and saw Ernest staring at her.

Ernest had come in off the street through the wooden double garage doors; Pauline was not sure how long he had been there, or how much of her sickness he had witnessed. She hated him at that moment and wanted nothing so much as to be as far away from him as possible.

"Tennessee," Ernest said quietly, "get her cleaned up and bring her back in, but not to the pool – take her up to her room." With that peremptory order, he turned and strode out of the garage.

It did not occur to Pauline at the time, but she later wondered what Tennessee thought about being given this nursemaid's job. Would Tennessee think it strange that her husband had not attended to her? In hindsight, she understood perfectly: Ernest did not care for illness or weakness and would not tolerate it. And of course, he would delegate what he considered a menial nursemaid task, to a man who he felt acted like a woman. If Tennessee was offended, however, he did not show it.

"Come on, silly, let's get you up and out of here, and away from this vileness," Tennessee tugged at her arm. "You need a bath, and another little snort to ward off the creepy willies." Pauline didn't respond, didn't protest as he pulled her out of the car, wrapped her in a towel that she supposed he had brought with him from the pool, and steered her toward the back door of the garage. "Onward and upward we go, dear child." With that, he led her stumblingly across the Cuban tile courtyard, through the soft Key West night, and into the back kitchen door. He led her upstairs into the bedroom and steered her toward the corner bathroom.

Pauline was grateful that someone else was taking care of things. She let him pull off her soiled dress and strip her to the skin. Tennessee gently guided her into the shower, and silently washed her off, head to foot. When the detritus of the evening was washed away, he wrapped her again in a clean towel, carefully dried her, and led her to the bed.

In one weird, spinning moment, Pauline wondered if Tennessee would try and kiss her. He stared down at her, and she watched him breathing. His hands twitched at his side, and then he was suddenly and completely still. After a moment, he reached down and pulled up the sheet to cover her.

"I'm going to get you a little toddy – I'll be right back." He left the room, and she heard his footsteps softly pad down the staircase as she fell asleep.

Pauline wakened hours later. The night was fully black now; only a sliver of moon shone its light through the tall side windows. She glanced at her bedside table and saw an old-fashioned glass, full of brownish liquid. The ice in it was long melted, forming a clear liquid layer on top of the whiskey.

She sat up, swung her legs over the side of the bed, and waited for her head to stop spinning. She pulled on her bathrobe and carefully walked down the long staircase. She turned down the back hallway and walked out onto the lanai.

Pauline gazed at her beautiful pool, pallid blue and shimmering in the moonlight. Ada had cleared away the leavings of the party. No evidence remained of the evening's antics.

Pauline looked at the velvety water in the pool; as always, it drew her in. She moved slowly toward the edge, kicked off her slippers and stepped down onto the ledge. She eased herself down onto the cool concrete and pulled up the bottom of her robe to keep it from falling in the water. She sat silently for a time, contemplating her pool, her trees, her moon.

Pauline heard a small rustle, a human sound, coming from the guest quarters behind her. She stood and pulled her robe more closely around her, tightening the sash as she stepped out of the pool. The door to the guesthouse was ajar and she wondered if Ernest could have invited Tennessee and Freddie to spend the night. Unlikely, she thought; that possibility was remote.

The front room of the guest quarters was dark, but a thin line of light glowed under the door to the back bedroom. Moving quickly, she crossed the room and turned the glass knob.

Ernest was splayed across the bed, eyes half-closed. Tennessee was standing over him, just as he had stood over Pauline at her bedside a few hours earlier. Freddie was nowhere in sight.

Tennessee glanced at her when she entered. His perpetual smile was gone, but he did not seem upset, merely wary.

"You're not the only one I had to take care of tonight," Tennessee said quietly. Tennessee looked at Ernest, now snoring loudly, and pulled the sheet up over him, just as he had covered her earlier. They both looked at Ernest and watched the thin material of the sheet rise and fall with his breathing. Tennessee walked to her side and kissed her tenderly on the cheek.

"I'll see myself out." Tennessee walked out of the guest quarters, and Pauline remained standing mute by her husband's bedside. She turned and left the guesthouse bedroom and went back out into the cool almost-morning.

Pauline slowly lay down on one of the chaise lounges and let herself, for a moment, relax. She saw the sky was beginning to lighten, and the moon had already fallen over the horizon. The night ended as it had started – quietly, alone by the pool.

PART
FIVE

~Harvest~

CHAPTER ONE

Key West, Florida, August 1939

Years passed, with uncountable repetitions of depressing evenings like the one with Tennessee and Freddie. Ernest's writing flourished; his years in Key West would become known as the most productive of his career. He was sketching out another novel, *For Whom the Bell Tolls*, set during the Spanish Civil War. Pauline often wondered what muse drove Ernest to select his artistic focus; this book, she would later find, was to be a foreshadowing of his final departure from her.

During his Key West years, Ernest wrote most of the body of work that would make him the most influential American writer of the twentieth century. His fame as a writer was blossoming, and he even had offers of movie options. And as her now-famous husband began to enjoy the avid reception and adulation of the public, Ernest pulled himself further away from Pauline.

As Ernest's his celebrity increased, his interest in Pauline diminished to a casual disdain. And as this indifference grew, Pauline felt a recurring urge to find a friend, to have some companionship other than that of Ada or Lorine or the children, and especially other than that of Ernest. She wanted to see Elizabeth.

Pauline had met Elizabeth Bishop a year earlier, at an artists' gathering in Key West. Elizabeth had struck her at the time as a very unusual woman; she interested Pauline. After that first meeting, they slowly entered into an easy friendship – aside from Jinny, the closest friendship Pauline would ever have with a woman.

Elizabeth was independently wealthy, erudite, flamboyant. A lesbian, she had blossomed in the casual freedom of Key West. The elegant, fluid poetry that Elizabeth created during her time on the island had captivated and stimulated Pauline.

In the year since Pauline had seen her friend, the two women had corresponded regularly, but Pauline always felt at somewhat of a disadvantage in that realm. Pauline was a good writer, but Elizabeth's talents were soaring, and even a simple letter from her could make Pauline cringe at the inadequacy of her own efforts.

Elizabeth's poetry had begun to attract national interest and she enjoyed a compounding fame in literary circles. Pauline knew all too well how fickle that fame could be – she had seen so many bright talents in Ernest's circle, in Paris, in New York, flash and then flame out. But Elizabeth's work had held to a steady upward trajectory. Her poetry was *luminous*, one of her favorite words. She used it often, and aptly. Pauline found it charming.

Pauline awakened one morning with a tremendous hangover, the residue from the previous evening's drunken gloom. The skin around her head felt tight, like a stocking, and she did not want to open her eyes fully – the light hurt too much. It was in this mood that she sat down to write a letter to Elizabeth.

With her hangover and depression dulling any latent feelings of insufficiency, Pauline poured her heart out. She told Elizabeth about the joylessness and sadness she was experiencing. And she asked Elizabeth, begged her, to come visit. Pauline needed her.

Pauline knew that the trip from New York would be no small labor for Elizabeth – she hated to fly, and she hated to leave New York. But Pauline also knew that, because of her especial attachment to Pauline, if she asked Elizabeth to come, she would come.

And Pauline was right. A little more than a week later she received a response from Elizabeth. In her florid, loopy handwriting, Elizabeth said that she would finish out the season in the city, and then come to Key West. She reminisced how much she loved and missed the island and bolstered Pauline's mood by telling her that she loved and missed her as well.

Pauline did not tell Ernest about Elizabeth's impending visit. She did not want to hear his rebarbative, combative insults and prejudices about her friend. In their early days in Paris, Pauline had viewed Ernest's machismo as attractive; but now she perceived that it was merely a thin bravado, covering up a core of insecurities. Pauline did not tell him about Elizabeth's visit until the day before she arrived.

"We're going to have a houseguest, Ernest," she revealed at the breakfast table, staring resolutely at her eggs as she spoke. She could feel his glare, and his silence was threatening. Pauline did not look up but continued to eat. Then she slowly raised her eyes to meet his.

"Who?" Ernest never used more words than he had to.

"Elizabeth. My friend, Elizabeth Bishop," Pauline said. "You remember her, she's a poet." She waited for the harangue to begin.

"Oh Gad, not her," Ernest snorted loudly. "I remember that half-talent, lunatic bard. Why on earth is she coming here?"

"Because, I invited her." Pauline kept her eyes on her plate and continued to eat. She did not look up, waiting for the explosion.

"What?" Ernest roared. His face was red, his eyes flaming. "You invited her here? She's not staying with us, I hope you understand that, at least." Ernest flung down his napkin. "Great Caesar's Ghost," he continued, his anger growing, "I

371

don't want that merman in my house. When she's here, she spends all her time in the pool, spouting liquidy poetry. And when she's not in the pool, she smells bad." Pauline's bile rose, and she slammed down her fork on the tablecloth.

"Smells bad? *She* smells bad?" Pauline shouted. "Ernest, have you ever caught a whiff of your own stench after you come home from that low-life dive you go to every night?" Her eyes were on fire; she felt that she wanted to strike him. Ernest glared at her. Then he spoke, softly, menacingly.

"My dear girl," he hissed, "you have become rather loose in your speech. I am surprised, and disappointed in you." Long ago, Ernest's dominant, "correcting" voice might have seemed to her to be an extension of his manliness. But now, she felt only disgust. She stood up from the table, the rest of her breakfast left on the plate.

"She will be staying here, as my guest," Pauline said icily. "If you cannot act with simple civility – both to me and to her – then I suggest you find somewhere else to sleep." She could tell that she had succeeded in shocking him. He had not been expecting such a bold retort.

"Find someplace else to sleep – *huh*," he responded carefully. Ernest rarely was at a loss for words, but he was now. Pauline felt a rush of blood, of adrenaline, as she watched the effect of her audacity play across the planes of his face. She turned and walked away.

As Pauline left the dining room, she felt her face relax into a grim smile, pleased and vengeful. She knew that her words would cost her, but she did not care. They had begun down a path from which there would be no retreat. They were now in the eye of the hurricane, beyond discussion, beyond persuasion, beyond return.

CHAPTER TWO

Elizabeth's ostentatious arrival was welcome and disconcerting at the same time. As the taxi deposited her at their front gate, Pauline smiled out the front window at her friend's garish, multi-layered caftan, printed with brilliant pink flamingos and lurid green palm fronds. Elizabeth wore over-sized, white-framed sunglasses that sat slightly askew on her nose, and she struggled with a large floppy straw hat that kept slipping off the back of her head. Pauline watched as Elizabeth engaged in a constant struggle to push the sunglasses up and the hat down. Pauline sighed. It was precisely the kind of outfit that was certain to engender Ernest's condescension.

Pauline walked out onto the front porch, just as Elizabeth was waving directions to the driver, gesticulating. Elizabeth pointed at which of the large suitcases she wanted pulled first from the trunk and pointed as to where on the sidewalk the driver was to place them.

The driver, phlegmatic and compliant, followed her orders in patient silence. For a moment, the sight of Elizabeth made Pauline apprehensive. She suppressed the thought that this visit was almost certain to create explosive tension with Ernest and began to walk swiftly down the front sidewalk, anxious to dampen any further spectacle.

Pauline paused at the large concrete fishpond, halfway between the front door and the street, and hesitated. Elizabeth was busy trying to tip the driver. She was stirring her arm around in her capacious handbag, pulling out handkerchiefs, lipsticks, scraps of paper, placing each successive find in the cupped hands of the driver. Pauline heard her mumble that her wallet was in there somewhere, and watched as Elizabeth continued to fumble around the bottom of her bag.

For some reason, Pauline felt a sudden absurd urge to run away, to dive into that little pool and swim through the bottom of it, to let it swallow her up and hide her. She brusquely shook her head at the escapist thought, and continued down the concrete walk to the street. Elizabeth had finally succeeded in paying the fare and was busy retrieving the detritus of her purse from the cabbie's hands and replacing it all in her bag.

"Elizabeth!" Pauline crooned. "I'm so glad to see you." She stepped forward, smiling, and embraced her friend, feeling the small, bony frame beneath the billowing caftan. They stood, arms around each other for several moments.

As Elizabeth held her, Pauline was surprised to feel her face crumple; she was shocked to hear herself begin to sob. Elizabeth held her friend more tightly, rocking her on the sidewalk until the tears subsided. Elizabeth broke the embrace and stepped back to look at Pauline, still holding onto her hands.

"Pauline, my dear, I'm glad to see you." She gazed at her friend lovingly, empathetically, "I can see that I'm needed." Elizabeth smiled at her and wiped the tears off her cheeks.

"Oh Elizabeth, I'm so glad you're here." Pauline bowed her head and quietly began to weep again.

"Alright, alright," Elizabeth urged. "Let's go inside. No need to make a pageant out here on the sidewalk for everyone to see." Pauline raised her head; Elizabeth beamed at her.

Her friend's presence was truly a balm, a respite, an oasis. Pauline had not realized just how terribly much she had really needed her, really needed a sympathetic ear and voice. They turned and walked arm in arm into the front hallway of the big house.

"Come get these bags, Ada," Pauline called back to the kitchen as they entered the house. Pauline could hear the washing of dishes, the soft familiar sounds of running water and china clinking against porcelain. Ada poked her head around the corner and yelled down the hallway.

"Be there in a minute," Ada barked. "I'll get them when I'm finished here." Ada never did anything just as Pauline told her to; she reacted in her own time. It was a constant, if minor, irritation. Pauline sluffed off the momentary annoyance and drew her friend down the hallway out onto the backyard patio.

"Come on, let's go sit down outside and have a drink. I've got champagne cooling." Elizabeth smiled at Pauline and stroked her arm.

"Of course, you do, my friend, of course you have champagne!" She grinned at Pauline, and they continued to walk toward the pool. Pauline had arranged two chaise lounges with a small, low table in between, facing the pool. She motioned for Elizabeth to sit. Pauline moved around the side of the other chaise, lowered herself slowly, and gazed at Elizabeth.

"I can't believe you're actually here, Elizabeth. I've missed you so." They stared at each other, not speaking. Elizabeth had become, in one way, more and more like Ernest: she used words cautiously, and with careful meaning.

"I can see that. Yes, I can see that," Elizabeth repeated. She stared around the manicured back lawn. "It's even more beautiful than the last time I was here." She cast her gaze in a slow circle at the garden, the pool, the arching coconut palms, the blazing heliconia and poinciana. "It's like a Garden of Eden, Pauline," and glanced over at her friend.

Pauline's face suddenly turned sorrowful, and Elizabeth quickly realized her misstep. "Well, angel, I guess not a Garden of Eden. Or perhaps maybe only in this way," she hesitated. "Perhaps a snake has wound itself around your ankles." Pauline did not respond; she stared dully at her feet.

Ada appeared between them, and leadenly placed an ice bucket on the low table, a slanting green bottle protruding from the top, glossy cubes of ice brimming on the surface. She thumped down two champagne bowls, dropped a linen towel on the table, and walked away without a word. The friends waited until Ada had returned to the house and noisily slammed the back door, and then they began to laugh.

"Come on honey, let's do that, right now," Elizabeth gestured to the bottle. "Let's try and get most of that inside us before the gargoyle comes back out." Pauline laughed, grateful to her friend for her humor and kindness. Ernest had left for the evening, not wanting to be around when Elizabeth arrived, so they would not have to contend with him. Pauline thought, *he'll probably stay out all night.* She shook her head: she didn't want to think about him now.

Pauline tugged the bottle out of the bucket, spilling icy cubes onto the surface of the small table as she pulled. She wrapped the bottle in the linen towel, and concentrated on the little wire bail, twisting and twisting until it was fully loosened, then discarding it casually beside her on the flagstones. She pointed the bottle toward the pool.

Pauline pressed her thumb against the rounded, mottled edge of the cork, and pushed. She turned the bottle, pushing harder with each turn, and finally the cork spewed off in a gentle arc and landed with a splash on the placid blue surface of the pool. They watched it bob a couple of times, then lay still on top of the water.

Pauline reached over for a glass, and poured the bubbly liquid carefully, almost to the top. She repeated the process with the second glass and handed the first to Elizabeth.

"Later, we'll have a contest to see who can find the cork," Pauline joked, and raised her glass. "Here's to good friends, Elizabeth." She smiled and stopped immediately as she caught her friend's frown.

"'To good friends'?" Elizabeth chided. "good grief, Pauline, I think we can do better than that." Elizabeth laughed, and Pauline chuckled back at her. Elizabeth raised her glass again and began a new toast.

"Here's to delight, and happiness, and excitement, and intrigue." Pauline smiled at her, and Elizabeth continued, "And here's to the improvident, the ill-considered, the unexpected, and the unreckoned." Elizabeth's smile broadened, and her good humor infected Pauline. "Here's to burping and farting, here's to deep and liquid and smelly human interactions, here's to honest pleasure, and dishonest compliments." Pauline started to lift her glass to her lips. "I'm not done!" Elizabeth barked at her. "Put that down."

Elizabeth continued her poesy, glass halfway between table and lips. "Here's to dirty, sandy feet, here's to the scent of seagrass in your hair, here's to sundried salt licked off your own skin." Pauline waited for more, glass held still in her hand. Elizabeth raised her glass higher and finished her toast. "And here's to you, my cockle shell, my pretty pink friend, my beautiful sea urchin." Elizabeth's smile widened and softened, and she tilted her head to one side. "Now," she said quietly, "Now we can drink."

They pulled their glasses to their lips and drank, deeply and reverently. They stared at each other over the tops of their glasses as they swallowed. The bubbles in the champagne floated and swirled. The two women continued to drink, wordlessly, smiling at each other.

They sat and drank and talked, and watched the night begin to fall. The birds had stilled, and the evening animal sounds had commenced: frog and cricket and owl. As these sounds continued, increasing, neither of them spoke, or needed to speak. Elizabeth reached over and took Pauline's hand.

"I am glad that I am here. Right now, this is where I am supposed to be." Elizabeth leaned her head back against the chaise and turned toward Pauline. "You don't need to tell me what's wrong, or why you asked me to come. It's enough that I am here, and that you are happy I'm here."

Pauline shut her eyes, and she could feel her tears begin again. She squeezed her eyes tighter, trying to stop the flow. She did not want to weep, not now. She just wanted to feel the warmth of her friend's hand, the softness of the evening trade winds, and forget the ever-increasing pain of each day. They continued to sit, silently, holding hands.

At length, Elizabeth turned to Pauline. "Let's take a swim." She grinned at Pauline impishly. "Yes, yes, yes, that's exactly what we need to do." The champagne had softened Pauline's speech and her thoughts, and Elizabeth's suggestion made her want to giggle with pleasure. They stood, walked back over the cold flagstones, and into the pool house.

Pauline squinted in the dim light and looked toward the back wall; bathing suits of varying sizes hung on hooks in the corner. Pauline always kept several suits, for men and women, just in case anyone wanted to swim but had not come prepared. Pauline paused in front of a pale green suit that she thought might fit Elizabeth, reached for it, and started to lift it off the hook.

"Do we really need those?" Elizabeth queried. Pauline gazed at her friend. Elizabeth had a quiet, simple way about her, belying her innate complexity. Elizabeth just stood and stared. Pauline lowered her hand. "It's a beautiful night, there is no one else here, and we've both seen ourselves before,"

Elizabeth said. "There's really nothing to cover up, and no need to do so." Pauline paused, then gave her a sideways grin.

"Of course not, Elizabeth. Of course not." They hung their clothes on top of the bathing suits and walked back out the narrow door of the pool house. The night had truly fallen by this time, and Pauline reached back to the wall and flicked on the pool lights.

It was always a theatrical moment, when the blue-green salt water lit up like a stage, waiting for its actors to enter and perform. Pauline walked back toward Elizabeth, waited a moment, then took her hand. They walked to the side of the pool.

Without sound or warning, Pauline felt rather than saw Elizabeth soar out over the water, launching herself in an arching dive into the warm saltiness of the pool. Her small body cut the surface and shimmered beneath the water. She sliced the water, again and again, and then after a time came up for air. Pauline sat down on the pool ledge and watched, fascinated.

Elizabeth moved her arms backward and forward, and Pauline smiled at the little feet paddling at the ends of diminutive legs. Elizabeth treaded water, and Pauline watched. The evening sounds of gecko and bull frog accompanied Elizabeth's gentle, swishing motion. She beckoned for Pauline to get into the pool.

Pauline slowly lowered herself from the edge, no splashes or unnecessary movement. She sank down under the water, and slowly came up again. Elizabeth was smiling at her.

"Look down," Elizabeth said, and pointed at Pauline's legs. Pauline hesitated, momentarily confused. "Look down," Elizabeth repeated, and Pauline followed her gaze, beneath the water, at Pauline's slowly moving legs. "You see your legs underneath the water, in this light?" Elizabeth continued to tread water, moving her arms in a wide arc on the shimmering water, her gaze directed below the surface. "Look at my legs, too. Same thing." Elizabeth smiled, teasing. "This light, this water, it's magical. It makes our legs look like luminous green frogs' legs."

Pauline was caught short. Elizabeth's words cut through the heavy sadness in her head. She looked down at Elizabeth's legs, then at her own, and she saw what her friend had meant. Their legs were so beautiful, so breathtaking, moving slowly, illuminated in the greenish glow of the sunken lights. They continued to move about in the water, unconscious of time, enveloped in the organic healing of the sea water.

Completely black now, there was no moon in the sky, and they were alone in their universe of salt water and conversation. Pauline felt the balm and comfort minister to the neediness of her heart.

As the night deepened, so did their conversation. It went on and on, in circles of clarity and confusion, they swam and splashed, and their words played on top of the water. Occasionally they exited the pool and wrapped themselves in warm, soft terrycloth robes, before throwing them off again and climbing back in the water. They opened more bottles of champagne. Elizabeth's power to listen and to respond incisively and with empathy drew out more and more of Pauline's marital predicaments.

Elizabeth had a profound talent to assist Pauline's thinking, to see things that Pauline otherwise would miss. As the night faded away to the sunrise, Pauline began to see a different vision, a clearer understanding of herself. As they talked, Pauline began to view her relationship with Ernest in distinct outline: Ernest had become all-consuming, and Pauline had been all but devoured. Elizabeth's empathy, compassion, understanding, and advice had led Pauline to a revelation. In truth, it had already been there, waiting for Pauline; Elizabeth just helped her grasp it.

As the new sun's rays touched the palm trees, the women climbed out of the pool and walked inside and upstairs to their bedrooms. Pauline smiled sleepily at Elizabeth, kissed her small white cheek, and they moved off to their individual slumbers.

Pauline crawled into her bed and thought about the clarity that the night had brought her. She realized, calmly, that what lay ahead for her would be difficult. But Elizabeth had helped Pauline realize that, while daunting, her future was not desolate, and that she would indeed survive. Pauline drifted off, to a dreamless, tranquil sleep.

CHAPTER THREE

Pauline knew all about it; she no longer pretended that she did not. During Elizabeth's brief visit she had spoken of it openly for the first time: Ernest, she believed, had taken a mistress. Pauline had reason for this suspicion for some time, but after Elizabeth left Ernest became open and unabashed in his affair.

Of course, he had engaged in flirtations before. Whether they were consummated or not, Pauline had always chosen to turn a blind eye. She had too much to lose, including her dignity, by confronting him. She knew from his experience with Hadley that he would not bow to a wife's pressure, in any way. He might be capable of feeling an incredible, overweening guilt, as he had after his infidelity with Pauline in Pamplona, but Ernest would always end up doing whatever it was he wanted to do.

Pauline decided that, just as Ernest was intent on getting his own way, just so would she. It became inevitable they were headed toward an implosion.

In several surreptitious visits to Ernest's writing studio, Pauline had found letters to Ernest strewn around his desk, signed from "Martha," or sometimes simply "M.". Ernest had made no apparent effort to conceal them. Just as he had baited Hadley at the San Fermín so many years before, he was now daring Pauline to say something about this new affair.

Pauline demurred; hadn't she been complicit in the same way? At least this new woman was not physically present, colluding openly in front of Pauline. This fact dredged up Pauline's long-buried guilt at the way she had treated Hadley. But she successfully repressed that emotion and focused her antipathy on Ernest.

He even began to talk about the woman openly in front of Pauline. He would refer to his "friend," in wistful, glowing terms. He goaded Pauline with his veiled comments. He began to talk, with loud braggadocio, about his efforts during the Great War, re-telling the stories of wounds he received as an ambulance driver in Northern Italy. He even began to talk about going to Spain, going to the front lines in that country's ongoing civil war. Ernest made clear his desire to feel the rush and excitement of the battlefield and, unimaginable to Pauline, the lustful draw of war. Ernest wanted to be there, to write about it as it was happening.

Brazenly, Ernest talked admiringly about the fact that his new "friend" was doing just that. He had first met her when she visited Key West, but now she was a reporter on the battle front in Spain. He did not hide his obvious veneration for this brave female war correspondent, nor did he make any attempt to conceal his attraction to her. And, Ernest told Pauline, the war had already been going on for three years; he needed to get there before it was over.

Just as Hadley had come to the realization that she could not measure up to Pauline in Ernest's eyes, Pauline realized that she could not compete with Ernest's new infatuation. She told herself that, whatever happened, she would not follow the ignominious footsteps of her predecessor. She would, like a Key West wrecker, figure out how she could salvage the most from this situation.

The final confrontation was not long in coming. One evening she went up to Ernest's studio, carrying a bottle of wine and two glasses. It was now only over alcohol that they could stand to talk with each other, to tolerate each other's presence. Rather than take the catwalk to his studio, she went out through the kitchen and up the wrought iron spiral stairs to the iron landing; he would have more opportunity to hear her coming that way. She knew it was not in her interest to surprise him.

When she got to the top of the steps, she stopped and listened. His typewriter had been clacking earlier; it was silent now. She walked through the open doorway. Ernest looked up at her from his desk, and his eyes moved from her face to the bottle in her hand.

"What have you got there, girl?" he said softly. He even managed a small smile. Pauline placed the glasses and the wine on his desk and turned the bottle so that the label was facing him. She did not speak, intending for him to read the label. She decided that, for starters, silence would be her best tack. He looked at the bottle and nodded approvingly. "Ah, a bottle from your nancy California boys."

It was Gallo wine, and Ernest's characteristically ill-mannered reference was to a long-ago friendship Pauline had made with the Gallo brothers during a trans-Atlantic cruise many years before. Ernest never believed that they were brothers; he maintained that they were lovers, and that the brother ruse was their cover story.

Pauline could never understand why Ernest was so quick to be unpleasant and accusatory. But she abandoned that mental corkscrew and reached for the metal one in her pocket. She turned to open the bottle and remained silent, grateful to have this task to focus on. She uncorked the wine and poured two generous glasses. She picked up the one closest to her and held it toward him, then picked up her glass and waited for a toast.

Ernest always preferred to be the one, in any group, who raised his glass first, and he was always the one with the salute. He liked to start the ceremony, and his toasts always presaged his mood and disposition. Pauline waited.

"Here's to better days, here and abroad," he said, raising his glass. Ernest stared steadily at her, and she could see the defiance in his eyes.

"Well, surely we need to wish for better days elsewhere. What would you like to improve here?" Pauline responded. She had cast down the glove, and he picked it up.

"Well, Pauline, I think it's obvious." He sipped and looked out the window. Then he surprised her. "I have loved you, dearly and completely. At the same time, you know that I feel I need to be elsewhere." He took a deep swallow, and continued. "Just as much as you need, Paulie, to be here in this house, on this island, I need to be in Spain."

He was not going to tell her he was leaving for another woman; like a coward, he was concealing that fact beneath his ostensible need to report on a war abroad. Pauline drank deeply from her glass. Her head tilted back, she continued swallowing until the glass was empty. Ernest smiled at her.

"You surely didn't drink like that when I met you, my little Catholic," Ernest said. "I believe I corrupted you." Although she had intended her broad quaff to be her own form of defiance, once again Ernest had deftly turned it to his advantage. Yet again, he had demonstrated that he held all the cards. Her bravado faltered; she struggled to find the perfect retort.

"Well, Ernest, if it's a war you're going to, I guess I can't complain." Her words were intended to belie the fact that she knew about Martha, even though Martha's opened letters lay on the windowsill beside him. Pauline felt her eyes rest on them for a second, then return to her glass. She knew Ernest had seen her notice the letters. She was trying to maintain her dignity. But Ernest was not content to allow her that. He cleared his throat, and then spoke.

"Well, yes, it's a war. And it's more than that." He paused, considering. "It's a part of my life that I need to restore. I need to hunt, to explore. I need to feel the blood in my bones again." His enigmatic words could be painting a portrait of a war zone, or of the pursuit of a lover. He enjoyed taunting her.

Pauline remembered his initial cowardice in not being able to tell Hadley outright about his affair with Pauline. He had even gotten mad at Hadley for confronting him about Pauline, after the fact of their affair had become undeniable. Ernest had been deft, for a time, at somehow making the whole situation Hadley's fault. Pauline knew, if she were not careful, he would turn this new affair with Martha into something that was her fault. She struggled to find the words to avoid that.

"Well, I guess you've made up your mind, Ernest. We'll miss you." The words were hollow, and she could not stop from sounding desperate. She poured herself another glass, leaving the bottle on his desk. She turned and moved toward the door. Fleeing from this awkward stand-off was the only way to not fall apart in front of him, not break down, not lose her *amour-propre*. She simply had to walk away.

"Is that all, Pauline?" Ernest's voice was low, enticing. She turned back to him once more. The look on his face contradicted his soft voice. He did not want to keep her; he wanted to bait her. He wanted to see if she would scream, cry, accuse.

Whatever she did, Pauline knew she was not going to allow that. She needed to keep whatever bargaining power she had left; she needed, desperately, to hang on to the self-respect left to her. Pauline answered him with her back.

She walked out, into the tropical night, into what she believed would be a new, independent chapter of her life. She knew, even then, she was going to have to fight him for it.

Elizabeth Ritter

CHAPTER FOUR

It was Ernest's last week in Key West, and he had made his travel plans. He began to refer wistfully to Spain's "bloody civil war," and espoused his desire to be on the front lines, dramatically reporting on siege after siege. Pauline knew he would be meeting his new inamorata there.

During that last week, Ernest had become more and more open about discussing his plans to meet up with another reporter – Pauline knew who it was. At first, he strove to make it sound like purely a work relationship, that Martha had paved the way with her publishers for him to accompany her on the front lines and in the field, and that this was somehow to be both an entrée for him and a kind of protection for her.

Pauline wondered if Martha would have been offended at the way Ernest was characterizing this; from what Pauline had heard about her, she would have spurned any thought that she needed a man's protection. Pauline's silence in the face of his increasingly explicit conversations about Martha was, she knew, a challenge to him. It came to a head on his last night at home.

"Well, my dear, I hope you won't pine away while I'm gone. And I don't expect that I will be able to communicate much, if at all – even by letter. I expect that I will be fully consumed." Pauline couldn't help it; she took the bait.

"Consumed by what, Ernest? Or by whom, should I dare ask?" There it was, the first time she had fallen into his trap and acknowledged that there was a woman he was going to. He stared at her.

"I don't think that's a profitable conversation for us to have at this point, Pauline." His dark brown eyes were frosty. This was what he had wanted, and at the same time he was angry that she had brought his affair out into the open. Just as he had gotten angry at Hadley, he now turned that same venom on her. "I wish you hadn't said that," he spat. "Not necessary, not productive, my dear. And leaving on that note puts us on a much different footing, you know."

Pauline realized that she had made precisely that same mistake that Hadley had made. Now it was her fault. Pauline felt like she had fallen into the vortex, once again into the eye of the hurricane. She had to regain some footing and let him know that there was a fight ahead. He could not be the first one to spell out where they were going; then he would be in total control. So, she leapt.

"I see, Ernest." Pauline's voice was steely, cool. "Well, I suppose if it's a divorce you have in mind, you'll get it. Believe me, you will get it. But you won't enjoy it." She glared at him. "I've experienced too much with you to let you off easily. I watched what you did with Hadley, and believe me, I learned from that." The room felt charged and expectant. Pauline thought that she had gained some advantage, simply by making the first volley. "After you leave tomorrow, I'll go see the Spottswoods."

Spottswoods, father and son, were the preeminent lawyers on their little island, famous for deftly handling all manner of delicate, personal, and often embarrassing legal matters, and they invariably got the upper hand for whichever client hired them first. Pauline knew that this was a bold chess move for her; Ernest was leaving in the morning, and she would be able to get to them before he could. He would be forced to fight a divorce from across the sea, with lawyers hired long-distance. Ernest knew that she had put him, at least for the moment, at a disadvantage.

"Well, it seems you've already thought a great deal about this, my dear," he said, coldly, "And what have you planned in that scheming head of yours, for the boys?"

Ernest had caught her off guard; she had not really thought about the boys. Her sole focus had been on maintaining her own position and power. Her two sons had always been merely an adjunct to her life, they did not necessarily figure in her decision-making.

"Well, the boys – they will be taken care of," she stammered. It was clear to him that she did not have much of an answer for him. He smirked.

"Ah, ever the mother hen. Well, Pauline, you can expect to see very little of them. You know they can barely stand to be in your presence. They merely tolerate you. Good grief, they prefer to be with that harridan of a nanny rather than spend even a little bit of their time with you." His words cut, even more deeply because she knew they were true. He continued. "Since you've got this already planned out, little Pauline, I'll follow through. I will have responses, not to you, but to your attorneys on whatever schemes you track out. And don't think I won't be able to fight you, even long distance. I will." He was so resolute, so firm, Pauline felted that he was moving toward a checkmate. Being enigmatic, at this point, was an attractive option.

"You will see, Ernest. This won't be easy at all for you." And she knew, at the same time, it was not going to be an easy road for her either.

CHAPTER FIVE

Ernest left. And soon after, so did the boys. Their departure with Ada was a sudden affair, staged as easily as if departing for summer camp. Ernest had penned a letter to his parents the night before his New York flight left for Spain, telling them that he was getting a divorce and that they were to send for Patrick and Gregory and keep them in Oak Park until his return. The plan, as he laid out to his parents, was that he would keep the boys, and Pauline would keep the house.

When Pauline first heard of these unilateral decisions on property and custody from Ernest's mother, she found that she was not displeased with the arrangement. The house was already in her name, and she had no desire to begin to act as a mother to the two boys. This was perhaps what Ernest anticipated, but Pauline was not content to let it end that way. She instructed the Spottswoods to begin the long and expensive process of getting everything they could for her monetarily.

The genteel attorneys were surprised and somewhat mystified by her immediate acquiescence to Ernest's demand for custody, but they were soon kept busy with her demands to secure for her as much of Ernest's money as they possibly could. If they thought her callous, the Spottswoods kept that to themselves. The more strung-out the divorce, the bigger their fees.

The next six months were filled with wrangling, over long-distance phone calls, with an increasingly recalcitrant Ernest. When it became clear to him that her primary focus was money, and how much she could get, he became even angrier and the fights became more and more venomous, more toxic.

At the end, they were arguing about the smallest details: an old savings account, a percentage point on the royalties of past and future books and movies, an antique chair. Pauline had the advantage of being on the ground in Key West, in front of the judge who would eventually rule on the divorce. And she had the venerable Spottswoods by her side. Sooner than she could have expected, it was over.

Ernest and Pauline were divorced almost one year to the day after he had left for Spain. She had heard and read about his exploits on the front. She had seen newspaper clippings and photographs detailing the famous author's reportage. In one of the pictures, she could see Ernest standing with a reporter's tablet in his hand, gesturing with it out over a ragged field, his other arm around a woman. It was Martha.

The look on Martha's face as she stared up at him was pure admiration. Pauline had once gazed at Ernest with that same look. She wondered what would become of Martha, and of that awe. She did not think Ernest capable of maintaining a woman's respect, and she surprised herself by feeling saddened at the thought. It would turn out that she was right.

Ernest's courtship and eventual marriage to Martha was brief and stormy. Apparently, his drunken rages and braggartry very quickly staled her attraction to him, and he soon became little more than an embarrassment to Martha. Indeed, Pauline understood that Martha used those exact words in her divorce complaint. Martha was a formidable woman, who discovered that this man she had admired was little more than an empty shell. Pauline found herself feeling a vague if fleeting sympathy for Ernest.

Pauline had ended up getting everything she wanted in the divorce: the house, the car, a fair amount in royalties from his books, and numerous artifacts she had used to decorate their home, pieces from all over the world. There were carvings and pelts from Africa, several paintings they had acquired during their time in Europe, all the Murano glass fixtures she had ordered from Italy, and any other artifact that Spottswoods had managed to glom onto for her. She was even able to retain a small cat sculpture that Pablo Picasso had made specifically for Ernest.

And of course, there were the cats. There was no way Ernest could take his beloved cats, and therein lie the odd conundrum of their final property settlement. His feline brood was the one thing Ernest highly prized that Pauline affirmatively did not want; she was, however, ultimately saddled with them, if for no other reason than geography. She had long ago lost any positive emotion for these felines; they were nothing now but an irritation to her. She ignored them as much as possible, sometimes even kicking them out of her way. They had grown to avoid her.

The cats became the sole responsibility of the estate's caretaker, Toby. Toby, the silent, gaunt character, given more to monosyllabic responses than explanations, had stayed on in Key West after Ernest's departure.

Toby had been unfailingly loyal to Ernest, and was sullen and terse in his communications with Pauline. He preferred to keep silently to himself in the small apartment above the garage and go about his duties as if Ernest were still the master of the house. Toby did not ask Pauline about his duties, question whether there was something she wanted done; Toby simply continued to engage in his manifold chores as if nothing in the household hierarchy had changed. If Pauline happened to come upon him as he carried out one of his daily tasks, Toby would abruptly walk away, and find something else to do.

Sometimes Pauline would watch him from behind the kitchen curtains as he bent over the cats' feeding bowls at the far end of the yard. Pauline could not hear him, but she was able to see that he was carrying on a conversation with the cats as they milled around his feet, waiting for him to fill their bowls. The cats would lean against his calves and rub luxuriously against his pant legs. Toby would gently swat them away, and then immediately reward them with a soft caress. As he stood among the cats, playing with them, a smile would crease his face.

For some reason, it disturbed Pauline to see this; it was a club from which she was excluded. She knew that it was silly that this bothered her; she certainly had not even wanted the cats. Pauline thought it ridiculous that this prosaic scene affected her. She would back away from the curtain, and wonder briefly why the denial of the dumb animals' affection troubled her.

Now, when Pauline looked around her home it felt as if she were looking at herself in a painting. Pauline, standing in her elegant living room, Murano chandeliers glowing softly above her head. Pauline, swimming alone in her magnificent pool at midnight. Pauline, seated at her massive dining room table, eating her dinner, the only occupant of the elegant room. Pauline, lifting the curtain to stare at the milling cats in the yard. She let the curtain fall.

CHAPTER SIX

It had been a few years since Didi had seen Key West. He had left as a young teenager, anxious to remove himself from the tucked-in household of his overbearing grandparents and wildly desirous of seeing the world outside the tiny tropical island. Now, after travelling the rails and working grain silos in North Dakota, slaughterhouses in Kansas, coalmines in Pennsylvania, Didi had returned to the island for his grandpa's funeral. His grandma still lived in the miniscule house, still spent her days sweeping the dust around in circles on the floor and boiling black beans on the stovetop.

The afternoon following his grandfather's funeral service at the Catholic church, Didi sat in the small kitchen, boots scuffing on the gritty linoleum, waiting for his grandmother to place a bowl of fragrant beans and rice in front of him. He took his first bite and sighed.

"Grandma, ain' had nothin' like this anywhere else. Gotta come home to Key West for this." She smiled briefly at Didi, then swatted him on the back of the head.

"Then what you go 'way for boy?" She sputtered, turning back to the stove. "You don' need to leave home to find anythin' you need. It all right here." She angrily stirred the thickening beans in the pot.

"You're right, Grandma, you're definitely right." Didi knew it was fruitless to argue with her. He bent over his bowl and continued to eat his supper. "Hey, tell me, what goin' on over at the big house?" Since his arrival, Didi had studiously avoided looking over the fence into the back yard of the mansion. He had focused solely on making the arrangements for his grandpa's funeral, buying groceries for his grandma, and trying to clean up the inveterate mess that always seemed to be the perpetual state of the little house. He had not wanted to be tempted by any of his boyhood distractions, if indeed any remained at the big house next door. His grandma turned, frowning.

"They always got theyselves a big mess over there," she jerked her head toward the fence. "Mr. Hemingway, he left a month ago or thereabouts, they fussin' and hollerin' all the time." She looked out the kitchen window at the neighboring back yard. "I seen it with my own two eyes, cain' miss they fightin.' I'm thinkin' he gone for good." Didi continued to stare at his meal, slowly eating. The beans were cooling down.

"You think anybody left in the house?" Didi asked his question, not looking up at his grandmother. She narrowed her eyes, evaluating her grandson. She remembered his boyhood fascination with Mrs. Hemingway: *not right*, she thought to herself, hoping that he had outgrown his childhood foolishness.

"She still there, but somethin' wrong with that woman. I think she ain' right in her head." She wanted to paint as unattractive a picture as she possibly could of her next-door neighbor. "Her boys gone too, and that nasty nurse they had. Only one lef' over there to help is ol' Toby, and he ain' too much of anythin' anymore neither." She felt she had covered the issue as broadly as she could, and was satisfied that she had been able to convey a completely negative narrative to her grandson. She ended with one last admonition, "Don't you think about lookin' around over there boy, ain' nothin' over there but trouble. You 'member your grandpa, the rows he had with Mr. Hemingway over those cats." Didi well remembered the loud cursing matches, in staccato Spanish, between his grandfather and the famous neighbor.

His grandpa had raised fighting cocks in the dusty back yard, a not uncommon pastime for expatriate Cubans, and

Ernest was continually increasing his brood of cats at the mansion. Inevitably, the cocks and cats engaged with one another, ending in either a feline or avian death. "Yeah," Didi's grandmother concluded, "you mess about wi' them folks you liable get yo' self kilt." She paused, pleased that she had completely covered the matter; the subject was closed, there was nothing more that needed to be said. Didi finished his meal and put the dirty bowl and spoon into the sink. He walked back to his boyhood bedroom, still the same graying coverlet on the bed, lay down and went to sleep.

Didi awoke after dark. The revolving beam of the lighthouse lit up the back wall of his room in slow, repetitive cycles. He looked at the travelling alarm clock propped open on the metal table beside his bed. It was just after midnight, and Didi stood and walked to the window. He stared up at the lighthouse, watching it revolve unhurriedly. He was still in his day clothes; he had fallen asleep without removing them. He got up and softly opened the bedroom door and looked out into the kitchen.

All the lights were off in the house. He could hear his grandma softly snoring in the next bedroom, her door still open so that she could see out into the living room. Didi smiled to himself; in the light from the streetlamp dimly coming through the front windows, he could see that his grandma still slept with her head at the foot of the bed. Still watching out for me, he thought. He walked back through the kitchen and noiselessly opened the back door.

The lighthouse was not the only light in the sky: the moon was full, high over the southwestern horizon. It lit up the evening, and Didi could see his way easily through the clumps of monkey grass and weeds in the back yard. He walked over to the fence.

He heard her before he saw her. There was the soft paddling of her arms in the pool, as well as the occasional gentle kicks of her feet on the top of the water. Didi stopped, mesmerized. She was there.

Just as she had always been, she was still there. He walked closer and peered through the close slats of the fence. He saw one quick glimpse of her in the pool, and then quickly turned away. *I'm not a boy anymore*, he thought, and chastised himself for even that brief glance. He walked quickly back to the house and sat down slowly on the ledge of limestone coral that served as a small back stoop at the kitchen door. Didi stared again up at the lighthouse.

He would probably not see her again, he thought. He could not imagine any scenario in which their paths might cross. Didi leaned back against the kitchen door and closed his eyes. He could see her in his memory, clear as glass, and felt the quickening of his heartbeat as he remembered her beauty.

Over all these years, he had never again seen anyone as beautiful as the woman who lived in the big house. Her memory was pristine, and pure. Nothing his grandmother said could influence Didi's remembrance of the woman. His devoted esteem for the beautiful woman in the mansion was unchanged.

Didi opened his eyes. Just as vivid as his memory of her was his recollection of the husband. From what his grandmother had said, he had continued to be the bullying, angry fool that he had always been; Didi wondered where the man had gone.

He stood, wiped the dust off the seat of his pants, and walked back in the house. Just knowing she was there was enough, still beautiful, still pristine in the water. He walked quietly back into his bedroom and fell asleep, resting in the untainted adoration of the woman.

In his dreams, however, he was plagued with his unalloyed abhorrence of the big man, roiling and burning in his chest, undiminished by the passage of time. Didi awoke, sweating, his fists clenched as he lay under the cool sheets.

EPILOGUE

The small figure marches up the dirt track, legs swinging, torso rigid, tanned arms barely moving with each effortful step. The shoulders are square and straight, and the gait is purposeful, but neither rapid nor slow. So many miles, so much time passed. But today is the end of the long journey. Today is the final day.

Eyes squinting, the large house is now in view, in the far distance up the hill. A huff of breath sounds into the early-morning summer air. Hair tousled but not unkempt, face browned with weather and travel. Clothes frayed, worn thin at the elbows and knees. The boots are the only remarkable piece of clothing: heavy good-grade leather, high tops bound up to the shins, tied neatly and tightly with new laces. The boots are evidence of priorities.

For the past month, the surveillance spot has been a secluded place in the northside woods behind the house, at a little declination in the landscape overlooking a ledge of lichen-covered limestone. From this vantage point, from sunrise to sunset, the daily coming and going of the wife and of the caretaker have been in full view. There has been no direct sight of Ernest, but there is no doubt at all that he is in the house.

Ernest returned six months ago from the hospital in Minnesota. He had been watched there as well, from the shelter of a doorway across the street from the hospital. In the snow and freezing wind, Ernest had taken long walks with the nuns, circling and circling around a frosty-white courtyard. After several weeks, he had been discharged from the hospital and the wife had come to pick him up. Under the large brick archway at the hospital entrance, Ernest had been wheeled out to the waiting car. He appeared to be much subdued, vacantly accepting instructions from the orderly who helped him into the passenger seat of the car. The wife had driven them slowly away, tires crunching through the frozen snow. And they had been followed.

Now, on this early July morning, the figure turns left off the dirt track and walks a large semi-circle trace, through the woods. Skirting the house by a wide margin, to the usual surveillance spot. Binoculars in hand, settling down to watch, and to wait.

The patterns are now familiar. The wife usually leaves in the late morning on her daily trips into town, and returns by mid-afternoon with brown paper bags from the grocery or hardware store, sometimes bright pink packages tied with ribbon from Ketchum's only ladies' shop. Sometimes she comes home with no parcels at all, but she always leaves and returns about the same time, almost every day. These daily outings, necessary or not, seem to be a respite for the wife.

The old caretaker's schedule is similarly predictable. Each day, just before the wife's departure, the stooped old man leaves his garage living quarters, and with effort raises the wooden garage door. Then he hobbles slowly to the back door of the big house. He pauses, as if waiting to hear her footsteps nearing the door. The old man opens the door, bowing slightly as the wife exits the house and walks to the garage. The old man waits for the sound of the car engine, watches the woman back out of the garage, and waves as she drives down the dirt track. Then he turns and enters the big house.

It is never more than five minutes before the old man reappears at the back door. Enough time to make sure that the wife is not going to return for a forgotten shopping list or a lipstick. Then the old man walks slowly back to the garage, not to return to the big house until just before the woman returns.

It is obvious that the old man is supposed to be watching over Ernest while the wife is away, but either does not like the task or feels it is unnecessary. *Probably the former*; it is too odious for anyone to be around Ernest for any length of time.

After a month of surveillance, the routines are predictable and dependable. After the wife leaves the house, there is always at least an hour when the big man is alone, unsupervised inside the rambling house. It will not take nearly that much time.

The plan had been reviewed dozens of times. It was based on memories of Ernest's predilections, weaknesses, and habits. There would be guns and ammunition in the house; that was a certainty. After the long stay in the hospital and the confinement to his home, he would now undoubtedly be further impaired, either by drink or medication, and probably both. Ernest never left the house, but his still-impressive silhouette was occasionally limned against a shaded window. When the silhouette moved, the motions were slow and ponderous. Not a difficult target.

It is just after five o'clock; the sun rises early in Idaho in July. The air is clear and cool. The larch and fir trees sway in the breeze, and a summer tanager, bright red against the morning sky, trills on a high branch. A good day to finish this.

At seven o'clock, the old caretaker leaves his apartment and moves around to the front of the building, where he bends to grasp the iron handle of the heavy wooden garage door. With much effort, he swings the door upwards. The opening of the door makes a scraping, metallic sound on its track.

The old man makes his slow, rambling way toward the back door of the big house. *Unusual.* The old man is rarely up this early.

405

The woman appears at the back door, walking toward the old man as he makes his slow trek toward the house. She has a coat draped over her arm and carries a large handbag. She is wearing a skirt, highly polished shoes, and a brightly patterned scarf is tied casually around her neck. The two stop, speak.

The binocular's focus wheel rolls beneath a dry finger, the lens zooms in on the woman's expression: it is calm today, almost smiling as she says goodbye and walks past the old man into the garage.

The old man stands at the back door, watches the woman pull the car out of the garage, waves as she drives away. Then he turns and enters the big house, and closes the back door. As is his habit, within five minutes the old caretaker appears again at the back door, stops, and gazes absently about the yard. The he slowly walks back to the garage, opens his apartment door, and goes inside.

It is obvious that the woman has left for the day. Her atypical clothes and expression indicate that she has plans for more than just her usual shopping. She has been too long under the daily burden and tedium of caretaking; she is taking a well-warranted respite. Perhaps the old man might check in on the invalid around lunchtime, but there will certainly be more than enough time. Enough time to finish this.

With the conviction of an unwavering purpose, Jinny reckons that the morning's unusual pattern is a sign – a clear omen that it is time for her plan to be executed, immediately. She had already decided that today would be the day; but the woman's early departure only confirms her choice. The universe is opening the way for her to move forward. For her, finally, to put an end to the suffering that Ernest has caused.

In the years prior to Pauline's death, Jinny had loyally nursed her sister in her lingering, agonizing illness. During those same years, Ernest had enjoyed his meteoric rise to fame, and heartlessly had continued to send frequent cruel, cutting letters to Pauline. Jinny was galled by Ernest's malice and vindictiveness and had watched over time as each dispatch sent Pauline deeper into sickness and depression.

After one particularly vituperative letter from Ernest, Jinny felt that Pauline had finally given up. Jinny had found her sister that evening dead in her bed, the letter from Ernest on the sheet beside her. Jinny had thought to herself, *he has finally done what he intended all along, he has finally killed her*. Something inside Jinny shattered.

And so, in the end, Jinny felt it was up to her to provide a fitting coda to her sister's long, painful, humiliating descent. Ernest had left a trail of hatred and disappointment in his wake everywhere he went; nearly everyone he encountered loathed and despised him. But it was Jinny who detested him most of all. For ten years after Pauline's death, Jinny had brooded and planned, and had been led to an inexorable conclusion.

For those who knew him, who had the misfortune to be within his sphere for any length of time, Ernest's considerable fame, his public deification, was a blasphemy. How could anyone venerate such a beast? It would be Jinny who would ultimately provide the conclusion. She would put an end to all of it, for everyone.

Jinny begins to make her way down out of the woods. She follows her well-trodden, circuitous path down to the dirt track. She pauses at the verge and breathes deeply. Then she begins to walk the track up the hill, directly toward the big house.

She reaches the front portico, three layers of curved brick embracing a large, semicircular porch, and climbs the steps slowly, purposefully. As she approaches the oversized front door, Jinny pulls a pair of leather gloves from her pants pocket and puts them on.

The impressive oak door looks menacing; it is tall and wide, and dressed in heavy wrought iron – handle, lock, hinges, and knocker. The knocker is incongruous, almost ludicrous: it is fashioned as a huge dragonfly, ungainly and grotesque. The surreal appearance of the knocker is a momentary perturbance; Jinny looks down at her feet, shakes her head and then, composed, reaches up and hammers the knocker down. Three ominous, slow hard claps, metal against metal. She waits, then repeats the thudding knocks.

After a few minutes, Jinny hears slow, plodding footsteps in the front hallway. The heavy doorknob turns slowly, almost furtively, and then clicks. The door is pulled open gradually, revealing the lone occupant of the house.

Ernest is still a physically imposing presence, large and barrel-chested. But the span and height of the physique is belied by the sickly countenance and appearance. His eyes are vacant, jowls droop, the wide mouth hangs slightly agape. There are food stains on the front of his shirt, his pants hang loose, and his ragged bedroom slippers are soiled and grimy. One of his bare heels is skewed off a dirty slipper sole and rests on the tile floor. Ernest stares at Jinny, expressionless and without recognition.

At first sight of him, Jinny is momentarily unnerved. More than three decades of accumulated hurt and volcanic anger cascade over her. Her titanic rage at what Ernest did to Pauline has been an ever-present entity in her life for years. His degradation of Pauline, his manipulation, his despicable disregard for her – Jinny has lived with it for so long and it consumes her still, ten years after Pauline's death. But she shuts her eyes tightly, grimaces, and shakes away the emotion. She has a job to do.

Jinny walks inside with staccato, rapid steps, then turns, reaches back, and closes the front door. She turns again and faces Ernest, who stands stolidly, planted and unresponsive. His gaze is empty and uncomprehending; he neither speaks nor moves.

Jinny does not give herself time or license to think; she acts automatically, and on plan. She walks quickly past Ernest and through an entryway on the right, into a large, imposing room circled by excessively tall oak walls rising to timbered rafters.

Her confidence is immediately rewarded: gun cabinets line the walls at the far end of the room, as she knew they would. Jinny walks swiftly toward them, past the numerous mounted heads on every wall – elk, caribou, bear – not noticing, not giving herself permission for any distraction.

She peers through the glass front of a long-gun case, and it takes just a moment for her eyes to rest on a double-barreled, twelve-gauge shotgun. She opens the case door, pulls out the shotgun and stares at it, briefly but intently. Mentally confirming the make and model of the gun, she chooses a weapon she knows how to handle. Ten years of practice and planning are coming to fruition.

Without hesitation, Jinny breaks open the action, and stares at the breech ends of both side-by-side barrels. As she had expected, both barrels contained shot shells; Jinny well knows Ernest's penchant for keeping his firearms loaded.

She snaps close the action, cocks the hammer, and walks swiftly and resolutely back to the front hallway, shotgun poised lightly in her right hand, the glove leather softly cradling the metal heart of the gun.

Back in the front hallway, Ernest stands motionless, impassive, and insentient. Again, Jinny's confidence is justified: Ernest's mental and physical incapacity leave him vulnerable and unwitting.

She acts in seconds, moving the shotgun almost parallel to the wide chest, the tip of the barrel under Ernest's chin and the finger guard almost touching his stomach. Without hesitation, Jinny pulls the trigger.

Ernest's head blows backward, and he falls heavily to the floor, newly lifeless eyes aimed ceilingward. Ears ringing from the shotgun blast, Jinny stares down at the body for only a moment. She quickly bends over, grabs the right hand of the corpse and pushes the right thumb through the shotgun trigger guard, pressing the pad of the dead man's thumb against the trigger itself. She pulls the fingers of his right hand over the top of the stock, and presses the limp thumb, palm, and fingers onto the metal.

She releases the dead right hand, allowing the gun to rest on the man's chest. She reaches over the supine body and picks up the deadweight of the left hand. Righting the gun, Jinny places the palm of the insensate hand on the gunstock, just below the trigger guard. Then she lets the left hand fall dully back to the floor.

Jinny stands, and takes a few shallow breaths. She bends over again, replaces the right thumb on the trigger, and holds it in place. Still bowed, she takes a step backward and pulls both gun and insensate arm up two feet above and slightly to the right of the body. In one brisk action, she jumps back and at precisely the same time releases both the hand and the gun.

Ernest's right arm falls heavily, out to his right side. The gun clatters to the floor, coming to rest at a forty-five-degree angle to the body, its stock pointed away from his right thigh.

The double barrels of the gun rest on the floor, nestled between Ernest's arm and side. The tips of the barrels are heavily covered with blood, as are the man's neck and chest. A widening, viscous pool spreads on the floor around Ernest's head. Blood spatter is sprayed out on the wall and staircase.

Jinny notes the position of the dead right hand, then gently rubs the forefinger base of her gloved right hand against the base of Ernest's thumb. She wants to make sure that gunshot residue can be found.

When she completes this last task, Jinny stands, turns, and walks out the massive front door, closing it softly behind her. The iron lock clicks. She has entered and exited the house in under five minutes. No one has seen her. It is seven-thirty.

Jinny moves quickly off into the woods, and disappears.

ACKNOWLEDGEMENTS

There are many people to thank for their assistance in writing this book.

Thanks to Kathryn Johnson and the Chevy Chase, Maryland Writer's Center. Your instruction, guidance, and insight helped create the shape and form of this novel. And your generous assistance in editing and framing the re-drafting was invaluable.

A profound thank-you to Paula McLain, whose novel, *The Paris Wife*, was a resource, a muse, and an unflagging encouragement. It was a joy to read you, and an even bigger joy to get to know you. Thank you for yielding the "Key West Wife" to me.

To Tom Hambright, Monroe County historian *extraordinaire* and keeper of the Florida History Archives at the Key West Public Library. Your unfailing ability to point me in the right direction in search of Hemingway facts and resources was incredibly helpful, as were your unshakable good humor and unerring instincts.

To my two very dear friends, Deb Wissinger Landis and Alice Gilmore Young: thank you, from the bottom of my heart. You loved me through a difficult first read of this manuscript. You are a great IDEA, my inspirations.

I am extremely grateful to the saintly Kim Dionis for expert advice and criticisms, which made this a much better book. You are a fantastic reader and editor, but more importantly you are a sweet and treasured friend.

To the Boalsburg Bookies, I am so thankful for the discussions, the laughter, and most of all the friendships.

To Doreen Diehl and Nasrin Saba, without whose never-ending friendship I could not get through the days. Let's go for another forty years.

To Jane Crandell, my dearest friend in Christ, who is my guide, my companion, and my delight. And to her daughter Doreen, for her insight, wit, advice, and Saturday morning breakfasts.

To my sister Isabelle, who put a copy of *The Enduring Hemingway* in my hands when I was fifteen. Who knew it would come in so handy?

To my brother Laird and to Sharon, your enjoyment of Key West propelled me to write a novel about the island.

To Katie, who continues to delight, amaze, and inspire me—since the day she was born. Your strength, intelligence, and honor never cease to encourage me. You are my sweetest angel.

To Drake and Erik, whose *joie de vivre* is contagious, and whose kind hearts are a joy to be around.

To Dave, my husband—you are solid, supportive, kind, generous, loving, and amazingly intelligent. Thank you for your suggestions and edits, and thank you for listening to hours of narration. There would be no love story without you.

BIBLIOGRAPHY

Chamberlin, B. *The Hemingway Log: A Chronology of His Life and Times*. University Press of Kansas, 2015.

Dearborn, M.V. *Ernest Hemingway: A Biography*. Knopf, 2017.

Diliberto, G. *Hadley: A Life of Hadley Richardson Hemingway*. Bloomsbury Publishing, 1992.

Diliberto, G. *Paris Without End: The True Story of Hemingway's First Wife*. Harper Perennial, 2011.

Farah, A. *Hemingway's Brain*. University of South Carolina Press, 2017.

McLendon, J. *Papa Hemingway in Key West, 1928 – 1940*. Popular Library, 1972.

McLain, P. *The Paris Wife*. Ballantine Books, 2012.

Hawkins, R.A. *Unbelievable Happiness and Final Sorrow*. University of Arkansas Press, 2017.

Hemingway, E. *The Sun Also Rises*. Charles Scribner's Sons 1926.

Hemingway, E. *A Farewell to Arms*. Charles Scribner's Sons 1929.

Hemingway, E. *Death in the Afternoon*. Charles Scribner's Sons 1932.

Hemingway, E. *To Have and Have Not*. Charles Scribner's Sons 1937.

Hemingway, E. *For Whom the Bell Tolls*. Charles Scribner's Sons 1940.

Hemingway, M. *How It Was*. Knopf, 1976.

Hotchner, A.E. *Papa Hemingway*. Random House, *1966*.

Hotchner, A.E. *Hemingway in Love: His Own Story*. St. Martin's Press, 2015.

Mellow, J. *Hemingway: A Life Without Consequences*. Houghton Mifflin Harcourt, 1992.

Moorehead, C. *Gellhorn: A Twentieth-Century Life*. Holt Paperbacks, 2004.

Reynolds, M. *The Young Hemingway*. W. W. Norton & Co., 1998.

Reynolds, M. *Hemingway: The 1930s*. W. W. Norton & Co., 1998.

Reynolds, M. *Hemingway: The Paris Years*. W. W. Norton & Co., 1999.

Reynolds, M. *Hemingway: The Final Years*. W. W. Norton & Co., 2000.

Reynolds, N. *Writer, Sailor, Soldier, Spy: Ernest Hemingway's Secret Adventures, 1935 – 1961*. William Morrow, 2017.

Scribner, Jr., C. *The Enduring Hemingway: An Anthology of a Lifetime in Literature*. Charles Scribner's Sons, 1974.

Spanier, S, Mandel, M., *eds. The Letters of Ernest Hemingway, 1929 - 31*. Cambridge University Press, 2020.

Questions and Topics for Discussion

1. The title of the book gives the plot away. Did the
    author successfully carry you forward throughout the
    book detailing the numerous characters who hated
    Ernest Hemingway? Did you guess correctly who the
    murderer would be? If so, how?

2. Discuss Pauline's relationship with Jinny. How did
    that relationship evolve over time? Is Jinny's intense
    devotion to Pauline believable?

3. By the time of the murder, do you believe Jinny was
    mentally unstable, or was she acting rationally in
    response to extreme provocation?

4. There are numerous racially- and socially-unjust
    scenarios throughout the novel (e.g., Ernest's bigoted
    comments about people of color and homosexuals;
    Pauline and Lorine's unquestioning acceptance of
    allusion to "slaves"). How did the comments affect
    your perception of the characters?

5. What was your reaction to Pauline's concept of
    "victim precipitation" regarding Hadley's
    obsequiousness toward Ernest?

6. The author attempts to capture numerous dialects
    throughout the novel (Key West, Arkansas,
    Wyoming). Does the use of writing "in dialect" offend
    you as a cultural appropriation, or is it an accurate

and respectful representation of the various characters' speech?

7. Was there a point at which you were exasperated at Pauline for putting up with Ernest? If so, was it continuous or did it culminate with any particular event? Was there a straw that broke the camel's back?

8. Did the author's note change your reading experience?

Thank you for reading.
Please review this book. Reviews
help others find Absolutely Amazing eBooks and
inspire us to keep providing these marvelous tales.
If you would like to be put on our email list
to receive updates on new releases,
contests, and promotions, please go to
AbsolutelyAmazingEbooks.com and sign up.

ABOUT THE AUTHOR

Elizabeth Ritter received a bachelor's degree from Penn State and a law degree from The George Washington University. She practiced law in D.C. for 25 years and taught at Georgetown University Law Center, specializing in financial market law. Elizabeth received appointments as legal counsel to six Presidential appointees in four administrations, and is a member of the D.C. Bar and the Bar of the Supreme Court of the United States. Elizabeth is married to Dave L. Gonzales, retired Executive Director of the Ernest Hemingway Home and Museum in Key West, FL; the couple lived on the museum property for seven years. They have three children, Katie, Erik, and Drake. Elizabeth and Dave reside in Key West, FL and Boalsburg, PA.

ABSOLUTELY AMAZING eBOOKS

AbsolutelyAmazingEbooks.com or
AA-eBooks.com

Made in the USA
Columbia, SC
02 January 2021

30142648R00241